J.A. JANCE

Books by J. A. Jance

J. P. Beaumont Mysteries

Joanna Brady Mysteries

and

LYING IN WAIT

J. A. JANCE

AVON BOOKS
An Imprint of HarperCollinsPublishers

This is a work of fiction. Names, characters, places, and incidents are products of the author's imagination or are used fictitiously and are not to be construed as real. Any resemblance to actual events, locales, organizations, or persons, living or dead, is entirely coincidental.

AVON BOOKS
An Imprint of HarperCollins*Publishers*
10 East 53rd Street
New York, New York 10022-5299

Copyright © 1994 by J. A. Jance
ISBN: 0-380-71841-3
www.avonbooks.com

First Avon Books paperback printing: January 1996

Avon Trademark Reg. U.S. Pat. Off. and in Other Countries, Marca Registrada, Hecho en U.S.A.
HarperCollins® is a trademark of HarperCollins Publishers Inc.

Printed in the U.S.A.

20 19

To Dirty Dick and the other displaced regulars. And to the good-sport charity auctioneers and attendees who make Seattle a great place to live and write. But most of all, to Thomas Blatt, a survivor and an inspiration.

LYING IN WAIT

Prologue

The old white dog studied me from her usual place as I stepped up onto the porch, but she made no effort to rise and greet me or even to lift her head off her paws. I walked over, squatted beside her, and gave her silky ears a gentle rub.

"How's it going, Mandy, old girl?" I asked. She leaned into my hand while her tail thumped halfheartedly on the wooden porch, but still she didn't scramble to her feet. Instead, she stared intently up at me through soulful, cataract-dimmed eyes.

Leaving the dog where she was, I rose and walked over to the door. My hand was raised and ready to knock when the porch light snapped on. The door swung open on well-oiled hinges before my knuckles made contact with the wood. My grandmother, Beverly Piedmont, stood before me in the open doorway with her wispy white hair glowing in a backlit halo around her head.

"Just a minute, Jonas," she said quietly. "I'll get my coat."

She came back to the door moments later. A green plaid wool coat that reeked of mothballs was folded neatly over one arm. The pleats in her shiny, silklike black dress made her appear to be far more substantial than she was, but as I helped her into the heavy coat, I noticed there was hardly any meat left on her stooped shoulders. The skin on her liver-spotted hands was as thin and brittle as parchment.

Once the coat was properly buttoned, I waited while she dug a clear plastic, accordion-pleated rain-hat out of her massive black purse. She unfolded the hat, placed it over her hair, and tied it under her chin in a neat bow.

"I'm ready," she announced when the rain-hat was securely fastened in place. "We can go now."

Matching my steps with her small, careful ones and angling my umbrella to fend off the falling rain, I walked her out to my car. When it had been time to go to the mortuary, it hadn't seemed appropriate to pick my grandmother up in my new Guard-red Porsche, but that was the only car I had. I had offered to rent a black limo, but she had turned that down because she didn't "want to put on airs." In the long run, it didn't matter, because I don't believe she even noticed what kind of car it was.

I eased her down into the low-slung seat. She sighed, closed her eyes briefly, and settled back against the soft plush leather. Pulling the strap out of its holder, I reached across her frail body and fastened the seat and shoulder belts around her. As the buckle snapped home, she sat up straight and grasped her purse firmly with both hands.

"Thank you, Jonas," she said in a voice that was surprisingly quaver-free. "Thank you very much."

Most of the time I go by the name of Beau or by my initials, J. P. Only two people in the world have ever called me Jonas—my mother, who has been dead for many years, and now my grandmother. It was only in the course of the last few months, after accidentally encountering my estranged grandparents' name and address in the phone book, that my mother's mother had emerged from the shadows of the long-buried past into the present. At eighty-six, Beverly Piedmont came into my life as both a puzzle and a blessing.

Now she was also a widow.

My grandfather and namesake, Jonas Logan Piedmont, was dead at age ninety-one.

I turned the key in the ignition, and the Porsche's powerful engine roared to life. With headlights slicing through sheets of slanting raindrops, we headed for Newton's Family Mortuary off Aurora Avenue, where Mr. Lloyd Newton, III, at age sixty or so, had been genuinely dismayed when my grandmother had told him in no uncertain terms that there would be no services for my grandfather.

"Absolutely not," she had announced determinedly. "At our ages, there aren't that many people still around that we know, and we only see them at weddings or funerals. These days there are a lot more funerals than weddings. Each time, someone else turns up missing. It's too depressing."

Her decree had brooked no argument. Mr. Newton had been forced to comply with reasonably good grace.

"Are you taking care of yourself?" I asked,

glancing in her direction as I threaded through evening traffic made worse by the steady downpour. A rain-slicked layer of newly fallen leaves covered the gutters and blocked Seattle's storm drains, leaving the streets awash. "Are you eating properly? Getting enough rest?"

"Mandy's the one you should be worried about," my grandmother returned with a shake of her head. "That crazy old dog won't eat a thing."

I remembered how Mandy used to sit for hours in mute companionship with my stroke-silenced, wheelchair-bound grandfather. She usually stuck close enough to his side that the slightest movement of his faltering hand would bring his flesh into contact with her patiently waiting head.

"Try bread and peanut butter," I suggested. "That's how Kelly and Jeremy get their dog, Sunshine, to take her arthritis medicine. Kelly claims there isn't a dog in the world that doesn't love bread and peanut butter."

Six months earlier, it would have been inconceivable to me that my daughter—Kelly, the complete airhead, as I once disparagingly called her—would end up passing out dog-care advice to her great-grandmother, but Beverly Piedmont nodded as though granting Kelly's suggestion serious consideration. "That sounds like a good idea," she said. "I believe I'll give it a try."

At the mortuary, we were ushered into Mr. Newton's private, rosewood-furnished office, where we were seated at a small conference table. The man himself appeared a few minutes later, carrying a small metal box in one hand and a file folder crammed with an unruly sheaf of papers in the other. Despite my grandmother's physical presence in the room and at the conference table, Mr. Newton's primary focus seemed to be aimed solely in my direction.

Before he said a word, he pushed an invoice toward me across the smooth expanse of polished wood. "We generally ask for payment upon receipt of the ashes. And I've made two certified copies of the death certificate. If you need more than two, just contact my office."

My grandmother's bony hand reached out and snagged the bill away from Mr. Newton's fingers before I could grasp it, but she left the death certificates lying where they fell. She groped in her cavernous purse and eventually came up with a checkbook. Meantime, I picked up the death certificates myself and studied the top one. On the line titled "Cause of death," it read, "Complications of flu, pneumonia."

I remembered back in August when the news broadcasts had been full of dire pronouncements about how this year's strain of Beijing flu was expected to be particularly bad. People had been urged to get flu shots, especially if they were in one of the at-risk groups.

The detective in me, the part that's worked the Seattle Homicide Squad for more years than I care to count, wondered how that one fatal bit of virus had managed to cross the Pacific Ocean and make its way into my grandfather's stubborn but failing system. Had it come into the house on a bill or with a stray piece of junk mail? Had it tracked him down on one of his infrequent trips to the grocery store or at the post office or in church?

And given that he was ninety-one, did it really matter?

Using a fountain pen, Beverly Piedmont finished writing the check in her old-fashioned, spidery hand. After blotting the ink and passing the check to Mr. Newton, she folded the bill neatly, placed it in the back of her checkbook, then carefully returned the worn plastic folder to her purse. When she reached out to pull the metal box of ashes toward her, her thin, bony hand trembled slightly.

"You don't have to do that, Grandmother," I said gruffly, taking charge of the box. "I'll carry it."

"Thank you," she murmured softly. Only then, after all that, did she bury her face in her hands and begin to cry.

I didn't get much sleep that night. I was up early the next morning. Standing on my twenty-fifth-floor terrace, I was drinking coffee when the fall sun came creeping up over the tops of the Cascades. The previous day's rainstorm had blown away overnight, pushed eastward by the arrival of a sudden high-pressure system. The storm had left behind it a layer of low-lying, moisture-heavy fog that clung to the ground like an immense down-filled comforter.

Looking out across Seattle's skyline from that height, I found that the city's streets were shrouded and invisible, as were most of the surrounding low-rise buildings. I could hear the muffled sounds of passing cars and buses in the street below, but I couldn't see them. Now and then I could pick out the sound of an individual car churning down the street, its progress marked by the distinctive hum of pavement-destroying tire studs. Here and there across the cityscape, the tops of other high-rise buildings loomed up out of the fog like so many huge tombstones, I thought. Or like islands in the fog.

Wasn't that the name of a book? I wondered.

No, it was *Islands in the Stream.* I had never read that particular Hemingway opus. My familiarity with the title came from working countless crossword puzzles.

That's what happens when you live alone. Your mind fills up with unnecessary mental junk like so much multipath interference on an overused radio frequency. Just as static on a radio keeps a listener from hearing the words, stream-of-consciousness interference keeps people who live alone from thinking too much. At least it helps. I had brought my grandfather's ashes home with me the night before. Even now, that discreetly labeled metal box was sitting on my entryway table. Sitting there, waiting. Waiting for my grandmother to decide what should be done with it.

I had asked her if there was some particular place where she would like the ashes scattered, or did she want an urn? Her answer was that she didn't know. She'd have to think about it. She'd let me know as soon as she made up her mind.

Chilled by the damp, cool air, I was headed back inside the apartment for another cup of Seattle's Best Coffee when the phone rang. Beverly Piedmont had been so much on my mind that somehow I expected the call to be from her, but it wasn't. It was Sergeant Watty Watkins, the desk sergeant from the Homicide Squad.

"How's it going, Beau? How's your grandmother holding up?"

"Pretty well, under the circumstances."

"Are you working today, or are you taking another bereavement day?"

"I'll be in. Why? What's up?"

"We've got a case that just turned up a few minutes ago, over at Fishermen's Terminal—a fatality boat fire. If it's a problem, I can assign it to someone else."

"Watty, I told you, I'm coming in. I'll take it. Who'll be working the case with me?"

"There'll be an arson investigator from the Seattle Fire Department, of course. As far as Homicide is concerned, pickings are a little thin. Detective Kramer and two of the other guys are off in D.C. for a training seminar this week. I'll probably team you up with Detective Danielson."

I was partnerless at the moment. Both of my last two partners, Ron Peters and Al Lindstrom, had been injured in the line of duty. For the foreseeable future, Ron was stuck in a wheelchair, and Al had just taken a disability retirement. Those two separate incidents had turned me into the Homicide Squad's version of Typhoid Mary. I was beginning to feel like an outcast.

For weeks now, I had been working by myself on the cold trail of a twenty-five-year-old homicide. The bullet-riddled skull had surfaced during the hazardous-waste cleanup of an import/export shipping company that had left Harbor Island in favor of cheaper rent in Tacoma. I had pretty well exhausted all possible leads on that musty old case. Frustrated at being exiled to a dead-end case and tired of getting nowhere, I was bored stiff and ready for some action.

Sue Danielson is one of the newest additions to the Homicide Squad. Not only is she relatively inexperienced, she's also one of the few female detectives on the team. Still, a partner is a partner. Beggars can't be choosers.

"Sue Danielson's fine," I said. "Is she there already? Does she have a car, or should I come down and get one?"

"She's right here," Watty replied. "I'll send her down to Motor Pool as soon as I get off the horn with you. She'll stop by Belltown Terrace to pick you up on her way north."

"Good," I said. "I'll be waiting downstairs."

And I was. Sue pulled up to the curb at Second and Broad in a hot little silver Mustang with a blue flashing light stuck on the roof. Some poor unfortunate drug dealer had been kind enough to equip the Mustang with a 5.0-liter high-output V-8 before unintentionally donating it to the exclusive use of the Seattle P.D. by way of a drug bust. As I crammed my six-three frame into the rider's side, I wished the bad guy had been taller. Short crooks tend to buy cars that are long on horsepower and short on headroom.

"How's it going?" I asked.

"Great," Sue said brusquely.

I was still closing the door when she gunned the engine and shot into traffic just ahead of an accelerating Metro bus that was lumbering down Second Avenue. Seattle police vehicles are supposedly nonsmoking in these politically correct days, but there was more than a hint of cigarette smoke wafting around in the Mustang when I got inside. Despite the cold, the driver's-side window was rolled all the way down.

I reached behind me for the seat belt as Sue

threw the car into a sharp right onto Clay and raced toward First.

"If you don't mind my saying so, from the way you're driving, I'd guess it isn't all that great," I said.

Sue Danielson made a face. "It's my son," she said. "Jared. He got himself suspended from school yesterday afternoon for fighting in the lunch line. He says one of the other kids stole his lunch money during gym. He claims all he wanted to do was get the money back. So the principal handed out a three-day suspension. Great punishment! How do those jerks figure? Since when is letting a teenager stay home by himself for three days a punishment?"

Ah, the joys of parenthood. No wonder the Mustang reeked of cigarette smoke. Sue Danielson was upset, and I couldn't blame her. Being a parent is a generally thankless can of worms. Being a single parent is even more so. But in police work having a partner whose mind isn't totally focused on the job can prove to be downright dangerous. Cops live in a world where even momentary lapses in concentration can be fatal.

"How old is Jared?" I asked.

"Twelve."

"Generally a good kid?"

"More or less," she said grudgingly.

"Let me give you some unsolicited advice, Sue. The only cure for a twelve-year-old male is time. Lots of it. Wait and see. By twenty, Jared will be fine."

"If he lives that long," she added.

"Where is he right now?" I asked. "At home?"

Sue nodded grimly. "Probably in the family room on the couch, watching MTV even as we speak. I dragged his ass out of bed before I left home and told him if he so much as poked his head outside the door, I'd kill him. Personally. And I left him with a list of chores to be done, starting with scrubbing the kitchen cupboards inside and out."

"That's all you can do for the time being, isn't it?"

"I guess so."

"Then forget about it. For right now anyway. Tell me about the case. Who's dead? Do we know?"

By then we were hightailing it down Elliott past the towering but invisible grain-terminal complex that was totally shrouded in its own thick mantle of fog. Sue is still relatively new to Homicide, but she's a good cop. Her jaw tightened momentarily at the implied criticism in my comments, but she took it with good grace. After a moment or two, her face relaxed into a rueful grin. "I guess I needed that," she said. "Thanks for the friendly reminder."

"The case," I insisted, still trying to change the subject.

She nodded. "The dead guy's on a boat up here at Fishermen's Terminal. Somebody from a neighboring boat saw the fire just after five-thirty this morning. By the time the fire department got there, the cabin was fully engulfed. They didn't know there was a body inside, though, until just a few minutes before Watty called you. I came in early to finish up the paper on yesterday's domestic in West Seattle, but I wasn't getting anywhere. I couldn't concentrate. I was glad the other two guys turned him down."

"Turned who down?"

"Watty. When he asked them if they wanted to work this case."

"Asked them?" I repeated. "I thought Watty's job was to assign detectives to cases. Since when did he start issuing engraved invitations?"

"Don't take it personally, Beau," Sue counseled. "You know how people talk."

"No, I don't. What's the problem? What are they saying?"

Sue Danielson shrugged. "That three's the charm. First Ron Peters and then Big Al."

So that was it. Those jerks. I had wondered, but this was the first time anyone had come right out and called a spade a spade. "You mean everybody really is scared shitless to work with me."

"Don't worry about it, Beau," Sue said with a laugh. "I told Watty I'm a big girl, and not at all the rabbit's-foot-carrying type."

"Gee, thanks," I grumbled. "I suppose, under the circumstances, I should take that as a vote of supreme confidence."

Sue clicked on the turn signal. We swooped off Fifteenth and tore around the cloverleaf onto Emerson. At the Stop sign, she paused, looked at me, and winked. "As a matter of fact, you should," she said. "Besides, now we're even."

"What do you mean 'even'?"

"You give me advice on child rearing, and I

help you get along with your peers. Fair enough. Tit for tat.''

Enough said.

The official name, the one used by the mapmakers who write the Puget Sound version of the *Thomas Guide,* may be Salmon Bay Terminal, but most Seattleites know the north end of the Interbay area as Fishermen's Terminal. It's the place where Seattle's commercial fishing fleet is berthed during the months when the boats aren't out on the Pacific Ocean, plying the waters between the Oregon Coast and the Bering Sea, trying to beat the foreign-owned, U.S.-registered vessels and each other to whatever remains of the once-plentiful West Coast fishery.

We raced through the parking lot outside Chinook's Restaurant and bounced over a series of killer, tooth-rattling speed bumps. Past two huge buildings marked Net Shed N-4 and Net Shed N-3 we darted up a narrow alley that was crammed full of fire-fighting equipment. We threaded our way as far as Dock Three where the fire lane out to the boats was full of trucks and a throng of firemen rolling and restowing equipment. Sue pulled over and parked the Mustang, leaving the blue light flashing on top of the vehicle.

It was early in November, and all the boats were in port. On the east side of the pier stood a long line of two-masted wooden fishing schooners. A few were old sailing vessels that had been converted from wind-driven to diesel propulsion. The others had been built with engines but had carried sails as well at one time. These old wooden boats, used by long-line fishermen to harvest halibut and black cod, were berthed down one side of the planked dock. On the other side were the seine-style—pilothouse-forward—long-liners. On Dock 4, next door to the west, were the salmon seiners, recognizable by their raised mainbooms and open afterdecks.

I wouldn't have known the difference if it hadn't been for Aarnie "Button" Knudsen, one of the guys I once played football with for the Ballard High School Beavers. The summer between our junior and senior years in high school, Button invited me to come work on his father's salmon boat. He told me it was a great part-time job, one he'd had every year from the time he was eleven.

I'm sure it would have been a good deal—if I had ever made it to the fishing grounds, that is. Unfortunately, it turned out I was a terrible sailor. I signed on, but by the time we reached Ketchikan in southeastern Alaska, I was so horribly seasick that Aarnie's disgusted dad gave up, put me off the boat, and finagled me a ride home. Who knows? Had things been different—had I actually found my sea legs and followed in Button's family footsteps—I might never have become a homicide detective. I might have spent my life slaughtering fish instead of studying slaughtered people.

Out beyond the buildings, we came to the place where the fire department had set up a perimeter by roping off the wooden pier at the point where it met a wider paved section. A group of old salts in coveralls, men I suspected to be mostly of Norwegian descent, stood talking to one another in subdued tones, all the while uneasily eyeing the charred wreck of a boat halfway down the dock.

I come down to Fishermen's Terminal sometimes, just to walk around. Early on a chill late-fall morning like this one was, it can be a seemingly idyllic place. Noisy gulls wheel overhead, appearing and disappearing, flying in and out of the fog. Water laps against the pilings. Boats shift and creak, occasionally thumping against the pier. But this idyllic setting is only that—a setting, like the flat backdrop painted on a stage.

The foreground holds the action where a troupe of men do the "work" of fishing—repairing boats and nets, cleaning fish-holes, hosing, painting, building bait benches and fish pens. I have utmost respect for these guys who, year in and year out, pit themselves not only against the unforgiving sea but also against the vagaries of international politics and government regulation. Most of them are independent as hell and more than slightly ornery—a little like the mythical cowboys of the Old West. Come to think of it, a little like me.

On this particular morning, I supposed that most of them had come to work early expecting to spend the day working on their wintertime maintenance logs. Instead of overhauling engines and preparing for the next season's first opener, however, they were stranded far from their boats on the landward end of the dock. From the grim looks on their faces, I realized word must have spread that someone was dead—most likely one of their own.

A uniformed harbor-patrol officer named Jack Casey glanced at Sue's I.D., nodded to me, and waved us through the barrier. "Any idea who it is?" I asked him on my way past.

Casey shook his head. "All I've heard from the firemen is that the stiff's too crisp to I.D."

"Oh."

Sue and I made our way down the dock. Even without having been told beforehand, I would have known we were walking into a fatality fire just from the appearance of the firemen we encountered along the way. They had done their job promptly and well. Not only had they managed to put out the fire, they had kept the blaze confined to only one boat—a schooner called *Isolde*. The flames hadn't spread either to the pier or to any of *Isolde*'s nearby neighbors. Even the *Isolde* herself hadn't burned on the outside, although the forward portion of the boat was heavily damaged.

In terms of fire-fighting success, that should have been a clear-cut victory. But the men and women I saw rolling up their hoses were a bedraggled, disheartened-looking crew. Someone had died in the blaze. Firefighters always take fire deaths hard, as though each and every person lost in a fire is a personal affront—a needless fatality they somehow should have been able to prevent. It's an occupational hazard, I understand all too well. Murder victims affect me exactly the same way.

A few feet from the *Isolde* a husky firefighter still in yellow coveralls and heavy rubber boots broke away from his companions and hurried toward us. "You from Seattle P.D.?"

Only when I heard the voice did I realize the firefighter was a woman, not a man. Her hair was cut short. Her broad shoulders were muscular, her at-ease stance seemed to reflect some kind of military training. In her early thirties, she looked tough but capable—the kind of woman who's instantly intimidating to a lot of men, but someone you wouldn't mind having on your side during an emergency.

"Detective Beaumont," I answered. "And this is Detective Danielson."

"I'm Lieutenant Marian Rockwell," she returned. "Seattle Fire Department, Arson Investigations."

Seattle's fire department has a team of arson investigators who carry weapons and are authorized to make arrests when necessary. Once the ashes and debris are cool enough to handle, the arson investigators are called in to do their stuff. They handle some fires entirely on their own, but when someone dies as a result of a fire, whether accidental or deliberately set, Seattle P.D.'s Homicide Squad comes into the picture. In those instances, we handle the investigation jointly.

"What's going on?" Sue asked.

"We got to it fast enough that it didn't have a chance to spread outside the fo'c'sle," Lieutenant Rockwell said, abbreviating the word "forecastle" to the approved nautical pronunciation of "foc'sul."

"One crew is just now finishing mopping up and checking for hot spots," Lieutenant Rockwell continued. "We should be able to go on board fairly soon now—as soon as the investigator from the Medical Examiner's Office gets here."

It's always a race between Doc Baker's folks and Homicide to see who reaches a crime scene first. We don't exactly keep score, but people from our squad always want to arrive before one of the M.E.'s somber gray vans. I was glad Sue Danielson had put the little Mustang through its paces.

"They'll show up eventually. Any idea whose boat this is?" I asked, taking out my notebook while Lieutenant Rockwell consulted one of her own.

"The guy who called in the nine-one-one report said it belonged to someone named Gunter Gebhardt."

"Nice Irish name. Pretty unusual for around here," I said.

"Why?" Sue Danielson asked.

Sue's from back East somewhere. Cincinnati, I think, so she could be forgiven for not knowing beans about Seattle's fishing fleet.

"Most of these halibut guys are born and bred squareheads," I explained. "An occasional Dane or Swede here and there, but mostly they're lutefisk-eating Norwegians through and through."

The soot-creased lines around Marian Rockwell's brown eyes wrinkled with amusement. "I thought so, too," she said. "No doubt the guy who made the initial call is. Alan Torvoldsen. Is that Norwegian enough to suit you? His boat's right across the way. He spotted the fire and called for help."

The very mention of Alan Torvoldsen's name rang a bell of memory that carried me right back to Ballard High. "You're kidding? Alan Torvoldsen? You mean good old 'Champagne Al'?"

"That's not what he said his name was," Marian Rockwell replied. "At least not in the report that came to me."

The Alan Torvoldsen I remembered was a couple of years older than I was. A senior when I was a lowly sophomore, he had been the big man on campus—a high-school playboy, someone who sported new cars, flashy clothes, and a ducktail with never a single hair out of place.

Just as Button Knudsen worked on his father's salmon seiner, Alan and his younger brother, Lars, spent summers on their father's halibut boat. The Knudsens were nondrinking straight arrows. The Torvoldsens weren't. Red Torvoldsen was never far from his flask of aquavit, and the boys were a matched set of hellions. Alan was two years older than I was, while Lars was two years younger.

Even in high school, Alan was a booze-drinking chip off the old block. According to BHS legend, "Champagne Al" Torvoldsen didn't go anywhere without at least one case of beer stashed in the back of his '56 Chevy.

The prom during his senior year was the pinnacle of Alan Torvoldsen's high school career. During the dance, he and his long-term girlfriend, Else Didriksen, were crowned king and queen of the prom. To celebrate, Alan invited everyone to an after-prom party to be held at the far north end of Carkeek Park. That infamous blowout—a party that is still spoken of in hushed tones at Ballard High reunions—came complete with fifteen cases of cheap champagne. It earned Alan Torvoldsen his lifelong nickname of "Champagne Al." It was also his undoing.

Cops busted the party only eight or nine cases into the program. The debauch may have been broken up early, but not nearly early enough as far as some disturbed parents were concerned. Before the arrival of the cops, several highly intoxicated young women—normally prim and proper Lutheran daughters of local Ballard area gentry—had shed not only important parts of their clothing, but several of their respective maidenheads as well.

A delegation of outraged parents descended on the principal's office early the following Monday morning. Looking for blood, they wanted someone to blame—someone who wasn't their own particular offspring. Alan Torvoldsen took the rap for everybody, and he paid big.

Despite a fair but unremarkable academic record, Alan was summarily expelled from school without ever being allowed to graduate. Within weeks, "Champagne Al" was drafted into the army and shipped off to Southeast Asia. Even at the time it had seemed like a miscarriage of justice to hold him accountable for everybody's drunken behavior, but that was the way things worked back then. Near as I can tell, nothing has changed.

Champagne Al got drafted and headed off for Vietnam. I finished up my high school career, and in the intervening years our paths had never once crossed. I hadn't even heard Alan Torvoldsen's name mentioned, not until now.

Audrey Cummings, King County's assistant medical examiner, showed up right about then, accompanied by my old buddy Janice Morraine, the second-in-command criminalist from the Washington State Patrol crime lab. Seeing them together, the old comics characters Mutt and Jeff came instantly to mind.

Audrey is your basic fireplug of a woman. Short, sturdy, stocky, no-nonsense, and a tad beyond middle-aged. Janice Morraine is tall and spare, angular where Audrey is round. Audrey is a nonsmoking vegetarian. Janice smokes like a fiend. Both of these talented women are sharp and politically adroit. Both of them have bubbled to the top in work situations where women have traditionally been excluded rather than encouraged. Young cops of both sexes who make the mistake of not according those two ladies the professional respect they deserve do so at their own risk.

Lieutenant Rockwell cast an appraising glance around the group. "Is this everybody?"

"As far as I can tell," Sue told her.

"This way, then."

Marian Rockwell passed out day boots for us to wear, then led the way toward the *Isolde,* followed by the rest of us. As I attached myself to the end of the line, I realized, for the first time, that in terms of Equal Opportunity, the investigation into the death of whoever had been on board the *Isolde* was breaking new ground—even in the politically correct world of Seattle P.D. All but one of the five investigators assigned to the case were women. Four to one.

Four of them and one of me.

Marian Rockwell was the only one of the group properly dressed for the grit and grime of a fire-scene crime investigation. The other women gamely hitched up their skirts and then scrambled over the wet, soot-encrusted rail and down onto a filthy deck covered with piles of wet, ankle-twisting coils of line, meandering hoses, and evil-smelling debris.

As I watched the women clamber over the rail one by one, I couldn't help thinking, You've come a long way, baby.

Because they had. All of them.

Decks of commercial fishing vessels make for treacherous going in the best of times. Now maneuvering on the *Isolde*'s deck was downright dangerous. It was covered with water topped by a layer of slick, oily slime that left zero traction and made walking hazardous. We waded our way forward past the last of the grim-faced firemen who were wrestling with an impossible tangle of hoses.

One of the firefighters caught my eye. "Good luck, fella," he said, just loud enough for me to hear him. I wasn't entirely sure what he meant, but I had a pretty good idea.

I smelled it almost as soon as I stepped on deck—an odor not unlike that of baked ham. As we neared the entrance to the fo'c'sle, the combination of residual smoke and charred rubber and wiring obscured the unmistakable odor of cooked human flesh.

The shattered hatchway door was the first thing I noticed. In an effort to reach the fire, someone— a fireman, most likely—had broken the hatch— splintered the middle of it, probably with an ax. But the edge of the door was still attached to the frame, held there by a metal hasp over which dangled a still-locked padlock. That padlock had been locked in place prior to the fire, by someone standing outside the closed hatch.

Janice and the others had gone on ahead, climbing over the sill of the hatch and disappearing down into the inside gloom. I paused outside long enough to jot a note, reminding myself to mention to Janice that the padlock as well as the remains of the hatch should be checked for fingerprints in case any had managed to survive both the fire and the firefighting.

Men my size aren't built for fishing boats any more than we're built for airplanes. I whacked my head on the hatch cover as I stepped down onto a makeshift metal ladder that had been placed in the companionway. The temporary ladder replaced the permanent one that, if not too badly charred, might well retain some critical fingerprints of its own.

Down in the darkened galley, with the interior lit only by the shallow light coming in through a fire-ax-created skylight, and with the water sloshing around my ankles, I found myself staring at a hellish scene.

It took a few moments for my eyes to adjust to the gloom. The fire hadn't burned long enough or hot enough for flesh to come off the bones. What I saw through the thick, smoke-dense air, was the still-recognizable form of an extraordinarily large man lying faceup on what was evidently the triangular, three-legged galley table. The cheeks of his face were strangely distended, like someone gathering up a mouthful of wind to blow out candles on a birthday cake.

It's funny what will strike you as odd in a situation like that. The first thing I thought about was a damn birthday cake. The second thing was the table.

Why was the victim lying on the table? I wondered. It didn't make sense for someone to be there. In bed? Yes. I could understand that perfectly. And I could see how someone might end up on the deck, especially if they were crawling on their hands and knees in an effort to avoid smoke and flames.

"What's he doing on the table?" I asked, moving forward to stand beside Sue Danielson, who had been next-to-last and who stood just ahead of me in line.

"Handcuffs," she replied, her voice tight and strained.

I saw them then, too. Three pairs of handcuffs, in fact. The man's shoulders were broad enough so that they almost covered the wide end of the three-cornered table, the part that was nearest the door. Bent at the elbow, his powerful forearms hung down beside and were fastened to the two chrome legs that supported the table's surface. Both wrists were secured to the table legs by locked metal cuffs. His legs dangled off on either side of the narrow part of the triangle with the ankles fastened together with cuffs just inside the table's third chrome leg.

Whoever had put the man there had meant for him to stay in exactly that spot. Permanently.

"Look at this," Marian Rockwell said, coming full circle around the far side of the galley so she was back behind me. Using a flashlight, she pointed to something in the sink. "The firefighter who found him said this was on the victim's chest. He had to move it so he could check vitals.''

We had come in single file. Since I was the last one in line, I was also the person closest to the sink. What I saw was a metal plate of some kind—a pie plate, maybe—with what looked like so many pieces of charred hot dog lying in the bottom.

"What is it?" I asked stupidly, squinting through the dim light.

"I think it's his fingers and toes," Marian Rockwell said in a hushed tone. "All twenty of them. I think they were cut off while he was still alive and left where he could see them. In fact, they were probably the very last thing he could see."

That announcement was followed by stunned silence. Homicide cops can't afford to be queasy, but right then a rebellious bubble of morning coffee rose dangerously in my throat. Behind me one of my cohorts made a strange, strangled noise that sounded very much like someone attempting to stifle an overwhelming urge to gag.

After first letting her breath go out in a carefully controlled *whoosh,* Janice Morraine was the one who spoke. "Okay, folks," she said. "Let's get the hell out of here. No one touches anything at all until after we get the police photographer down here to take pictures."

Her order was one we were all only too happy to obey. From a crime-scene-investigation standpoint, that was the only sensible solution. Too many people in a confined area at once are bound to disrupt things. In a crowd like that, someone can easily, if inadvertently, destroy a critical piece of evidence.

But it was also a good call in terms of people. We were every one professionals in a world where evidence of man's inhumanity to man is business as usual. But the idea of cutting off some poor guy's fingers and toes and then leaving him to burn to death went far beyond the range of mere murder. This was murder with all the trimmings— murder with mayhem and mutilation thrown in for good measure. We all needed a chance to decompress.

This time I led the way. After climbing back up the ladder, I stood by the smashed hatch and offered each of the four women a gentlemanly hand up as they followed me out. Only Marian Rockwell, agile as a cat, refused my offer.

Once she, too, was out of the fo'c'sle, Janice Morraine resumed command. She herded us all off the boat and onto the wooden pier.

"I want undisturbed pictures of the entire boat before anyone else goes back on deck," she said. "Somebody call downtown and see where the hell that damned photographer is. He should be here by now. Anybody got a cigarette?"

While she and Sue Danielson set about lighting up, I marched purposefully off down the dock, intent on tracking down Janice Morraine's missing photographer. I didn't have to go far. The "he" in question turned out to be another she—Nancy Gresham, a talented young woman who has been taking pictures for the Seattle Police Department for several years now. I met her hurrying down the dock, carrying her camera and a box of equipment.

She turned down my gentlemanly offer to carry her case. "Don't bother," she said. "I can manage."

"Suit yourself."

Nancy looked up into my eyes. "I was talking to one of the firemen on the way in," she said. "How bad is it?"

"About as bad as I ever remember," I told her.

"Coming from you, that's saying something," she returned.

"I guess it is," I agreed. And it was.

She continued on down the dock toward the *Isolde,* and I made as if to follow her, but Officer Casey, one of the patrol officers, came puffing down the dock. "Hey, Detective Beaumont," he said. "We've got a little problem here."

"What's that?"

He motioned with his head back down the dock to where another officer was manning the barricade. "There's a woman down there," he said.

"A woman?" I returned, trying to inject a little humor into what was an impossibly humorless situation. "Why would that be a problem? The place seems to be crawling with them. They're all doing their jobs."

Casey looked uncomfortable. "I know," he said in a way that told me he had missed the joke entirely. "You don't understand. She says she's his wife."

"Whose wife?"

"The dead man's," Casey answered. "Or at least I guess it's him. She says her husband is the owner of the boat. She wants to go on board. When I told her that was impossible, she went ballistic on me. Would you come talk to her, Detective Beaumont? Please?''

I followed Casey back down to the barricade, where a young officer named Robert Tamaguchi was arguing with a heavyset woman who towered over the diminutive officer by a good foot. Long before I reached the end of the dock, I heard the sound of raised voices.

''What do you mean, I can't go on board?''

''I'm sorry, ma'am,'' Officer Tamaguchi insisted placatingly, keeping his voice calm, reasonable, and businesslike. ''This is a police matter. No one at all is allowed on board.''

''A police matter!'' the woman repeated indignantly. ''You don't understand. The *Isolde* is my husband's boat. My boat. I want to see what's happened to it. You have no right. . . .''

I walked over to the barricade. ''Mrs. Gebhardt?'' I asked uncertainly.

A tall, thick-waisted woman with fierce, bright blue eyes and a long woolen coat to match looked angrily away from Tamaguchi and zeroed in on me.

''I want to know exactly what's going on here,'' she declared. ''I understand there's been a fire. I can see that. But why won't this policeman let me see what's happened to my own boat? And where's Gunter? He has to be here somewhere. His truck was out front in the lot.''

Behind the woman's heavy, angry features, there was a hint of someone I recognized, the shadow of someone I knew but couldn't quite place.

''And who are you?'' she demanded shrilly.

"Are you in charge, or should I talk to someone else? One way or the other, I'm going to find out what's happened."

Two distinct red splotches of irritation and anger spread out from both prominent cheekbones. With nostrils flaring and both hands glued to her hips, she looked fully prepared to take on all comers. She glowered at me, waiting for me to let her have her own way.

"I'm afraid I have some bad news for you, Mrs. Gebhardt," I said quietly, moving toward her, reaching in my pocket, pulling out my I.D. I held it up to her, but she stared across it without ever allowing her eyes to leave my face.

"What kind of bad news?"

"A dead man was found on board your boat about an hour ago now. It's possible he's your husband."

One hand flew unconsciously to her breast. "His heart," she murmured, eyes wide. "It must have been Gunter's heart. I've told him time and again that he had to lose weight. I tried to tell him it was bad for him to go on living the way he always had with all that butter on his bread and all those mashed potatoes. I tried to tell him he needed to go to the doctor to be checked out, get some exercise. . . ."

"I'm afraid it wasn't like that at all," I said.

"Wasn't like what?"

"The man on the boat didn't die of a heart attack, Mrs. Gebhardt. We believe he was murdered."

"Murdered!" she echoed in shocked disbelief. "That can't be."

"But it is. The investigators are down there now—taking photographs, gathering evidence."

"Else . . ." someone said tentatively behind her.

Mrs. Gebhardt spun around. A man stepped up out of the clutch of fishermen behind her. He was tall and lean and wearing a blue baseball-style cap with a Ballard Oil Company logo on the front. Worn Levis were held in place by a pair of wide red suspenders. The arms of his faded, still vaguely plaid flannel shirt were cut off halfway between the elbows and wrist.

"Alan?" she wailed in despair, moving toward him as she spoke. "Did you hear what he said? This man says Gunter may be dead. It isn't true, is it? It can't be true!"

"I didn't say we knew for sure," I corrected. "It is her husband's boat, though, and there is a dead man on board."

Else Gebhardt fell against the newcomer's chest. He gathered her to him with one hand and whipped off the cap with the other. As soon as he did so, I recognized him, even after all the intervening years. Alan Torvoldsen's ducktail was missing. In fact, only the smallest fringe of russet-colored hair remained in a two-inch-wide border from just over his ears and around the base of his skull.

"Al?" I said doubtfully. "Alan Torvoldsen? Is that you?"

He cocked his head momentarily, then a broad grin creased his face. "Beaumont? I'll be damned if it isn't J. P. Beaumont! Damned if it isn't!" He slapped the cap back on his balding head and then reached out to pump my hand. "What the hell are you doing here?"

I held out my I.D. close enough so he could see it, and he nodded. "That's it," he said. "You're a cop. I remember seeing the name in the papers. I kinda wondered if it wasn't you."

"It's me, all right," I said.

And then I looked at Else Gebhardt, sobbing brokenheartedly on Alan Torvoldsen's shoulder. I remembered Else Didricksen then; remembered her from years gone by as a tall, slender girl—a talented athlete in the days long before there had been any collegiate basketball programs for girls. There were few girl players back then, and even fewer scholarships.

I remembered that Else had started school at the U-Dub, as locals affectionately call the University of Washington, two years ahead of me, but I didn't remember ever seeing her on campus once I arrived there, nor did I remember hearing that she had finished.

"Else?" I asked. "Is this Else Didricksen?"

"Yeah," Alan murmured. "Look who it is, Else," he said, taking the weeping woman by the shoulders and bodily turning her around to face me.

"You remember this guy, don't you, Else?" Alan continued. "Jonas Beaumont. He was just a little pipsqueak of a sophomore the year we were seniors, but he was already a damn fine basketball player. Give him the ball, and he could run and jump like a damn jackrabbit."

Else Gebhardt looked up at me. "BoBo?" she said uncertainly.

It was the name that one year's batch of cheer-
leaders had stuck me with—a relic I had thought
buried in my past right along with my given name
of Jonas.

"That's right," I admitted reluctantly. "BoBo
Beaumont. It's me, all right."

Although her bright blue eyes were wild with
grief, Else Gebhardt smiled at me through her
tears. Her hands sought mine. "Please, BoBo,"
she pleaded. "Just let me on the boat long enough
to see if it's Gunter. I have to know."

"I'm not sure you should go anywhere near it,"
I answered dubiously. "The man on board—if he
is your husband—has been burned very badly.
You may not even be able to recognize him."

"I'll recognize him all right," she said
determinedly.

In the end, we compromised. At my direction,
the two uniformed officers reluctantly allowed
both Else Gebhardt and Alan Torvoldsen past the
crime-scene perimeter and onto the dock. I figured
there wasn't that much of a problem. It didn't
seem the least bit likely that Janice Morraine
would allow Gunter Gebhardt's widow access to
the burned-out boat, and I was right about that.
Janice didn't.

While Else waited on the dock, Janice Morraine
brought one of Nancy Gresham's police photos
over to the side of the boat. The grisly Polaroid
close-up she handed over to Else showed nothing
but the dead man's face. For a long moment after
Janice placed the small color photo in Else's hand,
she didn't look down at it. Once she was actually
holding the proof she had demanded, it seemed as

though she couldn't quite summon the courage to look at it.

At last, though, she dropped her gaze and held the picture out far enough from her so she could see it clearly. Time seemed to stand still on the dock. There was no sound at all and no movement. Then Else Gebhardt's features seemed to fall out of focus, and she fainted dead away.

Luckily, Alan Torvoldsen was there to catch her. I'm not sure anyone of the rest of us could have managed. None of the rest of us were strong enough—with the possible exception of Marian Rockwell.

Women don't seem to faint as much as they used to, at least not as much as they did in the old black-and-white movies my mother watched on TV once she was too sick to sew anymore. She spent countless sleepless nights in the company of one late movie after another.

And in those old thirties movies, when one of those pencil-thin female stars keeled over, there was always a strong leading man to catch her on the way down and deposit her on the nearest bed or couch, depending upon whether or not they were married at the time. My guess, though, is that none of those silver-screen beauties weighed nearly as much as Else Gebhardt.

The woman stood six-something in her stocking feet. Stark naked, she would have outweighed me by a good thirty to forty pounds. She outweighed Alan Torvoldsen, too, especially considering the full-length wool coat, but Champagne Al didn't seem to notice. He simply swept her up into his arms and strode off down the dock. Janice Morraine bent down and retrieved the picture before the wind blew the photo into the water, while I trailed off after Alan and Else.

"Where are you taking her?" I asked.

"To my boat," Alan grunted. "She needs a place to lie down."

"How far is it?" I asked.

His jaw stiffened with exertion and effort. "Just over there," he said, motioning with his head toward the next dock. "It's not far."

Maybe not as the crow flies, it wasn't far. Hitting a tennis ball, from one dock to another, even I could have managed it. But for a man carrying more than his own weight, down half the length of one dock and halfway up the other, it was a hell of a long way. Still, that's one thing I remember about Champagne Al from way back before he even had that name. He was always stubborn as hell. Stubborn and tough.

By the time we started up the other dock, beads of sweat popped out on Alan's brow. Else had come to and was already arguing. "Put me down," she insisted. "I'm all right. I can walk."

"I'll put you down when I'm good and ready," Alan Torvoldsen replied.

He finally stopped in front of one of the ugliest excuses for a fishing boat I had ever seen. Instead of the graceful old Torvoldsen family schooner *Norwegian Princess,* this was an old steel-hulled, T-Boat–class army lighter trying to pass itself off as a respectable member of the fishing fleet. The name of the boat was newly lettered on the stern— *One Day at a Time.* That name told me a whole lot about where Champagne Al might be coming from as well as where he'd been during the almost thirty years between then and the time when we'd been schoolmates together at Ballard High.

"Here," he said, setting the protesting Else down on her feet and turning to me. By then his whole face was drenched in sweat. Rivulets rolled down the back of his bald head and neck. He took off the cap and scrubbed away the perspiration with the sleeve of his shirt. "You hold on to her until I hop aboard," he ordered. "Then we'll both help her over the rail."

"I don't need any help," Else asserted, but she wasn't able to deliver. As soon as she tried to move under her own power, the wooziness returned, and once again she leaned against Alan for support.

In the end, it took both of us to help her climb aboard *One Day at a Time*. As he led her toward the galley aft of the pilothouse, I heard Alan Torvoldsen mumble something about ". . . one stubborn damn woman."

And although the remark was true as far as Else was concerned, I don't think Alan Torvoldsen had a whole lot of room to talk.

I climbed aboard and followed both of them into the galley, where I found Else Gebhardt seated on a narrow bench beside a tiny, bolted-down, Formica-topped table. She sat there with her elbows resting on the table and her hands clasped tightly to her face. It looked to me as though she was using her hands and fingers to physically hold back tears.

Without a word, Alan opened a locked cabinet with a key and took out a bottle of aquavit. Silently, he poured a generous shot into a glass and then placed it on the table next to Else's right elbow. Then he turned to me, one eyebrow raised and questioning.

I remember trying some of that potent stuff long ago. I know the heart-pounding, head-zinging rush. Even back in my most capable drinking days, I couldn't handle aquavit. "None for me," I said. "I'm working."

Champagne Al nodded sagely, returned the bottle to the cabinet, and turned the key in the lock.

"Drink it, Else," he told her kindly. "You need it."

But when Else Didricksen Gebhardt dropped her hands away from her face, there were no tears visible. Strangely enough, her grief seemed beyond tears. Shock works that way sometimes. Her face was pale, verging on gray, and the fierce blue light in her eyes had faded. She stared dully at the shot glass of liquor without making any effort to pick it up, almost without recognizing what it was.

"How is it possible?" she murmured. "Who would do such a thing?"

If she was expecting an audible answer to either of those two rhetorical questions, none was forthcoming—not from Champagne Al, and not from me, either.

Turning his back to her, Alan fiddled with the control on the galley stove, removed the cover plate, and then waited. When the well in the bottom of the stove filled with fuel, he lit one end of a twisted-up paper towel and used that to light the stove. Once satisfied that the fire was properly started, he replaced the cover, set a grimy coffeepot to heat, then turned back to Else, who had yet to touch her glass.

Alan studied her for some time but said nothing. Finally, he plucked a pack of cigarettes from his pocket, withdrew one smoke, and lit it with a wooden match he struck on his pants leg. He dropped the used match into a chipped, broken-handled coffee mug that was filled to within an inch of the top with an accumulation of ashes, spent matches, and dead cigarette butts.

Leaning impassively against the sink, Alan exhaled a plume of unfiltered Camel cigarette smoke that quickly filled the small galley. He seemed disinclined to say anything at all to break what was fast becoming an unnervingly long silence.

"I finally got Gunter to stop smoking," Else whispered sadly. "That seems pretty silly now, doesn't it? Stopping smoking may prevent lung cancer, but it doesn't make much difference if someone decides to murder you."

With no more warning than that, Else Gebhardt's tears returned. When two of them slipped silently onto the table, she quickly wiped them away. Meanwhile, Alan Torvoldsen remained oddly silent. It seemed as though the effort of carrying Else from one dock to the other had somehow robbed him of the ability to speak. Or the need.

"He was a good man, Alan," Else continued softly, her glance searching Alan's impassive face. "Gunter was a lot like you, you know," she added. "I've always been sorry about what happened. I'm sorry you two could never be friends. I think you would have liked him."

Alan Torvoldsen's eyes narrowed in a look that might have been anger or anguish, I couldn't tell which, and the fleeting expression disappeared before I had a chance to catalog it. With his eyes once more carefully veiled, he stared off over the disheveled graying hair on Else's once-blond head. His distant gaze seemed to drill a hole deep into the smoke-yellowed, years-old pinup calendar tacked to the bulkhead above and behind her.

The stark, empty expression on his face wasn't suitable for casual indoor use, or for mixed company, either. It came uncomfortably close to the thousand-yard stare I've seen occasionally on the faces of Vietnam vets who are going down for the count, unfortunate losers who are trapped in that crazed, memory-filled catch-all mental health professionals call Delayed Stress Syndrome.

Forgotten between his fingers, Alan's smoldering cigarette dribbled a trail of gray ashes across the already ash-strewn galley floor. When he noticed it finally, he shook the rest off into the mug-turned-ashtray he still held in his other hand.

"We won't ever know that now, will we, Else, so you could just as well forget it," he returned darkly. "Drink your drink."

The comment seemed blunt and unkind, and it was barked out more as a command than an invitation. Else's fingers inched uncertainly toward the glass. When her fingertips finally touched it, she looked up at him. "I'm sorry it happened," she said, "but thank you."

The words she spoke seemed strangely out of whack with what I thought was going on. It was as though she was talking about something else entirely—something that had nothing to do with either her husband's death or with the brimming shot glass sitting on the table in front of her.

It took a moment for me to put the pieces together. Embarrassed, I wondered if I hadn't inadvertently stumbled in on a private moment of loss and reconciliation that had been some thirty years in the making. It sounded as though Else was apologizing for marrying Gunter Gebhardt years before instead of Alan Torvoldsen.

Caught in that unexpected crossfire of intimacy in the cramped, smoke-filled galley, I felt suddenly isolated and invisible. It seemed as though the other two people had completely forgotten my presence. I was about to clear my throat to remind them when, as if on cue, the water in the coffeepot came to a sudden noisy boil. The rattling pot provided a much-needed diversion, shattering the moment and disrupting whatever it was that had passed between them.

When Alan turned to tend to the pot, Else picked up the glass and drained the generous shot in a single gulp. Her throat worked convulsively to swallow the burning liquid. Moments after she did so, her unnaturally pale face was suffused in a warm pink glow as the powerful alcohol blasted its way into her system.

"I should warn you," Else said. "I don't hold my liquor very well. It might set me off."

"That's all right," Alan said. "Crying's good for you."

He had taken two chipped but still usable coffee mugs down from the cupboard. He filled them with boiling water, spooned instant coffee into them, stirred thoughtfully, then handed one across the tiny table to me before picking up his own, proving once and for all that he hadn't forgotten my presence.

But his eyes settled on Else. "Especially at a time like this," he added. "When something terrible happens, everybody needs to cry."

One Day at a Time listed suddenly to one side. A quick tattoo of footsteps pounded across the deck. "Detective Beaumont," Officer Tamaguchi called from outside. "Are you in there?"

"Yo," I answered. "What's up?"

"We've got some kind of hit-and-run," he announced, when I opened the door, letting a burst of November chill into the stove-warmed galley. "It evidently happened earlier this morning—before the fire was reported. Sergeant Watkins seems to think the accident may be related to the fire. He wants you and Detective Danielson to get on it right away and check it out."

Alan was already sipping his coffee. The man's lips must have been made of asbestos. The liquid in my cup was still far too hot to drink. Reluctantly, I put my untouched steaming mug down on the table.

"I'll have to take a rain check," I said to Alan. "I've gotta go."

"That's fine," Alan said, waving at me with his cigarette.

I looked at Else. As far as I was concerned, Gunter Gebhardt's widow was no longer Mrs. Gebhardt. She was, instead, Else Didriksen—a schoolmate of mine, a former cheerleader who had once urged a long-legged, awkward kid called BoBo Beaumont on to basketball-court glory. That was back at a time when we had all thought our futures would be very different from the way they actually turned out to be.

"Else," I said. "I'll need to get in touch with you later. How can I reach you?"

Putting one hand deep into the pocket of her long wool coat, she pulled out a set of car keys and a wrinkled business card. She laid the keys on the table next to her empty glass, then handed me the card. On it was written the words, "Else Gebhardt, Consultant." That and a phone number was all.

"What kind of consultant?" I asked, as I pocketed the card.

"Seafood," she answered with a self-deprecating shrug. "What else would it be?"

What else indeed? "Look, Else," I said. "When you're ready to go home, one of the officers will be happy to give you a lift."

"I'm fine," Else said. "I can drive myself home."

"No, you can't," Alan replied.

"Why not?" Else argued with a sudden stubborn jut of her chin.

With a deft movement, Alan reached across the table in front of her, snatched up the keys, and stuffed them in his shirt pocket.

"Because I said so," he answered. "Because you've been drinking." He turned to me. "When she's ready to go, I'll see to it that she gets home."

His manner of saying it made it clear that he meant every word. And considering the effect I remembered from drinking aquavit, not driving anywhere under its influence was probably a damned good idea. I gave that point to Champagne

Al. One missing ducktail wasn't all that had changed about him.

When I started back out on deck, Else stayed where she was while Alan walked with me as far as the rail. "She'll be all right," he said.

I don't know which one of us he was trying to convince, me or himself.

"Where will you be?" I asked. "Give me your address in case I need to get back to you as well."

"This is the only address I have," he answered.

"You're living here on the boat? In the dead of winter?"

"It beats the hell out of where I was living before," he said.

I looked around at the ragtag wreck of a boat. I'm sure my skepticism showed.

Alan Torvoldsen grinned and flipped his cigarette butt over the side into the water. "If you think this is bad," he said, "you ought to try living on the streets." And with that, Alan hurried back inside the galley, closing the door behind him.

When I made it back out to the Mustang, Detective Danielson was already sitting in the driver's seat of the idling car, but I didn't see her at first. With one hand on the wheel, she was leaning across the car seat far enough to rummage in the glove compartment. When I opened the door, she slammed the glove box door shut in obvious disgust and sat up.

"I thought every car on the force was supposed to come equipped with a damned street map," she complained. "Somebody must have lifted it."

"Why do we need a map? What's up?"

"According to Watty, we're supposed to go see someone named Bonnie Elgin. I have her address right here. She lives on Perkins Lane, but where the hell is Perkins Lane? And how do we get there from here? Dispatch tells me it's right off Emerson, but I don't think Emerson goes all the way through."

That is an understatement if ever there was one. Sue Danielson was absolutely right. Emerson doesn't go "through" to anywhere, at least not anywhere useful and not directly.

Fishermen's Terminal is off Emerson on one side of Magnolia Bluff. Perkins Lane—one of Seattle's high-rent waterview property areas—is off Emerson on the other side of that selfsame bluff. It sounds easy enough, but between those two not-so-very-distant points, Emerson hopscotches around as though it were laid out by the proverbial drunken sailor. From what little I know about some of Seattle's early surveyors, it probably was.

I knew more about Magnolia than Sue Danielson did, and she settled down when I convinced her I could take us where we needed to go. Following my directions, she angled northwest on Gilman and Fort and then cut back down on Thirty-fourth Avenue West until it intersects with the westernmost section of West Emerson. No problem. In fact, it was totally straightforward.

Except for one small, unforseen complication. I got lost along the way—not physically but mentally. The route I outlined took us almost all the way to Gay Street. And to Discovery Park. And to the scene of a long-ago murder—the one that had brought an unforgettable woman named Anne

Corley across my path. Wearing a bright red dress and tossing her hair, she had sauntered purposefully into my life and changed everything about it.

It shocked me to realize that, for the first time, the identity of that murdered little girl had somehow slipped off the end of my memory bank. What was her name?

Too much time had passed. Too many murders. No longer did the answer come readily to mind, not even after several long minutes of silent concentration and mental urging. That wasn't fair, not when the end of that poor mistreated child's life had made such long-lasting changes in mine. Surely her name was far too important a detail for me to have forgotten.

I was still berating myself for my failed memory as we drove past those several fateful landmarks. The whole while, Sue Danielson was talking away a mile a minute, but I wasn't listening, wasn't paying attention. Encountering memories of Anne always stirs me with a terrible sense of loss—with an inconsolable aching for what might have been.

I'm sure if I had caught a glimpse of my own face in the rearview mirror right about then, I would have seen reflected back my own J. P. Beaumont version of Alan Torvoldsen's thousand-yard stare. And maybe for many of the same reasons.

"You say this is a hit-and-run?" I asked finally, as we turned right on Emerson once more and started to get serious about finding Perkins Lane. I figured it couldn't be that hard, since I knew it was right down on the edge of the bluff, near the water.

"You haven't been listening to a word I've said, have you?" Sue Danielson chided.

"No, I guess not."

"I don't blame you," she said. "It was bad, all right. When I first saw him, I almost tossed my breakfast."

It would have been impossible and pointless to attempt explaining to Sue Danielson why Gunter Gebhardt's charred remains had been the last thing on my mind as we traveled around Magnolia's winding streets. Far better to let her continue believing that I, too, was lost in thought, haunted by that day's murder rather than by one that had taken place years in the past.

It was just after nine A.M. when we came down the steep, fallen-leaf-cluttered incline that marks the beginning of Perkins Lane. The Elgins' house—a three-story, ten-thousand-square-foot giant—couldn't be missed. Other houses on the street were clearly of Pacific Northwest origin. This one with its pale rose stucco walls and gray tile roof might have been an Italian villa that had shipped out to sea and come to rest on the wrong coast. It was so new that glass stickers still lingered on some of the upstairs windows.

Although most traces of construction rubble had been removed, the scarred earth sat naked or else covered with bales of hay placed at key spots to prevent erosion. The bare rocky ground seemed to be waiting to see what hardy trees or shrubs could be tricked or trained into clinging to that steep hillside.

Two black Mercedes, one from the mid-eighties and one newer, sat side by side in the driveway.

Parked off to one side of the house was an old beater '76 Datsun station wagon that probably belonged to a housekeeper.

"That's cute," Sue Danielson said, wrinkling her nose. "His-and-her Mercedes."

"Don't be so sure about that," I said, once more unfolding my long legs out of the cramped confines of the Mustang. "For all you know, in this day and age, it could be his and his or even her and her."

Walking up to the house, I paused long enough to look at the cars more closely. The older of the two, a 500 SEL, was missing glass from the right front headlight. The fender surrounding the light was bent and buckled, and the grill had a crack in it as well. In addition to that, the hood ornament was missing. From what I knew of European auto repair, Bonnie Elgin was probably looking at several thousand bucks' worth of bodywork to make her slick but disfigured Mercedes look like new again.

Sue Danielson gaped openly at the imposing mountain of house. "I wouldn't want it," she announced with a disinterested shrug, and headed for the front door. "Too many bathrooms to clean."

Better detachment than envy, I thought. As a working cop, Sue Danielson wasn't likely ever to end up living in circumstances anywhere near this kind of opulence.

She gave the doorbell an angry shove, and a man opened the door almost as soon as the bell stopped chiming. He was around fifty years old— a fit specimen of upward mobility, dressed in an impeccable gray suit that was a perfect match for his hair. The man's mane of silvery hair was combed straight back in the classic style of a 1930s movie star.

"Bonnie Elgin, please," Sue said, opening her I.D. "I'm Detective Danielson, and this is Detective Beaumont. We're with the Seattle Police Department."

The man shook Sue's hand while his eyes drilled curiously into my face. "You're kidding me. Really? Detective Beaumont?"

I nodded. "That's the one."

Smiling, he turned to me and offered his hand. "Ron Elgin," he said. "Hang on a minute." Then he turned back into the house.

"Bonnie," he called over his shoulder. "You'll never guess who they sent. Detective Beaumont. Remember? The guy who donated the Bentley to the Rep."

I couldn't believe it. The damn Bentley again! Who was it who said that no good deed ever goes unpunished? Had a hole opened up in that columned porch, I would have been more than happy to have disappeared into it.

"Come on in," Ron Elgin said, totally unaware of my discomfort. He led the way into a marbled entryway with a spectacular vaulted ceiling. "Bonnie will be thrilled to meet you, Detective Beaumont," he continued. "And you, too, of course," he added with a polite nod at Sue. "My wife will be down in a minute. Would either of you care for some coffee?"

"Coffee sounds great," I said.

Sue nodded. "Coffee's fine," she said.

"Just go on into the living room and make

yourselves at home," Ron Elgin directed. "There's a new pot of coffee that should be ready by now. It won't take me a minute." He hustled off.

As instructed, I walked into the living room and wandered over to a bank of windows that overlooked the Puget Sound shipping lanes. The fog had lifted just enough to reveal a huge grain ship moving sedately toward the grain terminal.

"Great view," I said, in a lighthearted but vain attempt to change the subject. Sue Danielson wasn't about to be thrown off-track.

"What's this about donating a Bentley?" she demanded.

"It's nothing," I told her. "Nothing at all."

I would have been fine if Bonnie Elgin could have had the common grace and decency to back me up on that story. But she didn't. In her role as a member of the board of directors of the Seattle Repertory Theater Company, she had to come smiling into the living room, give me a big hug— as though we'd known one another forever—and thank me personally for my generous donation.

In terms of my ability to get along with Sue Danielson, my new partner, that was the worst possible thing Bonnie Elgin could have done.

As an unwed mother with little education living in the post-World War II era, my mother supported us with her hands. We lived in a tiny two-bedroom apartment over a bakery in Ballard. Mother took in sewing. The whole time I was growing up, she slept on the living-room couch. One bedroom was mine. In the other, Mom's treadle Singer sewing machine reigned supreme.

Over the years, she became an accomplished seamstress. The word seamstress sounds almost quaint now, like something out of another century, but that's what she was. She numbered some of Seattle's best-known names among her clientele, and not a few of them found their way to our door, climbing up the rickety stairs for fitting sessions.

I remember her telling me once that some of the society matron BB's—Bottle Blondes—Mother worked for didn't seem all that thrilled with their lives. "They may have all the money in the world, Jonas," she counseled, "but they're not happy. They don't appreciate the good things they have."

Bonnie Elgin was most definitely a society matron, but she was neither a bottle blonde nor was she unhappy. Her naturally graying, shoulder-length hair was pulled away from her face and secured by a big barrette. She came bounding down the circular stairway and into the spacious living room wearing a white tennis warm-up and an expansive smile.

Bonnie's doorknob-sized diamond twinkled as she held out her hand to Sue, then she hugged me as if we were long-lost friends.

"The way this morning started off, I didn't think anything good could possibly come of it," she said breathlessly. "But I'm very happy to meet you in person. Thank you so much for what you've done for the Rep. That Bentley of yours was a wonderful contribution. And it looks like it'll be an auction item again this year." Her face darkened. "The Guy Lewis trust, you know. The trustees decided to donate the Bentley for a second time. Of course, what happened to Guy and Daphne was a real tragedy. . . ."

I nodded, hoping to cut her off and steer the conversation into somewhat less volatile territory.

Years earlier, the Belltown Terrace Real Estate syndicate, of which I am a member, had bought a pre-owned Bentley. A chauffeur-driven Bentley on call to ferry residents around town was envisioned as a one-of-a-kind building amenity—something unusual with some real snob appeal. Unfortunately, that selfsame wonderful-sounding upscale amenity had turned into a mechanical nightmare. No amount of high-priced tinkering from a series of inept mechanics could get the damned thing running right. It broke down time and again, stranding residents in any number of inconvenient places.

In the end, and with me acting as point man, the syndicate had unloaded the British-made, decrepit albatross by donating it to a local charity auction. Months after the auction, both the unlucky purchaser and his wife had been murdered, but that's another story.

"Coffee anybody?" Ron Elgin asked cheerfully, joining us in the living room. He was carrying a beautifully inlaid wooden tray. On it was a vacuum carafe coffeepot, mugs, cream, and sugar. He set the tray down on a rosewood coffee table. "Detective Danielson?"

She nodded. He poured a cup and passed it to her. "Detective Beaumont?"

"Yes, please."

"Are you and Alexis Downey still an item?" he asked with a wink as he passed me my cup.

"Not really," I said.

"Too bad," he said. "She's a nice lady."

Pouring a third cup, Ron Elgin handed that one to his wife. "Are you going to be all right now?" he asked, regarding her solicitously.

Bonnie Elgin nodded and smiled gratefully as she took the cup from him. "Sure," she said. "I'm fine now, Ron. You go on to work. It was silly of me to let it throw me like that." She reached over and gave him a light peck on the cheek, which he returned with a husbandly hug.

"Well, you're getting good service," he replied. "With all the gang warfare and drive-by shootings in town, I never expected the police department to send out two whole detectives to investigate a harmless little fender bender."

Bonnie Elgin's smile disappeared. "It wasn't all

that harmless," she said seriously. "That man could have been badly hurt. For all we know, maybe he is."

"Do you want me to stay around for the interview?" Ron asked. "I will if you'd like me to."

Bonnie took a deep breath. "No, that's all right. You're already late for your first meeting, and I'm not nearly as upset as I was when it first happened. You go on."

"But you'll call if you need me?"

"Yes," she agreed. "I will."

"And don't forget to show them the wrench."

"No. I won't."

Ron turned back to Sue and me. "I do have to go," he said. "But I really appreciate your coming over right away like this. I didn't know Seattle's police department was this responsive."

Neither did I. Ron Elgin left his wife standing in the middle of the room, hurried to the double entryway doors, picked up a waiting briefcase, and disappeared outside.

"So you were the driver in this morning's hit-and-run?" Sue asked.

I was surprised by the kindness in her voice. Sue was right. I had been distracted during the drive from Fishermen's Terminal, and I hadn't paid that much attention. But hit-and-run drivers aren't usually accorded all that much courtesy, not even when they finally come to their senses and report what happened.

Bonnie Elgin nodded somberly. She settled into a huge but elegantly upholstered easy chair, balancing her coffee mug on one knee.

"I was afraid I'd killed him," she said with a

slight shudder. "I'll never forget the thump when I hit him. It was awful."

"Suppose you tell us about it," Sue suggested. "From the beginning."

"It was early," Bonnie said. "I left the house right at six-thirty. I was supposed to be in Kirkland at seven to meet with the contractor and the landscape architect. November's the best time to plant trees, you see, and seven was the only time we could all three get together. So I was heading over to the freeway. At that hour of the day, Emerson to Nickerson to Westlake is the quickest way to get there.

"I turned left onto Gilman and started toward Emerson. It was foggy. I don't think I was going very fast, but all of a sudden this guy ran out in front of me. I mean right in front. He didn't even look. I slammed on the brakes and swung the car to the left as hard as I could. But I hit him anyway, and he went flying into the air. The next thing I knew, the car was skidding, and I slammed into a signpost."

She stopped and shuddered.

"What happened then?" Sue asked.

"Naturally, I was scared to death. I thought sure I'd run over the guy and killed him, but actually I must have booted him out of the way. He landed up in a rockery along the street, in some kind of bushes. I got out of the car and went looking for him. When I finally found him, he was lying face-down and not moving. I was afraid he was either dead or else badly hurt.

"I ran back to my car and called nine-one-one on my cellular phone. I told them I'd hit someone and that maybe he was dead. And then, while I was still talking on the telephone, he got up all of a sudden and started to limp away. I put down the phone and went after him. He was bleeding. There was a cut on his face and another on his leg. His pant leg was torn to shreds. 'You're hurt,' I said to him. 'I've called the police and an ambulance. They'll be here in a minute.'

"He said, 'No! No ambulance! No police! I'm okay, I'm okay. Leave me alone.' And he kept right on walking. I couldn't stop him. He crossed the street, climbed down over the edge of the embankment, and disappeared in that greenbelt that runs along the railroad track."

"Then what happened?"

"I don't remember exactly. By then another car had stopped. The driver got out. He came over to where I was and asked me if I was all right. It didn't take all that long for a patrol car to show up—only a minute or two. And the aid car came right after that, but by then the guy was long gone. The cop who was taking the report acted like it was all a big joke."

"A joke?" I asked.

Bonnie Elgin nodded. "They all seemed to get a big kick out of it. One of them said it was the damnedest hit-and-run he had ever seen. I hit the guy, and then *he* ran. I told them I didn't think it was funny. After that, they more or less straightened up and tended to business.

"Since the fellow I hit was long gone, the medics insisted on checking me out, making sure I was okay. I told them they didn't need to bother. I was fine, except now I think maybe I bruised my knee when I banged it against the dashboard. Anyway, pretty soon the aid car left. The cops were about to start measuring the skid marks, but they never got around to it.''

"Why not?"

"Because all of a sudden all hell broke loose. There were sirens and ambulances and fire trucks coming from every direction. None of them came past where we were on Gilman, because they all turned off on Emerson to get over to the terminal. A minute or so later, somebody radioed the guys who were there with me. They told me they had been called to the fire along with everybody else. They gave me a case number and told me someone would finish taking the report later, and then they left. I have the case number right here, in case you want it.''

She reached into a pocket, pulled out a slip of paper, and handed it to me. I jotted down the case number. "What did you do then?"

"I called Ron," Bonnie answered. "Luckily, he was still home. He asked me if the car was drivable, and I told him I didn't know. So he came down to see. And it was. We got it home all right. I've called the dealer. He's sending out a driver to pick it up sometime this morning. He's bringing me a loaner.''

"Your husband said something about a wrench.''

"That's right. It's still in my purse. I'll go get it.''

"Tell us about it first.''

"When Ron got there, he turned the key in the ignition, and the car started right up. But then he noticed that the hood ornament was missing. You know about Mercedes hood ornaments, don't you? It's better now, but there was a real epidemic of hood-ornament theft a couple of years ago. We lost seven by the time it was all said and done. It's a small thing, really, but it drives Ron bonkers.

"As soon as he saw it was gone, he turned off the motor and said we weren't leaving until we found the damn thing. And we did, surprisingly enough. It's in my purse, too. That reminds me. I've got to remember to give it to the loaner-car driver so the body shop can put it back on the hood when they fix the car. Hang on. I'll go get them both while I'm thinking about it." Bonnie Elgin put her coffee mug down on a cut-crystal coaster and dashed off upstairs. She returned a few minutes later.

"It's bent," she said matter-of-factly, looking down at the shiny round chrome object in her hand. "I didn't notice that before. We'll probably have to get a new one anyway."

"Could I see the wrench?" I asked.

She handed me a small box-end wrench—about a $5/16$, although oddly enough, there were no markings on it to indicate what size it was or who had made it, either. And for some strange reason somebody had painted it with a solid layer of enamel.

Sue and I weren't playing with a full deck of information, but since we had been sent because Bonnie Elgin's hit-and-run supposedly had something to do with the homicide on the *Isolde*, it was best to treat the wrench as though it were an important piece of evidence. Better safe than sorry.

Using a cloth handkerchief and a glassine bag, I stashed the wrench in my inside jacket pocket. Meanwhile, Bonnie Elgin continued talking.

"I found the wrench first, before Ron caught sight of the hood ornament lying over against the curb. He said the wrench probably belonged to the guy I hit—that the impact most likely knocked it out of his pocket. He said that if we ever found out who that was, maybe we could give it back to him. Ron's a big believer in complete sets of tools."

"Me, too," I said.

"So do you need to look at the car?" she asked. "Or did the two cops get enough information on that earlier? I'm really not sure whether or not the man I hit was in the crosswalk. There is one around there, but I don't remember exactly where I was in relation to it when all this happened. Are you going to give me a ticket?"

"Mrs. Elgin," Sue Danielson explained. "We're not really here to investigate the automobile accident. That's up to Patrol. We're here because of a fatal fire at Fishermen's Terminal early this morning. It was discovered a few minutes after your accident. We have reason to believe it was an arson fire, so anyone seen running from that same general area around the time the incident occurred would certainly be a person of interest. What, if anything, can you tell us about the man you hit?"

"He was Hispanic," Bonnie Elgin said immediately. "I know that much. He had an accent. A heavy Spanish accent."

"You said he was injured and bleeding. Where?"

"There was a cut over his eye."

"Right or left?"

She stared for a moment and then gestured to an invisible point in space. "Left, I think."

"And his leg?"

"It was definitely the right leg. And that was bleeding, too. Pretty badly, I think. From a cut on his knee. My guess is that one will probably need stitches."

"What was he wearing?"

"Jeans. Tennis shoes. A jacket—a green jacket. Only a windbreaker, really. It didn't look like it was warm enough for this weather."

"Any identifying features—a beard, mustache, that kind of thing?"

"Not that I remember."

"How tall was he?"

"Not very. Only five-five or maybe five-six. And not very heavy, either. Medium build."

To me, five-five sounded smaller than medium, but that's all a matter of perspective.

"Which way did he go when he walked away?" I asked.

"The same way he came," Bonnie Elgin answered. "Back down the embankment to the railroad tracks. It seemed like he was more scared of talking to the police than he was of being hit by a car. Right then I couldn't understand why he was leaving, but if he was involved with the fire, I suppose then it all makes sense, doesn't it?"

"Yes," I said. "I suppose it does."

By the time we left Bonnie Elgin's house on

Perkins Lane, it was almost ten-thirty. The fog had
burned off fairly well. Out on Puget Sound, the
water was still mostly gunmetal gray, but here and
there overhead were occasional chips of pale
blue sky.

"Back to Fishermen's Terminal?" Sue Danielson asked as she started up the Mustang.

"Let's swing by that crosswalk on Gilman," I
told her. "I want to get out and take a look
around."

It wasn't difficult to find the location of the accident. A splatter of shattered glass marked the
point of impact. As far as that was concerned,
Bonnie Elgin was in luck. The glass was well
south of the crosswalk. Generally speaking, it's
not good to hit pedestrians at all. But if you have
to hit one, it's better not to do it in a marked
crosswalk. Everyone, from judges to insurance
companies, takes a dim view of that.

Sue parked the car. I got out and walked over
to the guardrail on the far side of the street. Heading down the embankment, a trail of footprints dug
deep into the soft, wet earth on the other side. The
person who had left those tracks had been in one
hell of a hurry. From where I stood, I could look
across the railroad cut and see the long creosoted
beams that formed the retaining wall for the bank
on the far side of the cut, but the metal tracks
themselves were out of sight.

Avoiding the footprints, I hitched my legs over
the guardrail and climbed down. Even stepping
carefully, the compressed mud squished beneath
my feet, bubbling up around my heels and into
my shoes. I stopped at the edge of the embank-

ment. Just below me, hunkered up against the retaining wall on my side of the cut, was a makeshift
tent. A blue tarp had been draped over a sheltering
framework of blackberry bramble. Inside was a
single box spring, minus the mattress, and the remains of a recent campfire.

I had stumbled uninvited into the home of one
of Seattle's homeless, and from the looks of it, so
had the injured victim of Bonnie Elgin's hit-and-
run. There were several bright red bloodstains on
the fabric of the box spring.

As I scrambled back up the incline to the guardrail, it struck me how little physical distance separated the Elgins' marble foyer with its magnificent
domed ceiling from this tarpaulin-covered hovel.
Existing almost side by side, both were part of
Seattle's Magnolia Bluff community, and yet they
represented realities so separate and alien that they
could just as well have been on different planets.

Or else in parallel universes.

5

Sue Danielson wanted to go straight back to Fishermen's Terminal and see what was happening there, but I persuaded her otherwise. Until members of the crime-scene team finished up with their physical examination of the *Isolde,* there wasn't all that much for a couple of stray homicide detectives to do but to stand around with our hands in our pockets and look useless and/or pretty, depending on your point of view.

So we turned off Emerson onto Twenty-third, parked in a triangular chuck-holed mire that passed for a parking lot and did an impromptu but thorough shoe-leather tour of the neighborhood. The strip of land on the far side of the railroad tracks contained a collection of small, one- and two-man businesses. We must have dropped in on ten or twelve offices and shops in the area bordered by Emerson and West Elmore. Most of them faced southwest and overlooked the railroad cut that sliced across the northeastern slope of Magnolia Bluff.

Looking out each succeeding window, I was surprised to learn that the blue tarp that seemed so exposed from directly above it was really well concealed from observers on the other side of the cut. The sheltering berry bramble that served as a tent pole not only provided support, it also offered camouflage. Only twice did we catch glimpses of the bright blue plastic. Both of those flashes were seen from businesses due east of both the tent and the crosswalk on Gilman.

Most of the people we spoke to were startled to learn that the makeshift shelter existed at all, that it lay—just out of sight—in what was, to all appearances, a permanent no-man's-land along the Burlington Northern's railroad right-of-way. I had hoped to find some observant witness able to tell us something about the tent's occupant and where we might find him. No deal.

The people we spoke to either feigned astonishment or else seemed downright uncomfortable to learn someone actually lived in a cut where hobos have traditionally hung out since the bad old days of the thirties. The issue of homelessness tends to disappear if you don't see actual living evidence of it up close and personal each and every day. The last person I talked to was a young woman who, despite the chill weather, was bundled up and sitting next to a concrete picnic table on the very edge of the bank. She clutched an oversized plastic traveling mug from the Chevron Beverage Club in one hand and a smoldering cigarette in the other.

In Seattle in the nineties, smokers are generally considered *personae non gratae*. People who smoke are required to slink outside with their cigarettes so they don't pollute the breathing mechanisms of their nonsmoking colleagues with their pall of secondhand smoke.

From the rim of cigarette butts that surrounded the table, this woman wasn't the only tobacco addict in the neighborhood who'd recently come here to smoke. Even in this alternating cold, wet weather, she was still sitting outside. I wondered how many of those outdoor smokers were courting the same kind of exotic pneumonia that had killed my grandfather.

When the woman saw me approaching, she pulled her coffee mug closer into her down jacket and guiltily moved the cigarette so it was below the level of the tabletop as though I were one of Seattle's smoke police. When I showed her my Seattle Police Department I.D., she seemed relieved to see I was only a homicide detective rather than some radical secondhand-smoke prohibitionist. The cigarette reappeared from under the table.

"Whaddya want?" she asked vaguely.

"Did you happen to see anyone unusual around here this morning, someone who didn't seem to fit in the neighborhood?"

She shook her head, tossing her mall-bang hair. "It was real foggy," she answered.

"Have you noticed a derelict—a tramp or street person—any time recently? Or have you seen anyone down near that blue tent on the other side of the cut?"

"What blue tent?" she asked, blowing a white plume of smoke into the air.

I pointed. "See that patch of blue over there on the face of the cliff?"

"Where?"

"Just above the timbers of the retaining wall. The blue you see is actually a tarp. It looks as though someone may be living there. I was hoping someone from here in the neighborhood might know who that person is or where I might find him."

The woman frowned. She gave me a doubtful look—as though she thought I was some kind of nut—and then looked in the direction I was pointing. "You mean somebody actually lives over there?" she asked finally. "No kidding?"

"No kidding."

"Well," she said. "I wouldn't know anything about that. Besides, why would somebody want to live down there in that hole with all those trains going past? They'd have to be crazy. What a stupid idea!"

She was young and more than slightly arrogant. She had a warm coat, wore a small diamond engagement ring on her left hand, and had enough extra money to squander two bucks per pack on her daily ration of cigarettes. Her whole attitude irked me. I suspected that she believed the reality of homelessness would never touch her personally. For her sake, I hoped she was right.

"What do you want him for?"

"There was a fire this morning over at Fishermen's Terminal, and . . ."

"I heard about that. Somebody died in it, didn't they?"

"Yes . . ."

She stood up, ground out her cigarette in the hard-packed earth beneath her feet, then pulled her

coat more tightly around her. "My boyfriend will
have a fit when he hears about the fire," she said.
"He's from Bellevue. He keeps telling me I
should find another job, someplace over on the
East Side. He thinks my working in the city is too
dangerous and stuff, know what I mean?"

I could have explained to her that every neighborhood has its own peculiar dangers, even ones
on the East Side of Lake Washington, but her cig-
arette/coffee break must have been over. She
headed across the street toward a tiny insurance
office without giving me so much as a backward
glance. No doubt there was a desk inside where
she toiled away feeding letters and numbers into
the keyboard and memory of some computer.

I found Sue already in the car when I showed
up back at the Mustang, shaking my head in frustration. "Nothing?" she asked.

"Less than."

"Are you ready to give up and call it quits?"

"I guess," I admitted. "For the time being. We
sure as hell aren't getting anywhere doing this."

By the time we got back to the *Isolde,* the
crime-scene perimeter had been narrowed. The official off-limits area was now small enough to
allow people access to other boats along the dock.
While crime-scene investigation is important, it
wasn't the only business that needed to be conducted on Dock 3 of Fishermen's Terminal that
cold November morning.

We returned to the scene of the crime and
learned that Audrey Cummings had already loaded
Gunter Gebhardt's body into her gray van and had
taken him back to the Medical Examiner's Office

up at Harborview Hospital to await an autopsy. Janice Morraine was busy lifting prints from the guardrail of the boat. With her glasses pushed up into her hair and with her brows furrowed in concentration, Janice was making her way along the rail of the boat, examining what she saw there under a beam of light from the wand of an Alternative Light Source box.

An ALS, as it's called in the trade, is an expensive but handy crime-fighting tool that allows crime-scene technicians to locate and lift prints from places and materials—tire irons, for example—where previously they would have been impossible to detect. Everything Janice did was under the watchful eye of the arson investigator, Lieutenant Marian Rockwell.

Janice didn't seem at all happy with that arrangement. I guess it goes with the territory. I suspect she's like a lot of people I know who spend their lives peeling back progressively worse layers of humanity's dark side. Most of us are loners who don't do well when it comes to working under the scrutiny of a closely observing audience, not even an admiring one. And I knew from personal experience that Janice loses all patience with anyone or anything that gets in the way of crime-scene progress.

When Janice glanced up and caught sight of Sue and me standing together on the dock next to the *Isolde,* she scowled. "Now what do you two want?" she demanded irritably.

I knew better than to take her exasperation personally. "Just looking for a progress report," I returned lightly.

Janice Morraine was not amused. Without stopping what she was doing, she motioned curtly with her head in Lieutenant Rockwell's direction. "Why don't you ask her?" Janice suggested. "She seems to be standing around with nothing to do but watch me."

With a number of people working on one homicide team, it stands to reason there'll be fireworks sooner or later, but this was much sooner than I would have expected. Marian Rockwell raised one eyebrow at Janice's surly comment, but she didn't rise to the bait.

"I've already collected my samples," Marian said reasonably. "It'll take lab verification, of course, but I'd say this was a communicating fire with two points of ignition. One of them was in the lower bunk on the starboard side. The other was on the victim's clothing itself. My first guess is that the accelerant was charcoal lighter, but it's too soon to tell about that for sure."

"What two places?" Sue Danielson asked with a puzzled frown.

"The mattress was lit first and allowed to get a good blaze going. That's the main source of ignition. The man was poured down with flammable liquid, probably about the same time the mattress was lit, but the victim didn't catch fire until sometime later, until after the other fire got going good. Eventually, because of the fumes, flames flashed over from the bunk area to his clothing. When that happened, that poor bastard was history. It looks to me as though terrifying him was as important as killing him. And if whoever did it was hoping to use the fire to cover up the murder, they didn't do a very good job of it.''

Isolde was riding low in the water. We were talking over the rumble of supplementary bilge pumps that had been pressed into service. They were hard at work purging the fish hole and engine room of all the excess water that had landed there as a result of the fire hoses.

Their ominous rumble was almost as dark as the thought that entered my head. "You said terrify. Do you think the victim was conscious when the first fire was set?'' I asked.

Sue Danielson shot me a quizzical look. "Does that matter?''

I shrugged. "It seems like if he was, he could have called out for help. Isn't there a chance someone might have heard him?''

Janice Morraine and Marian Rockwell exchanged meaningful looks. "I'm sure he was unconscious part of the time,'' Janice said. "At least I hope he was. But even if he had been wide awake when the fire was set, he wouldn't have been able to say a word.''

"Why not?''

Janice sighed. "Because somebody whacked off the poor bastard's family jewels and stuffed them in his mouth, that's why! Now will you two please get the hell out of here and let me concentrate on what I'm trying to do?''

"You bet,'' Sue breathed. "We'll be glad to.'' And she hustled off down the dock. I followed more slowly, with my hands stuffed deep in my pockets. If I could have crossed my legs, I would have.

"It's hard to imagine hating someone that much," I said to Sue, when I found her leaning against the Mustang. Marian Rockwell was there as well.

Sue nodded. "It sure as hell goes a step beyond the usual execution-style killing," she said.

"What it says to me," I added, "is that Gunter Gebhardt made himself an enemy. A serious, son of a bitch of an enemy. And someone with that kind of hard-assed grudge shouldn't be all that tough to find. People don't keep that kind of feud secret."

"All we have to do is ask the right questions, right?" Sue asked with just the smallest hint of sarcasm.

"Right," I answered.

I'm sure Sue Danielson had heard one version or another of this speech several times before. That's the big disadvantage of being the new man . . . person in Homicide—all the old-timers figure they have to take you to raise.

Marian Rockwell seemed to grasp the full import of our little Homicide Squad byplay. "My job's a lot easier than either of yours," she said.

"Oh? How's that?"

The arson investigator smiled without humor. "All I have to do is figure out what kind of accelerant this crazy asshole used," she said. "That's mostly a matter of simple chemistry. Spectrographic analysis. You two have to find whoever did it and why. When it comes down to why, I'm not so sure I want to know."

With that Marian Rockwell walked back up the dock where she once more took up a bird-dog position overlooking Janice Morraine's progress. Meanwhile, Sue stood gazing at the boat, as if just looking at the *Isolde* long enough would somehow reveal all the necessary answers.

"How about some lunch before we tackle all this?" I asked. "My treat."

Sue Danielson looked at me as though I were speaking some strange and incomprehensible foreign language. "Lunch?" she said blankly. "I don't think I'm particularly hungry at the moment."

"Maybe not," I told her, "but the way this case is going, we'd better grab something now while we can. It's likely to be a long day."

Sue glanced at her watch. "Oh, my God. You're right. It's after one. I told Jared I'd stop by and check on him during lunch. I wanted to make sure he's tending to business."

"Let's go do it then," I said, trying to sound more cheerful than I felt. Truth be known, I wanted to put Gunter Gebhardt out of my mind for the time being.

"In fact," I added, "if you'd like to, we could invite your son to come have lunch with us. How far away from here do you live?"

"Not that far," she told me. "Just on the other side of the Fremont Bridge."

A few minutes later, we pulled up in front of a bare-bones duplex on Dayton in the Fremont neighborhood. The place was a long way from lavish, but it was in a decent, settled part of the city. From the way the yards had been kept up and from the number of older, sedan-type cars visible on the street, I had an idea that some of those homes still housed the original owners—little old people who were just now making plans to sell off their bungalows in order to enter retirement or nursing homes.

"It's a long way from Belltown Terrace," Sue said defensively as she stopped the Mustang in the driveway in front of a minute garage.

"What do you mean?"

"Compared to where you live, this place must seem like almost as much of a dive as that bum's tent back there over the railroad tracks."

I felt a momentary flash of anger. I've never made a big deal of my money, one way or the other. All I want to do is to be left alone to do my job without having to justify where I live or how. I glanced at the house. It may have been a humble little place, but a big orange, black, and brown construction-paper turkey covered the entire lower half of the front door. A lot of time and effort and love had gone into that damn turkey. Sue Danielson didn't have anything to apologize for—certainly not to me.

"You pay the freight on this place all by yourself, don't you?" I asked.

She nodded. "Such as it is."

"With or without child support?"

"Mostly without," she admitted.

"So you earn this place, don't you?"

"Yes."

"Well, where I live is a goddamned accident, Detective Danielson. I'm living in the penthouse of Belltown Terrace because God reached out and struck my life with lightning once, not because I've earned the right to be there. So don't give me any crap about it. And while you're at it, don't give me any crap about where you live, either. Got it?''

After a moment, she smiled slightly and nodded. ''The guys down at the department are right about you, aren't they? You can be a crotchety old bastard at times.''

''Damn straight! Now, are you going to go get that kid of yours, or am I?''

''I'm going, I'm going,'' Sue Danielson said. And she did.

The instant Jared Danielson trailed out of the duplex on his mother's heels, I knew why she wanted to brain him. In fact, so did I. On sight.

He was a gangly, scrawny kid who shuffled along in unlaced high-tops. He wore a Depeche Mode sweatshirt, the sleeves of which ended several inches below his longest finger. Although early November means legitimately winter weather in Seattle, his legs were bare. His ragged jams seemed to be several sizes too large for his narrow hips.

I know the look. The oversized clothing means only one thing to me, and I was sure it sent the same insulting message to his mother. Jared Danielson was a gang wannabe.

The drooping crotch of his pants hung down almost to his knobby knees. Had I been walking behind him, I think I would have been tempted to give them a yank. It wouldn't have taken much effort to have dropped them around his ankles.

For some unknown reason, kids who insisted on wearing their baseball caps backward six months ago have now, for no apparent reason, collectively turned them bill forward. Jared Danielson was no exception. At least the maroon-and-gray Washington State University baseball cap perched on his head was turned in the right direction. The dark brown hair sticking out beneath it fell well below his shoulders, and a small gold hoop earring pierced the lobe of one ear. He sported a spectacularly black-and-blue bruise under his right eye.

I'm old enough and old-fashioned enough so that the combination of earring and shiner jarred. When I was growing up, a boy who wore earrings wasn't likely to be hauled into the principal's office for fist-fighting. I take that back. They got in fist fights, all right, but they usually weren't the ones who started them. This punk looked as if he had mouthed off to the wrong person.

Just one look at his typical twelve-year-old-tough-guy pout as Jared Danielson slouched into the backseat of the Mustang was enough to make me regret having offered to take the little ingrate along to lunch. But then, settling back into my own seat, I managed to find something positive in the prospect. Lunch with Jared Danielson was all I was in for. He was Sue Danielson's son. She was stuck with the kid for life.

"Where to?" Sue asked me, once she resumed the driver's seat.

Attempting to play the role of polite host, I turned to Jared. "What would you like for lunch?" I asked.

Jared glowered back at me and shrugged. "I dunno," he said.

"Fair enough. It's my call then. Let's try that little diner up on Forty-fifth," I said. "The one just across from the Guild Forty-five Theater."

Ever since the Doghouse Restaurant closed in downtown Seattle, I've felt like a displaced person. Over the past few months, I've auditioned a few other hangouts, but so far none of them quite measures up.

I hate to admit it, but I miss the thick gray haze of secondhand smoke. I miss the butt-sprung orange plastic booths with their distinctive, triangular tears and duct-tape patching. I miss the basic "Bob's Burger" with the onions fried into the meat. But most of all, I miss the crusty old-time waitresses who always knew how I liked my coffee and who saved me a daily collection of crossword puzzles from various abandoned newspapers.

The diner on Forty-fifth was trying hard—too hard—to achieve a "real" 1950s look and atmosphere. Their recipe for authenticity was missing several essential ingredients. What was needed was more grime, more cigarette smoke, a few nonconforming extension cords strung along the moldings, and some hash-slinging waitresses at least one of whom would have a racing form handily tucked in her apron pocket.

Jared skulked into the far corner of a booth. Sue slid in beside him. We had no more than picked up our menus when Sue's pager went off. She headed for the pay phone in the back. "Order me a burger with fries and a cup of coffee," she said on her way. "I'll be right back."

I turned to Jared, who was scowling at the menu. "What'll you have?" I asked, trying once again to break the ice.

"I dunno," he said. "A cheeseburger, I guess."

Such unbridled enthusiasm, to say nothing of gratitude. I wanted to slug him.

He avoided my gaze by staring out the window. "So what are you?" he mumbled sarcastically. "My mom's new boyfriend? Are you two going out or something?"

Boyfriend? Going out? If I had ever been tempted to cut the kid any slack, that just about corked it.

"The lady happens to be my partner," I explained as civilly as I could manage. "We're working a homicide case together. Period."

He looked at me then, his eyes angry and accusing. "Well," he said, "you're taking us to lunch. It seems like a date to me."

The waitress showed up at the booth and saved me from knocking the presumptuous little shit upside the head. I ordered burgers for Sue and me, then stewed while Jared unconcernedly ordered a cheeseburger and chocolate shake. I waited until the waitress left the table before I answered.

"Look, Buster. Your mother had to squander her lunch hour checking on a smart-mouthed kid who just happened to get his butt kicked out of school for the next three days. So for the record, I'm taking my partner to lunch. At the moment, however, I seem to be baby-sitting you, and it sounds to me as if you need it."

Jared Danielson was used to dishing out free-floating hostility to any and all comers. He wasn't used to taking it, especially not from a complete stranger. My returned volley of dispassionate animosity caught him off guard.

"I hate school," he said, as though that somehow justified his rude behavior. "I hate this town. I hate my mother."

"So give her a break. Go live with your dad," I said amiably. "Good riddance. You'll be doing your mom a favor. What's stopping you?"

For a moment, his chin jutted defiantly, then his face fell. "I can't," he croaked.

"Why not?"

Jared Danielson shrugged. The tough-guy mask disintegrated. His lower lip trembled, while his eyes filled with self-pitying tears. The surly, belligerent teenager faded into something younger and much more vulnerable.

"We don't know where he is," Jared answered, while his changing voice cracked out of control. "He's supposed to pay child support, but he doesn't. He left town, and Mom can't find him. She thinks he went to Alaska."

Sue Danielson came back to the table. "You two look serious," she said, her questioning glance shifting apprehensively between Jared and me. "What's going on? What are you talking about?"

For the first time, Jared Danielson's eyes met mine in a silent plea for help. "Football," he finally mumbled.

We were? I needed a second to take the hint. I took a clue from the WSU baseball cap still parked on his head and tried to follow his lead.

"How about those Cougs," I said, feigning an enthusiasm for collegiate football that I don't feel. "We were wondering who would win the Apple Cup this year—WSU or the U-Dub. Who do you think, Jared?"

As quickly as the boy had emerged from his hard little shell, he retreated back inside. "Who cares?" he muttered before lapsing once more into a stubborn, resentful silence, but not before I caught a glimpse of what was ailing Jared Danielson.

I never knew my own father. He died as a result of a motorcycle accident eight months before I was born. Days before he and my mother planned to elope, my father was headed back to the naval base at Bremerton after a date with her when the motorcycle he was riding skidded out of control and threw him directly into the path of an oncoming truck. He died two days later without ever regaining consciousness.

Faced with Jared Danielson's pain, I could see now how losing a parent you never knew was different from being willfully abandoned by a father you had grown to know and love. Having a parent die on you is a long way from having your father run away. One loss leaves a clean break that eventually heals. The other leaves in its wake a lifetime of hurt, of unanswered questions and emotionally charged blame.

In spite of myself, I felt sorry for Jared Danielson—baggy pants, smart mouth, and all.

I expected Sue to see right through the phony football ploy, but she seemed to fall for it. "Football," she said, sliding back into the booth. "That counts me out. Oh, by the way, that was Watty. Alan Torvoldsen called in and wants us to come by and see him sometime this afternoon."

"We can do that later. I'd rather go see Else Gebhardt first."

"Fine."

Jared ate his cheeseburger and drank his shake in sullen silence. Sue and I talked some over ours, but by mutual-if-unspoken consent, neither one of us said anything more about the case. When we dropped Jared back at the duplex, he didn't bother to say thank you. Or even kiss my ass. Not to me and not to his mother, either.

"Sorry he was so rude," Sue apologized after her son slammed the car door shut and sauntered off up the walk.

"Don't worry about it," I reassured her. "That's what twelve-year-old kids are like these days. Give him ten or twelve years. Maybe he'll improve with age."

"I hope so," she said.

I do, too, I thought as we headed for Ballard. For Sue's sake as well as Jared's.

Ballard as a district is considered to be Seattle's Scandinavian enclave. Whenever the king of Norway comes to town, somebody always schedules a ceremonial visit to Ballard. Whatever goes on there is headline-making news in the Ballard-based *Western Viking,* one of this country's two surviving Norwegian-language newspapers.

Ethnic jokes may be politically incorrect in the rest of Seattle, but down on Market Street, it's still open season on Sven and Ole jokes. People from Ballard don't necessarily see much humor in Garrison Keillor's tales of Lake Wobegon, because, as far as Ballardites are concerned, that's "yust the way things are." And when Ballard folks say "*Uff da,*" or "*Ja,* sure, you betcha," it's no "yoke." And it's not sarcasm, either. Even down through third-generation Sons of Norway.

Blue Ridge, the neighborhood where Gunter Gebhardt had lived with his wife, Else, is upper-crust Ballard, which isn't the oxymoron one might think. In Seattle, the price of houses always goes up the closer you get to the water, and the Gebhardts' house was on the view side and in a cleft at the bottom of Ballard's westernmost glacial ridge. The corkscrew street was named Culpeper Court.

The house Sue stopped at was a tidy if unassuming sandstone-veneer 1950s-era rambler. It may have been a "view property" once, but a newly constructed house with recently planted landscaping had been built directly across the street in a way that pretty much closed off the Gebhardts' visual access to the water and the shipping lanes.

Several cars were grouped in and around the driveway of the unfenced, meticulously mowed and landscaped yard. Three women, presumably friends, neighbors, or relatives of Else and Gunter Gebhardt, stood in a tight knot on the front porch. They eyed Sue and me suspiciously as we stepped up onto the porch from the manicured brick walkway.

"Can I help you?" one of them asked, but she moved in front of the doorbell and effectively blocked our access to it.

"We're police officers," I explained, displaying my badge. "Detectives. Is Else Gebhardt here?"

The women exchanged guarded glances, but finally, with a shrug, the one blocking the doorbell stepped aside. "Else's in the kitchen," she said. "Go to the end of the entryway and turn right."

In addition to Else, there were another seven or eight women milling about in the spacious country-style kitchen—middle-aged and older ladies who looked very much alike with their ice-blue eyes, more-than-ample figures, and blond hair going gray. Like the women outside the house, these turned on us as well with an unmistakable solidarity of distrust. Their collective message was clear. Mourners were welcome. Inquisitive strangers were not.

"Are you reporters?" one of them demanded.

This time, while Sue dragged out her I.D. and explained who we were, I caught sight of Else on the far side of the room. She was seated at a small desk that had been built into a bank of knotty-pine kitchen cabinets. Her back was to the room, and she was talking on the telephone.

"Please, Michael," she was saying, her voice controlled but pleading, her whole body tense with suppressed emotion. "Please put Kari on the phone. I've got to talk to her."

There was a momentary silence on Else's end of the line. The other women in the kitchen shifted uneasily. One of them offered Sue a cup of coffee more as a diversionary activity than out of any real interest in hospitality.

"Else's on the phone right now," the woman explained, edging Sue toward the door. "Wouldn't you like to wait in the living room until she's free?"

Sue seemed to take the hint, allowing herself to be herded toward and through the doorway, but something about the obvious discomfort of the women gathered in the kitchen, something about the tense set of Else Gebhardt's shoulders, kept me from following suit.

"Because I don't want to give you the message, that's why!" Else said sharply into the telephone mouthpiece. "This is important! I want to talk to Kari myself! Put her on the phone. Now!"

There was another brief pause. "Hello?" Else said a moment later, depressing the switch hook several times in rapid succession. "Hello? Hello? Why, that lousy little bastard! He hung up on me!"

"Else, such language!" an elderly woman exclaimed in a voice still thick with old-country inflections.

Across the room from where I stood was a small oak kitchen table. Seated at it, with her back to the window and with a sturdy wheeled walker stationed nearby, was a rosy-faced white-haired woman. She held a clattering cup and saucer in her palsied hand. Keeping her eyes focused on Else, the woman lifted the dainty china cup to her mouth and took a sip of coffee. When she put the cup back down, it rocked and rattled dangerously, but not a single drop of coffee spilled into the saucer.

"Be quiet, Mother," Else Gebhardt said sharply. "I'll talk about that rotten little creep any damned way I want."

Unperturbed, the old lady shrugged and took another sip of coffee. "I told Gunter he shouldn't have done that," she continued, her false teeth chattering loosely as she spoke. "I told him no good would come of it if he threw Kari out; that it would come back on you in the end. But would he listen? I'll say not. Not at all! Gunter Gebhardt never once listened to anybody else in his whole life!''

Else stood up and leveled a chilly, blue-eyed glare at the woman seated at the table. ''I'm warning you, Mother. I don't want to hear another word about it. Kari's father is dead, and I'm going to tell my daughter about this myself if I have to drive all the way up to Bellingham and break down the door to do it.''

Another woman moved quickly to the old woman's side. ''Please, Aunt Inge,'' she said soothingly. ''Let Else be. She has enough to worry about right now.''

But Else's widowed mother, Inge, wasn't so easily stifled. ''She certainly does,'' Inge Didricksen sniffed. ''And she should have started worrying about it a long time ago. She always let that man rule the roost like he was the king of Prussia. Now just see where it's got them!''

''Mother!'' Else exclaimed furiously. ''Drop it.''

From the way they were going at it, I figured Gunter Gebhardt must have been a bone of contention between mother and daughter since day one. Just then Else caught sight of me standing across the room. Her face flushed with embarrassment. ''I'm sorry, BoBo,'' she said. ''I had no idea you were here.''

''Detective Danielson and I came to talk to you, if you have time,'' I said. ''We need to gather some information about your husband. Is there some place a little more private than this? A place where we could talk?''

Behind me in the entryway, the doorbell chimed again. No doubt another group of sympathetic friends was arriving. Still holding the cup and saucer that had been thrust in her hand, Sue Danielson appeared in the doorway. Else looked from her to me and then down at her mother, who, totally unperturbed, continued to drink her coffee.

''Come on,'' Else said at last. ''We'll go downstairs. No one will bother us there. Just come get me if Kari calls back, would you?''

The woman, who was evidently a cousin, nodded and said she would. Meanwhile, Else turned on her heel and led us out the back door. Just outside, between the back door and one leading into the garage, was a cement slab. Yet a third door opened off it. Else paused before the third door long enough to extract a key from her pocket.

''Gunter always kept the workshop door locked,'' she explained as she worked with the key. ''He never liked having people go down there, but I can't see that it matters that much now. He didn't want people walking in on him when he was working. And, of course, I'm sure the collection itself is very valuable.''

Stepping into the darkened stairwell, Else switched on a single overhead bulb, dimly illuminating a set of heavily timbered stairs. Under the banister, on either side of the risers themselves, lay a pair of railroad ties. The rough wood had been notched to fit the steps to keep them from slipping. I saw them, but only enough to notice them, as Sue and I followed Else down the stairway and off across the darkened, dungeonlike basement.

The mistress of the house knew where she was going. We didn't. Stumbling forward in the dark, I slammed my knee into something sharp and hard. The pain of the blow was enough to make me yelp.

"What's wrong?" Sue demanded, groping for my arm. "What happened?"

"Watch out," I told her. "There's stuff around here that will break your leg." While we stood waiting for Else to switch on the lights, I rubbed my knee with one hand and reached out to touch whatever I had run into with the other.

It felt like a motor of some kind, and that wasn't too surprising. In the last few years, we've had a number of serious windstorms in the Puget Sound area. Damage to downed wires has sometimes knocked out power for as many as several days at a time. Feeling the metal object, I supposed it was one of those gas-powered generators that have become almost standard equipment in the basements of some storm-lashed neighborhoods.

A moment later, Else flipped another switch, and the room lit up. It turned out I was almost right. What I had thought to be a gas-powered generator was actually a small engine block for a diesel generator set, the kind fishing boats use to drive auxiliary generators and hydraulic pumps. For ease of moving, it was mounted on top of a raised four-wheeled dolly. I didn't find it at all surprising that Gunter Gebhardt would use his basement for off-season storage and maintenance of some of his equipment.

When the lights came on, Sue and I found ourselves standing at one end of what was apparently a single room that ran the entire length of the house. Unlike most basements I have known and owned, this one was clean and neat. The white tile floor gleamed in the glow of overhead fluorescent lighting. One end of the room was devoted to storage. There the carefully organized shelves held the kinds of tools and equipment you'd expect in the workshop of a boat-owning fisherman. And those didn't interest me very much. After all, if you've seen one bench vise, you've seen them all.

What intrigued me were the wooden display cases that lined the entire opposite wall. I started toward them, but Else stopped me.

"Don't move until I turn off the alarm," she said. I heard several electronic beeps from a keypad as Else punched in a code to turn off what was evidently a silent home-security system.

"Okay," she said. "It's off now."

By then I was already moving toward the well-lit, glass-enclosed curio cases. Metal locks had been slid in between the two separate glass panels that formed the front of each section of case. The glass shelves were lit from both above and below by a bank of fluorescent fixtures at the top and bottom of each case. And standing on the sturdy glass shelves were literally hundreds of tiny figures—toy soldiers, each standing on his own private base.

I remember having some lead soldiers of my own once back when I was a little kid. My set contained only a dozen soldiers in all—G.I.'s decked out in full combat regalia. I loved those damn soldiers, played with them every day, cried when I lost one, and begged my mother for more. But toy soldiers like that were too expensive for my single mother's limited means. Those twelve in that one set were all I ever owned.

It wasn't until I was in high school and found the last one lurking in a bottom dresser drawer that my mother told me, with no little shame, that my precious set of soldiers had come to me via a Toys for Tots drive at our church. Mother's obvious chagrin at having had to resort to charity was contagious. I threw away that last remaining soldier, although now I wish I'd kept him.

And so, those ranked figures on the well-lit shelves held a childish, almost magnetic attraction for me. Enchanted at the prospect and walking like one lost in a hypnotic trance, I moved across the glaringly clean tile of Gunter Gebhardt's basement floor. My mind was alive with anticipation, knowing that I would be delighted by the engrossing detail of what I'd find there.

And I was, too, but only for a moment. Only until I recognized the uniforms.

These were combat-ready troops all right— World War II–vintage soldiers circa 1940 or so. But these weren't my old G.I. pals, not by a long shot.

No, Gunter Gebhardt's soldiers were German troops, down to the last tiny, gruesome detail. On each hand-painted, khaki-colored uniform, the awful black-and-white swastika insignias were clearly visible.

I'm not sure why it surprised me so, but the shock on my face must have been readily apparent.

"Gunter's father was a piliot in the *Luftwaffe*," Else explained. "He was killed shortly before D-day. Gunter's been making these soldiers for years. It was his way of honoring a father he barely knew."

I only half heard what Else Gebhardt was saying. I was studying the collection of miniature soldiers in their painstakingly painted Nazi uniforms and thinking about my own father. He died just before D-day as well. Same war. Different side.

Looking around the basement now, I saw it through different eyes and felt as though I had been given a glimpse of not one but two dead men—an unsung war hero, a man who had presumably died honorably while fighting on the wrong side of a lost cause. And his son, who had spent his entire adult life living in a country where his father's wartime exploits would have been anathema to anyone Gunter chose to tell. Rather than discussing his father aloud, he had created this secret basement shrine.

I wondered if Gunter Gebhardt ever knew how

lucky he was. He had been fortunate enough to find a wife who had understood and accepted his need to honor his father. I saw Else Gebhardt in a whole new light as well.

"How did your husband happen to come to this country?" Sue Danielson asked.

Else beckoned for us to follow her and led us to a small workbench area where three tall stools were grouped around a waist-high countertop. We each settled on a stool.

"I've never been quite clear on how it happened, but somehow Gunter and his mother ended up in Norway after the war. Her name was Isolde. That's where the name of Gunter's boat came from. She married a Norwegian fisherman named Einar Aarniessen who happened to be my father's second cousin. When Gunter was in his mid-teens, both his mother and stepfather were killed in an automobile accident. When Gunter wanted to come to this country, my father sponsored him."

"That's how you two met?" I asked.

Else nodded. "I didn't know it then, but I think it was a put-up deal. My father wanted a son, you see—someone to fish with, someone to leave his business to. And since his only child was a girl— me—the best Daddy could hope for was a suitable son-in-law. As far as that was concerned, Gunter was perfect. He was a hard worker. He didn't smoke or drink."

Unlike a certain hell-raising boyfriend named Champagne Al Torvoldsen, I thought. I said, "Gunter didn't smoke, he didn't drink, and he needed a father."

"That, too," Else Gebhardt said with a wistful

little half-smile that made me wonder if she, too, was comparing those two very different young men as they must have been back then—the wild-haired, happy-go-lucky Alan and the straight-arrow, serious Gunter.

She gave me a searching look. "I suppose you knew we had to get married?"

I shook my head. What must have seemed like the central tragedy of her teenage years had been invisible to me and probably to most of the other kids at Ballard High as well.

"I mean, I had to marry someone," she added, "and Alan was long gone. My father saw to that. Fortunately for me, Gunter stepped in, but then I lost the baby anyway, when I was five months along. Our own daughter—Gunter's and mine—wasn't born until much later, when we were both beginning to believe we would never have a child."

Else shook her head sadly. "It's funny, isn't it, the things you think about at a time like this. Gunter and I had a good life together. He was a difficult person to understand at times, but we got along all right. I wasn't in love with him when we got married, but I came to love him eventually."

She was silent for a moment, looking across the room at the shelves filled with handmade soldiers. It seemed to me that she welcomed the chance to talk, to unburden herself of the secrets she had kept bottled up for years.

"It's strange. My father adored the ground Gunter walked on. My mother liked him all right at first, but later, especially these last few years, it seemed as though she resented every breath he took. Then there's my daughter, Kari. Not just my daughter, she's Gunter's daughter, too. Kari hasn't spoken to him or to me for almost four years now. And that boyfriend of hers wouldn't let me talk to her today, wouldn't even let me give her the news that her father is dead. I don't know if she'll bother to come to his funeral.''

Else Gebhardt stopped speaking and looked bleakly from Sue Danielson to me. ''I'm sorry to go blithering like this. You probably hear these kinds of sordid little tales time and again, don't you? And I don't suppose you stopped by expecting to hear all this ancient history.''

''It helps,'' Sue Danielson put in quickly. ''It allows us to form a more complete picture of who-all is involved. Besides you, who can tell us about your husband's associates, his working relationships?''

''If you ask around Fishermen's Terminal or the Norwegian Commercial Club, I'd imagine most people would tell you that Gunter drove a hard bargain, and that's true. He wasn't easy to get along with, but he was a man of his word. And there was no one in the world he was harder on than on Gunter Gebhardt himself.''

''He took over your father's fishing business?'' I asked. ''Or did Gunter buy your father out?''

A pained shadow crossed Else's face. ''My father had a heart attack at age fifty-seven. He was totally disabled for five years before he died. If it hadn't been for Gunter, Daddy and Mother would have lost everything—the house, the boat, the cabin on Whidbey Island.''

She shook her head. ''Nobody ever handed

Gunter anything on a silver platter. He worked like a dog to hold it all together. And it paid off. We own this house free and clear, BoBo. And the boat as well. We don't owe a dime on it, either. That's why, even these last few years when the fishing openers have been so short and when every man and his dog were out there trying to grab what few fish were left to catch, Gunter was still able to make it and do all right.

"We were lucky. For one thing, when the iron curtain fell, Gunter got in on the ground floor with some of the new joint-venture things coming out of Russia. For another, we didn't owe any money while everyone else was being eaten alive by interest rates."

Something was starting to bother me. Else Gebhardt was talking a blue streak, telling us all kinds of things we hadn't asked and didn't necessarily need to know. I wondered if we weren't being fed a line of some kind; if the tales Else was telling us were nothing more than a thick smoke screen designed to hide something else— something she didn't want to say.

"What happened last night?" I asked, inserting the question in a place where Else had most likely only paused for breath.

"What do you mean?"

"What was he doing down at the boat in the middle of the night in the middle of the winter?"

A slight flush crept up Else Gebhardt's neck. "He stayed there sometimes. Overnight."

"Why?"

"Because he wanted to."

I don't like boats much. They smell of diesel

fuel and grease and dead fish and mold. They're dank and damp and cold.

"Why?" I asked again. "In the winter, if someone can choose between sleeping in a hard, narrow bunk on a boat or in a nice warm bed in a cozy house like this one, you'd have to be crazy to choose the bunk."

"We had a fight," Else said quietly. "He left the house and said he wasn't coming back."

"What did you fight about?"

"My mother. She's the one thing we've always fought over. You see, this house belonged to my parents originally. We bought it from them, and Daddy used the money to buy an annuity for Mother, so she'd have some kind of pension income of her own. And Gunter promised my father that Mother could always live with us; that we'd take care of her for as long as she lived.

"Gunter was a man of his word. He took that promise very seriously, and he kept it. We both have. But it's cost me more than it has him. You don't know what it's like living with her day in and day out. Mother still acts like the house belongs to her, like we're only living here because she lets us. The towels have to be folded the way she likes them. Everything has to be done her way, and I don't have any say in it at all."

Else paused again, and I thought I could see how this was all shaping up. In the age-old battle between contentious in-laws, someone is always bound to be caught in the middle.

"Let me guess," I said. "Gunter gave you an ultimatum. He told you that you'd have to choose between them. Either your mother was out the door or he was."

Else shook her head. "No," she said. "That wasn't it at all. I told Gunter last night that I wanted to sell the house and put my mother in a retirement home. I've found one I think she'd like down in Gig Harbor. I told him that if he didn't agree to back me up on this and sell the house, I was leaving—that I'd go live in an apartment over someone's garage if I had to.

"I tried to explain to him that sometime before I died, I wanted to live in a house of my own— a place that belonged to me more than it did to my mother. A place where I could leave the dirty dishes in the dishwasher overnight without running it and no one would ever know about it but me."

"What did Gunter say?"

"No. Not just no, but *absolutely no*! He told me I was being silly and selfish. And then he left—stormed out of the house right in the middle of the fight. He just walked out the door, got in his truck, and went down to Fishermen's Terminal to spend the night. That's what's so unfair about it. Men can do that, you know. They can leave. Women can't. Somebody has to stay behind to take care of things. I had to stay here with Mother. I've had to do that my whole life."

Else Gebhardt's blue eyes suddenly brimmed with tears. "I feel so awful. I loved him. And I'm sorry he's dead. And I don't know what I'll do without him, but I'm mad at him, too, dammit! Because he got away, and he left me holding the bag. And because he didn't even bother to kiss me good-bye."

Just then a door opened at the top of the stairs. "Else?" a woman's voice called. "Phone."

"I can't talk to anyone right now," Else managed, choking down a sob. "Tell them I'll call back."

"It's Kari."

"Oh, of course," Else said, wiping the tears from her face and lurching to her feet. "Kari. Tell her I'll be right there. You'll excuse me?"

Sue and I nodded in unison. After Else left, I looked down at the notebook on the countertop in front of me. The page was blank.

"All this stream-of-consciousness stuff isn't getting us anywhere, is it?"

"Not really," Sue agreed. "But there's one thing I'm curious about."

"What's that?"

"Why does she keep calling you BoBo?"

I didn't much want to discuss it, but I figured I'd be better off getting it out of the way once and for all.

"It's from back in the old days," I answered shortly. "Back when dinosaurs roamed the earth. It's a nickname that dates from Ballard High School Beaver days, when the cheerleading squad used to give pet names to all the athletes."

"You two knew one another back then?"

"As well as a lowly sophomore ever knows the senior movers and shakers. You know how that goes. Else and Alan Torvoldsen were a real item back then."

"That's the guy she was going to marry? The one who knocked her up? Isn't he the same one Watty wants us to see later today?"

"That's right. In case you hadn't noticed, Ballard's really a small town stuck in the middle of a big city."

Sue Danielson nodded. "I'm beginning to figure that out," she said.

I got up and prowled around Gunter Gebhardt's compulsively clean workshop. Stored in one cupboard I found the collection of carefully crafted plaster molds he had used to create his army of lead soldiers. I also found the collection of paints and delicate brushes and files he must have used to do the finish work on the soldiers once they came out of the molds. Painstakingly making those soldiers must have been the sole creative outlet for a man with considerable artistic talent and capability.

The door at the top of the stairs opened, and the stairs creaked under the weight of heavy footsteps. Soon Else Gebhardt appeared from behind the partition at the bottom of the stairs. She was still crying, but she was smiling through the tears.

"Kari's coming down from Bellingham. Michael's bringing her down. They'll be here early this evening. I can hardly believe it." As far as I could see, it seemed reasonable that a daughter faced with news of her father's death would show up to help her mother. "What makes that so hard to believe?" I asked.

"You don't understand," Else replied. "The last time Gunter and I saw Kari was the night of her high school graduation. She cut us dead—refused to speak to either one of us. I thought it would break her father's heart."

"I heard you on the phone earlier. When all

this came up, how did you know where to call her, then?''

"Kari stays in touch with her grandmother—with my mother," Else answered.

No wonder Else wanted to be out from under her mother's thumb. Inge Didriksen was a problem. On more than one front.

The phone call from Kari seemed to have had a calming effect on Else. After that we settled down and took some more organized information from her. What time her husband had left the house the previous evening—seven. Where had he said he was going—the boat. Did Else know of anyone with whom Gunter was having difficulties—she did not. Was she aware of any business dealings that may have gone awry—not that she could think of.

The questions were straightforward, and so were the answers. That kind of basic interview may not seem like much in terms of drama or excitement, but the information gained usually forms the foundation of a murder investigation. It's like a baseline X ray on a cancer patient. It tells investigators where and when things started going haywire. It's the hub of a wagon wheel—an initial point for branching out and asking more questions.

As we walked away from the house and threaded our way through the collection of parked cars, I was struck by how commonplace and ordinary the house looked. Yet inside those sandstone walls there had been a world of multigenerational conflict—years and decades of parents and children at war with one another.

Of course, everyone tries to pretend to the outside world that his own family isn't at all like that, but maybe if you scratch the surface, most of them are just that way. Sue Danielson's family certainly wasn't absolutely smooth and trouble-free. The little lunchtime set-to with Jared had proved that.

I left the Gebhardts' home in Blue Ridge convinced that Else and Gunter's seemingly troubled existence, one filled with marital and parental strife, wasn't all that different from anyone else's.

Mine included.

Sue Danielson and I drove back to Fishermen's Terminal and hit the bricks, or rather the planks. We stumped up and down the separate docks, asking questions, talking to folks.

That first pass wasn't particularly productive. No one had seen anyone acting strangely the night before. No one had noticed anything out of the ordinary. When you're working a homicide investigation, those kinds of answers are to be expected, either because the various witnesses really haven't seen anything or because they don't want to become involved. It's also the reason why detectives seem to go back over the same ground, asking the same questions again and again.

Gradually, however, through the eyes of Gunter Gebhardt's peers, a complex picture began to emerge. "That damn hardheaded Kraut," as Gunter was referred to more than once, wasn't what you could have called Mr. Personality.

Despite thirty years spent working there, he hadn't been especially well liked in Ballard's fishing community. Grudgingly respected, yes, but not necessarily liked. A few people made wryly derogatory comments about Gunter's fishing capability.

I wasn't able to sort out if they were just making fun of him—which in Norwegian fishing circles pretty much goes with the program—or if Gunter Gebhardt really hadn't been all that good a fisherman. Still, not even his most outspoken critics faulted Gunter's general business acumen and sense of duty.

We spent almost half an hour with Dag Rasmussen, a grizzled and opinionated old salt whose boat, *The Longliner,* was berthed two boats away from the charred remains of Gunter Gebhardt's *Isolde.* Clad in greasy coveralls, Dag was elbow-deep in overhauling the main engine on his boat when we interrupted him.

"Gunter Gebhardt was one tough son of a bitch and hell to work for, too," Dag told us. Leaning on the rail of *The Longliner,* he seemed unperturbed by our dragging him away from his work.

"You have to remember that Kraut was still making money when lots of the other guys were falling by the wayside. And don't forget, either," Dag added, shaking a gnarled finger in my face, "after Henrik Didriksen's heart attack, Gunter was the one who held things together for Inge, and him only a son-in-law. I give him plenty of credit for that."

"What do you mean he was hard to work for, Mr. Rasmussen?" Sue asked.

Dag laughed and sent a brown wad of spittle arcing into the water between his boat and the one alongside. Several of his teeth were missing. The ones that remained were stained brown with tobacco juice. It reminded me why the Ballard area is sometimes referred to as Snoose Junction.

"He was big on busywork; always wanted the guys on his boat to work like dogs. Behind his back, they used to call him 'Gunter the Nazi.'"

Sue and I exchanged veiled glances. Those words might have been truer than anyone speaking them could possibly have suspected. Dag continued with his garrulous recitation.

"He didn't want to pay them nothing, either. He made up his own rules and docked his guys' pay for every infraction. Years ago, he opted out of the Vessel Owners Association. Said he was sick of settling up according to the set-line agreement when he wasn't getting nothing for it. That's about the time he stopped taking union crews and started negotiating his own deals."

"Why was that?"

Dag looked at Sue as if she must have just crawled out from under a rock. "So he wouldn't have to pay union scale," he answered simply.

"But people still worked for him anyway?"

"Ja, sure," Dag said. "You know how it is. The ones who need money bad enough don't give a damn about union wages, and the newcomers don't know the difference. They're just happy to have a job."

The possibility of union/nonunion difficulties was something to think about—a new wrinkle in our inquiry. If it turned out that labor relations had something to do with the case at hand, it wouldn't be the first time union wrangling had ended up as part of a Seattle P.D. homicide investigation.

"Would you happen to know the names of any of these nonunion crew members?" I asked.

"Hell, no!" Dag Rasmussen answered. "Most

didn't stay with him long. They got fed up and moved on. And the last few years most of 'em didn't speak English, leastwise not good enough so as you could understand 'em.''

"They're immigrants, then?"

"Yeah, foreigners of some kind."

"Where from?"

He shrugged. "I dunno. Mexico maybe. Or maybe farther south. Speak Spanish mostly, and don't know nothin'.''

Dag's words meandered off, spinning long, drawn-out, and dreary tales about the good old days when most members of the fleet had been born in Norway. Meanwhile, I wandered off on a separate tack of my own. Bonnie Elgin's missing hit-and-run victim. She had told us earlier that the injured man hadn't wanted to wait around long enough for either an ambulance or a police officer to arrive on the scene. She had also told us he was Hispanic. Was it possible he would turn out to be one of Gunter's nonunion fishermen? If so, that would be an unqualified Bingo.

I caught Sue's eye. She gave me a knowing nod that let me know I wasn't the only one making that potentially important connection. On our list of persons of interest, Bonnie Elgin's missing accident victim had just shot up to the very top. He was someone we would want to locate as soon as possible.

I jotted down a couple quick notes. One was to make arrangements to have someone pick up that bloody box spring and haul it down to the crime lab for analysis. The other was to try to lay hands on whatever initial reports Bonnie Elgin's accident might have generated.

It was possible the patrol officers who had responded to her frantic 9-1-1 call might have elicited some critical piece of information that she had inadvertently neglected to tell us. Years of doing this job have taught me that often the most mundane details—ones it's easy to overlook—turn out to be vitally important.

Well after five in the afternoon, Sue and I headed back down the dock, leaving Dag Rasmussen to return to his greasy engine overhaul. As we neared the Mustang, I reached into my pocket, pulled out the glassine bag, and examined the black-enameled wrench inside it.

"I guess we'd better get this down to the crime lab right away. And we'll need to make arrangements about getting that box spring picked up."

"Good thinking," Sue said.

I glanced up the darkening dock. Twice in the course of the afternoon, we had dropped by *One Day at a Time* in response to Watty's urgent lunchtime message to see Alan Torvoldsen. No one had been aboard Alan's boat either time. Now there was a light on inside, meaning he was most likely home. "How about paying a late-afternoon call on Alan Torvoldsen?"

Sue glanced at her watch. "Today's my turn to drive the car pool, and soccer practice gets over at six. If I don't leave before long, the kids will be left waiting in the park after everyone else goes home."

Such are the joys of single parenthood.

"That's okay," I said. "You go on and do what

you have to do. I can handle the Torvoldsen
interview.''

"But you rode with me," Sue objected. "How
will you get home?"

I laughed aside her concern. "I'm a big boy,
Sue. And Al's an acquaintance of long standing.
When we finish up with whatever he has in mind,
I'm sure he'll drop me off at Belltown Terrace."

She thought about that for a second. "All right
then," she agreed reluctantly. "Give me the
wrench. I'll handle both that and the box-spring
problem when I drop the Mustang down at the
department. It seems like cheating, though. I don't
like bailing out while you're still working. I like
to carry my weight."

I handed her the bag containing the wrench.
"Don't feel guilty. Believe me, Alan Torvoldsen
and I won't be working all that hard. My guess is
that he wants to shoot the breeze and talk over
old times. We'll most likely sit around and remi-
nisce about our glory days as Ballard High School
Beavers. It would bore you to tears."

"You're just afraid I'll pick up a few too many
stories about BoBo Beaumont and carry them back
down to the department, aren't you?"

"You wouldn't do that, would you?" I asked
apprehensively.

Sue Danielson grinned. "Not on your life. I'm
a great believer in what goes around comes
around. I'd be mortified if Paul Kramer or one of
those other jerks on the fifth floor ever got wind
of the fact that in high school people used to call
me Suzy Q."

Sue Danielson walked away and left me standing there on the end of the dock. She got in the Mustang and drove off before I realized what she had done—that she had given me the gift of trust. She was long gone before I had gathered my wits about me enough to realize I hadn't said thank you.

As I headed toward *One Day at a Time,* I noticed how cold it was. Once again a pall of thick fog was settling over the city. I stepped aboard Alan's boat and knocked on the galley door.

"Who is it?" he called from inside.

"Beau," I said.

When Alan came out, he was carrying an old corduroy jacket. The baseball cap had been replaced by a worn watch cap. He emerged grumbling, in a cloud of cigarette smoke.

"What the hell took you so long?" he demanded. "I was about to give up on you."

With that, and clearly expecting me to follow, he strode off down the dock, back the way I had come. Old times may be old times, but I didn't like his attitude. I resented his trying to lay on some kind of guilt trip about how late I was in getting back to him, especially since Sue and I had been trying to track the man down all afternoon.

"Look, bub," I told him brusquely. "Get off your cross. My partner and I stopped by twice earlier today. No one was home."

"Oh," he said. "I went out to check on something. It took longer than I thought. I guess we're not all that late, though. Happy hour runs until seven."

"Happy hour?" I echoed.

That was the last thing I needed—an escorted

happy-hour tour of Seattle with some supposedly reformed drunk who was about to fall off the wagon in a big way. Not only that, we were going in his car, and he was driving. Good planning.

I tried to stall. "Hey, Alan, how about if we sit around and shoot the breeze some other time? I don't do the happy-hour scene anymore. I didn't think you did, either."

Alan stopped beside a much-dented Mercury Cougar that dated from somewhere in the mid-eighties. The car was silver except for the right front fender, which was white. He looked at me across the top of the vehicle.

"This isn't a social visit," he said tersely. "I want to talk to you about Gunter Gebhardt, and I don't want to do it here."

Enough said. I stopped trying to argue my way out of it and went along for the ride. Using the term "ride" loosely. Alan Torvoldsen's Cougar beat walking, but not by much.

The passenger door opened only from inside. Most of the car's headliner had come loose from its moorings, so I sat with an unwelcome scarf of smoke-saturated felt draped around my ears. The lights from the parking lot revealed an overflowing ashtray. The ashes, apparently free of butts, formed a small white mound that resembled a miniature sand dune, puffs of which blew off when we opened and closed the doors. None of the dash lights worked, and it took three tries before the starter kicked in, but once Alan got the engine to turn over, the damn thing did run. Noisily so, however. And once we started moving, I realized the

Cougar's suspension system was totally shot. So was the muffler.

I figured the first cop who saw or heard that wreck moving in traffic would haul us over. No such luck. Where *do* you find a cop when you need him? Without incident, we rumbled through Ballard, making our way up Fifteenth and turning right on Eighty-fifth. The whole while we were driving, Champagne Al didn't say a word, and I followed his lead.

We stopped in front of a dingy-looking bar with a collection of Harleys parked haphazardly outside on the sidewalk. Great, I thought. Just where every homicide cop in the world wants to spend the evening happy hour—in a biker bar.

The sign outside said Club 449, but the sign just inside the door proclaimed, ABANDON ALL DOPE YE WHO ENTER HERE. Another, written in big red letters, said NO DRUGS. NO WEAPONS. NO GANG ATTIRE. NO EXCEPTIONS. Oh. That Club 449.

I guess I must have heard about Club 449 at an AA meeting somewhere, but before that evening with Alan Torvoldsen, I had never been there. It's owned and operated by a now-sober bartender who, once he stopped drinking, didn't have a comfortable place to socialize. He missed the bar scene so much that he started a joint that had all the right ambience for some displaced boozers, a place they could call home.

The number in the name, 449, refers to a page in *Alcoholics Anonymous,* known affectionately among AA members as "the Big Book." That page deals with acceptance. And looking around, I would have to say Club 449 was a pretty damn accepting place. Some of the customers were downright scary-looking, as were the ramshackle, dingy surroundings.

The room was furnished with a collection of battered cocktail tables and run-down chairs. The big dance floor was empty. The place was smoky and noisy, but it was nevertheless surprisingly familiar. It reminded me of all those places where I squandered large chunks of my misspent youth.

There were bursts of raucous laughter from a group of guys playing darts, while the sound of breaking pool balls crackled occasionally in the background. A guy with a stringy ponytail that ended below his belt fed a steady stream of quarters into a rumbling, sputtering video game. A compact-disc-playing jukebox shrieked out music that didn't at all match the mute MTV images gyrating on the TV set mounted above the bar. Next to the color screen and within easy view of the bartender was a small black-and-white monitor showing a series of interior views of the bar as seen through the watchful eye of a constantly scanning video camera.

Club 449 boasted all the things you'd naturally expect to find in a bar—with one notable exception. Booze. Instead, the hand-lettered blackboard menu offered a selection of seltzers. Happy hour there referred to all espresso drinks. A buck a shot.

Seltzers and espresso may sound trendy, but Club 449 bore not the vaguest resemblance to a yuppie "fern bar." Far from it. The no-nonsense message was clear. "If you're clean and sober, you're welcome."

As any reformed drunk can tell you, clean and

sober doesn't come easy. Some of those folks look as if they had just stepped out of detox and were hanging on to sobriety one fingernail at a time, to say nothing of one day. And although they may have all been sober, they weren't necessarily all on the up-and-up.

On the wall above the nicked and battered bar, next to the menu, was a second hand-lettered sign. This one was entitled BAD CHECK LIST. I counted twenty-six names on the list in all. Three had been crossed out. That meant three out of the twenty-six must have come in to make their bad checks good. I guess 23-to-3 is measurably better than 26-to-0, but it doesn't make staying in business very easy.

The bartender looked like someone who belonged to one of those mondo Harleys parked outside. He wore faded Levi's, leather boots, and a black T-shirt with a pack of cigarettes rolled into the sleeve. A line of complicated tattoos ran from his wrist up his arm until the pattern disappeared under the cloth of his shirt. He had a bulbous and much-flattened nose, but when he caught sight of Alan Torvoldsen, he grinned, and his eyes crinkled a friendly welcome.

"Hey, Al," he said. "How's it going? Whaddya want, the usual?"

Alan nodded. "And what about your pal there?" the barkeep continued. "What'll he have?"

The question was addressed to Alan as though I were some kind of nincompooop totally incapable of ordering for myself.

I'm a self-respecting Seattleite. When called

upon to do so, I can speak espresso with the best of them. "I'll have an Americano," I told him.

The bartender nodded. "Coming right up," he said.

Instead of settling on a bar stool, Champagne Al threaded his way down the bar to a newspaper-cluttered table sitting just inside the front window. Behind us, in a locked display case, was a collection of AA tokens and memorabilia, all for sale.

Alan swept the papers aside, settled into a chair, and motioned me into another. He shook a Camel out of the package in his shirt pocket, then lit it, leaned back, and stared off into space. For a man who supposedly wanted to talk to me, he was having a hell of a time getting around to it.

"What's up, Alan?" I asked him, hoping to prime the pump. "You look like a man with something on his mind."

He squinted at me through the smoke. "I guess you know about my baby brother," he said.

"What about him?"

"Lars is dead," he said softly.

I remembered Lars Torvoldsen as a fuzzy-faced kid two years younger than I was. Lars tried like hell to live up to his big brother's reputation, but he never quite managed. Lars was neither a good enough athlete nor a fearless enough thug.

"I'm sorry to hear that," I said.

Alan nodded. "Five years ago, the *Princess* went down in the Gulf of Alaska. Guys from another boat hauled me out of the water, but Lars didn't make it. We never found him."

"I didn't know anything about it."

The bartender brought our coffees. I paid.

"I guess I'm not surprised you didn't know," Alan said. "Boats go down all the time. Other than the local Ballard paper, it rarely makes page one. As far as most reporters are concerned, what's one dead fisherman more or less?"

He was right. Commercial fishing boats do go down every season—salmon seiners, longliners, crabbers. Anyone who thinks fishing for a living isn't dangerous ought to stop by Fishermen's Terminal and check out the memorial they've built down there. It lists the names of all the members of the fishing fleet who have died each decade. There's a whole new set of names cast in bronze every single year. Often one surname will appear two or three times when fathers, sons, brothers, and cousins who worked together on the same vessel end up dying together as well.

"We were partners, you know," Alan continued. "From the time our dad died, we were equal partners, but mostly I was so drunked up that Lars had to carry me. And he never complained about it. Always passed it off like it was no big deal. Like, 'He ain't heavy, he's my brother,' or something equally dumb."

Alan Torvoldsen blinked, shook his head, and ground out his half-smoked cigarette. "Shit!" he muttered. "I guess I still miss him."

"Alan ..." I began, but he held up his hand and silenced me.

"Now that I've started, let me finish. Lars was always a good kid—a good man, I mean. When he went down, he had a nice wife—a pretty wife who loved him and who was seven months pregnant. He also had a three-year-old son. The previ-

ous year had been a pisser. We barely made
enough for me to scrape by, and I didn't have a
family to support. So when Lars ran short, he more
or less stopped paying some of the bills, including
insurance on the boat and his own life insurance."

The Torvoldsens' family boat—The *Norwegian
Princess*—had been one of the graceful old two-
masted schooners. Compared to it, Alan's *One
Day at a Time* was little more than a sea-going
scow.

"That's where the family boat went?"

Alan nodded. "But it was only a boat, you
know? I should have been grateful just to be alive,
but did I fall down on my knees and thank God?
Hell no! I blamed Lars. Said it was his fault that
we were ruined, and then I climbed on my pity-
pot, got drunk, and stayed drunk. Finally, about a
year ago, Aarnie Knudsen—you remember Button,
don't you?"

"I remember Button."

"He tracked me down in a beat-out dive down
in Astoria. He told me I'd better come home because my mother was dying. So I did. My mother
was happy to see me, even after all that. It was
just like the story in the Bible about the damn
prodigal son. She died two days later. I haven't
had a drink since."

I've heard some pretty dramatic drunkalogues
in my time. We weren't even in a meeting, but
Champagne Al's story put gooseflesh on my legs.

"What I've done in the last year," he continued, "is to try figuring out why I'm still alive. If
Lars is dead and I'm not, there must be some
reason, some plan. I've tried to make amends for

what I didn't do before. I'm doing what I can to help Krissy—that's Lars's wife . . . widow. I spend every Sunday afternoon with my nephews. They're cute kids, but life without a father is pretty damn tough.''

He stopped talking as though he had used up all the words at his command, but something was still missing. We sat there in silence while the jukebox blared behind us. He lit another cigarette.

''Alan,'' I said finally. ''I don't understand why you're telling me all this.''

''Because I want you to know who I am now,'' he returned gravely. ''You probably remember me from the old days. It's taken almost thirty years, but I've finally grown up. I'm not Champagne Al anymore, and I'm man enough to tell you that although I may have been married five times, I've only been in love once. Else Didriksen is the one who got away, Beau. And maybe I still care too much. But when I tell you what I'm about to tell you, I don't want you to think it's sour grapes talking.''

''When you tell me what?''

''Gunter Gebhardt was a rotten son of a bitch,'' Alan Torvoldsen said through clenched teeth. ''He had a girlfriend on the side. She lives in a house up on Camano Island.''

''How do you happen to know where she lives?''

''Because she showed up in the parking lot down on the dock today. I'd seen her before, lots of times. I saw her driving around in the lot just before I called down to the department looking for you. I thought maybe you'd get there in time to talk to her, but you weren't in. When she left, I followed her home.''

"Who is she? What's her name?''

"That I don't know, but I can give you her address. She's a looker all right. She's maybe all of twenty-five, and she's got a figure that won't quit.''

He pulled a ragged scrap of paper out of his shirt pocket and handed it over. A street address had been penciled on it in a careless, masculine hand.

"Can I keep this?''

He nodded. "All I ask is one favor in exchange.''

"What's that?''

"I've seen this same broad coming and going from the *Isolde* off and on for months now. I kept hoping that someday someone would tell Else about it or that maybe she'd find out on her own. When you tell Else about this, it's going to be real tough on her. Even with Gunter dead, it's still going to break her heart. So don't tell her how you found out, okay? Whatever you do, don't tell her it came from me.''

I raised the cup that still held the dregs of my Club 449 Americano and toasted Champagne Al Torvoldsen in a heartfelt salute.

"You've got it," I said. "My lips are sealed.''

Alan Torvoldsen dropped me back at Belltown Terrace around nine-thirty. Our newest doorman, Kevin, let me into the lobby, where I stopped long enough to pick up my mail and punch the Up button on the elevator. When the elevator door opened, there was a dog inside—a dog and no one else. And not just one of those little, yappy waste-of-fur dogs, either. This was a big dog—tall, blond, and pointy-nosed. An Afghan maybe. Or perhaps a Russian wolfhound.

Whatever kind of dog it was, standing on all fours, its nose came right to the bottom of my tie. Fortunately, the tail was wagging.

"There's a dog in here!"

"That's just Charley," Kevin said, as though explaining the obvious. "Lives on nineteen. Haven't you two met before?"

"Never. What's he doing in the elevator?"

"Just riding around. Must get bored in the evenings sometimes, locked up in an apartment all day. Gail—the owner—lets Charley spend half an hour or so just before bedtime, riding up and down in the elevator and meeting people."

"He rides up and down all by himself?"

"Don't worry. Charley's very friendly."

"Thank God for small blessings."

Charley moved aside, giving me room enough to join him in the elevator. On the way up, I tried punching nineteen. The door opened on that floor, but Charley looked up at me quizzically and made no move to get off. Instead, he rode on up to twenty-five with me. When the door slid open on my floor, he started forward eagerly, as though he wanted to bail out right along with me.

"No, you don't, pal," I told Charley, barring the way. I was thankful that we were alone and that no one was there to hear me talking to a damn dog. It's bad for the tough-guy image.

"This is where I live," I added. "No dogs allowed."

Before exiting, I hit nineteen one more time for good measure, punched "door closed," and then made sure Charley was still safely inside when the elevator car started back down. I didn't know Charley's owner, Gail, from Adam's off ox, but someone would have to have a serious talk with the woman. Having a dog wandering around loose in a high-rise luxury condo building didn't seem like such a good idea to me.

I let myself into my apartment and started to put the mail down on the entryway table. I usually let it accumulate there for several days before I finally force myself to sit down and go through it all at one time. But the metal box was still there. My grandfather's ashes were still there. I put the mail on the dining-room table.

The red light on my answering machine was blinking steadily. Ralph Ames, my attorney, gave me the machine years ago. It's starting to wear out. Every once in a while, it goes crazy and either eats a tape or garbles a message. Or else it gets stuck in a loop and repeats my message over and over without ever sounding the beep that would allow someone else to leave one for me. Ralph keeps telling me that I ought to get rid of it and sign up for voice mail with the phone company, but I don't want to.

I know all about voice mail. We have it on the phones down at the department. I prefer the machine. With the answering machine, if I'm home, I can screen my calls. When I hear the voice on the recorder, I get to decide whether or not I want to pick it up. With voice mail, there's no way to screen calls. It's potluck; either you answer or you don't. Voice mail may come with a lot of fancy new bells and whistles, but it doesn't come with blinking lights. My old-time machine does. I can count the number of blinks and know exactly how many calls I've had without even picking up the phone.

In this case, there had been only one. I decided arbitrarily that one message could wait, at least until after I had something to eat. By then it was a long time past my noontime burger.

I went into the kitchen and used the last two crusts of bread to make myself a peanut-butter-and-honey sandwich. Reminded by a mouthful of peanut butter, I made a mental note to call my grandmother to check on how her dog, Mandy, was doing. Then I grabbed a glass of milk from the fridge and made my way to the recliner. Once

I settled in, I punched the Play button on the machine.

"Detective Beaumont," a familiar African-American voice said. "How you doing, my man? This is Rocky Washington from down at the crime lab. Janice Morraine asked me to call you. Says to ask you how come you're hanging out with folks from the Pentagon or maybe the Joint Chiefs. Give me a call back. I'll be here until eleven."

Rocky is a recent graduate from the University of Washington who is now serving an apprenticeship under the careful tutelage of Janice Morraine. Rocky has a quick mind and a great sense of humor. At work he speaks in perfectly articulated English, so he was clearly having fun and playing around when he left the message.

Joking is fine. We all need a little of that to lighten the load at times, but I couldn't figure out what the hell he was talking about. Pentagon? Joint Chiefs?

I picked up the phone and dialed the crime lab. Rocky answered the phone himself.

"Rocky, this is Detective Beaumont. What's up? I don't know anybody who works for the Joint Chiefs of Staff."

"We figured you did," Rocky answered. "If not them, maybe NASA. I mean, who else would have a solid-gold wrench? I suppose you've heard about all their two-hundred-dollar toilet seats."

"Wait a minute. Did you say solid gold?" I demanded.

"You got it. Nine-point-one ounces. The way I figure it, at three-thirty or so an ounce, that makes it your basic three-thousand-dollar wrench. And totally useless, besides. Gold's too soft to use on anything.''

I couldn't quite believe my ears. ''You mean the wrench Bonnie Elgin found, the one Sue Danielson dropped off, is made of solid gold?''

''Didn't you hear me the first time? The whole thing is covered with a thick layer of enamel, so you couldn't tell it right off. But after I finished lifting the prints, I put it under a microscope. I found a tiny chip in the enamel that was invisible to the naked eye. But the chip I saw looked like gold to me, so I measured the specific gravity. Sure enough. It's gold all right.''

''I'll be damned,'' I said.

''Me, too,'' he agreed. ''There were a bunch of prints on the damn thing. Who-all handled it?''

''Bonnie Elgin. The lady who was driving the car. And maybe her husband, although I don't know for sure.''

''Find out for me, would you? If he did, we'll need both of them to come in to give us a set of elimination prints.''

''Okay,'' I said. ''No problem. It's not all that late. I'll give them a call right away.''

After dropping off Rocky's call, I located the Elgins' phone number in my notebook and dialed them up. Bonnie herself answered, but there was a lot of noise in the background, as though there was a party going on. I identified myself and asked her if this was an inconvenient time to talk.

''It's fine,'' she said. ''Go ahead.''

''We need you to come down to the department tomorrow morning so we can take a set of fingerprints.''

I heard a quick intake of breath. "That sounds bad."

"No. We're just trying to save the taxpayers a little money. It's expensive to run prints through AFIS." I caught myself talking cop jargon and backed up. "Sorry, that's the Automated Fingerprint Identification System," I explained. "By taking your fingerprints and comparing them to the ones lifted off the wrench, the print technician can tell which ones need to be processed and which ones don't. By the way, did your husband touch the wrench?"

"No. I'm pretty sure he didn't."

"Ask him, if you can. If he did, we'll need him to come in to be printed as well. Then, in addition to the prints, while you're down at the department, I'd like to set you up with our staff artist. Maybe you can put together one of those Identi-Kit sketches so we can have a little better idea of what this guy looks like."

Bonnie sounded doubtful. "I don't know if I can remember all that well. Is it important?"

From my point of view, I thought having a sketch was vital, but I didn't want to spook her. "Let's just say that we have uncovered some additional information. It's looking more likely than ever that there's a connection between the man you hit and the one who died in the fire at Fishermen's Terminal. So, yes, it could be very important."

Bonnie Elgin paused, but only for a moment. "What time do you want me there?"

"Is nine too early?"

"No. I'm up and out long before then. Nine will be fine."

After we rang off, I started to put down the phone. Then I thought better of it and dialed my grandmother. She had told me that she never goes to bed before the end of the eleven o'clock news. She answered on the second ring.

"Just thought I'd check and see how you're doing tonight."

"We're doing fine, Mandy and I," Beverly Piedmont returned. "She did manage to have a little something to eat. Kelly's right about the peanut butter. Mandy loved it, except for getting some stuck to the roof of her mouth. After that she ate a bite or two of her dog food as well, so she seems to be feeling better. I let her out for her walk a little while ago. Now we're sitting here waiting for the news to come on. What are you doing?"

"I just got home a few minutes ago. I'm going to kick off my shoes and unwind for a few minutes, then hit the sack early."

"It sounds as though you work too hard, Jonas," she chided gently, her voice full of grandmotherly concern. "You have to remember to take time to smell the flowers every day. Life's much too short if you don't."

"Thank you," I said, and meant it. "I'll try to remember that."

When I put down the telephone receiver, I did finally kick off my shoes. Then I sat back in the creaking leather recliner and gave my grandmother's advice some serious thought.

It had been a day that had brought me face-to-face with my own mortality. It's one thing to deal with homicides on a daily basis. That's my job, and Gunter Gebhardt's death was far more work than it was personal.

The knowledge that my grandfather's ashes still waited on the entryway table brought death into much too close proximity. Not only that, hearing about what had happened to Lars Torvoldsen— someone I still saw as a kid I grew up with—hit me where I lived. Last but not least in that regard, Karen Livingston, my ex-wife, was never far from my thoughts. The two of us had been divorced for a long time, but she was still the mother of my children and the grandmother of little Kayla. Karen had also just finished up undergoing her third round of chemo in a little less than two years.

Damn.

So what if Champagne Al had developed a slight paunch and no longer had any reason to use H. A. Hair Arranger. I didn't use it anymore, either, but that was more because of my perpetual crew cut than because my hair was falling out. Still, Al and I had cause to count our blessings. The two of us were still alive and in reasonably good health. For how long? I wondered morbidly. How does that old saying go? First you get old, and then you die.

On that cheery note, I must have dozed off for a little while, lying back in the recliner and probably snoring. I'd like to believe I didn't drool, but I was sound asleep when the telephone at my elbow startled me awake.

"Hello?" I answered uncertainly.

"Detective Beaumont?"

"Yes."

"My name is Jacek," the man said. "Detective Stan Jacek."

I cleared my throat and tried to sound more on top of things. "Where are you from, Detective Jacek? And what can I do for you?"

"I apologize for calling so late, but I was just talking to Rocky. You know, Rocky Washington down at the State Patrol crime lab? I'm not sure why, but he said I should give you a call. He thought you'd want to talk to me about this, even if I had to wake you up to do it."

I wasn't the least bit sure Rocky knew what the hell he was talking about. Glancing at my watch, I saw it was late, all right—twenty after eleven. I remembered Rocky Washington telling me he was due to be off shift by now. With the budget problems in the crime lab, something must have happened to keep him working overtime, something important.

"Talk to me about what?" I grumbled. "And where did you say you're from?"

"Sorry, I guess I didn't. I'm from the Island County Sheriff's Department up in Coupeville on Whidbey. We had a little problem here on Camano Island tonight. A fire. As I understand it, Rocky's on his way up here right now in one of the evidence vans. He's the one who gave me your number, by the way. He said he didn't want to take the time to call you himself."

A fire on Camano Island? The words caused an uncomfortable tightening in the pit of my stomach. "What kind of fire?" I asked.

"A house fire," he answered. "One fatality. That's the only one we've found so far. Some of the house is still too hot for anyone to go inside, but from what I could see of what's left, it looks as though the place was pretty well tossed before the fire was set.''

''A robbery then?'' I asked.

''Possibly,'' he returned.

''Any witnesses?''

''None so far, and I'm not too hopeful about that, although we're starting to check out the neighbors right now. The house sits off by itself in a swale down near the water, so there aren't clear sight lines from any of the nearby houses.''

By the time Jacek had told me that much, I was able to guess the rest, especially in view of the Rocky Washington connection. Jacek's investigation and mine had to be linked in some way. The fire on Camano Island had something to do with the earlier fire at Fishermen's Terminal. Using my shoulder to hold the telephone receiver to my ear, I fumbled clumsily in my notebook, trying to locate Alan Torvoldsen's scrap of paper—the piece of paper on which he had penciled the Camano Island address of Gunter Gebhardt's cute little side dish.

Once I had the address in my hand, I still didn't want to blurt out the information to Stan Jacek. Homicide cops are generally cautious folks who believe in playing their cards close to their chests. We don't willingly share information with others, and that's possibly one of the things that accounts for the high divorce rate among members of homicide squads. We especially don't like sharing information with someone we don't know who is clearly a member of an opposing team.

I wanted Stan Jacek to have to talk before I did, and that may sound childish. It's probably a holdover from some long-ago game of darers-go-first.

"What makes Rocky Washington think I'd have any interest in a beach house out on Camano Island?" I asked guardedly.

As soon as I heard Detective Jacek sigh, I knew I had won the first round.

"I saw the victim," he admitted. "It's pretty rough. You don't happen to have a queasy stomach, do you, Detective Beaumont?"

The careful way he asked the question, his tone of voice. It all fit.

"Let me take a wild guess," I said. "Was the corpse mutilated, by any chance? Did this arsonist of yours take the time to whack off all the victim's fingers and toes?"

"All of them," Jacek answered at once. Then, when his brain caught up with his mouth, when he realized exactly what I'd said, there was a long pause. "How in the hell did you know about that?" he demanded. "Did Rocky already call and tell you?"

"No," I answered. "He didn't."

"But how . . . ?"

"That means either I'm some kind of mind reader," I interrupted, "or else we're both working the same case."

"The same case?" he echoed. "How could that be?"

"We had a fatality fire here in Seattle earlier today—a boat fire down at Fishermen's Terminal first thing this morning. One dead male, burned to a crisp with all of his missing fingers and toes toasted to potato chips in a pie plate that was left sitting on his chest.''

The phone line went silent for a moment, then Jacek said, ''You're absolutely right. If it's not the same guy, we've got a helluva trend starting.''

I was already slipping on my shoes. ''Where are you right now?'' I asked.

''I'm out on Camano, but I told Rocky I'd meet him over in Stanwood. Have you ever been here?''

''Once, years ago. For a Memorial Day picnic.''

''Rocky Washington hasn't even done that. The roads and lanes can turn into an impossible maze if you don't know exactly where you're going. I figured it would be easier for me to meet Rocky in Stanwood and lead him out here than it would to try giving him directions over the phone.''

''How long ago did he leave?''

''Not very long ago. He was just heading down to get the van when I called you.''

''Good,'' I said. ''If you're meeting him, you can meet me, too. I'll be there as soon as I can, and it won't take long. I'm far enough north of the Public Safety Building that I may actually beat him there. Where will you be?''

''As you come into Stanwood, you'll see a blinking red light with a grocery store and shopping center on the far right-hand corner. I'll be waiting there, in the parking lot. What'll you be driving?'' he asked. ''That way I'll know what to look for.''

''A Porsche 928,'' I said. ''Guard red.''

''Right,'' he said, ''and I'll be in my Rolls.''

He paused for a moment, then said, "You're kidding about the Porsche, aren't you?"

"No, I really will be driving a 928."

"What the hell kind of cop are you?" he demanded. "Narcotics? Vice?"

I figured Detective Stan Jacek didn't need to know that this was a special-order 928—one I had purchased to replace another one that had been blown to bits months earlier in a propane explosion down in Ashland, Oregon. So I didn't tell Jacek any of that.

"I'm nothing but a plain old detective," I answered. "Same as you."

Dead on my feet, I finally crawled into bed at four in the morning and set the alarm for seven. The alarm woke me. As soon as I managed to shake the cobwebs out of my head well enough to be able to talk, I called Sue Danielson at home.

She sounded disgustingly chipper and wide awake. "I hope you had a good night's sleep last night," I told her.

"As a matter of fact, I did. Why?"

"Because the ball's in your court this morning," I said. "There's a whole lot to be handled, and unless I catch an hour or two of sleep before I come into the office, I'm not going to be worth diddly-squat."

"I take it you and Alan Torvoldsen tied one on last night?" she returned.

It's funny, but when a dedicated drinker lays off the sauce, it's invisible to most people. Once you've established a reputation as a boozer, the reputation sticks, regardless. That was something Champagne Al Torvoldsen and J. P. Beaumont shared in common.

"Actually, I spent most of the night alternately sweating like a pig or freezing my ass off, prowling around the scene of a house fire up on Camano Island. It was still hot in places.''

''A house fire on Camano Island?'' Sue asked. ''Why would you want to do something like that?''

''Because Detective Stan Jacek of the Island County Sheriff's Department asked me to. By the time he called me, he already knew it was a fatality fire, and he was hoping I could help him figure out who the victim is. We did pick up a letter from the scene—actually from a singed white Cadillac parked in the driveway outside the house. One of Jacek's deputies found it.

''It was addressed to somebody named Denise Whitney, and the address was the same as the burned house. The letter was signed 'Mom,' and the envelope had an Anchorage, Alaska, return address. By now I'm sure Detective Jacek's followed up on that, trying to locate next of kin.''

''Wait just a minute,'' Sue interrupted. ''How come this Island County detective is pulling you in to investigate his case?''

''Because,'' I said, ''we think it may be the same perpetrator as whoever killed Gunter Gebhardt.''

As briefly as possible, I brought Sue up to speed, telling her everything I could remember, starting with the phone call from Detective Jacek at 11:00 P.M. I told her about the grisly copycat connections between the Camano Island homicide and our own. I explained, however, that there were some notable differences between the two separate blazes.

For instance, the one on Camano had been

started by setting fire to piles of newspaper scattered in separate rooms throughout the house. Unlike the blaze on the *Isolde,* there were no apparent signs of a liquid accelerant in most of the house, but that was a long way from conclusive. It was possible that subsequent arson investigation would reveal the use of accelerant in that part of the house that had still been too hot to handle by the time I left the scene to return to the city.

Attempting to be thorough, I became so caught up in telling the story that I never saw it coming. When I finally finished my recitation and shut up, I was dumbfounded to find that Sue Danielson was steamed—at me.

"How come you didn't call me right away?" she demanded angrily. "You should have let me know the minute all this came up."

"Detective Jacek's call didn't come in until after eleven. I figured you were sound asleep in bed by then. Besides, you've got kids at home to worry about. You can't spend half the night traipsing around all over the countryside with them there by themselves."

"Wait a minute here, Detective J. P. Beaumont," she bridled. "Wait just one goddamned minute! Since when do you have the right to make those kinds of decisions for me? I'm a big girl. And in case you haven't noticed, I'm also a sworn police officer. I've been working outside the home all my life, and all my kids' lives, too.

"Jared Danielson may be a jerk at times, but he's not a baby. I started out working night shift at the Communications Center while he was still in diapers. My sons Jared and Chris both understand that my job is what keeps food on the table and a roof over our heads. They know there are times when they have to look after themselves because I can't always be here.''

"I stand corrected," I said, although I was sitting on the edge of my bed at the time. When faced with that kind of an unexpected, cross-gender firefight, I've learned to shape up and apologize right away. Somebody told me once that the first rule of holes is that when you're standing in one up to your eyeballs, stop digging.

In this instance, that strategy worked.

"So what is it you need me to do?" Sue asked, sounding somewhat mollified.

I explained the bit about the solid-gold wrench, then, and told her Bonnie Elgin was due at the department at nine to have her fingerprints taken and to work on an Identi-Kit sketch of our missing hit-and-run victim.

"Bonnie most likely will need to be walked through the process, have her hand held a little," I said. "Evidently, she's never been involved in anything like this before, and I think she's nervous about it."

"I can certainly understand that," Sue said briskly. "What else needs doing?"

"Be in touch with Detective Jacek." I gave her both his phone as well as his fax number at the Island County seat in Coupeville. "As soon as we can get a photo from Else, we need to fax Jacek a picture of Gunter Gebhardt—one taken while he was still alive."

"What's that for?" Sue asked.

"For him to show to the neighbors on Camano.

I have a feeling Gunter may have been spending a good deal of time up there.''

''And what makes you think that?''

Sue's last question brought me face-to-face with my second sin of omission—I hadn't yet briefed her on my conversation with Alan Torvoldsen, either.

''I believe Gunter Gebhardt was playing the field,'' I told her. ''I heard it first from Alan Torvoldsen earlier last night, but I heard it again from people who live around the fire scene. Camano Island is one of those places where nothing much happens. The fire was like a neighborhood picnic. Everybody in town must have showed up last night to find out what was going on. Jacek and I talked to most of them, including the real estate man who sold the place to the new owners two years ago.

''The realtor remembered there was something odd about the deal—that the house was bought by a corporation of some kind, but he couldn't remember the name last night. Another neighbor, a woman who works in the post office over in Stanwood, said that the woman who lived in the house, a Denise Whitney, claimed it was hers. She said she owned it along with somebody else. Detective Jacek and I think that other person may actually have been Gunter Gebhardt.''

''I suppose it's safe to assume that Denise Whitney was quite a bit younger than Gunter,'' Sue said.

''Evidently,'' I replied. ''From everything I hear, she's on the downside of twenty-five.''

''It figures,'' Sue said.

She had kept her cool while I passed along the dope Alan had given me about Gunter's sweet young thing. Rather than risk landing once more on my partner's wrong side, I was scrupulous about not leaving anything out. I went ahead and told her what he had said about still carrying a torch for Else, Gunter's widow. When I told Sue that, she turned thoughtful on me. "It wasn't him, was it?"

"Wasn't who?"

"Your old friend Alan Torvoldsen. You just told me he's still in love with Gunter's wife . . . his widow. What if he's had a grudge against Gunter—first for stealing Else out from under his nose, years ago. Think about it. First he loses Else. Then thirty years later, he finds out the guy who did marry her is screwing around behind her back."

Unfortunately, the exact same thought—that Alan might have had some reason to be after Gunter—had occurred to me as well. I hadn't exactly rationalized my way around it, but I'll admit I hadn't sat down to scrutinize it too closely, either.

"I can see why Alan might be pissed off at Gunter," I said, "but why would he take out the girlfriend?"

"I don't know, but you did say he knew where she lived, didn't you?"

I nodded. "Yes. He said he followed her home when she showed up down at the *Isolde*."

"Which means he was at the scene of the crime the day of the murders."

"That's right. But by the time the Camano Island fire started, he was back here in Seattle. And remember, he has an airtight alibi for that time.

He was with me, drinking *espresso* at Club Four-four-nine up in Greenwood.''

Sue seemed prepared to accept that notion, at least for the time being. ''What time do you expect to show up at the office yourself?'' she asked, changing the subject.

''I'll plan on being there by ten,'' I told her. ''I should be on the job by the time you and Bonnie Elgin finish with the sketch.''

''All right,'' Sue said. ''See you then.''

I was dog-assed tired. I slipped down into the comfort of the still-warm covers, and it didn't take five minutes for me to fall back asleep. I slept the sleep of the just—for all of twenty minutes. That's when the phone rang. Captain Lawrence Powell was on the line—an irate Captain Larry Powell.

''Detective Beaumont,'' he said. ''Who the hell appointed you as spokesman for the Homicide Squad?''

''Excuse me?'' Shoving my feet out of bed, I put them flat on the floor. I tend to think better sitting up. ''What are you talking about, Captain Powell?'' I mumbled sleepily. ''What's going on?''

''You know very well that it's against departmental policy for officers to make any kind of unauthorized statement to the media regarding the progress of an ongoing investigation, particularly a homicide.''

''Statement to the media?'' I echoed. ''What are you talking about?''

''Have you read this morning's *P.-I.*?'' Larry Powell asked. ''And isn't Maxwell Cole some kind of buddy of yours?''

The *Post-Intelligencer* is Seattle's morning paper. I don't take it myself, and I don't read it, either. As a matter of fact, I don't read any newspapers at all, except when unavoidably provoked into doing so. I try to limit my journalistic intake to relatively harmless items like crossword puzzles and comics. I encounter enough blood and guts in my own life—the real stories—without having to have reporter-revised versions of those same events polluting the flavor of my breakfast coffee.

Maxwell Cole is another story entirely. He's a regular columnist for the *P.-I.* He uses his three-times-weekly forum, "City Beat," to take journalistic potshots at anyone handy. His favorite targets happen to be police officers. Max is a former fraternity brother of mine from my days at the University of Washington. Even then he was a pain in the ass, and thirty years of practice have allowed him to raise his level of assholosity to something of an art form.

I rubbed the grit out of my eyes. The corneas felt as if they were made of etched glass and the lids of sandpaper.

"What's he saying about me now?" I asked wearily.

"It's not about you," Captain Powell responded. "Want me to read it to you?"

"Not especially," I said, "but go ahead."

" 'Ron and Bonnie Elgin, ace procurers of auction items for Poncho, Seattle's premier arts fund-raising event, are busy attending to months of pre-party planning. Much to their surprise, yesterday they found themselves embroiled in Seattle's most recent murder.

" 'According to sources close to the case, Seattle police officers are combing the city, looking for a young Hispanic male who was seen running from the scene of yesterday's tragic and fatal boat fire on board the *Isolde* at Fishermen's Terminal in Ballard.

" 'The fleeing suspect evidently suffered a close encounter of the worst kind when he ran into the path of a vehicle driven by Bonnie Elgin. Despite injuries serious enough to merit medical attention, the man fled the scene on foot without waiting long enough to have his injuries attended to by a Medic I unit that had already been summoned by a call to nine-one-one.

" 'It sounds as though the missing suspect's wounds were fairly extensive, and it doesn't seem like it should be all that difficult to find him. Of course, that all depends on how hard someone is looking.

" 'Rumor has it that these days Seattle's Finest are spending their time trying to learn how to work their newest crime-fighting tools—laptop computers—which were purchased at taxpayer expense with the understanding that they would offer cops high-tech aid in taking criminals off the streets.

" 'I have a feeling our men in blue are spending so much time learning keystrokes that they can't be bothered with doing their real jobs—like actually looking for suspects and making arrests.' "

"Where the hell did Max come up with all that crap?" I demanded.

"That's what I thought you'd tell me," Lawrence Powell returned grimly. "And once I find the guy who blabbed, I'm going to bust his nuts."

"Look, Captain. I never talked to Maxwell Cole about this case. And I didn't talk to anyone else in the media, either. Somebody else must have told him, but it wasn't me."

"Sue Danielson maybe?"

"I doubt it."

"According to Watty, she's the only other Seattle Police Department detective assigned to this case."

"It wasn't Sue," I asserted. "She wouldn't shoot off her mouth to the media any more than I would."

"Maybe you're right," Powell returned. "And then again, maybe you're not. In any case, Beaumont, it's your problem now. I want you to find the source of that leak, and I want it stopped. Is that clear?"

"Yes, sir."

"And I want it done today."

When I put down the phone that time, I didn't even bother crawling back under the covers. There was no point. Instead, I staggered out of bed and headed for the bathroom and a much-needed shower. I had taken a shower when I came home from Camano Island but I wasn't sure one shower was enough to wash the soot and smoke off my body and out of my nostrils. It sure as hell wasn't enough to wash what I had seen out of my mind.

I left Belltown Terrace and drove straight down Clay to Western. A short twenty minutes after I got off the phone with Captain Lawrence Powell, I was standing in the reception area of the *Seattle P.-I.*

Times have changed in the country, and not necessarily for the better. In the old days, it was possible to walk into an airport or a radio station or a newspaper office without having to go through a whole security rigmarole. Compared to getting into the *P.-I.,* breaking into an armed camp would have been easier.

"I'm sorry, but Mr. Cole isn't available," the receptionist told me with a blandly sweet smile. "He's on special assignment today."

"Where?"

"I'm sorry, I'm afraid I can't give out that information."

"When will he be back?"

"Probably later on this week. For sure by next Monday morning."

Captain Powell hadn't given me until Monday. He wanted results today. Now. And so did I.

"Is he calling in for messages?"

"I'm not sure. Somebody up at the City Desk could probably answer that better than I can."

The switchboard phone rang, not once but three separate times in a row. And each time the receptionist handled the phone before coming back to me. It's the same kind of song and dance that happens in auto-parts stores or hardware stores where the important person on the phone always takes precedence over the poor hapless boob who is actually standing in front of the counter with money in his hand waiting to buy something.

The receptionist came back to me eventually. She looked at me as though she'd never laid eyes on me before. "May I help you, please?"

"Maxwell Cole, remember? You were going to

connect me to the City Desk.'' By then I was no doubt clenching my teeth.

The light came on. Dim, but a light. ''Oh, that's right. Sorry. Just step to that phone over there.''

In the long run, the City Desk folks wouldn't or couldn't give me a straight answer on Maxwell Cole's whereabouts, either. But someone did finally agree to connect me with the ''City Beat'' voice-mail line.

''Max,'' I snarled into the phone. ''This is Detective Beaumont. I need to talk to you. ASAP. And I mean talk in person, not just play telephone tag back and forth on these damn voice-mail networks.''

I left both my home and office numbers on the voice-mail message and then stalked back outside, where my 928 waited next to the curb. Even after maneuvering through downtown morning rush-hour traffic, I parked in the garage on James and still made it into the Public Safety Building and up to the homicide digs on the fifth floor a good fifteen minutes before Sue Danielson.

''What are you doing here, Sleeping Beauty?'' she asked when she caught sight of me. ''The last time I talked to you, I thought you were going back to bed.''

''So did I,'' I grumbled. ''Right up until Captain Powell called to ream my ass out.''

''What about?''

I handed her a photocopy of Maxwell Cole's column, one that had magically appeared in the middle of my desk by the time I arrived at work. Sue read the column in silence, then gave it back to me.

"Where did he get his information?" she asked.

"That's what Captain Powell wants to know. It wasn't from you, was it?"

Her eyes narrowed. "Are you accusing . . . ?"

I cut her off, stopping her in midreply. "No, I'm not, but I had to ask. Forget it. Powell gave me orders to find the leak. I'm going through the motions, that's all. But if you didn't talk to Maxwell Cole, and if I didn't, who else is there?"

"The two guys from Patrol who took the initial report and Bonnie Elgin herself."

"Wait a minute," I said, remembering my late evening phone call to the Elgins' house. There had been a lot of noise in the background. "That has to be it."

"What does?"

"When I called Bonnie about the prints, it sounded as though there was a party going on. Maybe there was. I'll bet either Maxwell Cole was there in person, or else one of his big-mouthed sources was."

"When Bonnie shows up for fingerprinting, we'll have to check that out," Sue Danielson said.

"Yes," I agreed. "We certainly will."

As it turned out, I was nowhere near the Public Safety Building by the time Bonnie Elgin and Sue Danielson finished up with the prints and sketch.

About 9:15 A.M. Detective Stan Jacek came wandering back through the fifth-floor maze of cubicles and found me sitting at my desk, holding up my head and working on paper. *Paper* paper. Somebody needed to let Maxwell Cole know that not everybody at Seattle P.D. had a handy-dandy laptop computer at his or her disposal.

Stan hadn't slept any longer than I, and he was equally grouchy. "How can people stand living and working in a place like this?" he demanded irritably. "It took me ten minutes just to find a parking place."

I've never visited Stan Jacek's home turf up in Coupeville, but it's safe to assume that parking isn't that much of a problem in the downtown area of Island County's county seat on Whidbey Island.

"It's no big deal," I said. "All you have to do is be born in a parking place, and then you're set."

Detective Jacek wasn't up for that kind of early morning quip. "Very funny," he said. "You want to come for a ride or not?"

143

"Where to?"

He pulled out a notebook and thumbed through the scrawled-on, dog-eared pages. "Remember the letter we found in the Caddy parked out in front of the house last night?"

"The one signed 'Mom'? What about it?"

"I finally managed to track that back to the woman up in Anchorage who wrote it," he answered. "She and her husband are flying into town later on today. She's willing to help as much as she can, but she doesn't have access to any of her daughter's more recent dental records. They'll bring along whatever they do have."

The condition of the dead woman's body had meant that dental records would be necessary to establish a positive I.D. My heart went out to those two unfortunate parents—to any parents—forced to set out on that kind of devastatingly awful mission. They might be hoping for the best, yet I'm sure they were dreading the worst.

"It's going to be rough on them," I said.

Jacek nodded. "I'll say. In the meantime, the mother gave me a line on their other daughter—Denise's older sister. Her name is Deanna Meadows. She lives down in Kent in a place called Fairwood. Ever heard of it?"

I shook my head, but then there are lots of places in the Puget Sound area that I've never heard of.

Jacek shrugged and continued, "It doesn't matter. I've got an appointment with her about forty-five minutes from now. I thought maybe you'd like to ride along."

For an answer, I stood up and put on my jacket. "Lead the way," I said.

We crossed Lake Washington on I-90 in fog so thick that the water was invisible. We might have been driving in a universe made of cotton balls. Detective Jacek was far too aggressive a driver for me to be able to doze off and catch forty winks. Instead, I stayed wide awake the whole time, gripping what I call the "Oh-shit bar," and thinking about all those fog-caused multicar pileups that happen every year on that long stretch of California freeway they call "the Grapevine."

I was relieved when we finally turned off Interstate 405 onto the Maple Valley Highway. Valley population and traffic has far outstripped the capacity of that piece of rural two-lane road, and it's certainly had its share of head-on collisions, but at least there Stan Jacek slowed down to a relatively sane sixty.

For all the ease of finding our way, we might just as well have been traveling in the middle of the night. The fog was that thick. But as we rose up out of the valley onto a plateau, the sun began to burn through the haze.

We meandered around a housing development that had been built around the perimeter of a golf course. For golf-course houses, the places were fairly modest. The new cedar shake roofs told me the development must be about twenty years old. The little kid tearing up the middle of the street on a Big Wheel was probably the child of a second generation of owners.

The house we stopped in front of was much newer construction than some of its neighbors. It was one of those new phony French-château places with a three-car garage that covered almost the whole front of the house except for a front porch three stories tall. The porch light was so far up on the wall that you'd need an extension ladder just to reach it and change the lightbulb. A brand-new white Infiniti, still wearing temporary plates, sat by itself inside one open garage door.

"Yuppies," I muttered to myself, thinking the people who lived there were probably ex-Californians who deserved to have to use a ladder just to change a lightbulb. "Definitely yuppies."

Detective Jacek must have thought I was saying something important. "Huh?" he asked, pulling his finger back from the doorbell without pressing the button. "What did you say?"

"Never mind," I told him. "It's nothing."

Deanna Meadows turned out to be a woman in her early-to-mid-thirties. She wore a thick terry-cloth bathrobe. Her carrot-colored hair was pulled up on top of her head with a dark blue band of some kind. It looked as though she had started out wearing makeup, because two twin trails of drowned mascara still lingered on her cheeks. There was nothing besides the dead mascara to cover the fine sprinkling of freckles on her cheeks. She had been crying. When she opened the door, she was still sniffling.

Detective Jacek introduced himself and showed her his I.D. Deanna nodded. "I remember. You're the one I talked to earlier."

"And this is Detective Beaumont of the Seattle Police Department. He's working on this case as well."

Deanna Meadows led us into a spacious living room. Looking beyond the living room and out through the dining-room picture window, I could see one of the fairways on the golf course outside. That smooth expanse of green, evenly mowed-and-manicured grass provided a backyard that was long on lush and low on homeowner-driven maintenance. The thought crossed my mind that maybe not having to spend every Saturday pushing around a lawn mower outweighed the hazard of an occasional golf ball bouncing in through a window and landing on the dining-room table.

"I'm sorry things are in such a mess," Deanna Meadows apologized.

Mess? I didn't see much mess. A few scattered newspapers were strewn around on the floor. There were two coffee cups sitting on an end table along with a pile of soggy, crumpled tissues. Other than that, the room was spotlessly clean, with no sign of kiddy-type debris anywhere. Unless there was an ever-vigilant nanny stowed somewhere upstairs, it was safe to assume that Deanna Meadows and her unnamed husband—she was wearing a wedding band—were childless.

Deanna motioned for Jack and me to sit down on the green-and-white living-room couch. "Coffee?" she asked.

We both accepted gratefully. While she hurried off to the kitchen to make it, I examined the two rooms that were visible from where I sat. They were furnished in a tasteful, uniformly comfortable style. The house seemed like some kind of safe haven in which Detective Jacek and I, along with our ugly reason for being there, provided the only jarring notes.

Deanna Meadows was talking when she came back into the dining room, shouldering open the swinging door between that room and the kitchen.

"I was on the phone with my aunt just before you got here," she said. She paused long enough to pass us mugs of coffee and to offer cream and sugar.

"Aunt Mary is my mother's sister. I was all right for a while, but as soon as she started talking about Denise, it set me off all over again. I don't know what's the matter with me. I just can't seem to stop crying. It's hard to believe that it's happened—that she's really dead."

Sipping his coffee, Detective Jacek nodded sympathetically. "I'm sure this is all very difficult for you—and having us show up so soon like this must seem pretty heartless. But in order to solve cases we have to gather information as quickly as we can."

Deanna nodded. "I know," she said. "Mom told me. I promised her I'd do whatever I could to help."

"What can you tell us about your sister?" Stan Jacek asked. "Her neighbors up on Camano Island knew her name and recognized her on sight, but she doesn't seem to have sought out friendships with any of them. No one could tell us much about her background—about where she came from and all that sort of thing."

Deanna blew her nose. "I'll tell you what I can, but I have to watch the time," she said. "My folks left Anchorage by plane this morning. They're due in at Sea-Tac two hours from now. I'll have to leave before too long to go pick them up.''

''That's where you're from—Alaska?''

Deanna nodded. ''Not originally. My folks moved up there from Dayton, Ohio, during the oil rush. They liked it so much they never left.''

''What do your parents do?'' I asked.

''My father used to be a minister,'' she said. ''Now he's the chief administrator in a convalescent home.''

''That's a big change.''

Deanna Meadows shrugged. ''He pretty much had to do it. Dad just couldn't bring himself to stand up in front of people and preach Sunday sermons when his own family life was in such disarray.''

''How so?'' I asked.

''Because of Denise,'' Deanna answered, with more than a trace of bitterness in her voice. ''It was always because of Denise. Isn't that why you're here?''

''I'm not sure,'' Jacek said. ''Maybe you'd better tell us.''

It took a while for Deanna Meadows to answer. ''I guess you've heard all the bad talk about preachers' kids,'' she said at last. ''About how awful they are.''

''I've heard rumors to that effect,'' Jacek agreed, ''but from what I hear, teachers' kids are just as bad . . . or maybe even a little worse.''

''*Some* of them are,'' Deanna asserted, placing careful emphasis on the word ''some.'' ''Not all, but some.''

''So you're saying your sister went haywire?''

"She didn't *go* haywire; she always *was* hay-wire, but I don't think anyone realized it at first. As a little kid, she was so pretty. She got good grades and was smart as a whip—a lot smarter than I ever was. They tested her at school once. Her scores were off the charts. Genius-level I.Q. But she had this dark side to her, mean almost.

"As far as Denise was concerned, rules didn't exist. Not for her, anyway. Only for other people. The first time she got busted for soliciting, she was thirteen years old. She told my parents she was going to a slumber party with some of her friends from school. Instead, she was downtown trying to hustle visiting businessmen."

"Thirteen's pretty young," Stan Jacek agreed.

I think he said what he did only to reassure Deanna Meadows; to make it easier for her to continue. I knew I'd seen hookers in Seattle who hadn't seen their twelfth birthdays yet, and I'm pretty sure Jacek had, too. Maybe even in Coupeville.

"What happened?" I asked.

"The cops called my parents. Dad went down to juvie to get her; to bail her out. On the way home, he asked her what she was thinking of; how come she did it. She said she did it for the money, because she didn't get enough allowance. She told him she'd figured out that she could make more by the hour screwing—although she called it something much worse than screwing—than he did after twenty years of being a minister."

"That must have been hard on him," Jacek said.

Deanna laughed a harsh, raw, humorless laugh.

"*Hard* is hardly the word for it!" she exclaimed. "Denise killed something in my father when she told him that—robbed him of something important—his dignity. He took it personally. Having Denise act like that made him feel like his whole life was a fraud, a joke. He must have thought he had failed his entire family."

There was a long pause while Deanna Meadows gazed off into the middle distance and collected her frayed emotions. When she spoke again, I could hear the unvarnished bitterness behind her words.

"Of course, I was there and doing all right. While Denise was out raising hell, I was busy finishing up my last year in high school and getting good grades, but that didn't seem to matter. It didn't count. I don't think anybody even noticed. That's what they say. The squeaky wheel is always the one that gets the oil."

"What happened after your father brought Denise home?" Jacek asked.

Deanna shrugged. "He must have written his letter of resignation that very night and turned it in the next day. He never preached another sermon. I used to love his sermons. He and Mom were both hurting, but Denise didn't give a damn. My parents tried to pick up some of the pieces—tried to glue them back together. They did all the things parents do, like going to counseling and all that, but it didn't work. Nothing worked. Denise didn't want to get better because she didn't think there was anything wrong with her.

"Eventually, my parents just gave up. They had to. They ran out of time and energy and money all at the same time. They couldn't afford to keep on fighting. By then, my father had gone back to school to get a degree in hospital administration, and my mother was working as a receptionist in a doctor's office. Denise ran away for good when she was fourteen. I was already down here, going to school on a scholarship. I met a guy here at school. Gary's the best thing that ever happened to me. We ended up falling in love and getting married.''

"And Denise?''

"She dropped out of sight completely. No one heard from her for years and years. Then, about a year and a half ago, out of a clear blue sky, she turned back up. Someone rang my doorbell one morning, and when I opened the door, there she was. 'Hi,' she says with this big grin on her face, as though nothing had ever happened, like the years in between the last time I saw her and right then didn't exist.

" 'It's your baby sister,' she says. 'Remember me?' ''

Deanna closed her eyes as if remembering for a moment before she continued. "I was so shocked, I could hardly believe it. I mean, we all thought she was dead, but there she was, big as life.''

"You let her in?''

"Of course I did. Wouldn't you if your long-lost sister showed up when you'd spent years thinking she was dead and buried? Not only was she alive, she looked like a million dollars.

"She was all dolled up—healthy and tan. She's a brunette, not a redhead like me, so her skin always turns—turned golden brown whenever she went out in the sun. She looked like one of the models you see in commercials for Caribbean cruises.''

''And?''

''She came in for a while. We sat down and talked.'' Deanna Meadows frowned. ''I guess I'm naive. I thought maybe she had changed. I hoped she had done the same thing I did—that she had grown up and become a responsible adult. But she hadn't. She said her boyfriend—she called him Gabby or Gebby—something like that—had just given her a new car, one of those little Cadillac convertibles. White and black with a white leather interior. Anyway, she had decided to take the car out for a spin and look me up while she was at it. I still don't know how she found me.''

Jacek leaned forward in his chair. ''Was Gabby or Gebby the boyfriend's first or last name?'' he asked.

Deanna frowned. ''I don't know. I don't think she ever said. I did ask her if she and her boyfriend were, like, engaged or something. She just laughed and said she'd never marry him because he was too old for her.''

''Did she tell you anything else about him?''

''Not really, because she didn't stay for very long after that. And I was glad when she left. I didn't like being around her. It was almost like getting over being sick and then having a relapse. I felt like the whole time she was here she was making fun of everything I stood for and believed in. I think that's how my father must have felt, too, that time in the car.''

Deanna Meadows started crying again. For the next few minutes, there was nothing for Jacek or me to do until Deanna Meadows got herself back under control.

"It's so hard to understand," she said finally, when she could talk again. "I loved her once. Denise was so cute when she was little. I used to like to dress her up and show her off to my friends like she was some kind of living, breathing doll. Much better than a Barbie. But then she changed, and I never knew how or why.

"Part of me still loves her, I guess. Part of me still misses the little girl she once was, but part of me hates her, too. For what she did to my parents. For what she did to me. I think I've hated her for a long time. If she's dead, I'm sorry. At least I cry like I'm sorry, but still . . ."

Once again Deanna broke off and couldn't continue. I understood. There's very little distance between love and hate, and often death obliterates the distance between the two entirely. They fuse into a paralyzing turmoil of opposing emotions, one that's almost impossible to bear.

"So after she left your house that day, did you see her again?" Jacek asked gently.

Deanna shook her head. "No," she said. "I never saw her again, but I told my parents where to find her. I felt like they needed to know she was okay—that their daughter wasn't lying dead in a ditch somewhere."

Detective Jacek nodded. "That's how we found you and your mother both," he explained. "Through a letter your mother had written to Denise at the Camano Island house."

As soon as he mentioned the word *mother* Deanna glanced down at her watch. "Oh, my God," she wailed. "It's late. I've got to go get dressed and put on some makeup."

"Just a couple more questions, if you don't mind," Detective Jacek said. "When Denise was here, did she say anything more that you can remember about her boyfriend?"

"No, not really. Just that he had plenty of money and that he was willing to spend it on her."

"Would your sister have been involved in something illegal?" Jacek asked.

"Of course," Deanna answered at once. "Prostitution is illegal, isn't it? At least most places."

"I mean besides that. It looks as though her house may have been searched before it was burned, as though someone was looking for something."

"You mean like drugs?" Deanna asked.

"Possibly," Jacek answered.

Deanna drew a sharp breath. "The guy on the TV news said something about a 'torture killing.'" Deanna's tear-reddened eyes focused directly on Jacek's. "What exactly does that mean?"

Detective Jacek sighed. "I'm sorry that turned up on the news. It wasn't supposed to."

"Are you saying someone tortured her because they wanted her to tell them where something was hidden, like cocaine or something?"

"That's one possibility," Jacek said. "Whatever the killer was looking for, either your sister knew where it was or she didn't. Either she told them or she didn't. We can't tell which."

"But even if she did know where and what it was, even if she told them where to find it, who-ever it was still went ahead and killed her anyway."

"Yes," Detective Jacek agreed. "That's also possible."

"You said 'they.' Do you think there was more than one?"

"No. Not necessarily. That's just a manner of speaking. He. She. They."

Deanna Meadows leaned forward in her chair, her eyes searching Detective Jacek's face. "Tell me," she said. "Exactly how bad is it? I need to know so I can tell my parents so they can be prepared."

Detective Jacek put down his coffee cup and stood up. "It's pretty bad, Mrs. Meadows," he answered. "If I were you, I'd tell your folks to plan on a closed-casket service."

The statement was simple, brief, and to the point, but it answered the question. It told Deanna Meadows what she needed to know.

I had to give Stan Jacek plenty of credit for the diplomatic way he pulled that one off. I don't think I could have handled it better myself.

Before Stan and I finally left Deanna Meadows' driveway in Fairwood, Detective Jacek made arrangements to come back later in the afternoon to talk to her parents, John and Ellen Whitney, and to pick up Denise Whitney's dental records.

After putting in an all-nighter, both Stan and I were running out of steam. We didn't talk much as we drove back down off the plateau. When he suggested a lunch stop in Renton, it sounded like a good idea to me.

The place he chose was one of those cutesy-pie named-but-faceless joints that nowadays seem to litter freeway off-ramps everywhere. They're part of what I call the continuing Dennyfication of America.

Going from one of those standardized chains to another, it's impossible to tell them apart. Only the overhead signs outside are different. Inside they're all laid out in exactly the same manner. All the interiors look as though they were designed by the same silk-flower-crazed, California-based interior designer. The restaurants come complete with identical wood-grain Formica booths, colorful see-and-eat picture menus, and limp, half-cooked hash-brown potatoes.

One bite of my leathery hamburger threw me into a fit of nostalgia for the Doghouse. Chewing on that tough, overdone, and tasteless chunk of mystery meat made me long for one of my old eat-at-all-hours standbys—a chili dog or a grilled tuna with potato chips and pickles on the side. And remembering that reminded me of something else from the Doghouse—a guy by the name of Dirty Dick.

He was one of the old band of Doghouse regulars. To the outside world, that group constituted an oddball collection from all walks of life, but inside the darkened bar and gathered around the organ, they formed an informal, tightly knit choral society.

Dirty Dick was one of the sing-along songfest directors. Each person had his or her own signature song; his own particular number. Dirty Dick's perennial favorite was a bawdy, fun tune called "Aunt Clara."

It had been months since I last heard it, but with a little mental prodding, the words gradually surfaced. "Aunt Clara" is the story of one of those old-time "fallen women." When caught in the act, Aunt Clara is driven out of town in disgrace. While everyone back home predicts a sorrowful, shameful end, Clara heads off for France, where she lives happily ever after and marries far above her station, not once but several times. Four dukes and a baron and maybe even an earl. I'm not absolutely sure about the earl part because I'm not all that good on lyrics. Near as I recall, the chorus goes something like this:

We never mention Aunt Clara,
her picture is turned to the wall.
She lives on the French Riviera.
Mother says she is dead to us all.

It wasn't much of a stretch for me to make the mental leap from good old Aunt Clara to Denise Whitney. I wondered if a grieving John and Ellen Whitney had turned their younger daughter's picture to the wall. More likely, they still thought of her the same way Deanna did—as a beautiful, bright child who had nonetheless turned out badly and for no discernible reason.

A silent Stan Jacek was also lost in thought as he systematically forked his way through a slab of particle-board ground beef. He had ordered meat loaf, but the food on his plate bore little resemblance to that displayed on the colorfully illustrated menu.

"Denise Whitney reminds me of 'Aunt Clara,' " I said between bites. Not privy to my meandering stream of consciousness, Stan Jacek assumed I was talking about a real person.

"Too bad," he said. "I guess everybody has a kook or two hiding in the family closet. My first cousin Jim is undergoing sex-change therapy. As far as my aunt and uncle are concerned, he could just as well be dead."

"Dead's permanent," I said.

"According to Jimmy—that's what he/she wants us to call him now—so's the operation. But don't tell me, tell my uncle. What's this about your aunt?''

Stan Jacek was talking real stuff. I felt foolish admitting to him that I didn't have an Aunt Clara at all, and that I was really referring to the heroine of a barroom ditty. When I finished telling him the whole story, though, Stan Jacek agreed with me.

"I can see why you thought of it," he said. "Clara and Denise do seem to have a lot in common. Except it sounds as though the song has a much happier ending."

"That's right," I said. "I doubt Denise Whitney ever made it as far as the French Riviera."

"Not even close."

Jacek didn't need me hanging around while he picked up the dental records. Truth be known, I wasn't eager to talk to or meet Denise Whitney's bereaved parents. Talking to relatives of murder victims is one of the parts of this job that never gets any easier no matter how many times you do it. Parents are especially tough, no matter how old or screwed-up the children are.

Besides, I had the legitimate excuse of needing to go back to the office and put together a paper trail. I suppose reports do serve some useful purpose. When it's time to go to court, they help reconstruct who said what to whom, and when. But most of the time, they feel like a necessary evil that makes the departmental brass feel as though their grunts are actually working.

Sue Danielson was at her own desk when I walked by. "How'd it go?" I asked.

For an answer, she handed me a copy of an

Identi-Kit sketch. I studied it for some time and then started to give it back.

"Keep it," she said. "That's your copy." I folded up the piece of paper and put it in my pocket.

"Bonnie Elgin did a good job," Sue continued. "We were through with the whole deal, prints and sketch both, by eleven o'clock. After we finished up, I went down to the Millionair Club to have lunch with a guy named Edward G. Jessup."

The Millionair Club is a Seattle social service agency that provides meals, medical care, and temporary job placement to the homeless. I've eaten there on occasion as my part of the new police chief's policy of community outreach. Plain meals, made of donated food, and served cafeteria-style, don't make for a trendy luncheon-dining experience. But then, having just come from my board-like burger in Renton, who was I to talk?

"Sounds like you're dining out in style," I said. "So who's Edward G. Jessup? A new boyfriend? Does your son Jared know about this?"

Sue smiled slightly in response to my teasing, but her answer was serious. "Jessup is a former Magnolia Bluff resident who used to live on a box spring under a blue tarp."

"Good work! How did you find him?"

"He found me. Or rather, his job-placement counselor did. The guy was there last night when the evidence van picked up his box spring. The crime lab tech told him it had something to do with a homicide investigation. He went into the Millionair Club for a job call this morning and talked to his job-placement counselor about it. The counselor went through channels and tracked me down.

"The counselor was downright belligerent with me—said he was tired of Seattle P.D. picking on his clients just because they're homeless. He was ripped because we'd 'illegally confiscated' Jessup's property. Not only that, he said Jessup was prepared to take a blood test, if necessary, to prove the blood wasn't his."

"Did you schedule a blood test then?" I asked.

"Naw," Sue Danielson said with a casual shrug. "I decided not to bother."

That sounded like sloppy police work to me. "Why not?" I demanded.

"Because Edward G. Jessup wasn't home when Gunter Gebhardt's boat caught fire. The man has an airtight alibi."

"And what would that be?"

Sue grinned. "He was in the King County Jail overnight," she said smugly. "Drunk and disorderly. He was booked at twelve-oh-three A.M."

You win some; you lose some. "That's airtight all right," I agreed. "So what's next on your agenda?"

"I plan on spending the afternoon checking emergency rooms around town to see if anyone remembers treating Bonnie Elgin's hit-and-run victim. What about you?"

I gave her the *Cliff's Notes* summary of my morning with Detective Stan Jacek and Deanna Meadows, then I settled down at my desk and went to work. I checked voice mail for messages. There weren't any. I dialed Maxwell Cole's number at the *P.-I.*

"Leave your message at the sound of the tone," Max's cheerful recording told me in his own voice. "I'll get right back to you."

Like hell he would. He hadn't so far. I didn't bother leaving another message. I didn't want to give him the satisfaction of knowing I'd called back.

As far as writing reports is concerned, my intentions were good. What was it my mother used to say? Something about the spirit being willing but the body weak. My body was weak, all right.

I started off like gangbusters, but the greasy lunch combined with serious sleep deprivation zapped me before long. By two-thirty, I had nodded off at my desk with my pen trailing aimlessly across and off the edge of the paper. I was dead to the world when Sergeant Watkins stopped by and woke me up.

"Maybe you ought to go home and grab some shut-eye," he suggested. "I wouldn't mind, but you're snoring so loud no one else can concentrate."

"Snoring? Was it really that bad?" I asked.

Watty shook his head and grinned. "Naw," he said. "No louder than a buzz saw. How are you coming on your paper, by the way? Captain Powell wants a status report ASAP, particularly on the Maxwell Cole leak."

"Tell him I'm working on it," I said.

I pushed the reports I had completed across my desk. Standing in the doorway to my cubicle, Watty pulled out a pair of reading glasses and then scanned through what I had written. When he finished, he took off the glasses and stowed them in his pocket.

"If I'm reading the time lines right, you must have spent most of the night up on Camano Island. I know for a fact you've been on the job since eight o'clock. You've had what, three hours of sleep?"

"Something like that, give or take."

"No wonder you look like hell. Go home. Get some sleep."

"But Sue and I were going to . . ."

My objection was strictly *pro forma*. Years ago, when I first came to work on the force, being up all night didn't faze me. Back then, a case would grab my attention and keep it. If I had to, I'd work round the clock, then sleep eight hours straight and be back on top of things again. I can't do that anymore. I'm like an aging rubber band that no longer bounces back to quite its original shape. I must be getting old, but come to think of it, I didn't recall ever seeing Watty use reading glasses before, either.

In any case, he cut me off in midsentence. "I said go home, and I meant it."

With no further discussion, I swiped the remaining papers off my desk and stuck them in a drawer. Then I stood up and pulled on my jacket. "Middle age is hell, isn't it?" I said.

Watty shook his head. "It beats the alternative," he replied. "Now get out of here before Captain Powell lays hold of you."

Usually, I'll toss off some kind of smart-ass comeback, but this time I was too brain-dead. And I'm glad I didn't. Watty was well within his supervisory rights to send me home. I was too damn tired to be out on my own recognizance.

After I retrieved my 928 from the parking garage on James, it was all I could do to stay awake long enough to drive home, park the car, and stagger from my parking place to the elevator. I was so tired, I think I might have welcomed some company in the elevator—even an unaccompanied dog. It would have given me something to lean on.

I didn't bother to stop for the mail, and I barely glanced at the blinking answering machine in the living room. I left it to its own devices without hitting the playback button. The messages would have to wait. I headed straight for the bedroom, where, after a moment's contemplation, I pulled the telephone jack out of the wall, stripped out of my clothes, and fell into bed. I slept for twelve hours straight. If I had any dreams—good or bad—I was sleeping too hard to remember them.

When I woke up, I was totally refreshed—bright-eyed and bushy-tailed, as we used to say. I was also starved. The only problem was, it was three o'clock in the morning—not a good hour to discover that the cupboard is bare. A cursory inventory of the kitchen revealed that other than a bag of whole-bean coffee that I keep in my freezer, there wasn't a stick of edible food in the house.

When Karen and I split up, that was one of the first and hardest lessons I had to learn about living on my own. Food doesn't automatically transport itself from grocery-store shelves to refrigerator and cupboards or table. Someone has to go to the store and actually bring it home. And meals—especially balanced ones—don't appear on the table magically. They require advance planning and preparation. When it comes to cooking, I'm a complete flop.

Food considerations, odd hours, proximity, and loneliness were the several factors that had caused me to gravitate to the Doghouse. At three o'clock that morning, I missed it more than ever.

I glanced outside. It was foggy again—foggy and cold. I pulled on some clothes and walked out to the living room. I hadn't taken the messages off the machine earlier, and there was even less sense in doing so now. You can't call people back at three o'clock in the morning. Closing the front door on the blinking light, I headed downstairs.

I think Donnie, Belltown Terrace's graveyard-shift doorman, was most likely snoozing at his desk, but he lurched to his feet as soon as the elevator door opened.

"Mr. Beaumont," he said, a little too eagerly. "You're up and around early. Or is it late?"

"Early," I said. "Do you know a good place to get breakfast around here at this time of day?"

"Here in the Regrade?"

I nodded. "Someplace within walking distance."

"There's Caffè Minnie's," he suggested helpfully. "It's just down the street."

I've been in Caffè Minnie's a time or two. It's at the corner of First and Denny, one of those oddball spots where Seattle's various early-day surveyors couldn't come to any kind of sensible agreement. As a result, the corner lot is triangular, and so's the building that sits on it.

Caffè Minnie's has an eclectic crowd. Some are

of the purple-haired, earringed sort, while others are of the vacationing schoolmarm variety as well as assorted types between the two extremes. Caffè Minnie's late-night customers tend to view anyone who looks like a police officer with suspicion verging on outright hostility. I wasn't up to that.

"No," I said. "Not my style."

"How about Steve's Broiler up on Virginia?"

I had tried Steve's as well. For some reason, I found it depressing. "I don't think so."

"What about the Five Point?" he asked. "It's over on Cedar at Fifth, just under the Monorail."

"The Five Point isn't open, is it? I thought they closed early—around eleven."

"Not anymore. After the Doghouse closed, they went twenty-four hours."

"Oh," I said.

It was amazingly quiet on the street. As I walked, the lateness of the hour combined with the muffling qualities of the fog gave me the sense of being the only person left alive in downtown Seattle. But when I reached Cedar, there were three empty Farwest Cabs lined up on the street.

The neon sign in the window of the restaurant, the one that says COOK ON DUTY, gave the fog outside a ghostly pink glow. The fog was so thick, in fact, that from the front door I couldn't see as far as Chief Sealth standing in his winter-dry fountain a few feet away in the middle of Tillicum Square.

Right inside the door, a wooden cigar-store Indian waited beside the cash register. Back in my drinking days, I didn't venture into the Five Point much. For one thing, the black-and-white tiles on the floor, counter front, and ceiling can be a little disorienting when you're operating under a full load of McNaughtons.

Furthermore, legend has it that back in the old days, a Five Point bartender once asked me to leave when I tried to strike up a serious conversation with the wooden Indian. I don't remember the incident, but that doesn't mean it didn't happen.

Alexis Downey—my sometime girlfriend—didn't like the Doghouse; didn't approve of it. While the Doghouse was still open, I once offered to take her to the Five Point for a Sunday-morning breakfast. She refused to go. I could have handled it if her objection had been based on smoke or greasy food. I was thunderstruck when it turned out to be on the grounds of sexual discrimination.

I'm not sure how Alex heard about the men's rest room at the Five Point. Through the creative use of a periscope, users of the urinal—presumably all male—have an unobstructed view of the top of the Space Needle. Alex told me she wasn't setting foot inside the place until women could take advantage of the same view. I took this to be a new front in Seattle's potty-parity war between the sexes.

The sign on the front door of the Five Point made no mention of rest-room inequality. Instead, it announced SMOKERS WELCOME. NONSMOKERS BEWARE. That statement pretty much covered it.

Inside the small dining room, a predictable pall of cigarette smoke hung in the air. It may have been the middle of the night, but it was also the first of the month. The place was crowded with

what seemed like a group of regulars. Four oversized cabdrivers—a crowd all by themselves—
took up the better part of three tables.

There was only one empty seat left at the
counter. I slipped into it. I had barely started looking around to get my bearings when someone
slammed a full cup of coffee onto the counter in
front of me. Some of the coffee slopped over the
top onto the Formica.

"It's about time you got around to dropping
in here. What'll you have—bacon and eggs, hash
browns crisp, whole-wheat toast, and a small OJ?"
The voice was familiar. So was the peroxide-blond
beehive hairdo.

The waitress was Wanda, one of my old favor-
ites from the Doghouse.

"Wanda!" I exclaimed. "What the hell are you
doing here?"

"Whaddya think? I'm just working to wear out
the uniform." She grinned. "Besides, I'm way too
young to retire. Now are you going to order or
what? I don't have time to stand around here jaw-
ing all night."

"You're right," I said. "I'll have the usual."

"By the way," she returned. "For future reference, that's a number four."

Wanda hustled off. I'm not that good a judge
of women's ages. Perpetually blond hair tends to
throw me off, but if I were going to guess, I'd
say Wanda was somewhere right around seventy.

When she came back with my orange juice, she
slapped a slightly used, grease-stained newspaper
on the counter in front of me.

"Sorry it's so messy," she apologized. "This

is the only one I could find where somebody
hadn't already worked the crossword puzzle. Do
you need a pencil?''

"No, thanks," I said. "I've got one."

I opened the paper up to the right page. First
I read "Mike Mailway," then I started working
the puzzle.

For the first time in months, I felt as though I'd
come home.

13

James Gleason, the author of that morning's *New York Times* Crossword Puzzle in the *Seattle P.-I.*, must have been my blood brother. Or maybe he's a twin, and the two of us were separated at birth. Whatever the connection, we were on the same wavelength. I banged my way through the entire puzzle without a single hitch or hang-up. I finished it completely in twenty minutes flat—while I was eating breakfast.

Only when I was in the process of refolding the paper to leave it for the next guy did I see a copy of Bonnie Elgin's Identi-Kit sketch right at the top of the front page in the local news section. It was good positioning for that kind of piece. I know for a fact that people read that section of the paper more than any other.

It's easy to close our eyes and ignore what's going on in Washington, D.C., or to gloss over the latest episode of bloodthirsty carnage in Bosnia or the Middle East. It's a lot more difficult to blind yourself to what's going on in your own backyard. Readers tend to skip over the blaring headlines on the front page in favor of devouring in detail—down to the last sentence—what's happening at home. For some reason, news of murder and mayhem next door is almost always more compelling and more interesting than systematic genocide as it is practiced in other, more distant parts of the world.

Seeing the picture there in the *P.-I.* served notice to me that Sue Danielson had kept right on working throughout the afternoon. She had talked about visiting hospitals with our missing hit-and-run victim's picture, but she must have faxed copies to some of the media as well. I doubted she had actually stepped inside that heavily guarded, impregnable fortress—the *Seattle Post-Intelligencer.*

I gave Sue credit for both initiative and hustle, especially considering the fact that her partner *du jour* had spent most of the afternoon and all of the evening literally lying down on the job. I allowed myself only the smallest twinge of guilt. After all, Sue hadn't spent the previous night poking around in the still-warm ashes of that house fire up on Camano Island.

Intrigued by the reproduction of the sketch, I broke my own protocol and actually read the accompanying article. In brief, it said that detectives were looking for the man depicted in the picture as a ''person of interest'' in the fatal fire at Fishermen's Terminal two days earlier. The reporter went on to say that there was some speculation about his possible link to another fatal arson fire as well, one that had occurred the following day on Camano Island.

The reporter stated that although the two fires were thought to be related, investigators had so far declined to comment on the possible connection between them. Gunter Gebhardt was mentioned by name. Denise Whitney was not.

I was relieved that the appalling details of the murders themselves had been left out of the article. As a police officer, I found it comforting to know that not every aspect of Stan Jacek's and my two separate investigations had become public knowledge. More important than not disrupting our work, the fact that some of the gory details were missing from the article also served to spare the victims' families considerable pain.

Now that I was buoyed by my decent night's sleep, the food, a successfully completed crossword puzzle, and a little camaraderie with an old friend, even reading a newspaper didn't get to me. I left the Five Point and sauntered back to Belltown Terrace feeling almost human.

Once in my apartment, I was impatient to get to work, but common sense prevailed. Four-forty-five was way too early to show up for my shift down at the Public Safety Building. The guys on night duty would have thought I'd lost my marbles. That hour was also still too early to begin returning phone calls, but I did settle down in my recliner to take the messages off my answering machine.

The collection of calls was about what you'd expect in a downtown high-rise. One enthusiastic telemarketer wanted to know if I wanted to subscribe to *The Wall Street Journal*? It could be delivered directly to my door. No, I did not. Someone else wanted to know if I'd like to subscribe to a credit-card protection program. I didn't bite on that one, either.

Heather Peters called from downstairs where she lives with her father, Ron Peters—one of my former partners—and her stepmother, Amy. Sounding like a very dignified and old-for-her-age eight-year-old, Heather informed me that she now had a weekend job that would pay ten dollars a day for four whole days, but that she would tell me more about it later when she saw me in person. Way to go, Heather!

The next call was from Maxwell Cole. Unlike voice mail, my old answering machine doesn't time-date the calls, but since this message came in after Heather's, Max must have called me back fairly late in the day—sometime after three o'clock or so.

"Hey, J.P.," Max said. "Long time no see. How's it going?" He spoke in one of those gratingly familiar, hail-fellow-well-met tones that comes across as phony as a three-dollar bill.

"Sorry about playing what you call telephone tag, but I'm down here in Olympia on special assignment, paying a visit to Ulcer Gulch. I think I may be on the trail of a little graft and corruption."

Ulcer Gulch is a snide in-crowd code name for the crowded hallway in the State Capitol down in Olympia where lobbyists can hang out and rest up between sessions of heavy-duty legislative arm-twisting. Legislators and their Olympia-based peccadillos are a little outside Max's normal "City Beat" investigative-journalism territory, but I didn't question it. After all, Camano Island is outside my usual jurisdiction boundaries as well.

"There's no way for me to receive a phone call here at the moment," Max continued, "and it's hard as hell to make outgoing calls. I had to lie like a son of a bitch for permission to make this one. I'll have to get back to you tomorrow or the next day, J. P. Hope that's soon enough." Click.

"No, it isn't soon enough, thank you very much," I said irritably, talking back to the machine since I couldn't talk back to Maxwell Cole himself. Shaking my head, I ground my finger into the Erase button and sent Max's voice whirling into the great beyond. It was easy for him to put off talking to me until it happened to be convenient for *him*—tomorrow or the next day or even the day after that. Max didn't have to face a pissed-off Captain Lawrence Powell when he reached his office later that morning. I did.

The next voice on the machine I recognized at once. It was my grandmother, Beverly Piedmont.

"Hello, Jonas," she said, keeping her now-familiar tone brisk and businesslike. "It's late Thursday afternoon, right around five, I think. I don't want to make a pest of myself, but it's so quiet around the house here today that I'm driving myself crazy. Not that your grandfather talked all that much, mind you. He was a man of few words even before his stroke. I'm sure you know what I mean.

"I guess I must be feeling lonely. Anyway, if you're not already busy, maybe the two of us could have dinner together tonight. My treat. We could go to the King's Table." Her voice faltered unmistakably. "Your grandfather and I didn't go out to eat often, you see, but King's Table was one of his favorite places. It was easy to get his chair in and out, and it's not terribly expensive."

Beverly Piedmont took a sharp breath. "Oh, dear," she said. "I'm afraid I'm sounding like a big crybaby. As I said, if you're too busy, just ignore this. It's not as though there isn't any food in the house. I can always open a can of soup or something, and we'll have dinner together some other time. Bye."

Awash in guilt, I looked at my watch as if I could make it run backward. I hadn't ignored Beverly Piedmont's plaintive message, but she had no way of knowing that. The message was a good twelve hours late, and dinnertime was long gone.

Damn! That's the story of my life. It seems as though when someone I care about needs something, I always fall short of the mark. I'm never quite where I'm supposed to be when I'm needed. I never quite make the grade.

I saved that message for later and went on to the next one.

"BoBo," said Else Gebhardt. "You probably won't get this until morning. It's sometime after midnight. I apologize for calling so late, but this is the first time I've been able to get to the phone.

"I really appreciate your giving me a card with your home number on it. I need to talk to you as soon as possible—in person. And alone, please, if you don't mind. It'll be hard enough to discuss this with you. I don't think I can discuss it at all in front of a stranger or even over the phone."

There was a pause. Else Gebhardt took a ragged breath that was just one choke short of a sob.

"I've had three reporters show up here at the house earlier today. This afternoon. They were all asking me what the connection is between Gunter's death and some fire that happened up on Camano Island last night. Night before last, now. I told them I hadn't heard about any fire and that I had no idea what they were talking about. Do you?"

I nodded silently to myself.

"BoBo," she continued, "if you can shed any light on all this, I'd really appreciate it if you'd stop by and let me know. I feel so . . . so confused.

"And then there's Kari. She and Michael finally drove down from Bellingham earlier tonight. She went to bed just a few minutes ago. I'm thankful to have her here, but that's another reason I waited so long to call.

"Kari was in terrible shape when they first got here. Hysterical. Couldn't stop crying. She kept saying it was all her fault—that somehow she was the cause of what happened to her father—almost as though she killed him herself.

"Of course, I told her that was ridiculous, but she didn't seem to pay any attention. I think it's hitting her so hard because they were . . . well, you know . . . she and Gunter were . . . estranged."

This time Else was unable to suppress a series of sobs that rose in her throat and temporarily choked off her ability to speak. Her audible anguish, captured in all its misery on the recording, flashed through the machine and into me—emotions transformed to electrical shocks.

Bad as Else Gebhardt's suffering was right then, I knew it would only grow worse once she learned about the existence of Denise Whitney and the young woman's relationship to Gunter.

Eventually, Else's voice came back on the recording. A little stronger and steadier, more under control.

"Sorry," she managed. "I didn't mean to fall apart like that. Anyway, I'll be up early in the morning. If I go to sleep at all, that is. So call me any time after six or else stop by. I really do need to talk to you."

I erased that message. Alan Torvoldsen had dodged the bullet, that damned lucky stiff. I was the one who would be stuck with the thankless task of revealing the fact that Gunter Gebhardt had made a mockery of his marriage vows.

The next hour seemed to take forever. My coffee dipstick wasn't registering quite full, so I made another pot and then sat in my recliner, sipping coffee and considering what I had learned about the people I so far knew to be part of Gunter Gebhardt's life. More often than not, murderers are found within the realm of the victim's circle of acquaintance.

In other words, Gunter was a whole lot more likely to have been bumped off by someone he knew than by someone he didn't. And by someone who knew him well. The savagery of the crime didn't point to random violence perpetrated by a passing stranger. The killer was someone twisted who reveled in human suffering—someone with an appalling grudge against Gunter and Denise both. Which of those two was the primary target?

I wondered. Was it one or the other or both? That was the basic starting point. Until we understood that, the investigation had no focus. We were shooting blind.

My instinctive choice for primary target was Gunter. That's probably nothing more than prejudice on my part. The reading we'd been getting on him was a mixed bag. Yes, he had done good things—including rescuing his financially failing in-laws, but there were plenty of other things that weren't nearly so commendable.

And that's when I started thinking about Gunter's twenty-two-year-old daughter, Kari. Naturally, Else had categorically dismissed her daughter's self-incriminating admission of guilt. And why not? Mothers are almost universally like that. Else had attributed Kari's emotional distress to the fact that Gunter had died without ever resolving the quarrel between them.

And that was possible. But I wondered if that was all of it. Exactly how long had Kari Gebhardt and her father been at war? I asked myself. How long and why?

I happened to know there were things about Gunter Gebhardt that his wife and widow didn't yet suspect. What about Kari? Had she somehow learned her father's ugly secret? What if she had discovered not only the existence of Denise Whitney, but also of the concealed financial assets that allowed her mother's rival to live in isolated splendor in the house on Camano Island.

As the father of a more-or-less unpredictable daughter, I'd like to think that torture patricide isn't something well-brought-up girls do—not even when they learn awful truths about their daddies screwing around behind their mommies' backs. Still, irate daughters have committed murder on occasion. Had that happened here? Or if Kari Gebhardt wasn't tough enough to do the dirty deed herself, might she not—in defense of her mother's honor—have found someone else to do it for her?

After years in Homicide, I have more than a nodding acquaintance with killers. Some of the most disturbing perpetrators—the ones I consider to be the scum of the earth—are the contract-killer types, the ones who murder for hire and see their job as nothing more or less than a business transaction. Some of them are willing to do anything for money—anything at all. And a scary few take inordinate pride in a job well done—the bloodier the better.

I left my apartment at a quarter to six and drove through Seattle's third day of unremitting morning fog. When I got to the top of Greenbrier, I had to dodge out of the way of a fire-engine-red Jeep Cherokee that came surging up the rise and almost ran me off the road. I would have had a few choice words about drivers of bright red cars, but I didn't. After all, I happen to be the driver of a bright red car myself.

I arrived at Else Gebhardt's Blue Ridge house at exactly the same time as the delivery boy for the *Post-Intelligencer*.

I picked up the paper from where he had tossed it in the driveway and carried it into the house. It seemed to me it was probably fortunate that the paper and I arrived at the Gebhardt house at precisely the same time. At least it gave Else someone familiar to lean on as the tawdry details of her dead marriage began to unravel in public.

Maybe I was kidding myself, but I wanted to believe that my being there would help.

I had a single, overriding reason for not wanting to be the one who gave Else Gebhardt the damning news about her husband—I knew how much it would hurt.

Faced with this kind of after-the-fact revelation of betrayal, people are always quick to trot out that useless old saw "The truth will set you free." Use of that particular quote always causes me to respond in kind with a line of my own, with the title of a song from Gershwin's *Porgy and Bess*— to wit, "It Ain't Necessarily So."

I know from personal experience that a painful truth learned about a departed loved one—news that arrives after that person's death—is more than merely hurtful. It can be paralyzing. I'm not hypothesizing, either. I know that pain personally because I've been there, and years later, it still hurts.

I've wondered sometimes, in the years since Anne Corley died, how would I have reacted if things had been different. For instance, if I had been given a clear-cut choice to go either way— to know the truth about her or to spend the remainder of my life in blissful ignorance—which would I have chosen? Would I have opted for truth or would I have clung blindly to those few precious moments and memories? Yes, having to come to terms with the "real" Anne Corley inalterably changed me. Grieving over her loss forced me to grow up. Was loving and losing worth it? I don't know.

Some days—like the day I first held Kayla, my granddaughter, in my arms—I can say unequivocally that life since Anne was well worth the pain. But other times, I'm not so sure. The jury's still out.

On occasion I give myself little pep talks and try to convince J. P. Beaumont that of course he loved Anne Corley unconditionally. That's a hell of a lot easier to say or contemplate as long as she's dead and safely buried up in Mount Pleasant Cemetery. I'm afraid the reality of living out our lives would have been a whole lot tougher. For one thing, we would never have been able to live together as man and wife, not with me working homicide year after year and with her locked away, either in a prison or else in a facility for the criminally insane.

So Anne Corley was on my mind that morning when I sat in Else Gebhardt's cheerfully decorated kitchen, telling her what I suspected to be the sad truth about Gunter, her philandering and now-dead husband. Else's sallow, haggard features became even more so as I related what I knew of her husband's illicit connection to Denise Whitney and of the still-smoldering love-nest hideaway on Camano Island.

The problem for Else Gebhardt was entirely understandable. I believe that while Gunter was alive, Else gave him his husbandly due in the form of willing and unconditional love. Now she was finding out too late that rather than treasuring her devotion, he had hurled it back in her teeth. I told her as diplomatically and gently as I could, yet she seemed to shrink under the hurtful impact of my words.

"How long did you say she's lived there?" Else asked listlessly when I finished my series of revelations. Her face was strained and pale. There didn't seem to be any spunk or fight left in her. Two days earlier, when she was arguing with Officer Tamaguchi on the Fishermen's Terminal dock, her features had been alive with anger, outrage, and exasperation. Now she seemed to have simply given up. My sense was that the fire of life in Else Gebhardt was about to sputter and go out.

We were seated at the small oak table in the well-lit kitchen of her house on Culpeper Court NW. Two coffee cups sat on the table before us. By then mine was empty. Else's, still completely full, had grown cold without her ever having touched it.

"Two years," I answered.

"How can you be sure Gunter bought it?"

"The purchaser was a corporation named Isolde International. What do you think?"

"Who's Isolde International?" she asked. "I've never heard of them."

"It's the company that purchased the Camano Island house," I told her. "The corporation commission lists your husband as president. Denise Whitney is on the books as vice president."

"Oh." Else frowned, absorbing the information.

"But where did he get the money to buy an extra house?" she asked. "I remember two years ago. It was a real tough season. We were all right, but only because we weren't carrying a whole lot of debt. I ..."

"Is it possible Gunter came into an inheritance of some kind?" I interrupted. "Did he sell off some equipment, maybe?"

"No." Else looked at me, her eyes narrowing. "You think he was involved in some kind of illegal activity, don't you?" she said accusingly. The spark inside her lit up a little, gave off some heat. "Smuggling, drug-trafficking, is that what you mean?"

"I suppose it could be something like that," I conceded reluctantly, not wanting to plant unsubstantiated ideas in her head. "What I can tell you is that some of the rooms of the house on Camano Island were left pretty much intact. Our investigation of those has turned up evidence that those rooms for sure, and most likely the others as well, were thoroughly searched before the house was torched.

"At this point, it's impossible for us to tell whether or not the killer found what he was looking for. We don't know what, if anything, is missing, since we have no idea what was there in the first place."

Else shook her head several times, more determinedly with each successive shake. "I can't believe Gunter would have been mixed up in anything like illegal drugs, but then ..." She paused and backed off. The glowing ember inside her dimmed once more.

"Come to think of it, though, I wouldn't have thought he'd have anything to do with another woman, either, so I guess you can't set much store by my opinions."

A door opened and closed somewhere else in the house. Moments later, Inge Didriksen propelled her creaking, wheeled walker across the living-room floor and into the kitchen. Else raised a cautioning finger to her lips and shook her head.

"Shhhhh," she whispered. "Don't you tell her. Let me do it."

But Inge's hearing was far better than Else knew, or else she had come much closer to the kitchen than either of us realized.

"Don't tell me what?" Inge asked sharply, pushing over to the kitchen counter and pouring herself a cup of coffee.

A small wire basket—a pink-and-white webbed-plastic bicycle basket—had been welded between the two uprights near the handlebars of Inge Didriksen's walker. Despite the shaking of her palsied hand, the old woman somehow managed to lower a full coffee cup down into the basket. Then, without spilling a single drop, she maneuvered herself, the walker, and the steaming coffee cup over to the kitchen table.

Else waited until her mother was seated at the table before she took a deep breath. "Mother," she said, "Detective Beaumont has discovered that Gunter had a girlfriend. Now she's been murdered as well, most likely by the same person who killed Gunter."

Inge Didriksen looked harmless enough. Comic almost. She was wearing a dainty, lace-edged housecoat. The topmost button was fastened properly, but she had skipped the second one, leaving the rest of them crooked. Her thinning hair peaked at the top of her head, making her resemble a white-haired Woody Woodpecker. Her eyes, huge behind thick glasses, focused on her daughter.

"Oh, that," Inge said. "My stars, Else! Are you just now finding out about her?"

I don't know who was more taken aback by Inge Didriksen's surprising revelation—Else Gebhardt or Detective J. P. Beaumont. I know Else's mouth gaped open, and mine probably did as well. Else's already pale face faded to ashen, but the spark came back to life in her voice.

"Mother!" she exclaimed, her voice tense with outraged indignation. "Do you mean to tell me you knew about this? You knew Gunter was carrying on an affair, and you didn't bother to tell me?"

Inge took a delicate sip of her coffee. "You know I make it a practice never to interfere between husbands and wives," she replied primly.

"Only when it suits you," Else retorted angrily. "How did you know about it?"

"She was here one day. I saw her."

"Here?" Else asked in shocked dismay. "Right here in my house?"

"My house," Inge corrected blandly. "But, yes, she was here. At least I believe it was the same one. A brunette, wasn't she?" The old woman peered at me slyly over her coffee cup and waited for confirmation.

In less than two minutes, that little no-holds-barred verbal exchange between Else Gebhardt and Inge Didriksen taught me more about open warfare between mothers and daughters than I ever wanted to know.

"Well?" Inge prodded. That's when I finally realized she was looking at me and waiting for me to answer.

"Yes," I said. "A brunette."

"When?" Else demanded. The fire was back in her eyes now—her eyes as well as her voice.

"When did I see her?" Inge returned after another question-deflecting sip of coffee.

"Yes."

"It must have been three years ago, now. Maybe a little more. Yes, three, I think. It was just after Kari came back from being an exchange student. And it must have been around this time of year, too. I remember I was going to go with you to spend the day at the Christmas bazaar, and then I didn't because I wasn't feeling well. I believe my arthritis flared up."

"Stick to the point, Mother," Else insisted.

"I'm sure Gunter had no idea I stayed home," Inge continued. "If he had, they never would have come here in the first place. After you left for the bazaar, I must have fallen asleep. When I woke up, I heard voices—someone laughing—a woman's voice laughing. I thought you must have come home early, but then the back door slammed shut. I looked out the window and saw them. They were just leaving the house. I sat on the edge of my bed and watched the whole thing."

"And never told me," Else breathed. "You knew about it, and you never said a word!"

"What good would telling you have done?"

Inge returned petulantly, with an air of offended innocence.

"If I had known and chosen to leave then, I would have been three whole years younger than I am now," Else replied with commendable self-control. "I would have been a hell of a lot smarter a hell of a lot sooner."

"Please don't swear, Else," Inge scolded. "I've told you time and again, that kind of language isn't at all necessary or ladylike."

"I'll talk any damn way I want to!"

My pager went off right then. The number displayed on the tiny screen was from the Seattle P.D. Homicide Squad. Sergeant Watty Watkins's extension, to be specific. I recognized the number. Normally, I ignore my pager until the second or third try. This time I welcomed the interruption.

I don't like being a party to petty domestic disputes. Witnessing Inge Didricksen pick away at her daughter reminded me of a crow I once saw snap the head off a helpless baby sparrow that had fallen out of its nest. But the crow was only doing what came naturally. There was something almost malevolent about Inge Didricksen.

"Could I use a phone for a moment?" I asked.

Else nodded curtly toward the built-in desk across the kitchen. "You can use the one here if you want. Otherwise, if you need some privacy, there's one in the family room and another in the bedroom."

"This one will be fine."

Hurrying across the kitchen, I picked up the phone and dialed Watty's number. The phone was answered by Chuck Grayson, Sergeant Watkins's counterpart on the night shift. I was surprised when Grayson answered the phone, but I went ahead and asked for Watty.

"What've you been smoking, Beau?" Grayson replied with a laugh. "Watty isn't here yet. It's only seven o'clock. He won't show up for at least another half hour. Longer if traffic's backed up on I-Five."

I glanced at my watch and was startled to see it was only seven o'clock. I had been up and around for hours. It didn't seem possible that shift change hadn't happened yet.

"Somebody paged me," I answered, without bothering to attempt an explanation.

"It was me," Chuck returned. "I tried your home number first. When no one answered, I tried the pager. And it worked like a charm. You're calling back, aren't you?"

"Right. What's up?"

"First off, there have been three calls so far from someone named Maxwell Cole. Isn't he that columnist . . . ?"

"That's the one," I said, cutting Grayson off before he could finish asking. "Maxwell Cole can wait. Anything else?"

"That's about what I figured. More important, there's somebody here waiting to see you."

"Already? Who?"

"She says her name's June Miller."

"Doesn't ring a bell. What does she want?"

"Try the name John Miller. Does that one sound familiar?"

"Sergeant Grayson, could we please stop playing games and cut to the chase?"

"How about former congressman John Miller? June Miller, as in Mrs. John."

"Okay, okay. Mrs. John Miller, married to a former congressman. What does she want?"

"To talk to you. Now."

"What about? I'm working a case. I'm trying . . ."

"Which case? Fishermen's Terminal?"

"That's right."

"According to Mrs. Miller, that's the one she wants to talk to you about."

"What about Sue Danielson? She's my partner on this. Couldn't this Miller woman talk to Sue?"

"She says Maxwell Cole directed her to see you and no one else." Maxwell Cole strikes again. "Sergeant Grayson . . ." I began, but he never let me finish.

"Detective Beaumont," he said, "John Miller may not be a currently elected public official, but he still has a lot of influence in this town. And no one at Seattle P.D. is going to like it if one of our very own homicide detectives flies in the face of all that clout. Do I make myself clear?"

Sometimes I'm a very slow learner, especially when it comes to politics. "I'll be there as soon as I can," I said at last.

"How soon?"

"Fifteen minutes."

"Make it ten. I'll tell her you're on your way."

I turned back to the kitchen table, where Inge, sitting alone now, continued to sip away at her coffee. She seemed totally unaffected by the distress she had caused her grieving, middle-aged daughter.

It went against my upbringing—against everything my mother ever taught me—to think of that sweet little old lady in her crookedly buttoned housecoat as an unmitigated, cold-blooded bitch, but that's what Inge Didriksen was—that and more. In spades.

"Where's Else?" I asked.

"She said she was going back to her room to lie down," Inge answered. "She said she hoped you wouldn't mind showing yourself out."

"I can manage."

I pulled one of my business cards from my wallet and placed it on the table in front of her. "Would you mind giving your granddaughter a message for me?" I asked.

"What kind of message?"

"That's my number at Seattle P.D. Would you please ask her to give me a call as soon as she wakes up?"

"I can do that," Inge Didriksen agreed. "Although I don't know when that'll be. Young people these days sleep until all hours, you know."

Inge's cloudy blue eyes met and held mine for a very long time. It was a challenge. I think she was waiting to see if I would say anything about the way she had treated her daughter.

"I never liked him, you know," she said with a small, almost imperceptible shrug.

"Never liked who?" I asked, playing dumb.

"Why, my son-in-law, of course," she replied. "Gunter. Who else did you think I was talking about?"

Who else indeed? But with Else out of the room, I was free to ask this strange old woman a few questions that might possibly serve to open up some of the darkened corners of the Gebhardt family history.

"Why did Gunter quarrel with your granddaughter?" I asked. "And when did it happen?"

Inge dropped her gaze, as if the strain of holding my eyes was suddenly too much for her.

"You'll have to ask Kari about that," Inge answered demurely. "I couldn't possibly tell you. You see, I make it a practice never to interfere in my children's affairs."

Like hell you do, I thought savagely as I stalked out of the house, closing the door behind me.

Inge Didriksen interfered, all right, but only when it happened to suit her.

15

As I left Else's house on Culpeper Court and started back downtown, the words "wife of a former congressman" conjured up a certain picture in my mind. The image of the imagined June Miller that formed in my head was of someone as tough and cantankerous as Betty Friedan, only not nearly as pretty.

Sergeant Chuck Grayson was still on duty and fighting his way through a deskful of paperwork when I stopped in front of it.

"Where is she?" I asked, starting for my cubicle.

"Whoa, there," Grayson said. "You didn't think we'd stash somebody like her in your office, did you? That place is a wreck."

I ground to a halt and glanced pointedly at the tumbled mass of scattered papers on Sergeant Grayson's desk. "Pardon my saying so, Sarge, but when it comes to wrecks, you don't have much room to talk. Where did you stow her then?"

"Upstairs," he answered. "In that little conference room next door to the chief's office."

It figured. It wouldn't have surprised me if June Miller had been granted a personal interview with the chief of police while she was waiting for me to show up. "She didn't happen to say what all this is about, did she?"

Grayson shook his head. "Nope. Just what I told you on the phone. It has something to do with your deal up at Fishermen's Terminal. Whatever it is, it was important enough for her to show up here at six-twenty A.M. By the way, have you ever met this woman before?"

"Never."

Grayson grinned. "Lucky you," he said. "You're in for a real treat."

"Sure I am," I replied. "And no doubt the chief will give me the rest of the day off when she and I get finished."

"I wouldn't count on that," Grayson said.

I didn't break my neck going back to the elevators. The idea that police officers are "public servants" tends to go to some people's heads. Maybe that was the same reason John Miller was a former congressman instead of a current one. Maybe he resented the idea of being on call twenty-four hours a day.

Right that minute, I know I did. Public servant be damned! June Miller had stopped by the department, without benefit of an appointment, a full hour and a half before the beginning of my shift. Nonetheless, she still expected me to show up, Johnny-on-the-spot, at her beck and call. And since she was far too good to wait in my humble cubicle, she had been ushered up to the more plush surroundings of SPD's "executive" level to wait for me there.

Who the hell does she think she is? I grumbled

irritably to myself as I stepped onto the Public Safety Building's crowded, slow-boat elevator. The goddamned queen of Sheba?

Fortunately, the elevator is very slow, and by the time I stepped off it almost a minute later, I had pretty much come to my senses. After all, if a citizen shows up to *voluntarily* help with an investigation, the least the detective involved can do is not act like a total jerk.

The chief's conference-room door comes complete with a single sliver of glass window in it that allows someone outside in the lobby area to peek inside. Presumably, that's so the person outside can tell exactly what's going on before entering the room and disrupting the proceedings.

The furnishings are Danish modern—cheap Danish modern. They consist of a credenza, a single oval-shaped oak table, and eight matching chairs. There is a ninth chair as well. The cloth and basic pattern of that one are the same as that on the other eight, but that ninth one is a captain's chair with armrests on it. Seattle's chief of police may be in favor of the common touch, but when he's involved in something that requires the use of this particular conference room, you can bet the captain's chair belongs to him and nobody else.

That Friday morning, when I paused outside the door and peeked in through the window, there was only one person in the room. Not surprisingly, June Miller had chosen the captain's chair as the one in which to sit.

To say the woman was striking would do June Miller a serious disservice. Even sitting down, I could tell she was a tall woman with chin-length

white-blond hair, a lithe, slim body, a long, elegant
neck, and the erect bearing of a West Point graduate. Her hands were gracefully draped over the
ends of the armrests. Her long, slender fingers—
one studded with a very impressive diamond—
curled slightly around the wood as if she were half
asleep. Yet, the moment I pushed open the door,
she was on her feet and wide awake, hand out-
stretched. A pair of startling ice-blue eyes sought
mine.

"Are you Detective Beaumont?" she asked.

"Yes. What can I do for you?"

"I came to tell you that he didn't do it."

Mrs. Reeder, my senior English teacher at Ballard High School thirty years ago, used to be a
stickler for faulty pronoun reference. I remember
the speech pretty much verbatim, even after all
these years, because she delivered it often—on an
average of once a week.

"You hounds," Mrs. Reeder would shriek,
striking terror in our hearts and rapping her knuckles on the chalkboard for emphasis. "You must
not use a pronoun unless a noun clearly precedes
it. Unless one naturally follows the other, what
you write becomes so much babble. People can't
make heads nor tails of it."

In this case, that same edict should have applied
to speaking as well as writing. I had no idea what
June Miller was trying to tell me. "Who didn't do
what?" I asked.

"The man you're looking for," she returned
with an exasperated furrowing of her smooth
brow. "The one whose sketch is in the newspaper
this morning. I'm telling you he didn't do it—

didn't do any of the things the article hints he did."

I motioned June Miller back into the seat she had vacated and then settled into an adjoining one myself.

"You make that statement as if you know it for a fact," I said.

"Oh, yes," she agreed, nodding. "I do know it."

"How?" I asked.

"Because he told me," June Miller answered staunchly, as though the matter were already settled once and for all. "Because he said he didn't do it, and I believe him."

"Does this person have a name?" I asked.

June Miller nodded. "His name's Lorenzo," she said. "He happens to be a friend of mine."

"Lorenzo what?"

"Do I have to tell you that? His last name, I mean."

The truth is, she did. It's a felony to withhold information in a homicide case, but I sensed that this was no time to play scare tactics.

"It would be helpful," I said, leaning back in the chair. "What brought you here so early this morning, Mrs. Miller?"

She glanced at the floor, chewing on her lip. "Maxwell Cole gave me your name," she said. "John and I know him. I guess you know John is my husband?"

I nodded but didn't comment.

"We met Max years ago at a campaign function, and we've more or less stayed in touch. I called him last night to ask his advice. He told me you had some connection to all this—that you were the person I should talk to.''

It was funny that June Miller could slice through the ''special assignment'' bullshit and reach Maxwell Cole in Olympia when J. P. Beaumont couldn't. Of course, I had a feeling that there were any number of bureaucratic, red-tape tangles that June Miller could cut her way through without ever having to resort to use of her husband's political prestige.

''And how does Maxwell Cole happen to know so damn much about my case assignments these days?'' I asked, attempting to control my irritation. It wasn't right for me to allow fallout from his and my longstanding animosity to land on an innocent downwinder named June Miller.

''He said he was at a party given by Ron and Bonnie Elgin. Something about a charity auction. From the way he talked, I thought you were there, too.''

Thanks to June Miller, I now had a name to attach to the leak Captain Powell wanted plugged. Unfortunately, the name was mine. And when the good captain came around looking to lop off heads, mine would be first to roll. The fact that the leak was inadvertent wouldn't help my cause in the least. Bonnie Elgin must have mentioned it to some of her party guests when she got off the phone from talking with me. It was my fault for not cautioning her to silence.

It was not yet eight o'clock in the morning, but already this was feeling like a very long day. ''I wasn't at the party in person,'' I said, ''but go on.''

"Of course, I already knew about Gunter Geb-hardt's murder," June Miller continued. "In fact, I more or less expected someone to come talk to me about it before now, but according to Max, I guess you've been too busy following other leads to get around to interviewing the neighbors."

"Neighbors?" I sat up straighter. "Wait just a minute. Where do you live?"

"On Culpeper Court. Right across from the Gebhardts' house. We just had our house remodeled."

"So you knew Gunter and Else Gebhardt?"

June Miller dropped her gaze and pursed her lips before replying. "We aren't exactly best friends," she said.

"What does that mean?"

Raising her chin, June Miller's eyes met and held mine without flinching. "Gunter Gebhardt was a ..." She paused, searching for the right words, then shook her head. "He wasn't a very nice neighbor," she said lamely, leaving me with the impression that she had backed away from say-ing something much stronger.

"I'm not all that grief-stricken that he's dead, either. Of course, I'm sorry for Else and Kari."

"You know them fairly well then?"

June nodded. "Before she left home, Kari used to baby-sit for my son, Brett. I know this will be hard on Kari and her mother, but don't expect me to shed any tears for that unpleasant man. I won't, not at all."

Every time she mentioned Gunter, June spoke with such carefully controlled vehemence that it made me wonder what was behind it. "I take it you and Gunter had some difficulties?'' I suggested.

She ran her hand over her already smooth hair, then took a deep breath before she answered. ''He threatened to hurt Barney, to get rid of him.''

I was sure she had just told me her son's name was Brett. ''Who's Barney?'' I asked.

''Our dog. A terrier. We named him Barney as a joke. You know, after the guy who used to be on TV—Barney Miller?''

''I see,'' I said.

''Threatening Barney would have been bad enough all by itself, but Brett and the dog were right there together. You see, Barney's batteries had run down. . . .''

''His batteries?''

Had I missed something? At first I had thought we were discussing a real dog, but the only ones I know that require batteries are the little stuffed ones toy stores sometimes set to yapping in shopping malls.

''For his collar,'' June Miller explained. ''We have one of those invisible fences. There's a battery on Barney's collar. If he crosses a certain line in the yard, the collar zaps him with a little shock. But it only works as long as the batteries are charged. We're supposed to replace them every four months, but every once in a while, I'll get a pair that runs down sooner than the four months.

''Barney's a smart dog. I don't know how he knows when the batteries are running low, but he does. As soon as they quit, he's out of there. Once I found him all the way up on top of Greenbrier, headed downtown.

"Anyway, this one time, Barney got away. Brett saw him go. He ran inside to get the leash. By the time he came back outside, Barney was across the street, leaving a doggy calling card in Gunter Gebhardt's precious front lawn. I came home a few minutes later. I had just run up to the store to pick up a couple of things for dinner. Brett's old enough to leave alone every once in a while, for a few minutes at a time, anyway. It never occurred to me that anyone here in the neighborhood would think of hurting the dog or deliberately scaring my child."

"What happened when you came home?"

"Brett and Barney were both inside. Brett was scared to death and crying. He told me Mr. Gebhardt told him that if he ever caught Barney in his yard again, he was going to get rid of him. My first thought was that Brett was making a big deal out of something that wasn't all that serious. My son has a very active imagination. But he wasn't making it up, Detective Beaumont. Not at all.

"After I put the groceries away, I left Brett where he was, and I went across the street to clean up the mess and see what I could do to straighten things out. The mess was already gone, of course. Gunter had evidently taken care of that himself. I rang the bell. When he came to the door, he yelled at me. Told me the same thing he'd said to Brett. That if Barney ever came in his yard again, he might just disappear."

"How long ago was this?" I asked.

"Right at the beginning of the summer. Just after school got out. It's almost six months ago now, because I marked it on the calendar. Now

I'm replacing the batteries every three months, just to be on the safe side. I'm supposed to put in a new set next week.''

"I can see this is all very troubling for you, Mrs. Miller," I said sympathetically. "But what you've told me so far is a long-standing problem. I don't think you've been here since six-twenty this morning waiting to tell me about Gunter Gebhardt threatening your dog."

"No," she agreed. "You're right. I came because of Lorenzo. I would have come anyway, but when I realized it was over that worthless man— over Gunter—I had to do something about it, something to help."

I'm the kind of person who doesn't sort through his pocket debris on a regular basis. Stuff I remove from pockets one night when I'm on my way to bed tends to be reloaded, as is, when I dress the next morning.

Reaching into my jacket pocket, I pulled out my copy of Bonnie Elgin's Identi-Kit sketch and placed it on the table in front of June Miller.

"Is this your friend Lorenzo?" I asked.

June nodded. "Not exactly, but close."

"You know why we're looking for him?"

"Not really."

"Because he was seen running through the neighborhood adjacent to Fishermen's Terminal a few minutes before the fire was discovered on Gunter Gebhardt's boat. He ran into the street and was hit by a passing vehicle."

"I know some of that. I read the newspaper while I was waiting. But I knew about it before then, too. I heard about it last night."

"How?"

"From Maria. Lorenzo's sister. She came to *Beso del Sol* looking for me. Lorenzo sent her to find me and to ask me to help."

I had seen *Beso del Sol* in the Wallingford district. It looked to me like an ordinary Mexican-food joint. My first thought was that maybe the Millers were Mexican-food junkies and went there often enough to be considered regulars, but June Miller soon disabused me of that notion.

"I go there once a week for the salsa dancing."

"Salsa dancing?" I asked, still wondering if this had something to do with food. "What's that?"

For the first time since we'd started talking, the woman actually smiled—a dazzling, white-toothed smile.

"It's a hobby of mine," she said. "I walk around Green Lake in the morning, and I salsa dance three or four nights a week. Some people jog. I dance."

"You and your husband both?"

She shook her head. Her hair, free of any noticeable layers of spray or goo, shimmered and then settled softly back around her face without a single strand out of place. "John doesn't go," she said. "At least not often. He stays home with Brett."

Typical male, I couldn't help wondering if former Congressman Miller wasn't riding for a fall. My face must have given my dirty mind away.

"It's not like that," June Miller said quickly. "People really do go there to dance, nothing else. It's not a pickup joint."

"You go dancing at *Beso del Sol* three or four

nights a week, and that's where you met this Lorenzo person?"

"I don't go there every night," June Miller corrected. "The dancing moves from place to place. Sometimes it's at the New World. Sometimes Latitude Forty-seven. Sometimes at the Ballard Fire House. And yes, *Beso* is where I first met Lorenzo. He's a very good dancer."

"What else can you tell me about him?"

"He's scared, Detective Beaumont. Maria told me he's scared to death. I'm sure he ought to have his leg sewn up, but he refuses to go to the doctor."

"If he didn't do anything, why's he scared?" I asked. "What's he scared of?"

"The police."

"Why?"

"He's from Guatemala."

"So?"

"Do you know anything about human-rights violations? Amnesty International?"

I'm always so caught up in that home-grown variety of human-rights violation known as murder that I don't have to go looking for it beyond our borders.

"It's not top on my list of interests," I admitted.

"When it comes to police brutality—to police operating out of control—Guatemala used to take the prize. That's why Lorenzo's family came here in the first place. His older brother was killed by two policemen. Lorenzo was in the room when it happened. He's scared the same thing will happen to him here."

"This is Seattle," I said.

"I know," she agreed. "I went to see him last night. Maria took me to their apartment. I talked to him and tried to explain all that. But he was so upset by what he had seen and heard that he could barely talk. Even to me. It really shook him up."

"What did?"

June Miller took a deep breath. "Lorenzo's brother was tortured to death," she said softly. "By two police officers. Lorenzo works two jobs these days—one as a gardener. But he's also a trained mechanic. He was helping Gunter Gebhardt do some work on his boat. On the side. For cash. But when he came to work that morning . . ."

She paused, then stopped altogether.

"What?" I urged impatiently.

June Miller took yet another deep breath. "I don't know what he heard or saw because he won't tell me. But it must have been awful."

As far as I knew, no mention of Gunter Gebhardt's mutilation had appeared in any of the local media. This wasn't something June Miller had heard from Bonnie Elgin or from Maxwell Cole, either. The room grew silent.

"You're telling me Lorenzo saw Gunter Gebhardt being tortured?"

"He didn't say that to me," June Miller answered. "But he must have seen something."

"Why do you say that?"

"Because of what Maria told me. She says that ever since, whenever he falls asleep, even for a few minutes, the nightmares start up again. The same nightmares that kept him awake for years after his brother died."

"You have to take me to see him," I said softly.

"Yes," June Miller agreed. "I know I do. But you can see why I don't want to."

And indeed I could.

"When can I talk to him?"

"Tonight. Maria said she'll try to bring him to the Ballard Fire House. That's where the salsa dancing is tonight. I told her I'd try to make arrangements to bring you there as well."

Salsa dancing in Ballard? Not the Ballard I knew—or used to know. "What do I do?" I asked.

"Just show up around ten o'clock or so. Pay the cover charge. I'll meet you inside. There's a band. The dancing doesn't really get under way until around eleven."

"What do I wear?"

"What you have on is fine."

"I have a partner, you know. Her name's Sue Danielson. Is it all right if she comes along?"

I knew I'd be in a whole lot of trouble if she couldn't.

"Do you dance?" June Miller asked.

"Not me."

"How about your partner?"

"We work the Homicide Squad," I said. "The subject of dancing has never come up."

"You can bring her along," June agreed. "But it'll be better if she knows how to dance."

16

After my interview with June Miller ended, I escorted her as far as the elevator lobby. Leaving her there, I jogged down the stairway to the fifth floor.

"See me," said the yellow Post-it note pasted at eye level on the doorway to my cubicle. It was signed with the scrawled initials of Captain L. Powell.

See me, I thought, heading for the Homicide Squad's command post. Words to live by.

Years ago, that kind of summons would have struck terror in my heart, especially if I knew that the reason behind it was a screwup of my own making. But things have changed since then. The truth is, I no longer need this job. I work because I want to. That kind of economic freedom does put a slightly different spin on things when the boss comes around chewing ass.

When I first heard Johnny Paycheck sing his trademark song "Take This Job and Shove It," it seemed like an impossible dream. It's reality now—for me anyway. Anne Corley's generous legacy made that possible. And now that I have a choice, I find it's a whole lot easier to be forgiving of Captain Powell's occasional foibles, to say nothing of my own.

On the fifth floor, we refer to Captain Powell's fully windowed interior office as "the fishbowl." I went straight there, carrying the still-smoldering Post-it with me. I could see from outside that the captain was busy on the phone, so I meandered over to the desk where Sergeant Watkins had assumed his usual position.

"Did Sue Danielson find you?" Watty asked. "She was by looking for you a few minutes ago. I told her Chuck Grayson said you were around—upstairs somewhere—but I couldn't be any more specific than that."

"Did she say what she wanted?"

Watty shook his head. "Last thing I heard, I think she was headed downstairs to the crime lab."

I nodded in the direction of the Fishbowl. "What's he want?" I asked.

"I wouldn't know," Watty answered.

Since Sergeant Watkins is Captain Powell's right-hand man, that seemed unlikely, but I didn't argue the point.

About that time, Captain Powell put down the phone. Then he sat there frowning with his hands steepled under his chin, staring at the molded black plastic instrument as though it had just delivered news of the end of the world. The grim set to his jaw boded ill for my coming interview, but I figured I could just as well get it over with. As I started toward the Fishbowl's perpetually open door, Watty gave me a cheery thumbs-up sign.

As a high school student, I earned spending

money by hawking popcorn and sodas in Ballard's now-defunct Baghdad Theater. Watty's gesture reminded me of some of those old gladiator films. There was always a scene in the dusty amphitheater when the doomed gladiators clapped themselves on their armored chests and announced ever-so-solemnly, "We who are about to die salute you."

Watty and I are about the same age, and most likely he grew up watching the same movies I did. I took heart from his raised thumb. After all, in the movies a thumbs-up from Caesar meant the bloodied gladiator lived. Maybe there was hope for me.

I tapped lightly on the doorjamb.

"Come," Powell called out.

Being summoned to Captain Powell's Fishbowl bears an uncommon resemblance to being called to the principal's office back in grade school. My instincts then, as now, were to get my licks in first, to hurry and blurt out my side of the story before anyone else could get a word in edgewise.

"Sorry, Captain, but it's all my fault," I said, not giving him an opportunity to take the first shot. "I tracked down the leak on the story in the paper, and it turns out to be me. I didn't realize it, but at the time I called to discuss the Identi-Kit sketch with Bonnie Elgin, she and her husband had a houseful of company—including Maxwell Cole himself. I made the mistake of not warning Bonnie to keep a lid on. . . ."

"Forget it, Beau," Captain Powell interrupted. "Those things happen. That's not why I called you in here. I need your help. Have a chair."

I shut up and sat.

"I guess you know what they say about shit—
that it rolls downhill?"

After twenty-some years on the force, this was
not news. "So I've noticed," I said.

Captain Powell nodded gloomily. "Me, too."
He plucked a single piece of paper off the morass
on top of his desk. "No doubt you've seen this?"

I glanced at the memo. The bar at the top said
it came from the office of Kenneth Rankin, Chief
of Police, Seattle P.D. It was addressed "To all
Squad Leaders," of which Captain Powell is one.

Seattle's recently appointed police chief, Kenneth Rankin, is on a one-man campaign to get cops
out of their patrol cars and into the community. To
that end, the chief's staff has generated a steady
flurry of printed pages that gradually filter across
desks and down channels to the men in blue—
something that also may change if Rankin's radical proposal to get police officers out of uniform
gains approval.

To be honest, there have been so many memos
flying around that most people have developed a
certain immunity. I, for one, had just about given
up bothering to read them.

The piece of paper in my hand was some long,
wordy dissertation on the value of police-officer
visibility and volunteerism in the community. The
general gist of the memo was that Seattle Police
Department officers were being asked to use their
off-duty hours—whenever those might be—to take
part in community-service activities and projects.

I suppose the basic philosophy behind all this
is the idea that if a punk and a police officer work

side by side cleaning up garbage out of a park or off a beach one weekend, they're not quite so likely to shoot one another the next time they meet on the street. The concept sounds fine on paper, but it doesn't translate all that well into practice.

For one thing, it wasn't at all popular with the rank and file. Seattle's finest—those public servants sworn to serve and protect—weren't exactly running over each other in their eagerness to give up their off-duty time. Neither were their wives and families. Furthermore, the punks of this world—the real baddies—were far too busy selling drugs or shooting one another to be bothered with cleaning up garbage-strewn parks.

I handed the paper back to Powell. "What about it?"

"The chief's riding the individual squad leaders pretty hard about this. In fact, that was his second-in-command on the phone just now, calling to ask for a progress report. By Monday, each individual squad is supposed to come up with some game plan for that squad's community participation."

"What does all this have to do with me?"

"Watty and I were talking it over a little while ago. He said you might be able to help."

"How?"

"You're involved in things like this, aren't you, Beau? Don't I remember you donating a car or something to one of the charity auctions?"

Not the damned Bentley again, I thought, but Powell continued without detouring off into any specifics. "Watty said he thought you might know some of the people who are involved in this kind of do-gooder crap—someone who could point us in the right direction.''

"What exactly did you have in mind?"

"Well,'' Captain Powell said, "we need to come up with something that will actually do some good, won't take up too much time, and will get the chief off my back. Do you have any ideas?"

It took some time, but I did come up with one. The idea, when it came, was almost blinding in its sheer brilliance.

"Captain Powell,'' I said, barely concealing the smirk that wanted to leak out the corners of my mouth. "This is one time when you've come to the right place at the right time."

"How so?"

"I happen to know just the person you need to talk to—one who can put you in touch with all the movers and shakers around town. She'll hook you up with one of the charity auctions for an item like 'Coffee-with-a-cop' so fast it'll make your head spin."

Captain Powell frowned. "Are you kidding? Coffee with a cop?"

"It would probably sell like hotcakes."

Powell picked up his pen and held it at the ready. "All right," he said. "Who is she? What's her name?"

"Bonnie Elgin,'' I answered triumphantly, dragging my ragged notepad out of my pocket. "I have her number right here. You can tell her I suggested that you call."

It must have sounded do-able, because Captain Powell was looking almost cheerful when I left his office. As for me, I was still grinning when I made it back to my cubicle.

There were two messages on the voice mail—one from Kari Gebhardt and one from Sue Danielson telling me she was on her way down to the crime lab. I returned Kari's call first. Sounding young and uncertain, she was the one who answered the phone.

"This is Detective Beaumont," I told her.

"Oh, right," she said. "My grandmother told me to call you. What do you want?"

"I'm a member of the team investigating this incident with your father. Is there a time when my partner and I could get together with you to talk?"

"I don't know. I'm awfully busy. And I don't know how much help I could be, either," Kari answered evasively. "I wasn't even in town when it happened."

"It's just routine," I assured her. "And it shouldn't take too long. We're gathering background information—that kind of thing."

"I can't do it this morning," Kari said. "Mother and I are leaving in a few minutes to go to the mortuary."

"Early this afternoon is fine, if that would be more convenient."

"Where?" Kari Gebhardt asked.

"Detective Danielson and I could come there to the house, if you'd like," I offered.

"No. Not here," Kari said quickly. "I'd rather meet you somewhere away from the house. And not in Ballard, either. Everyone here knows ..."

"Would you like to come to my office down here at the department?"

"No," Kari said. "Not that. How about Caffè Minnie's at First and Denny up in the Regrade. Michael and I go there sometimes when we're in town. Michael's my boyfriend."

I didn't tell her that I had already heard about Michael from Else. "What time?" I asked. "Say, one-thirty?"

"Yes," she replied. "Mother and I should be done making arrangements by then."

"Good. I'll see you there."

"One more thing, Detective Beaumont. Would it be all right if Michael came along?"

My first choice was naturally to speak to her without the presence of a support system. For a twenty-year-old whose father had been murdered, she was surprisingly under control. Over the phone, there was no hint of the inconsolable grief her mother had worried so about the night before. On the other hand, seeing both Kari and her boyfriend together might give me some insight into what had gone on between Kari and her father.

"That'll be fine," I told her. "Bring him along. Detective Danielson and I will meet you there."

As soon as I got off the phone with Kari Gebhardt, I called down to the crime lab looking for Sue Danielson.

"She's still here," the crime-lab receptionist told me. "Do you want me to put her on the phone?"

"Don't bother," I said. "This is Detective Beaumont. Tell her to wait there. I'll be right down."

I found Sue and Janice Morraine in one of the back labs standing in front of a table examining several unrecognizable pieces of metal, some of which were covered with what looked like charred charcoal.

"What's that?" I asked, looking at Janice. "Have you been trying to cook again?"

Janice Morraine's lack of culinary skill is almost as legendary as my own. My quip provoked a glare from Janice and a quick hoot of laughter from Sue Danielson.

"It's a melted pruning shears," Janice Morraine replied stiffly. "From the basement of the house up on Camano Island. Tim Riddle, the arson investigator, found it."

Camano Island. Melted pruning shears. Putting the two together, I didn't much like the answer those two items combined to make. "And why would a melted pruning shears be so interesting?"

Janice looked at me as though I were hopelessly stupid. "What if I could prove someone used them to whack off a few fingers and toes?" she asked. "Would you be interested in them then?"

"Yes," I said. "I suppose I would." I didn't add that June Miller had just told me that her friend Lorenzo was a part-time gardener. But before I could go into any of that, Sue took off on another tack.

"Tell him about what you found in the truck," she said.

"What truck?"

"Mr. Gebhardt's truck," Janice Morraine answered. "I don't know if you remember, but it was at the scene of the fire, and we impounded it, just in case. What we found turns out to be very interesting."

Janice moved back to the first table and picked up a copy of an evidence inventory-control sheet. "For starters, airplane tickets for two to Rio de Janeiro in the names of Denise Whitney and Hans Gebhardt."

"You mean Gunter."

"I mean Hans." She shrugged. "At least that's what it says here. According to his widow, the dead man's legal name was H. Gunter Gebhardt, so Hans may very well be his real given name. In addition to the tickets, we found fifty thousand dollars' worth of those slick, new two-person, either/or traveler's checks. There were also two fully packed, brand-new suitcases."

"It sounds as though he and the side dish were on their way out of town at the first available opportunity."

"That's the way it looks to me," Janice answered.

"What were the times and dates on the plane tickets?"

"The afternoon of the day he died."

I shook my head. Poor Else, I thought sadly. Poor, poor Else.

A few minutes later, Sue and I were trudging up the stairwell to the fifth floor. On the way, I told her about our afternoon appointment with Kari Gebhardt before going into my meeting with June Miller.

"By the way," I said casually, as we started through the fifth-floor maze of cubicles. "What do you know about salsa dancing?"

Sue stopped dead in her tracks. "Don't tell me

you're into salsa dancing, too. I've never seen you there.''

Hello. Did everyone in the world know about salsa dancing except me?

"You mean this is something you know about?'' I asked in dismay. "You actually go to these places and do it?''

"Sure. I can't go very often because of the boys. But it's great fun. Some of those Latino guys are great dancers.''

"Have you ever seen a tall, willowy blond there?''

"Almost every time I go,'' Sue sighed. "She always makes me feel like a total frump. Do you know her? Is she a friend of yours?''

"Actually, her name is June Miller. I just spent an hour talking with her upstairs. She lives across the street from Else and Gunter Gebhardt, who— incidentally—offered to shoot her dog last summer when Barney—the dog—left a pile of doggy doo in Gunter's front yard. Furthermore, June Miller happens to know our hit-and-run victim, who turns out to be a part-time gardener named Lorenzo.''

Sue is quick. She never missed a trick. "A gardener?'' she repeated. "You mean like someone who might be missing a pruning shears? Where do we find him?''

"That's where the salsa dancing comes in,'' I explained. "June Miller has offered to introduce us tonight at the Ballard Fire House.''

"Of course,'' Sue said. "Today's Friday, isn't it?''

"What does Friday have to do with anything?''

"On Fridays salsa dancing is at the Ballard Fire

House. But why talk to this Lorenzo guy at a dance?''

"June said he's terrified of cops. She claims that's why he ran away from the accident. I told her we'd meet her there around nine-thirty or ten.''

"You think it's on the up-and-up?''

"Enough so that I agreed to go. Not enough for me to do it without a backup handy.''

Sue started into her own cubicle, but she stopped again just inside the doorway. "By the way, Beau, do you know how to dance?''

"Not very well.''

"You'll learn,'' Sue said. "It's easy. You'll pick it up in no time.''

I left her and headed for the relative safety of my own cubicle and desk. I hoped she wouldn't slip and tell her son Jared about where she was going that night and with whom.

If he once heard about us going salsa dancing together, that lippy kid would never again believe that his mother's and my relationship was strictly professional.

17

I told Sue Danielson I was going home for lunch. We're not in the kind of business where it's fashionable to "do" lunch. The implication behind what I said, of course, was that I'd be dining on a homemade sandwich of my own making. The last part was a little white lie. There wasn't a scrap of bread in the house, and nothing to put on it if there had been. I solved the lunch problem by grabbing a sandwich from the downstairs deli, the one on the ground-floor level of Belltown Terrace.

Famished, I inhaled the sandwich, then turned my attention to my real reason—my shameful, nonmacho, secret reason for coming home at lunchtime. To take a nap. Even I could see the folly of getting up at three o'clock in the morning and following that with a late-evening stab at salsa dancing. There was a time when I would have thought nothing of such an arrangement, but age begets wisdom. Now I have better sense.

I set an alarm for one-fifteen and stretched out full-length in the window seat. The fog had burned off early that day. With the sun headed south for the winter, the southwestern exposure of the building as well as my living-room window seat were

220

both drenched in a splash of warm sunlight.
Within moments I fell sound asleep.

Sue had agreed to pick me up in a departmental
car. I hoped it wouldn't be the Mustang again. So
when I woke up at one-fifteen, there was plenty
of time between then and our one-thirty appointment for me to check for messages. The only new
one was from Ralph Ames, my attorney, calling
from Phoenix to say that he would be in town on
Sunday afternoon to work on our quarterly trust
report. Did we want to get together? He'd call
back later to try setting something up.

In addition to the call from Ames, there was
one saved message as well—the call from my
grandmother, Beverly Piedmont. Guilt-ridden
again, I dialed her up right away.

"Sorry. I didn't get your message until late last
night when it was too late to call back."

"Oh, that's all right," she replied. "Don't
worry about it. I was just feeling sorry for myself.
I shouldn't have bothered you."

"It's no bother. What about dinner tonight? I'll
have to go back to work later on in the evening,
sometime after nine. But I could take a break earlier than that—say, around five-thirty or so."

"I don't want to be in the way, Jonas. Are you
sure it isn't too much trouble?"

"I'm sure."

"Where shall we go?" she asked. "The King's
Table? It's a buffet. There's one right down here
on Market."

"No," I said. "It'll be a surprise. And it's also
my treat."

"But . . ."

I stopped her in midobjection. "No buts, now. Just be ready by the time I get there."

I had to break the connection, then, because my call-waiting buzzed. When I switched over to the other line, Sue Danielson was calling to let me know that she and the Mustang were both waiting downstairs.

Caffè Minnie is barely three blocks from Belltown Terrace. It was still crowded with late-lunch customers, so the only available four-top table was located in the triangular, window-lined front dining room—not the best place for conducting any kind of confidential conversation. By one-thirty Sue and I were settled at the table and sipping coffee out of clear glass cups. Kari Gebhardt and her boyfriend arrived ten minutes later.

Even without an introduction, I would have recognized Kari anywhere. Six feet tall, blond, and blue-eyed, she seemed a carbon copy of her mother as I remembered her back when Else Didriksen was a senior at Ballard High School. The only real difference was a ranginess and muscle tone in Kari that pointed more to participating directly in athletics rather than sticking to the sidelines and serving on a cheerleading squad.

The young man she introduced to us as Michael Morris was a good five inches shorter than she was. My initial impression of him was that he was a handsome little shit with light brown, wildly curly hair, chiseled features, and an attitude. Tight-lipped, he sat down, crossed his arms, grunted his order for coffee, and then glowered at me while Kari ordered hers. I wondered what his beef was and was it with me or with Kari?

The uncomfortable tension between the two young people was immediately obvious. Kari seemed near tears, which wasn't all that surprising. Considering what was going on in her life, God knows there was plenty of reason for her to cry. But still, from the way she and Michael sat at the table—not touching; avoiding one another's gaze—I wondered if they hadn't quarreled on their way to the restaurant. If so, I had the distinct impression that the fight was far from over—only postponed for the time being.

"I don't know why she has to come see you like this," Michael said huffily, glancing around the noisy room once our waiter had delivered two more cups of coffee. "What do you want to talk to Kari for? She wasn't even in town when her father died. She was home in Bellingham with me."

"This interview is strictly routine," I explained. "When someone is murdered, the only way homicide detectives can get to know the victim is through talking to people who knew him."

My explanation wasn't enough to mollify Kari Gebhardt's self-appointed defender. "Why now?" Michael demanded. "And why today? Hasn't Kari been through enough? I mean, she and her mother just finished making funeral arrangements."

"I know it's a difficult time for you right now. For *all* of you," I added, letting my gaze linger on Michael's defiant face. "And I realize how painful it must be to have to endure this kind of interview along with everything else, but you must understand we can't afford to wait until later. With every hour of delay, the killer's trail grows that much colder, and we're that much less likely to catch him.''

"Please, Michael," Kari said. "You know we have to help. For Mother's sake if nothing else.''

Kari's appeal caused Michael's expression to soften a little, but his arms remained folded across his chest. "Go ahead and ask your damn questions then," he said. "Let's get this over with.''

Sue started off with the basics—names, telephone numbers, addresses, that kind of thing. When she asked for their addresses and phone numbers in Bellingham, Kari flushed before she answered. "You won't give that information to our families, will you? About where we're living, I mean.''

Neither Sue nor I made a comment, and Kari rushed on. "Michael and I share an apartment up at school. I had a female roommate to begin with, but she moved out at the end of last semester. I never quite got around to telling my grandmother that Michael and I were living together. Sharing expenses cuts down on costs for both of us, but I don't think Granny would approve. And I *know* Mother wouldn't.

"When we've been here in Seattle, Michael stays on Mercer Island with his folks, and I've stayed with a girlfriend. This time . . .'' She broke off.

"I can see how this time things are different," Sue finished, and Kari nodded gratefully, relieved that she didn't have to continue. She seemed to be having difficulty making her voice work without dissolving into tears.

From the looks of them, I guessed that expenses

weren't all Kari Gebhardt and Michael Morris were sharing. I remembered what it was like back when I was a horny young man. And it isn't so long ago that I've forgotten how such men think. For a sexually active young adult, it's a real come-down to go from living together to being split up into separate celibate sleeping arrangements in dis-approving parental households. It's like a hotshot shift boss being booted back to the gang.

I wondered if Michael's role as Kari's surly de-fender wasn't a guise used to cover a more general distress that stemmed from the fact that Michael Morris currently wasn't getting any. He probably expected to die soon of pure sexual deprivation. I felt like telling him that doing without isn't fatal. In the long run, it's all part of the educational process.

"What are you two studying up in Belling-ham?" I asked. I thought but didn't add, "besides the obvious."

It was an icebreaker-type inquiry, designed to bridge the necessary gap between presumably easy questions and tough ones. To my surprise, my sup-posedly innocuous question wasn't innocuous at all. The quick warning glance that passed from Michael to Kari put me on instant alert.

Kari was the one who answered. "We're history majors," she said. "When we graduate, we both plan to go for advanced degrees."

"What kind of history?" I asked.

"Twentieth-century," Michael Morris replied.

Kari looked at him, one eyebrow raised and questioning. "I told you on the way here, Mi-chael," she said. "I'm going to tell them everything." She ignored the almost imperceptible shake of his head and forged on.

"We're both interested in World War Two, Detective Beaumont. Particularly the European front. We're doing a joint independent study project on the Holocaust that may eventually evolve into a joint Master's project as well."

I'm not a golfer, so I've never hit a hole in one. The feeling, however, has to be similar. With that one effortless question and without even having to dig for it, we suddenly had a pretty good idea of what it was that had gone wrong between Kari Gebhardt and her father.

Closing my eyes, I could visualize the rank upon rank of Nazi toy soldiers standing on the shelves in Gunter Gebhardt's locked basement. A lover of Nazis would be prone to think of what had happened to Jews in Hitler's Europe more in terms of "Final Solution" than as "Holocaust." Justification rather than horror. Rationalization rather than responsibility.

For some inexplicable reason, Kari, the Nazi-lover's very own daughter, had opted to identify with the slaughtered victims rather than with the perpetrators who were her father's heroes.

This was nothing short of a fundamental disagreement, but then that's how generation gaps usually work. Often, American children in particular seem to be programmed to oppose their parents' most cherished beliefs. I figured Kari was just keeping up her end of the bargain.

"Did your father know anything about this study project of yours?" I asked.

Kari shook her head. "Since he wasn't paying

a dime for my schooling, I didn't think it was any of his business. I'm not a dependent, you know. I'm on a scholarship, although when I need help, Granny usually slips me a little something."

That figured. Inge Didriksen strikes again. Everyone should have such a noninterfering mother-in-law.

"Tell us," Sue Danielson said, "what was your father like?"

For the first time, tears sprang to Kari Gebhardt's eyes. "He was a liar and a cheat," she answered.

Kari's tears proved to be too much for Michael. Frowning, he uncrossed his arms, leaned forward, and took her hand. "You don't have to do this, Kari," he whispered urgently. "You don't have to put yourself through this. Let's just go." He stood up.

I sensed that Kari was about to tell us something important, while Michael was ready to cut and run. "She does have to, Michael," I said. "Willingly withholding information in a homicide investigation is a felony. Now sit back down."

He sat, and I turned my attention back to Kari.

When detectives ask questions, they usually have some notion of what the answers will be. We had spent two days nosing around in what had turned out to be Gunter Gebhardt's very unsavory recent past. What we had learned pretty much agreed with Kari's simple assessment. Her father had indeed been a liar and cheat. I half expected her to tell us that years earlier she had somehow stumbled across irrefutable evidence of her father's womanizing—with some distant predecessor of

Denise Whitney. I thought that would be the real basis of her feud with her father. I would have missed the mark by a country mile.

"He lied to us," Kari Gebhardt murmured. "He lied to Mother and me about everything."

"Everything?" Sue asked. "What do you mean?"

Kari paused, as if uncertain whether or not to continue. The noisy clatter of a nearby table being cleared of dishes by a green-haired busboy filled Kari's sudden silence. I was afraid she'd quit on us altogether, but she didn't.

"My father was born in a town in Bavaria, a place called Kempten. He always told us that his father was a pilot in the Luftwaffe, and that he was killed during World War Two."

"We already heard about the pilot part from someone else—your mother, I believe," I said. "Wasn't he shot down over France?"

"That's just it," Kari said, her voice breaking as she spoke. "He wasn't. That's all part of the lie along with everything else. When I was little, I used to be fascinated by all those soldiers. I'd go down in the basement and watch for hours while Dad worked on his collection. He always told me the soldiers were from his father's army, and that's why he made them—out of respect for his father. I didn't have any idea what the German Army stood for, and I didn't really come to grips with the awful reality of what went on during World War Two until I was in high school.

"I spent part of my senior year as an exchange student in Frankfurt, Germany. When we had a break from school, I hitchhiked down to Kempten and looked up the records myself. My grandfather, Hans Gebhardt, wasn't in the Luftwaffe at all. Ever. He was S.S. A Nazi guard at Sobibor.''

She whispered the last word with what sounded like wrenching revulsion, as though she could barely stand to say it aloud. Her eyes met mine. They seemed to be pleading for understanding. It was as if she expected me to recognize the full implication of what those strange sounds meant.

Certainly when the words ''Nazi,'' ''the S.S,'' and ''guards'' are all used in the same breath, several awful images come inevitably to mind— Auschwitz; Dachau. Photographic images of skeletal, emaciated people with shaved heads staring hopelessly out through barbed-wire fences. But the word ''Sobibor'' meant nothing to me.

''What's that?'' I asked. ''A concentration camp?''

Kari looked at me through tear-filled eyes. She shook her head, bit her lip, and didn't answer. Couldn't. Finally overcoming his own reluctance, Michael Morris spoke up in her place.

''Not a concentration camp,'' he answered. ''Not a work camp. Sobibor was an extermination camp. A death camp in Poland. The official record says the Germans killed two hundred fifty thousand people there in a little over a year. But that total only counts the ones who were transported there by train. Lots more came by truck or bus or on foot. Those weren't counted in the official total.''

Michael spoke softly but determinedly, each word enunciated with horrifying clarity. ''However they arrived, once they were inside the gate, guards gave a speech welcoming them to a work camp. Dirty and exhausted from the trip, their hair was cut off, and they were ordered to strip for cleansing showers. But gas came out of the shower heads, not water. They died like dogs being slaughtered in a pound.

"Afterward, the corpses were burned, the ashes used for fertilizer. The countryside for miles around that place is still littered with human bones."

I glanced at Kari. Her face was pale, but she appeared to be under control.

"Maybe your father was ashamed of what his father did," I suggested. "With your grandfather gone, maybe it was easier for Gunter to rewrite his father's death as a pilot than to. . . ."

"Kari's grandfather isn't dead," Michael interrupted. "We believe he's alive and in hiding someplace. He was an S.S. guard and a deserter besides, and people are looking for him. I hope to God they find him, too," he added bitterly.

"But, Michael," Kari blurted, "what if they killed my father while they were trying to find my grandfather? I was mad at Dad. I hadn't spoken to him in years because of the way he *acted* about what his father did; because he lied about it and covered it up. But that doesn't give these men the right to kill him. That makes them just as bad as my grandfather was."

Voices were rising. Other people in the restaurant were beginning to stare. "Wait a minute," I said. "You're telling us that someone came looking for your Nazi war-criminal grandfather, and you think they're the ones who killed your father?''

Kari nodded. ''I'm sure of it,'' she said.

I looked around the room. There weren't that many people around, but some of the customers seated at other nearby tables seemed entirely too interested in what was going on at ours.

''I'm sorry,'' I said. ''This isn't something we should be discussing in such a public place. I'm afraid we're going to have to ask you to come down to the department after all. At least there we'll have some privacy.''

This time there was no objection from either Michael Morris or Kari Gebhardt.

■18■

Breaking up an interview at a crucial juncture like
that is always a tough call, but Seattle's still a
small enough town when it comes to discussing
something that volatile. I opted for privacy over
continuity.

I considered the privacy issue so important, in
fact, that I was even willing to risk moving the
interview to one of the interrogation rooms at the
Public Safety Building, if need be. Interrogation
rooms can be pretty scary places for someone
who's never seen one before. Out of deference to
Kari and Michael, Sue Danielson radioed ahead in
search of a more suitable alternative.

We lucked out. The conference room next to
the chief's office—the same one in which I'd spoken to June Miller hours earlier—was free for the
remainder of the afternoon. We went there, but
even in reasonably comfortable surroundings, it
wasn't easy to restart the interview.

"Maybe we'd better go all the way back to the
beginning," I suggested.

"Back to Sobibor?" Kari Gebhardt asked,
blinking uncertainly.

"That would probably be best," I answered.

Kari took a deep, steadying breath. "There was an uprising at Sobibor in October of 1943. According to the records, my grandfather was still a guard there at the time. The mass escape from Sobibor was the only successful one out of all the Nazi camps. That day five hundred fifty prisoners scrambled through and over the barbed-wire fences and ran from the compound. Of the three hundred who actually made it to the woods outside the prison, only forty-seven were still alive by the end of the war. In the course of the uprising, approximately twenty-seven Ukrainian guards disappeared. Eight German guards also disappeared and were presumed dead."

"Hans Gebhardt was one of those?"

Kari nodded. "After I came back from Germany, I confronted my father about Sobibor, about my grandfather's role there, and about Hans Gebhardt's status as a deserter. Father denied every bit of it. Said it never happened. He claimed I was making the whole thing up. After that, I never had anything more to do with him." Her voice diminished to the merest of whispers. "Until three days ago, that is," she added.

"What happened three days ago?"

"That's when the people Michael told you about came to our apartment in Bellingham. They asked all kinds of questions about my father—where he worked, what he did. I felt like I had to warn him, and I did—even though Michael begged me not to."

I turned my attention full on Michael Morris. "Why?" I demanded.

"Because I didn't want that slime to get away."

"Kari's father?"

"No, her grandfather. I never thought Gunter would be in danger as well. That didn't occur to me. But I wanted them to catch the old man."

"They who?"

"Simon Wiesenthal's people. They were sure they were on the right track, and I didn't want them to lose him."

Michael's knowledge about the noted Wiesenthal Nazi hunters, his single-minded determination that Hans Gebhardt not escape capture, and the defiant way in which his eyes met mine suddenly switched on a lightbulb in my head.

"Michael," I asked, "are you Jewish?"

He nodded. "Half. My dad's Irish." His answer went a long way toward explaining his attitude.

"And you, Kari?"

"Lutheran," she answered, "so far."

"And how, exactly, did you two meet?"

"At school," Kari replied. "Toward the end of our freshman year, a Holocaust survivor came to the university to speak as a guest lecturer. Michael and I didn't know each other then, but we both went to hear the talk."

Michael nodded and took up the story. "I saw her at the lecture, and I knew what was said affected her. It affected all of us. After the lecture was over, a group of us went out for coffee. Somehow, Kari and I started talking. Long after everybody else had gone home, we were still there and still talking."

"What about?" Sue asked.

This time it was Michael's turn to draw a deep breath. "About the Holocaust. We talked all night.

I told her about my family, and she told me about hers. My mother lost most of her aunts and uncles in concentration camps. She's still bitter about it, even now. And yet, here was Kari—the grand-daughter of one of the very monsters my mother had warned me about—and she didn't seem like a monster at all. She was my age. Just listening to her talk, I knew she was every bit as horrified about what the Nazis had done as I was.''

Once the dam was breached, Michael Morris couldn't seem to stop talking. ''That's almost two going on three years ago now,'' he hurried on. ''We've been together ever since. We've talked about getting married, but my mother's dead set against it. Like it was okay for her to marry my father, but it's not okay for me to do the same thing. Mother doesn't say so straight out, but she'd really like Kari and me to break up so I can marry some nice Jewish girl.

''And even though her family died in the Holo-caust, she doesn't approve of what we're doing—tracking down the various escaped survivors, writ-ing to them or to their descendants or relatives, trying to learn exactly what happened to them dur-ing and after the war. Mother says Sobibor has become an obsession for both Kari and me. She says it's not a healthy foundation for a relationship.''

It crossed my mind that Michael's mother might be right about that, but I didn't mention it to either Kari or Michael. In the meantime, Sue went back to the death-camp story. ''What did happen to those death-camp escapees?'' she asked.

Sue Danielson had been sucked into wondering

about the desperate and virtually hopeless fates of those survivors in exactly the same way Michael and Kari had become caught up in their compelling stories. Part of it is the hope that a sliver of good could somehow emerge from such appalling evil. And once you heard about such terrible, inhuman suffering, it seemed unthinkable and disrespectful to turn away.

Michael shrugged. "Fewer than twenty of the escapees are still alive. A few of the German officers were tracked down and tried at Nuremberg. Some of them got as little as three years for their part in killing all those people. One of them, the commander at the time of the uprising, was sentenced to sixteen years. We read an interview with him after he was released from prison. His comment about the war was that '. . . it was a very bad time for the Germans.' "

Shaking his head in apparent disbelief, Michael repeated the phrase. " 'For the Germans'! I can't believe the man's hypocrisy! How could he even think such a thing, much less say it?"

With that, Michael lapsed into a brooding silence. I waited a moment before I pressed on. "Tell us what happened to the guards."

"We haven't had much luck tracking them. The Ukrainians pretty well disappeared into post–World War Two Soviet territory and never resurfaced. The same goes for the Germans."

"Including Hans Gebhardt?"

"That's right," Kari answered. "Until those two men showed up at the apartment."

"Did they carry I.D.?"

"Yes."

"And did their papers identify the organization by name?"

"Oh, yes," Michael said. "One side of the I.D. card was in English; the other was printed in Hebrew."

"I never heard of the Wiesenthal people killing anyone," Sue objected pensively. "I thought they always worked inside the law and turned the people they captured over to the local court system."

"These people may or may not be who they say they are. It's always possible the I.D. they showed you was fake. If they're involved in all this, it certainly doesn't sound like they're operating inside the law this time," I said. "Regardless of justification, these people don't get to be judge and jury. If they killed Denise Whitney and Gunter Gebhardt, they'll have to answer for it in our courts. That's the law."

"The law!" Michael repeated, snorting in disgust. "What good does that do? Look at Nuremberg. All those guys got was a slap on the hand— like the guy who was sentenced to three whole years in prison. What kind of deal is that? After murdering that many people, here he is, walking around at seventy-five, as free as a bird. My mother's family is gone, and his isn't. Not only that, we're all supposed to buy into the idea that he's paid his debt to society. In full. What a load of crap!"

Michael Morris was absolutely right on that score—serving a total of three years for killing 250,000 people didn't seem to balance the scale.

Not even close. Still, the alternative to courts of law is anarchy.

"Let me remind you one more time, Michael," I said. "That guard was actually at Sobibor. Denise Whitney and Gunter Gebhardt were not. Even if they've helped Hans Gebhardt avoid apprehension—even if they've shielded him for years—they may be guilty of harboring a criminal, but that's not a capital crime. They didn't deserve to die for doing it."

Michael made a face and nodded. "I know," he allowed grudgingly. "That's why we're here."

"Tell us what you can about the men who came to visit you last week," Sue said. "Didn't you say there were two of them?"

"Yes."

"Did they give you their names?"

Kari looked at Michael, and he answered. "Yes. One was Moise something. Rosenthal, maybe. The other one, the older one, was Avram Steinman. That struck my funny bone. Moses and Abraham working together."

"Can you give us a description of the two men?"

"They were both white. Medium build. Steinman was quite a bit older than we are, like about Kari's father's age. Your age. The other one was closer to us or maybe a little older. Thirty or so. The older one had a pronounced accent. The younger one spoke American English. He had brown hair, almost the color of mine."

"Were they in a car? On foot?"

"I don't know. I suppose they had a car, but I didn't see it."

"How did they find you?"

"Maybe they talked to some of the people we wrote to—one of the escapees."

"And why did they come to you?"

"They wanted us to help them," Michael answered. "After the letters we'd exchanged with some of the survivors, I'm sure they thought we would."

"What exactly did Hans Gebhardt do at Sobibor?" Sue Danielson asked.

This time it was Kari who answered. "They told us he was in charge of extraction. After the bodies came out of the gas chambers and before they were thrown into the fire, some of the prisoners—ones who were kept alive for a time solely to serve as part of the work crews—had to go through all the bodies and remove the gold teeth. That gold, along with gold from confiscated jewelry, was melted down into bars and shipped back to Germany. At the time of the Sobibor prison uprising, an entire truckload shipment of gold disappeared."

"The Wiesenthal people think your grandfather stole it?"

Kari nodded. "That's what they told us. They think he did it with help from one or more of the missing Ukrainian guards. They told us that over the years, and one by one, the guards have turned up dead, but no one had ever found any trace of my grandfather until just recently."

"Did they say what that trace was?"

"No."

"Where do they think the gold is now?" I asked, thinking at once of the solid-gold box wrench Bonnie Elgin had found lying in the street.

"They think it may have ended up in the Eastern bloc right after the war, but they believe most of it has been smuggled out in the course of the last few years," Kari answered. "On fishing boats."

"To your father?"

She shook her head. "By my father," she answered. "Through his joint-venture connections in and out of the former Soviet Union. They seemed to think my father knew where his father was all along. I think they were hoping Dad would tell them what he knew."

In view of the two unused airplane tickets to Rio, I thought I had a pretty good idea of where Kari's grandfather might be holed up. By now, the Wiesenthal operatives knew that, too.

"Michael and I were just doing research," Kari continued. "I think that's what called the investigators' attention to us. I think someone—maybe one of the survivors we interviewed—noticed my name and made the connection to my grandfather. And that's why those men came here, looking around and asking questions."

Kari's eyes once more filled with tears. "After they left, I called Granny to ask what she thought I should do. She told me just to stay out of it, to let well enough alone. I asked her advice, and then I ignored it. I guess I thought that if he helped them, it would make things better. And that's why this whole mess is my fault. I brought him to their attention.

"You see," she added, "I hated my father, but I never meant for him to die. And it's hurt my mother real bad. I can't stand what it's doing to her. It breaks my heart."

At that juncture, Kari Gebhardt finally fell apart completely. She put her arms on the table, rested her head on her arms, and sobbed brokenly for several minutes. I sat there and listened to her and waited for her to stop, but the whole time I was listening, I was thinking about Sobibor. I think Sue was, too.

It was late when we finally finished up with the interview. We had spent another full hour and a half going over and over everything they could remember about their Nazi-hunting visitors. It wasn't very illuminating. The first available appointment we could make for them to visit with the Identi-Kit artist was for the following Tuesday. The artist doesn't work weekends, and Monday would be entirely taken up by the funeral.

Kari and Michael left. Sue and I returned to the fifth floor, where she had some phone calls to make. I could have waited for her and hitched a ride home, but I wanted to walk. I thought the exercise might help clear my head and shake off some of the horror of what we had learned.

I thought about the men claiming to be Wiesenthal Nazi hunters as I made my way down a pedestrian-crowded Third Avenue. My natural inclination would have been to root for Nazi hunters—to cheer them on. But not if they had invaded my home territory and murdered people on my watch.

Back at Belltown Terrace, I grabbed a quick

shower and changed into one of the two Brooks
Brothers suits Ralph Ames had forced me to buy.
Without my lawyer/fashion adviser's counsel, I'd
look a whole lot more like Eddie Bauer than I
would anything else. Once I was dressed, I placed
a call to the Four Seasons Olympic. I wanted to
be sure they'd have plenty of room to squeeze
my grandmother and me into the Georgian Room
for dinner.

Why did I want to take Beverly Piedmont to
the Four Seasons? Maybe it was a way to distance
myself from the horrors I'd been hearing about all
afternoon. But also, I think, it had something to
do with pride.

I had been to the Georgian Room on several
occasions with Ralph Ames, and I wanted to take
Beverly Piedmont someplace nice. Maybe it was
showing off, and maybe it was nothing more than
a misguided desire on my part to pamper her, to
make my grandmother feel as though there was
still someone in her life who cared about her,
someone she could lean on if she ever needed to
do some leaning.

Once I had her in the car headed back downtown, I began to have misgivings. Since I didn't
have any viable alternatives in mind, I stuck to
the original plan with the exception of parking in
the garage off Fifth and Seneca instead of driving
up to the posh front entrance and using the valet
parking.

The trouble started as soon as we walked up the
stairs from the lobby to the entrance of the Georgian Room. We stopped beside the maître d's station behind a laughing, somewhat noisy group of

well-oiled diners. There were several men in tuxes and women in long, sequined gowns, and from what conversation we overheard, they were evidently on their way to the opera.

Beverly Piedmont looked down at her plain but neat coat and dress. "I shouldn't be here," she whispered self-consciously. "I'm not dressed well enough."

"You're fine," I said reassuringly, urging her forward.

The unfailingly polite maître d' took her modest wool coat and showed us to a linen-covered table, where he graciously helped my grandmother into her chair. While she examined the elegant room, I stole a glance at the menu. These were definitely not King's Table prices. If she caught a glimpse of the toll, she'd balk, and we'd be out of there in a flash.

Before she even had a chance to look at the menu, I shifted hers out of reach, closed mine, and waved away the sommelier.

I knew from being there with Ralph that the Georgian Room always has available an elegant fixed-price dinner, from soup to nuts, literally. The set five-course dinner offered the advantage of taking all the options out of ordering. The food was bound to be good, and it would keep my grandmother from reading the menu too closely. It would also keep me from trying to explain what any of the listed food actually was. Despite the name Beaumont, French and I are not exactly on speaking terms.

My menu sleight-of-hand may have been a slick maneuver, but Beverly Piedmont has a few jumps

on me in terms of years and experience. She didn't
fall for any of it.

"This place is very expensive, isn't it?" she
observed, watchfully examining the room while
she picked at her squash-soup appetizer.

"It's all relative," I said.

"I'm not a blind date, Jonas," she chided gently. "You don't have to impress me."

Touché. She had me dead to rights. Neither of
us said a word while the busboy whisked the appetizer dishes out of the way of a waiter poised to
deposit our entrées.

"Your grandfather was not a mean man; he just
had no idea how to bend," Beverly Piedmont said.
"In retrospect, I can see that what he did to your
mother was heartless. It was only days after your
father died in that motorcycle accident that Jonas
and I found out our daughter was pregnant. He
wanted her to give you up, and she refused. They
had a terrible fight. I have to say your mother gave
as good as she got. After that, there was no turning
back for either one of them. And not for me,
either.

"Through the years, it broke my heart to know
that my only grandson was growing up right here
in Seattle, almost under my nose, and yet I
couldn't have anything to do with him. With you.
I suppose I could have ignored your grandfather's
wishes—done something underhanded and gone
behind his back—but that's not the kind of person
I am.

"I'm an old woman now, Jonas," she continued. "I never got to hold you when you were a
baby or to save your first tooth in my jewelry box

or to watch you unwrap your very first Christmas presents. Or any Christmas presents at all, for that matter. Now that I'm alone, I want to make up for lost time. I promise not to be a pest, but I do want to spend time with you, to get to know about who you are and how you think.

"And there are things I want to tell you, about what your mother was like when she was a little girl. About the places we lived when she was growing up and the things we did. Does that make any sense?"

I nodded. That's all I could manage.

"The food is very nice here," she went on, "but you don't have to take me to fancy restaurants. We could go someplace like Zesto's or Dick's Drive-In, or we could just sit at the house and talk. Mandy would like that. I swear that dog is lonely, too."

Beverly Piedmont put down her fork and then fumbled in her purse until she located a white lace-edged handkerchief, which she used to dab at her eyes.

It's a funny thing about Adam's apples. On special occasions, mine swells until it is approximately the size of a basketball. When that happens, I find it very difficult to talk. Impossible even. Rather than embarrass us both, I reached into my pocket and dragged out my notebook.

On the first blank page, one just beyond my hastily scribbled notes about Hans Gebhardt and Sobibor, I wrote myself a note. I put it in a spot where I was sure to stumble across it first thing the following morning.

"CALL KELLY," I wrote, printing my daugh-

ter's name in large capital letters. ''INVITE TO
T-DAY DINNER.''

Who says you can't learn from someone else's
mistakes?

19

Sue Danielson and I had agreed to drive to the
Ballard Fire House in separate vehicles. It was
later than it should have been when I dropped my
grandmother off at her house and headed that way.

Back when I was a kid, the Ballard Fire House
was still just exactly that—a firehouse. That was
its *raison d'être* from the old horse-drawn fire-
engine days back in the early 1900s. Sometime in
the early seventies, the firemen moved into more
modern quarters, and the old firehouse was transformed into a trendy sort of night-club/restaurant.
It has operated in that guise ever since.

The Fire House was evidently a popular place.
I had to park two blocks away. When I reached
the entryway alcove, I found both Sue Danielson
and June Miller waiting for me. Former congressman Miller was nowhere in evidence, and I had
to look twice before I recognized Sue.

I'm used to seeing Detective Danielson in her
work mode down at the department, dressed in
what passes, I guess, for women's business attire—skirts, blazers, sensible heels—if heels can
ever be said to be sensible, that is—and in blouses
so prim, they leave absolutely everything to the

imagination. The outfit she wore salsa dancing had barely any blouse and even less skirt. As soon as I saw her legs, I realized with a shock that I'd never noticed them before. It made me wonder if I'm getting old.

Dressed as she was, Sue was no slouch, but next to June Miller, I could see why Sue might have felt a bit drab in comparison. The wife of the former congressman was pencil-slender, but still curved in all the right places. She wore a sophisticated long black dress with an attention-capturing, knee-high slit up one side. Inch-wide straps ran across otherwise bare shoulders. She didn't walk. When she moved, she glided.

While I stopped at a table and forked over the cover charge, June and Sue went on inside and staked a claim to a spot three tables from the dance floor and right on top of the bank of electronics handled by the band's chief soundman.

I caught up with the women just as the band began revving up. "Your husband won't be joining us?" I shouted to June over the cacophony.

She shook her head. "Not tonight," she yelled back, followed by something totally incomprehensible.

"What?"

"Brett's having some friends for overnight."

More's the pity, I thought.

A cocktail waitress came by, and we ordered drinks—tall 7-Ups with lime all around. No wonder there was a cover charge. The Ballard Fire House wasn't making any money on drinks at our table, and it turned out that most of the others were pretty much the same way. Whether the drinks had booze in them or not, people tended to nurse them rather than swill them down. As far as I could see, most of the people came there to dance, not to drink.

And I do mean dance with a capital *D*.

People hit the dance floor the moment the band—a twelve-member, all-male outfit named Latin Expression—finished tuning up and struck the first note of the first number. Thanks to Ralph Ames, I've been in enough Mexican restaurants to have a nodding acquaintance with mariachi music, which generally sounds to me like Polish polka with a south-of-the-border twist. And the words "salsa dancing" had made me think that what I was in for was a group of round, sausage-shaped guys wearing sombreros and glitzy Cisco Kid costumes. Wrong.

These were good-looking young men in white shirts, splashy up-to-the-moment ties, and double-breasted suits. The two backup singers were as energetic and as well orchestrated as the Supremes. The three singers belted their hearts out in what sounded to me like Latino-beat rock, and I never understood a single word—for two reasons:

Number one: Everything except the between-song patter was in Spanish. Listening to it reminded me of a disastrous recent date with Alexis Downey where I had been force-fed a Chinese-made art flick. Alexis had assured me in advance that we were attending a must-see film with some of her friends and that she knew I was going to love it. I didn't come close to loving it—I didn't even like it, and I don't think English subtitles would have helped.

Number two: The music Latin Expression
played at the Ballard Fire House was far louder
than the small space could accommodate, which
made it much too loud for me. I remember telling
my mother once long ago that you can't have too
much bass. Latin Expression proved me wrong.
The deafening roar of the bass guitar thrummed in
the tabletop and shivered the back of my chair.
The decibel level may have turned my ears to
mush, but it didn't seem to faze the dancers.

They were there to dance, and dance they did.
To every single song. There was none of this
phony hanging back and waiting to see who would
go first, or if the band would play fast tunes or
slow ones or something in-between. People
grabbed partners and headed for the dance floor
as soon as the first note blasted through a pair of
two-story-high collections of speakers stacked in
the front corners of the room.

Sue and June were old hands at this. Within
minutes they both saw people they knew and recognized from other salsa-dancing venues. Guys
stopped by the table long enough to shout dancing
invitations to the two women. Soon both my ta-
blemates were led onto the crowded floor, where
they danced their hearts out to numbers that could
have been rumbas or sambas or tangos or some
variation on all of the above. Fortunately, no one
asked me to dance.

Everyone seemed to be having a good time. Everyone but me. Somewhere in the middle of the
third number, someone turned on a red-and-yellow
rotating spotlight that flashed across the gyrating
figures on the dance floor and then splashed di-

rectly into my eyes. I was already tired, and blinking to dodge the flashes of light almost put me to sleep—in spite of the ear-shattering volume.

In other words, salsa dancing wasn't my favorite. And it was odd to realize that a culture so alien to me was thriving right there in the middle of Ballard—what was once strictly white-toast Ballard—only blocks from the apartment where I had lived as a boy growing up. Times do change.

I was truly lost in a crowd, a fifth wheel. While musical numbers followed one after another, I sat there all by myself with no one to talk to and nothing to do but watch. To keep myself occupied and awake, I tried putting all the little pieces together: salsa dancing and Sobibor. Two murders and a hit-and-run. Thousands of gold teeth and a gold wrench. And Nazi toy soldiers standing in rows.

The sudden thought hit me with the force of a lightning bolt and left me feeling sick and shaken. What about those damn soldiers? I wondered. What if they weren't made of lead at all? What if they, like Bonnie Elgin's wrench, were made of solid gold?

As soon as the thought crossed my mind, I was torn. On the one hand, I didn't want to miss the meeting with Lorenzo. On the other, I couldn't wait to get my hands on one of those soldiers in the basement of the Gebhardt house on Culpeper Court. Even considering it was almost eleven, I was sure Else would let me examine the soldiers for myself. Checking the metal content wouldn't require the professional services of someone like the crime lab's Janice Morraine. Just hefting them would be enough to tell me what I wanted to know. Or else I could scrape off some of the paint and see whether or not there was gold concealed beneath the enamel.

My distress must have showed. June Miller came back to the table for a sip of 7-Up. She offered reassurance and counseled patience. "They'll be here pretty soon," she said. "Maria gets off work around eleven."

There was no point fighting the music and trying to yell out an explanation. That was hopeless. Against my better judgment, I slouched deeper into my chair and listened to the boom of a complicated conga-drum solo. From then on, though, with my mind still working overtime, I kept one eye on the door. My vigilance was rewarded when, through the haze of cigarette smoke, I spotted a man and a woman who paused just inside the doorway.

The two of them, a man in his thirties and a somewhat younger woman, entered the room cautiously, as though they expected the Ballard Fire House to be furnished with armed land mines rather than tables and chairs. The man looked like a young Cesar Romero. He wore gray slacks, an open-necked white shirt rolled up at the sleeves, and no tie. Walking with a noticeable limp, he went to the nearest corner and sank into a seat directly in front of the stacked speakers.

Great, I thought. We'll never be able to talk there.

The woman, presumably his sister Maria, appeared to be several years younger. Her dark hair, crinkled as if newly loosened from tight braids, fell almost to her waist. She stood near the door, surveying the room with quick, nervous glances that betrayed her anxiety. Eventually, she must have spotted June Miller. That wasn't difficult, since June's blond hair glowed like a pillar of yellow flame among the other, mostly dark-haired dancers. As soon as June smiled and waved, the young woman turned to the man and nodded.

June had given me strict orders not to approach either one of the newcomers until she personally cleared it with them. What I did do, however, was make my way, between songs, onto the dance floor, where I reclaimed Sue Danielson from the apparently pleasant clutches of a young Latino man with whom she had danced several dances.

The man spoke little or no English, but he danced with the verve and flair of a professional. Invariably, he had returned Sue to our table with a courtly bow to her, and with a politely deferential nod to me as well. I did my best to return the favor when he relinquished Sue to me on the dance floor, but he seemed genuinely mystified when, instead of dancing away with her, I dragged her back to our table.

"They're here?" she asked.

"Just came," I answered. "Maria's the young woman standing just to the left of the door. Her brother's seated at the table right in front of the speakers."

"Should I go get June?"

"She said for us to stay put, remember?"

June had spent much of the evening dancing with a balding gentleman who must have been close to sixty and who seemed to be the most

capable dancer in the room. While I squirmed with
impatience, a laughing and unconcerned June
Miller danced two more interminable numbers
with her smooth-move partner. Just when I was
about to go cut in on him as well, the band finally
took what I considered a well-deserved break.

Instead of returning to our table, however, June
hurried over to the new arrivals. After a moment's
conference with Maria, June turned and beckoned
to Sue and me.

Carrying what little remained in our three
drinks, we threaded our way across the room. As
we neared the table, I was surprised, as I often
am, by how closely the Identi-Kit artist had managed to capture Lorenzo's likeness.

He wasn't a large man; but he was sleek, like
a racehorse, and compactly built. Almost hidden
behind the cloth of his unbuttoned shirt was a gold
crucifix that glowed in the dim, overhead lights.

Gold again, I thought. That particular commod-
ity seemed to be everywhere at the moment.

"Detective Sue Danielson and Detective J. P.
Beaumont, this is Maria Hurtado and her brother,
Lorenzo," June was saying.

Maria, seated beside her brother, rose to her feet
and then tentatively shook hands, first with Sue
and then with me. Lorenzo didn't move, and he
didn't offer his hand, either. His eyes stayed full
on my face.

"How do you do," he said formally.

There were only four chairs at the table. I rus-
tled up a fifth and then sat in that one with Sue
and June on either side of me and with both the
Hurtados facing us. From the way he watched me,

I knew it was no accident that Lorenzo had chosen the chair he was seated on. From that vantage point, he could observe the entire room. Whatever the real story behind his brother's death back home in Guatemala, it had left Lorenzo Hurtado a cautious survivor.

Still holding my gaze with his, Lorenzo used casual and unhurried movements to extract a package of cigarettes from his pocket. He offered the cigarettes around the table. When no one took one, he did so himself, shaking a cigarette loose from the pack, which he then returned to his pocket. He lit the cigarette with a steady, tremble-free match. June had told me Lorenzo was frightened of cops. If that was the case, he was doing a hell of a good job of covering it up.

Once the cigarette was lit, Lorenzo was the first to speak. He did so slowly and deliberately, as if taking scrupulous pains so as not to be misunderstood.

"I didn't do it," he said.

"Didn't do what?" I asked, playing dumb.

"I did not kill Señor Gebhardt, and I didn't see who did it, either."

"But you were there when he was killed?"

"Yes," Lorenzo said. And then, "No." And then, "Maybe."

"Look, you can't have it both ways," I insisted. "Were you there or weren't you?"

The lights around us reflected on the smooth, closely shaved skin of Lorenzo Hurtado's narrow face, capturing a slight involuntary tic. "I don't know for sure if I was there or not when Señor Gebhardt died," Lorenzo answered. "But he was still alive when I stepped onto the boat. I know that because I heard him.''

"What exactly did you hear?" I asked.

Lorenzo closed his eyes and shuddered. He swallowed hard, then opened his eyes again and stared at me while a stream of ashes spilled unnoticed from the smoldering and forgotten cigarette clutched between his fingers.

"You are a policeman, Detective Beaumont." It was a statement, not a question.

The music wasn't playing, but even so, Lorenzo Hurtado spoke so softly that I had to strain to hear him. I nodded.

"Señora Miller says things are different here; that it isn't the same as it was back home in Guatemala when my brother died. So maybe you don't know what it's like. Have you ever heard the sound of someone being tortured?"

Suddenly, Lorenzo Hurtado was the interrogator and I the mere questionee. "No," I answered truthfully. "I have not."

His eyes narrowed. Although they appeared to be staring directly at me, I don't think he was seeing me so much as he was seeing something else, recalling a witnessed event from long ago— a terrible, intimate ghost from his own past.

"There is a time," he said slowly, measuring his words. "It comes almost at the end, when there are no more cries for help or mercy, when there is no more begging. I heard no words on the *Isolde* that night, only a groan. It is the nightmare sound of someone consenting to die, Detective Beaumont. Of someone wanting to die. It is the sound

I think of now when the priest reads to us about Jesus 'giving up the ghost.' ''

Lorenzo Hurtado paused and shook his head. ''Before that night on the *Isolde,* I had heard that sound only once before when I was a little boy of eleven. When it comes in my dreams, it keeps me awake even now. Because, Detective Beaumont, once you hear it, you never, ever forget.''

''You're saying you came on the boat, heard this terrible noise—the sound of someone being tortured—and then you just left? You didn't even try to help?''

''I ran,'' he whispered. ''I ran as far and fast as I could.''

''Judge not, jerk,'' I berated myself, while a single tear welled up in the corner of Lorenzo Hurtado's eye and coursed a glistening track down his cheek. He made no effort to brush it away. For a time, no one at the table spoke, although Maria Hurtado was weeping openly.

''I know now that I should have tried to find help,'' Lorenzo continued finally. ''I don't know what happened to me. Maybe if I hadn't run away, Señor Gebhardt would still be alive. I should have tried to help, but I didn't. I pray to the Holy Mother every day, asking for forgiveness.''

Shoulders heaving, Lorenzo caught his breath, sighed, and looked away. Call it gut instinct, but there was no question in my mind that Lorenzo Hurtado was telling the absolute truth.

Clearly, although the man was right on the edge, someone had to keep asking questions, and I was elected. ''After you heard the groan, tell us exactly what happened then.''

Lorenzo shuddered and cleared his throat before he spoke again. "I guess I panicked. Maria's a nurse. She works at the V.A. Hospital. She says what happened to me is a flashback. You think what's happening now is what happened that other time. What *is* gets all mixed up with what *isn't*. I don't remember all of it. I think I may have hidden somewhere for a while. My shoes and clothing were covered with mud, but mostly I ran."

"Until you were hit by the car?"

"Yes. I don't remember that exactly, either. I mean, I don't remember how it happened, but yes. The car hit me."

"And then?"

"After I got away from the lady in the car, I went home."

"Where do you live, Lorenzo?"

"Capitol Hill. Maria and I share an apartment there, with our mother."

"How did you get home?"

"I called Maria from a pay phone. She had dropped me off for work, and she came back to get me."

"And bandaged your leg?"

"Yes."

Since Maria was a nurse, there had been no necessity for them to seek medical treatment for the cut on Lorenzo's leg. That explained why his description and the Identi-Kit sketch hadn't rattled any chains of recognition at the hospital emergency rooms where Sue Danielson had made inquiries.

"What were you doing on the *Isolde* at that

hour of the morning? What time was it, four-thirty? Five?"

"Five. Señor Gebhardt asked me to come to work then. He said we had a lot to do that day, that we needed to get an early start."

"What exactly were you doing?"

"Getting the boat ready to go out. I was supposed to help him overhaul the engine starting next week, but he called me on Sunday. He said he had decided to put off the overhaul until later. He said while it was still good weather, he wanted to take the boat out for one last test before we started working on it. I did some other work on the boat the day before, on Monday, checking the equipment, fuel, and fluids—making sure everything was right. Mostly I helped him load stores on board. The next day he told me he wanted me to come help him load on everything else."

"What everything else?"

Lorenzo raised his shoulders and shook his head. "I don't know. He said it would be hard work, that it would take all day."

"There was a wrench," I said, "a small box wrench that was found near the scene of the car accident. The lady who hit you found it in the street after you left. Do you know anything about that?"

He nodded. "It was on the deck of the *Isolde* when I came on board," Lorenzo said. "I stepped on it and almost fell down. I'm sure it was one of Señor Gebhardt's tools, and I was afraid I had left it out overnight. He was careful about his tools. I was going to return it to the toolbox without letting him know it had been left out. When I picked it up to put it in my pocket, it felt funny, and I wondered why it was covered with paint.''

Sue Danielson had been quiet throughout the interview. She didn't keep still because she's some kind of shrinking violet or because I'm particularly brilliant. The truth is, interrogations can shatter like glass with too much handling or interference. Because Lorenzo focused on me and seemed so concerned with whether or not I believed him, Sue simply assumed it was better to leave well enough alone.

Now, though, she stirred. "How long had you known Gunter Gebhardt?" she asked.

"Five years."

"How did you first meet him?"

"Through my cousin, and one of my cousin's friends. They went to work for him, fishing, and they asked me to come along. We made good money."

"Was he hard to work for?" Sue asked.

"It was a job," Lorenzo answered. "He paid us, and the checks didn't bounce."

"You didn't have any trouble with him?"

"No," Lorenzo answered. "No trouble," but for the second time, that same involuntary tic I had seen before flitted across the man's tense jawline. He glanced reproachfully at June Miller as if to say that exactly what he had feared would now happen—that we would blame him for Gunter Gebhardt's murder.

Lorenzo stood up, as did his sister. "My leg hurts," he said. "I want to go home."

Sue looked at me questioningly, one eyebrow raised. I shook my head, indicating we should let

him go. After all, we had come so far in the process that I didn't want to risk alienating him by
pressing any further right then. Besides, the band
was tuning up again. Sitting there right on top of
the speakers, as soon as the music started, we
wouldn't be able to hear a word.

As the first notes of the next number blasted
out of the speakers, I got up and followed the
Hurtados out into the night.

"Wait a minute," I called after them as they
started down the streetlight-lit sidewalk.

Lorenzo swung around angrily. "What do you
want now?" he demanded.

For an answer, I pulled out my copy of the
Identi-Kit picture—the one with Lorenzo's own
likeness staring out from the paper.

"Have you seen this?" I asked, handing it over
to Lorenzo.

He glanced down and studied the picture for a
moment. Then he nodded and handed it back.
"Yes," he answered. "I've seen it."

"So has everyone else in this city," I told him.
"Including the third party who was on the *Isolde*
with you and Gunter Gebhardt the night he died."

Beside him, Maria inhaled sharply. Her hand
rose reflexively to her throat. Lorenzo's eyes rose
to meet mine. "What are you saying?" he asked.

"Two people are dead so far," I answered. "If
the killer believes you saw him and can possibly
help lead us to him, he may very well come looking for you. Thanks to this, we found you, and
the killer may be able to do the same thing. Sometimes, in cases like this, we'll put a witness in

protective custody, but I don't think that would work too well here. Do you?''

Lorenzo looked at me but said nothing.

I knew I was bending the rules, but it sure as hell wasn't the first time. "If I were you," I continued, "and if I had anywhere else to go, I would take my mother and sister and go there. At least for a while."

Lorenzo's questioning gaze held mine for a long moment. Finally, he nodded. "I have another cousin," he said. "His name is Sergio Hurtado, and he lives in Yakima. I can take my mother and go there. Maria can't miss work, but she can stay with friends."

"Does your cousin have a phone?" I asked. "Can I call you there if I need to?"

"Yes," Lorenzo answered. "Yes, you can."

"Is he listed in the telephone directory?"

Lorenzo nodded. And then he offered me his hand.

As we shook, I realized the entire process had been a test, from the moment the two of them stepped inside the door of the Ballard Fire House. It had been a life-and-death examination on the subject of trust, and although there were still many unanswered questions, I knew I must have passed.

20.

By the time we left the Ballard Fire House, it was far too late for even the former BoBo Beaumont to pay a call on Else Gebhardt. Besides, I was beat. And the bone spur on my heel was kicking up again. I told myself it came from just watching all that salsa dancing, but it probably had a lot more to do with stumbling around in the dark out at the Camano Island fire two nights before.

In any event, I took off for home, where I dosed myself with prescription anti-inflammatories. The directions on the bottle said that the medication was to be taken with food. Since there wasn't much of that lying around loose in my bare-bones kitchen, I followed the pills with a chaser of peanut butter. A generously rounded tablespoonful. I figured since peanut butter seemed to be good enough for the other old dogs in my family, it was probably good enough for me.

And it worked, too. Soon after I crawled into bed, the throbbing in my foot lessened enough for me to fall asleep. During the night, I dreamt, not surprisingly, of salsa dancing.

Ralph Ames, who is often an overnight guest in my high-rise condo, has made a crusade of bringing me out of the technological Dark Ages. He had prevailed on one of his electronics/computer-whiz friends to design a dazzling system for my apartment that can do everything but bring me coffee in bed. If I carry a little electronic wafer in my pocket, I can set the thing to automatically adjust lights and music as I move from room to room.

The system also includes a wireless pagerlike controller and intercom that can, from any room in the apartment and without benefit of telephone, answer and open my apartment door as well as the door to Belltown Terrace's outside entrance. It's a great gimmick—if I'd just remember to wear it. Most of the time it stays parked on the counter in the bathroom, which is where I most often have need of it.

That was the case the next morning when the doorbell rang just as I stepped out of the shower. It was the bell to the apartment.

Belltown Terrace is a secured building. That means no one is supposed to enter without being buzzed in by either a resident or allowed in by the doorman. If the doorman lets a guest inside the building, he's supposed to call and check to see whether or not the arriving person is expected and should be allowed to proceed. In other words, whoever was standing at the door to my apartment should have been one of my fellow residents, a neighbor from inside the building.

And she was. "Hi, Uncle Beau," Heather Peters chirped through the pager. "Can we come in?"

Heather and Tracy Peters are the daughters of Ron Peters, a former partner of mine. After a disabling line-of-duty injury left him wheelchair-bound, he and the girls moved into a unit on one of the lower floors of Belltown Terrace along with Amy, the physical-therapy nurse who became his second wife. Never having had any nieces and nephews of my own, I appreciated being allowed to borrow the girls on occasion.

"Sure, Heather," I said, pressing the button. "I'll be out in a minute. Just let me get some clothes on."

Eight-year-old Heather had said "we." I assumed that meant she and her ten-year-old sister would both be waiting in my living room. I was wrong.

I came down the hallway a few minutes later to find both Heather Peters and an amazingly large Afghan hound—who was either Charley, the elevator dog, or Charley's twin—enthroned on my window seat. Heather's arm was around the dog's shoulder, and they both sat with their backs to the room, peering down through yet another morning of Puget Sound's late-autumn fog.

"Hey, what's he doing in here?" I demanded.

"Charley's a she," Heather corrected primly. "She's named after the perfume."

"Well, get her down off my window seat."

When ordered to get down, Charley complied, but not without a baleful look at me. She sighed, disdainfully shook her footlong ears, and then flopped down at Heather's feet.

"Have you ever met Charley before?" Heather asked.

"Only once. In the elevator. Is that where you found her?"

"Oh no, I'm taking care of her for the whole weekend. I told Amy and Dad that I'm taking her for a walk, but I need your help."

I come from an era when people who owned dogs usually had yards to go with them. When the dog needed to be walked, the owner simply opened the door, and the dog walked itself. No one carried pooper-scoopers and plastic bags back then.

"I don't walk dogs, Heather," I said, stopping in the kitchen long enough to pour the first cup of coffee from the morning's second pot. The last statement sounded grouchy, even to me. When Heather's face fell in disappointment, I modified my position some. "At least I never have up till now," I added.

Heather brightened instantly. "Did you know it's Amy's birthday today?"

Amy Peters is Heather's stepmother. "I had no idea."

"I know what I want to get for her birthday present—Frangos. You know, those chocolate things?" Heather prattled on. "She just loves Frangos. I've got enough money, but my dad's too busy to take me to the Bon. I could walk there by myself, if I had Charley along to look out for me, but then what would happen to her when I went inside the store?"

What indeed? Forty-five minutes later, I was cooling my heels on the corner of Fourth and Stewart outside the Bon Marché, one of Seattle's premier department stores. I stood there hoping to God none of my fellow police officers would see me doing dog-sitting duty with that arrogant, snooty animal. Charley and I seemed to be of the same mind—we were both pretending we'd never seen each other before, which is hard to do when you're on opposite ends of the same leash.

Much as I hate to admit it, Charley was an exceptionally well-behaved dog. Although nearly as tall as Heather, the dog obeyed all instructions issued by her diminutive keeper. Head held high, Charley pranced along beside Heather when we walked, or sat with her narrow nose high in the air while we waited for lights to change at intersections.

Heather is a cute kid in her own right; always has been. Charley is a beautiful dog, and the two of them were a winning combination. Just like any ordinary regular uncle, I got a boot of pride out of the way passersby craned their necks to take a second look.

We spent some time window-shopping downtown and sauntering through the Saturday morning throngs at the Pike Place Market. I told myself I was just minding my grandmother—taking the time to stop and smell the flowers. Along the way, I picked up some groceries. With the gourmet cook Ralph Ames due to arrive the next day, I couldn't afford to be caught foodless in Seattle.

Back at Belltown Terrace, I said good-bye to Heather and Charley in the elevator, put away the groceries, then picked up the phone and dialed Ashland, Oregon. Jeremy Todd Cartwright III, my recently acquired son-in-law, answered the phone.

"Kelly's outside with the kids. Want me to go get her?"

Kelly runs a day-care center out of their newly

remodeled home, so she is often "outside with the kids." One of those kids, Kayla—short for Karen Louise—is my only grandchild.

"Don't bother. I can talk to you. Do you and Kelly have any plans for Thanksgiving?"

Jeremy paused. "We had talked about going down to Cucamonga, to visit Dave and Karen, but Dave called the other day and says he doesn't think Karen will be up to having company."

Karen Livingston, my first wife and Kelly's mother, has been battling cancer for more than two years now. Dave, her second husband, is a good guy, one I've come to respect more and more over the years. But the fact that Karen didn't want company for Thanksgiving, not even her new grand-daughter, was not good news.

"Besides," Jeremy added gloomily, "I'm not all that sure the old van would make it that far. The clutch may be on its last legs."

"How about coming up here?" I suggested.

"Kelly would probably like that, but I still don't know about the van making it over the passes between here and Eugene."

"Talk it over with her," I said. "I don't need an answer right this minute, but if you want to come, we can see about flying you up from Medford."

Jeremy's reply was interrupted by my call-waiting signal.

I make it a point not to switch calls when I'm on the phone with someone long distance. That seems rude to me. When call-interrupting starts buzzing in my ear, that's the time when I long for the good old days when a dialed telephone offered only one of three uncomplicated results—an answer, a busy signal, or no answer. Life was simpler back then, in more ways than one.

". . . expensive?" Jeremy was asking, when I could hear him again.

"Don't worry about the money," I told him. "What matters is whether or not you want to come."

"I'll check with Kelly right away," Jeremy assured me. "We'll get back to you with an answer as soon as we can."

Even though we didn't rush in finishing up the call, as soon as I put down the phone, it rang again. Whoever was calling was persistent enough to stay on the line for far longer than I would have.

"Hello," I said.

"Beau?"

"Yes."

"Detective Stan Jacek here. What do you think of the latest?"

"The latest what?"

"The autopsy results, of course. I faxed them down to Seattle P.D. about half an hour ago."

"Look, Stan, it's Saturday," I pointed out. "This may come as a surprise to you, but I have no intention of going into the office today. I'm trying to learn how not to work twenty-four hours a day, seven days a week. I've already put in a helluva long week, and the Seattle Police Department's new chief isn't all that keen on sanctioning excess overtime. I figure Monday should be time enough for me to take another crack at all this."

"Are you saying you'd rather I hang up now, then, so you don't get the news until after you've actually punched in on the time clock Monday morning?''

It seemed to me Stan Jacek was being a bit testy. ''Cut the sarcasm, Stan. We're already on the phone. Go ahead and tell me. What autopsy results?''

''It's not her.''

Now I was completely baffled. ''Who's not her?''

''Denise Whitney,'' he answered. ''The dead woman isn't Denise. The dental records don't even come close to matching the ones her parents brought down from Anchorage.''

That blew me away. Once again my none-too-limber mental rubber bands were being stretched to the limit. One minute I was talking to my son-in-law and hoping to arrange a visit with my grandchild over the holidays, and the next I was back in the dark world of murder. A place where things you thought were straightforward suddenly weren't. And it wasn't even my case.

''If the dead woman isn't Denise,'' I said, ''who the hell is she?''

''Good question,'' Jacek answered. ''We're checking missing-persons reports all over the Pacific Northwest—from northern California to Vancouver, B.C., and from the coast as far east as Montana. Nothing so far.''

''What about him?''

Now it was Detective Jacek's turn to be bumfuzzled. ''Him who?''

''If Denise isn't Denise, is Gunter Gunter?''

''I guess,'' Stan Jacek answered. ''At least they didn't say anything to me about him. But then

Gunter's your case, not mine, so they probably wouldn't have told me regardless. You'd better check that one out for yourself. I'll let you go, so you can get back to whatever it was you were doing.''

''Oh, no, you won't,'' I replied. ''Now that you've dragged me back into a work mode, there are a few things I need to go over with you as well.''

In the next ten minutes, I gave Stan Jacek a brief version of what had gone on since he and I last parted company outside the Public Safety Building. I told him about Sue Danielson's and my intriguing interview with Kari Gebhardt and Michael Morris, and the results of my salsa-dancing foray. I told him about Lorenzo Hurtado's revelation that Gunter Gebhardt had been making hasty and ultimately futile preparations to leave town.

''It sounds as though as soon as Kari told him someone was looking for him, he tried to beat it, but the killer or killers got to him first,'' I concluded.

''Sounds like,'' Jacek agreed, ''but why would he be getting the boat ready to ship out when he already had a plane ticket stashed in his car?''

''Good question.'' And it was.

''And what about those Wiesenthal guys,'' Jacek continued. ''I always thought they played it straight up.''

''So did I, and so does everyone else,'' I told him. ''But it occurs to me that having an international reputation for being absolutely above suspicion is a reasonable reason for checking them out, don't you think?"

"You do have a point," Jacek allowed grudgingly. "An organization like that is bound to have an occasional bad apple or else someone who tags along behind them. We should look into that. Can you go interview them?"

"Sure. If I can find them."

"And how do you do that?"

"Beats me. Call the FBI, maybe? I'll give it some thought. If I come up with any bright ideas, I'll let you know, and you do the same. In the meantime, now that my day off is totally screwed, I could just as well drop by Else Gebhardt's and ask for the use of one of her husband's soldiers."

"What soldiers?"

Oops. "Didn't I tell you about the toy soldiers down in Gunter Gebhardt's basement?"

"Not that I remember."

"They're handmade replicas of Nazi soldiers," I said, making up for my oversight in not telling him earlier. "As far as I can determine, making those miniatures was Gunter's sole hobby. Last night, when I was talking to Lorenzo, I had this sudden brainstorm that maybe they were made of gold, just like that wrench Bonnie Elgin found after the hit-and-run. And where better to hide them than in plain sight?"

"You think they're made from all those melteddown teeth?" Jacek sounded aghast. Even second- and third-hand, Kari and Michael's revelations about Sobibor had hit Stan Jacek as hard as they'd hit me. "That's nauseating. How could he?"

"That's a question I don't even want to think about," I told him.

"But it adds up," Jacek said eventually. "Are you going to check it out, or shall I?"

"I'm closer," I told him.

So when I got off the phone with Detective Jacek, I simply put my jacket back on and headed for the parking garage. Duty called. At least that's what I told myself all the way downstairs in the elevator.

Even though it was early November and winter cold, at least it wasn't raining. So during that chill afternoon drive to Blue Ridge, I had to make my way around the last few end-of-season die-hard garage sales. And once I reached Culpeper Court, I expected to have to fight my way through another collection of friends and relatives to gain admittance to the Gebhardt residence. To my surprise, no one seemed to be around.

More surprising still was the orange, black, and white FOR SALE BY OWNER sign that had been stapled to a wooden stake and hammered into Gunter Gebhardt's otherwise-pristine front lawn.

Because of my job as a homicide cop, I naturally come in contact with lots of grieving relatives and friends. I have more than a nodding acquaintance with several of this city's best-known grief counselors. They differ on some points, but they all agree in advising traumatized relatives to avoid making any precipitous decisions about moving out of the family home or selling property too soon after the death of a loved one.

In the days and weeks following a death—sudden or otherwise—the decision-making faculties may be badly impaired by the overwhelming weight of confusion and loss. Sad but true, there are plenty of vultures loose in the world who make their fortunes by finding and preying on such people.

Even knowing how unwelcome unsolicited advice can be, I was determined to give Else Gebhardt the benefit of my feelings in that regard. I stepped up onto the front porch and rang the bell.

Else answered the door herself, dust rag in one hand and broom in the other. "Why, BoBo," she said, "what are you doing here?"

She seemed to be in far better emotional shape than I would have imagined, so there was no point in shilly-shallying around. "I came to see if you'd lend me a sampling of Gunter's soldiers," I said, going straight to the heart of the matter. "I want to have it analyzed down at the crime lab to see if there's any way to trace the source of the metal."

Else led me into the freshly cleaned living room where vacuum-cleaner tracks still lingered on the carpet. The furniture had been totally rearranged.

"Cleaning seems to make me feel better. I need to be doing something instead of just sitting around brooding," she explained, putting the dust rag down and motioning for me to take a seat on the sofa.

"Now what's this about tracing the metal the soldiers are made of?" Else asked, once she was seated beside me. "Why would that be so important? They're just made out of lead, aren't they?"

I couldn't bring myself to answer that question straight out. Else wasn't ready to hear about Sobi-

bor, and I certainly wasn't ready to tell her. Before
I spoke, I listened for the sounds of other people
at home, but the house was quiet. We seemed to
be alone.

"I'm not entirely sure, but it might be," I
hedged. "We have to check everything."

"Well," Else answered, "you're too late.
They're gone."

"Gone? What do you mean gone?"

"I sold them, not two hours ago. I wanted them
out of my house. If they had asked for anything
else of Gunter's, I would have sold that, too."
Else's voice was bitter.

"You sold them?" I must have sounded like a
witless echo. "To whom?"

"To some men who came by to look at the
house."

"What men? Who were they? Someone you
knew?"

"Two men, an older gentleman and a younger
one. They said they were driving in the neighborhood and saw my sign. I had just put it up half
an hour earlier. The young man is getting married
in a couple of months, and his parents are going
to help them buy a house."

"You showed the house to them, then. The
whole thing? Even the basement?"

"Of course I showed them the basement. And
while we were down there, they happened to see
Gunter's soldiers. They both got very excited
about them. Evidently, someone in their family
collects miniature soldiers."

"German soldiers," I added.

"Yes, well, maybe the men are German, too,

come to think of it. At least the older one might be. It sounded like it anyway. He spoke with what sounded like a German accent."

"But the younger one didn't?"

"No. He's American. I'm sure of it."

A younger man and an older; one with a German accent and one without. Else's description sounded more than vaguely similar to Michael and Kari's portrayal of the two Simon Wiesenthal operatives who had visited their apartment in Bellingham.

"Did the younger one happen to have brown curly hair?" I asked.

Else frowned. "As a matter of fact, he did," she answered. "Why, do you know something about him?"

I did know some things, and I suspected much more. Why the hell hadn't I acted immediately on my hunch about those damn toy soldiers? They probably were solid gold.

Knowing I'd been totally outmaneuvered, I asked Else the bottom-line question, even though I didn't really want to know the answer. "How much did you sell the soldiers for?"

"Five hundred dollars for the whole shebang," she answered, with a smile that showed she was pleased with the bargain she'd struck. "Cash and carry. The two of them loaded the soldiers into boxes and took them away. Now I'll be able to use those shelves to display stuff in a few weeks when I have my moving sale."

That was probably the opening when I could have administered my prepared lecture about the evils of making too-hasty decisions; when I should

have warned her that if she acted too quickly, she
might be taken to the cleaners. I didn't waste my
breath. There wasn't much sense in going to the
bother when, likely as not, the cleaners had already come and gone.

Else was watching my face. "You do know
something about those two men, don't you?"

I nodded.

"Did they have something to do with Gunter's death?"

"It's possible."

She paled. "And I let them into the house when
I was here by myself? I shouldn't have done that,
should I?"

"No," I agreed. "You shouldn't have. Now,
where's Kari?" I asked.

"She took my mother to have her hair done. I
wanted to be here alone. I wanted to do some
work—some real physical work. . . ."

"I understand all that, Else," I said. "You don't
have to explain, but you really shouldn't be here
by yourself right now, and under no circumstances
should you allow any more strangers into the
house whether you're alone here or not,
understand?"

"Yes."

"And for the moment, I want you to take down
the For Sale sign."

"No," Else Gebhardt said determinedly. "I'm
not taking it down for you or for my mother or
for anybody else. Maybe people think I'm being
disrespectful by trying to sell it when Gunter isn't
even buried yet, but they don't understand. My
husband betrayed me, BoBo. Gunter played me for

a fool. No wonder he wanted my mother with us. As long as I was locked up here in this house looking after her, he could go about doing whatever he damn well pleased.''

She paused and then added, ''Well, that's over. Gunter's dead, and so is his girlfriend.''

The part about the girlfriend certainly wasn't entirely true since I now had proof that Denise Whitney hadn't perished in the Camano Island fire, but I didn't even attempt to interrupt Else Gebhardt's angry tirade.

''I'll do the right thing by Gunter, even if he didn't deserve it,'' she continued. ''I'll play the part and see to it that he's properly buried, but I'm through being a doormat, BoBo. I want out of this house, and I want out of it now. This was my mother's house and Gunter's house. It's never been mine, and I won't stay here a minute longer than I have to.''

Else finally ran out of steam.

''In other words,'' I interjected, ''you won't take down the sign?''

''No! I certainly won't! Why should I? If the soldiers are all those two men were after, why would they come back?''

''You're right,'' I agreed. ''They might not. But somebody else might.''

''I don't think so,'' Else returned.

I'm not very good at changing women's minds, and Else Gebhardt's mind was definitely made up—too much so for me to tackle the problem directly. I simply went around it.

On my way back downtown, I took a swing by Fishermen's Terminal. There was a single light on in Champagne Al's *One Day at a Time*. When I knocked on the galley door, he answered with a book in one hand and a cigarette in the other.

In the course of a five-minute visit, I didn't tell Alan Torvoldsen much, only that I was worried about Else Gebhardt being alone in her house up on Culpeper Court and that I wished someone, preferably a friend of the family, would keep an eye on her. Just to be on the safe side.

From the expression on his face when I finished, you'd have thought I'd just handed a lifepreserver to a drowning man. I left the boat a few minutes later. As I headed out the door, Champagne Al was already standing in front of the smoke-filmed mirror, carefully combing into place what little remained of his flaming-red hair.

21.

I understand that there are lots of people in the work force today who are into telecommuting. They work at home. I'm not one of them. I'm used to working at work. There's something about the workaday, slightly grubby ambience of the fifth floor that helps me think and focus. Since focusing was what I needed to do, I headed straight for my cubicle in the Public Safety Building.

It only took a moment to retrieve Stan Jacek's fax containing the Jane Doe autopsy findings. It took a hell of a lot longer than that to digest same.

Because the Camano Island victim's body had burned so completely, there was virtually no soft tissue remaining on the bones. Even so, many of the circumstances were similar to the ones we'd found in the Fishermen's Terminal incident. The victim's fingers and toes had all been removed and left to time-bake in a charred pie tin on top of the body. However, because of the condition of the tissue, it was impossible to discover whether the mutilations had occurred before or after the victim's death.

From my point of view, however, the biggest

problem with the autopsy was that it dealt with the wrong person. If the dead woman wasn't Denise Whitney, who was she? And, for that matter, if Denise wasn't dead, where the hell was she? One more time, she had put her family through an emotional ordeal not unlike being tossed in a Waring blender. Had she done this to them herself, willingly? Or was she also among the killer's victims—a missing corpse, rotting and waiting to be discovered?

And then, of course, there was my other problem—the guys who might or might not be Simon Wiesenthal operatives. I hadn't a doubt in my mind that the two men who had paid their timely visit to Else Gebhardt, the two wheeler-dealers who had aced me out of Gunter's soldiers, were the same ones who had called on Kari and Michael up in Bellingham. So—were these characters really on the trail of Hans Gebhardt, or were they actually on the trail of the gold? Both, or neither?

The mire was so deep now that I didn't know what to think. Maybe Hans Gebhardt was still alive, and the Wiesenthal agents were doing exactly what they claimed—tracking him to ground. But there were other possibilities. What were the chances that Gunter Gebhardt's long-missing father was, in fact, long dead, and the story about searching for him was nothing more than an elaborate cover?

The Simon Wiesenthal organization. How do you go about contacting them? I wondered. After a few moments of reflection, I tried my old standby—I dialed Information—and came up winners, twice over. Within minutes I had numbers for the Simon Wiesenthal Foundation in both New York and Los Angeles. But neither office was open at five-something o'clock Pacific Standard Time on a November Saturday afternoon. And what I had to say wasn't something that could be trusted to the impersonal discretion of a taped voice-messaging system.

I could hear myself saying, "I'm a detective up here in Seattle, and I've got these two guys who may or may not be yours and who may or may not be wandering around the state of Washington killing people. Would you mind having somebody get back to me on this?"

Like hell they would!

So the question was, how to find out more about Moise and Avram without tipping my hand? If they were true-blue, then it might not hurt anything to check them out in a straightforward, official-channel fashion. But if they had gone bad—if they were renegades using their official credentials as free tickets to get away with murder—then any kind of official inquiry might be enough to send them dodging for cover.

Someone once told me that true creativity is 50 percent saturation, 49 percent perspiration, and 1 percent inspiration. After sitting there in the silence of my cubicle in a near-catatonic state for more than an hour and a half, after doing the hard work of turning the same questions over and over in my mind, inspiration finally struck at five minutes to six.

That's it, I thought. Picking up the phone, I dialed my old partner, Ron Peters.

As soon as he answered the phone and I heard

voices and laughter and dishes clattering in the background, I remembered it was Amy's birthday. It sounded as though I had called right in the middle of a party.

"I hope I'm not interrupting anything."

"It's just family," Ron answered. "We're just setting the table."

"This won't take long, then. Do you happen to have Tony Freeman's home telephone number?"

Captain Anthony Freeman is the head of the Internal Investigations Section of Seattle P.D. He's a well-respected straight-shooter. He was also the one supervisor in the whole department who had been able to see beyond Ron Peters' wheelchair to the fact that a trained detective's abilities were being vastly underutilized in a permanent assignment to the Media Affairs section. Ron was now working full-time as an I.I.S. investigator.

I also happened to know that, despite the fact that he bore a Gentile-sounding name, Tony Freeman was Jewish. As a matter of fact, he once gave me a memorable ass-chewing that had to do with my using a Yiddish word that he personally found offensive. What he said wasn't at all mean-spirited, but it wasn't the kind of thing you forgot, either. Ever since that rebuke, the word *schmuck* has been excised from my spoken vocabulary.

"I have his number," Ron answered, "but it's unlisted, and I'm not supposed to give it out. Why do you need it? What's up?"

I was off on such a wild-goose chase that I wasn't eager to discuss it with anyone right then—not even Ron Peters. "It's about the boat fire at Fishermen's Terminal," I said.

"You don't think a police officer is involved, do you?" Ron asked.

"No, nothing like that. But I do need to talk to Tony. Could you maybe call him and see if you can get him to call me here?"

"Where's here?" Ron asked.

"I'm in the office," I answered. "At my desk."

"On Saturday?"

"Don't hassle me about it. Someday maybe I'll get a life."

Ron laughed. "Okay," he said. "I'll see what I can do. And if for some reason I'm not able to raise him by phone, I'll give you a call back right away."

But the person who returned my call barely two minutes later was Captain Tony Freeman himself. "Hey, Beau," he said. "I understand you wanted to talk to me. What's going on?"

"What do you know about the Simon Wiesenthal Foundation?" I asked.

It was an unexpected question, one that caught Tony Freeman slightly off guard, but there was only a brief pause. "Some," he answered. "That's the organization devoted to tracking down Nazi war criminals and bringing them to justice. What about them?"

"I think we may have a couple of them wandering around loose in Seattle at the moment," I told him. "And from what I've found out so far, they may be up to no good."

"Maybe you'd better bring me up to speed," Captain Freeman said.

And so I did, in as orderly a fashion as I could. When I finished, Captain Freeman was silent for a long moment. I could almost hear the wheels grinding through the telephone wires.

"If those two guys have turned, for one reason or another," he said gravely, "then they'll have gone to ground, and you'll never find them. If they're playing it straight, you won't have any trouble."

"Meaning?"

"Call the name-brand hotels and find out if they're registered guests under their own names, or at least under the names they gave those two kids up in Bellingham," Freeman answered. "If they are registered, most likely they'll be eating kosher meals, and that takes special arrangements. One of the local caterers that keeps a kosher kitchen would be providing the meals and delivering them, ready-to-eat, to the hotel. I could probably get you a list of the possible caterers if you like, but at this hour on a Saturday, that might be tough.

"So, if I were you, I'd start by calling area hotels. Call, ask for them by name, and see if the hotel operator puts you through to a room."

"Good idea," I said. "I don't know why I didn't think of that myself. I'll see what I can do."

"One more thing," Tony Freeman added. "I don't think the Wiesenthal group operates under any strict budgetary considerations, so I'd start at the top. Don't bother checking with Motel Six. Their expense account would do much better than that."

If you ask for advice, my position is you'd better be prepared to take it. So I started at the top, both in terms of quality and alphabet—with the

Alexis. I figured I'd end up at the Westin when I
hit the bottom of the list, but it turned out I didn't
have to go that far. I hit pay dirt in the *S*'s when
I got as far as the Sorrento.

As soon as the phone started ringing in a room,
I slammed down the receiver. They were there, in
a local hotel, and checked in under their own
names—or at least under their most recent aliases.
That meant Captain Freeman was right. Had Moise
and Avram been crooked, they wouldn't have been
nearly that easy to find. Now what?

I sat there for several minutes, pondering my
next move. Should I hie myself up to the Sorrento,
call from the lobby, invite them down for a drink
in the bar? No, that didn't seem wise. After all,
although these two men weren't really police officers, I had to believe they were trained professionals. They might take a very dim view of being
tracked down in a strange city by a lone local cop
who shouldn't have had any idea who they were
or what they were up to. And if they decided to
get physical about my interfering in their lives, no
doubt they would both be fully capable of handling themselves in a crisis.

Once upon a time, I wouldn't have thought
twice about waltzing up to the Sorrento all by myself, but age and wisdom and scars all go hand in
hand. In this line of work, you either get smarter
or you die, so after a few moments of consideration, I looked up Sue Danielson's home number
and dialed it.

"'lo," a surly young male voice answered.

"Hello," I said. "Is your mother there?"

"I'm on the other line," Jared Danielson said. "Could you call back later, after I'm done?"

"No," I said. "I can't call back later."

I have very little patience with the self-appointed gatekeepers of the world, whether they be officially sanctioned receptionist types or simply self-centered teenagers who don't want to relinquish the phone to anyone else, especially to someone so undeserving as a mere bill-paying parent.

"This is business," I answered abruptly. "And it's important. I need to speak to your mother right away."

"Okay," he said. "Just a minute."

It was actually quite a bit more than a minute. It was more than two minutes, but I'll be damned if I was going to give up.

Eventually, Sue's voice came on the phone. "Hello. Is this call for me?"

"Yes, it's for you, dammit!"

"Beau?"

"Yes. I'm calling from down at the department. Tell Jared the next time he doesn't put me through to you right away, I'm going to come over and personally ream his ass."

"What a good idea." Sue laughed. "I'll pass the word. Now, what's happening?"

"Have you had dinner yet?"

"No. We spent the afternoon painting the kids' bathroom. I told the boys we'd order a pizza later on, but I haven't quite gotten around to that yet. We're still cleaning up."

"Go ahead and order pizza, but just enough for the boys."

"What about me?" she objected. "I'm starved."

"Put on your glad rags. We have to pay a call on yet another joint, but don't wear your salsa-dancing costume. I don't think the folks who hang out in the Hunt Club at the Sorrento speak salsa dancing. How long will it take for you to meet me there?"

"An hour maybe. I'll have to jump in the shower."

"I'll see you there, but tell that son of yours for me that this isn't a date, either."

When Sue hung up, I thumbed through my note-book until I found Michael Morris' telephone number at his parents' home on Mercer Island. A woman answered my ring. When I asked for Michael, I could hear the curiosity in her voice as she handed him the phone.

"Hello, Michael," I said. "Detective Beaumont. Are you busy?"

"We were about to sit down to dinner," he answered. "I'm not home all that often, and my mother invited friends over."

"What are the chances of your bailing out?"

"Maybe my mother wouldn't kill me if I told her it was urgent, but why? What's up?"

"I need you to come down to the Sorrento with me to help identify the two men who visited you and Kari up in Bellingham."

"You've found them?"

"I think so, but I need your help to be sure."

"How soon do you need me?"

"As soon as possible. Don't go to the hotel. I'm here in my office in the Public Safety Building. Come here first," I told him. "There's a guard downstairs. You can't come up to the fifth floor, but he'll call to let me know you're here. We'll ride over to the hotel together."

"Don't you want me to go get Kari so she could be there, too?"

"No," I said, "let's leave Kari out of this for the time being. She might have more of a conflict than you do when it comes to all this."

"Oh," Michael Morris said after a moment's thought. "I see what you mean," he added. "I'll be there just as soon as I can."

Michael and I arrived early, even after swinging by Belltown Terrace so I could put on something a little more appropriate for the rarefied atmosphere of the Sorrento. We commandeered a table in the well-appointed lobby—a table that allowed us an unobstructed view of both the front entrance and the elevator. We drank coffee, watched, and waited until Sue arrived.

Once again, she looked surprisingly good. After I ordered another coffee, one for Sue, I told her so.

She grinned. "Every woman looks good in a little black dress," she said. "But I came prepared." The matching evening bag that dangled by a string over one shoulder had a peculiar bulge and weight to it. I was glad to see she was carrying.

"Good," I said while Michael Morris' eyes bulged. I don't think the idea of real guns and real bullets had ever crossed his mind until that very moment.

The plan was simple. Sue and I took our positions—Sue in the wing-backed chair nearest the door that entered the lobby from the stairwell, and I at a point across from both the elevator and the main entrance. Michael's job was twofold. First he was to use the telephone and call to see if either Moise or Avram would answer the phone. If so, Michael was to tell them that he had important information to share with them. Hopefully, using that ruse, he could charm one or the other of the two men into coming down to the lobby for a conference.

That done, Michael was to position himself so he could see as much of the lobby area as possible and give us a prearranged signal as soon as either man appeared in the lobby. From that point on, Michael was ordered to leave everything else to Sue and me.

When Michael went over to use the phone, my heart started beating faster in my chest. The prospect of some kind of physical confrontation always gets the adrenaline flowing. I'm sure Sue was affected the same way. That's a conditioned response with cops—a way of life.

We couldn't hear exactly what Michael was saying while he was on the phone. When he finished the call, he retreated to his assigned chair and slumped down in it while Sue and I kept watch on the lights over the elevator door. Moments after Michael regained the chair, the elevator began rising from the ground floor in answer to a summons. It stopped on Four, and the down arrow came back on.

When the elevator door slid open, only one man stood revealed in the opening—a man of about my age, weight, and height. Glancing warily from side to side, he stepped into the lobby. Michael Morris rubbed his chin—the affirmative signal we'd been looking for.

As the man moved forward, so did I. "Mr. Steinman," I said, cutting off his access to the entrance and holding out my I.D. "I'm Detective J. P. Beaumont with the Seattle Police Department."

He stopped and glanced toward the door that opened from the stairwell where Sue Danielson—fetching, in her "little black dress"—was watching for Moise to make a not-unexpected appearance.

There is a tense life-and-death moment in every police officer/citizen contact—even the simplest traffic stop—when everything hangs in the balance. It must be similar to the way a tightrope walker feels suspended above a gasping crowd, frozen in the blinding glare of a spotlight. One misstep, one slight miscalculation, and disaster follows.

For a moment, we were all frozen in time and place, then the door to the stairwell swung open, and Moise appeared in the lobby. He stopped just inside the door and stood, reconnoitering. He reminded me of a lithe young cat—prepared to lunge forward but hanging back, waiting to see if it was necessary.

With his backup in position, the older man's shoulders relaxed, and he turned to me. "What can I do for you, Detective Beaumont?" he asked.

"You can tell me exactly who you are and what you're doing here."

"Would you like to see my identification?" he asked.

"Yes, but take it out very carefully."

He slid his hand into the inside breast pocket of his coat and brought out a slim leather holder. He flipped it open and handed me an embossed plastic card. One side I couldn't read at all—it was written in Hebrew. The other side said only, *Avram Steinman, Simon Wiesenthal Associates.* There was no address—only telephone and fax numbers with a prefix that belonged to neither New York City nor L.A.

I looked at the I.D. card for a moment, then handed it back. "What are you doing here?" I asked.

"I'm a hunter," Avram Steinman said. His speaking voice carried only the slightest hint of an accent. "I'm here investigating missing Nazi war criminals. How about you?"

"I'm with the Seattle Police Homicide Squad," I said. "I'm looking for a murderer."

Avram Steinman's eyes never stopped scanning the room. He was every bit as on guard as I was, maybe even more so, but his anxiety didn't carry over into his speaking voice.

"Maybe we should talk then, Detective Beaumont," he said, with a smile of wry amusement touching the corners of his mouth. "It sounds to me as though you and I are both in the same business."

Tim, Ralph Ames' favorite waiter on the staff at the Georgian Room, once told us about his most surrealistic shift in a lifelong career of waiting tables. It happened, he said, the first night of Operation Desert Storm. While bombs were tearing hell out of the swimming pool in the El Rashid Hotel over in far-off Baghdad, war protesters were swirling in a riotous mass up Seattle's Fifth Avenue right outside the gracious walls of the Four Seasons Olympic. War or no war, protesters or no protesters, the niceties of hospitable dining remained unaffected. Inside the Georgian Room, all that happened was that a piano player upped the volume.

I recalled Tim's comment vividly as I sat in the elegant, dimly lighted Hunt Club at the Sorrento while the Simon Wiesenthal manhunters happily devoured their specially prepared kosher meals and spoke, with a physician's clinical dispassion, of Hans Gebhardt and Sobibor. Plates of regularly prepared Hunt Club–quality food came and went from in front of Sue Danielson, Michael Morris, and me. Maybe Sue and Michael ate some of theirs. I barely touched mine. I have no idea now what the food was or whether or not I tasted it.

In my day-to-day work, I see plenty of common street-thug mentality—the kind of thinking that makes life cheap enough so smart-assed kids regularly blow each other away over something as negligible as a forty-dollar World Series bet.

Moise Rosenthal and Avram Steinman were ostensibly law-abiding citizens—at least when they were on U.S. soil. But I had heard allegations that Wiesenthal tactics occasionally resorted to kidnapping in faraway places like Buenos Aires. What that really meant was that Wiesenthal operatives could be presumed to be both smart and dangerous. When necessity dictated, they were capable of making nice, but they weren't above going for the jugular, either.

Both men exuded the intensity of hunters on the trail of someone or something. Their brand of single-minded focus was a trait I recognized all too well. I see it in myself every day—whenever I look in the mirror. In the course of my life, I've learned that the idiosyncrasies that seem entirely understandable and familiar in me are often the very ones I find most disturbing when I encounter them in someone else.

Moise Rosenthal and Avram Steinman bothered me. I found them so troubling, in fact, that at first I had difficulty staying tuned in to the conversation.

"Part of the problem in prosecuting the Germans who participated in Sobibor," Avram was saying, "was that there were so few survivors, not only among the prisoners, but also among the German personnel who were in charge.

"From the very beginning, the German High Command ran the place with a skeleton crew. Large numbers of guards weren't necessary because the people who were sent to Sobibor weren't prisoners in the ordinary sense of the word. They arrived dazed and ill, weak and exhausted from a hellish boxcar trip. In the summer, some prisoners perished in transit from heat and thirst. In the winter, many died of numbing cold. After exiting the trains, they were herded from the railroad siding into Sobibor's gas chambers within hours of their arrival."

"In other words, not that many guards were necessary," Sue Danielson interjected.

Avram nodded. "Right. The ranks of guard survivors were further reduced, not only by the number of those killed during the October uprising, but also by the ones who simply disappeared afterward. At the time, most of those were reported as either dead or missing in action. After all, the Germans didn't want it known in the ranks that they were having a desertion problem. Things were bad enough for them right then that it could have encouraged others to follow suit."

"I understand that Hans Gebhardt was among those who either went underground after the war or who were thought long dead," Sue said. "I'm wondering about the others, the guards and officers who were tried, convicted, and given their obligatory slaps on the hand during the trials at Nuremburg. Was your organization instrumental in bringing any of them to trial?"

"Yes," Avram said. "We were involved in some of those cases. But what we're talking about here is another kind of trial altogether, other trials besides the ones at Nuremburg.''

''What do you mean?'' I asked.

Avram ignored my interruption and continued. ''While the German High Command was totally focused on waging and losing a war, a few minor details slipped through the cracks. Sobibor was one of them. Those in charge knew approximately the number of prisoners who had been sent to the camp while it was in existence. According to the law of large numbers, they also knew about how much of what they called *das neben-produkt* —side-product—should have resulted from that many bodies. In the final accounting, gold from Sobibor turned up short.''

''I thought Germans always kept meticulous records,'' I said.

''Supposedly, and up to a point, they did. From the time the gold was melted into bars and turned over for shipment, there's a complete paper trail, even now. The missing gold was stolen long before it entered that officially documented path.''

''Stolen by whom?'' I asked.

''Hans Gebhardt, no doubt,'' Avram answered.

''Certainly he wasn't acting alone,'' I supplied. ''Who else would have helped him? Other guards perhaps? Some of the prisoners?''

''Maybe both,'' Avram said. ''A young lieutenant named Lars Weber was in charge of Sobibor's accounting. . . .''

''He was in on it?'' Michael Morris interrupted. ''I remember his name from Kari's and my research. Lars Weber was tried in Nuremburg and imprisoned for a while—only for six months or so. According to one of his surviving relatives, he died shortly after being released.''

"He died as a result of one of those other trials I was telling you about,'' Avram answered quietly. "The unofficial ones. They were conducted by some of the earliest and most vicious gangs of what we now call neo-Nazis. They wanted to re-group and reorganize. They were broke and look-ing for money. By then someone must have realized that a large amount of gold from Sobibor was missing.''

"After he was released from prison, Lars Weber got a job doing reconstruction in Berlin. He disap-peared one afternoon on his way home from work. A passing car slowed down, a door opened, and he was pulled inside. He returned home three weeks later. His five-year-old daughter found him outside the front door early one morning. He had been dumped off during the night. He had been severely burned over two thirds of his body. All his fingers and toes were missing. Gangrene set in. He died two weeks later.''

A burned body. Missing fingers and toes. This was clearly an identifiable M.O.—an inarguable connection.

Sue's eyes met mine across the table, but neither of us gave anything away. Unfortunately, Michael Morris wasn't a cop. He didn't know better.

"Fingers and toes!'' he exclaimed. "That's the same thing that happened . . .'' Too late, I silenced him with a reproving glare. He subsided meekly back into his chair.

"You're saying Lars Weber was in on it then?'' Sue asked.

Avram shrugged, "Maybe. Maybe not. The daughter—Erika—did very well in school. She grew up, became a member of the Communist party, and went to work for a branch of Stasi— the feared East German secret police. She dropped out of sight shortly after the fall of the Berlin Wall. We've been looking for her for the past several months."

"Why?"

"One of our affiliated organizations maintains a data base on the status of known Nazi war criminals—those who have already served their prison terms as well as those who have never been apprehended. When two of the missing Ukrainian guards from Sobibor turned up dead—murdered, or rather executed—under similar circumstances hundreds of miles apart, we started looking into it."

"Those guards were murdered?" Michael asked. "We checked on them. Kari and I were told they all died of natural causes."

"As far as we can tell," Avram answered, "six of the guards are dead. Some of them did die of natural causes. Two of them did not. Neither did the sons of two of the others. You must understand that the term 'natural causes' becomes very flexible in some jurisdictions when inquiries are being made by someone from outside that jurisdiction."

"You said 'similar circumstances,' " I prompted. "Can you be more specific?"

"Burned," he answered. "Almost beyond recognition, but not quite. In each case, the fingers and toes were removed but left with the body. As a warning, perhaps."

"To whom?"

"To whoever had the gold. We believe Erika Weber Schmidt was serving notice to all concerned that she was coming looking for the gold her father had once been accused of stealing."

"Whether or not he did it," Sue said. Avram nodded. "Do you think she was acting alone or in concert with someone else?"

"That we haven't been able to determine. Our assessment is that Erika Weber Schmidt is more than capable of doing it. She's a trained killer. More to the point, she's an unemployed trained killer, or at least she was."

"What does that mean?"

"We now have reason to believe she has gone to work for one of the newer and more radical neo-Nazi splinter groups."

"What you're giving us is a lot of ancient history," I interjected. "I'd like to know what brought you here to Washington last week when you showed up at Kari and Michael's apartment up in Bellingham."

Avram looked questioningly at Moise, who nodded. "A few days ago, while checking Erika Schmidt's back trail, we stumbled over the names of Michael Morris and Kari Gebhardt. One of the survivors mentioned having been interviewed by someone named Gebhardt. Since Hans Gebhardt was one of the missing German soldiers from Sobibor, it struck us as more than just a coincidence. We came here as soon as it was possible to make suitable arrangements. I should imagine Erika located Gunter in much the same way."

"Mr. Gebhardt's murder is our fault then, isn't

it?'' Michael murmured, his face ashen. ''Kari's father died because our research called her attention to him.''

''Don't blame yourselves,'' Moise Rosenthal said, speaking for the first time since Avram had begun his narrative. ''Gunter Gebhardt died because the neo-Nazis are trying to build an entrance ramp to the information superhighway. It's illegal for them to sell books denying the reality of the Holocaust, and the existence of the death camps. Instead, they're setting up a complicated computer network they plan to use to spread their propaganda. To do that, they need money.''

''We've been convinced for some time that Erika wasn't acting entirely on her own. For one thing, most former Eastern bloc workers don't have enough money to do the kind of traveling she does. They just don't have the wherewithal to pay for tickets. There's also the matter of navigating a complicated bureaucratic maze in order to secure the proper exit papers and visas.

''I personally am convinced that Erika Schmidt is working for one of these neo-Nazi entities, although we're not yet sure which one. They're providing seed money and helping her cut through red tape. In exchange, once the missing gold is found, they'll be reimbursed for their up-front expenses, then they'll split the profits with Erika.''

Michael Morris fidgeted in his chair. ''What am I going to tell Kari?'' he said. ''Here's her father, an innocent man and . . .''

''I wouldn't be so sure about the innocent part,'' Moise cautioned. ''For years Gunter Gebhardt has been involved in a joint venture with someone in

Vladivostok. I believe he went into it solely in order to establish a cover that would allow him to smuggle his father's gold out from behind the iron curtain.''

Moise Rosenthal sat back in his chair. He looked at Sue and me and smiled as if to say it was our turn. Now that he had told us what they knew, I believe he expected us to return the favor. Unfortunately, I wasn't in any mood for show-and-tell. Impeccable manners to the contrary, I still had a feeling Moise and Avram were playing us for fools. They had only told us as much as it suited them to tell. One important oversight was the fact that so far they hadn't mentioned a word about the toy soldiers they had bought from Else Gebhardt.

I stood up. ''Excuse me for a moment, would you?''

Moise nodded graciously. I made my way to the nearest pay phone and punched in the directory-assistance number for eastern Washington.

''What city, please?'' the operator asked.

''Yakima,'' I answered. ''I'm looking for someone named Hurtado. First name Sergio.''

Within moments I was speaking to Lorenzo Hurtado himself. I didn't beat around the bush. ''Tell me something, Lorenzo,'' I said. ''Was Gunter Gebhardt fishing or smuggling?''

''I am not a smuggler,'' Lorenzo answered. ''I am an honest man. So is my cousin. We worked hard for Señor Gebhardt. We caught the fish. We cleaned them. We unloaded them onto the ships.''

''What ships?''

"The Russian ships. American ships can't go into Russian ports."

"When you unloaded the fish, did you take anything on board?"

"Only food and supplies. Just enough to get back home. Señor Gebhardt would ship some spare parts and tools over ahead of time, so if anything broke while we were out, we'd have replacements. He said things they made in Russia weren't any good. He only wanted American."

"He didn't load on anything else?"

"Nothing else."

If Lorenzo was telling the truth, that pretty much blew the smuggling theory. Frustrated, I returned to the restaurant where the plates and dishes had given way to brandy snifters and cups and saucers.

"Look," I said impatiently. "Let's not play games. I know where you two were this afternoon. I know what you did. When did you figure out that those soldiers in Gunter Gebhardt's basement were made out of gold? Was it before or after you lied your way into Else Gebhardt's house to buy them?"

For a moment, there was dead silence around the table, then Moise said, "Those soldiers aren't gold, Detective Beaumont. You can check them yourself. They're made out of some other metal. Lead, maybe."

The soldiers weren't gold? There went my latest pet theory, shot straight to hell!

"Where is the damn gold then?" I demanded. "If Gunter didn't use it to make the soldiers, what the hell did he do with it?"

A tweak of amusement turned up the corners of Avram Steinman's mouth, wrinkling the corners of his eyes and twisting his face into a wry grin. "That, Detective Beaumont," he replied, "is what we were hoping you could tell us."

There was some stiff small talk after that. Moise and Avram were looking for information that neither Sue nor I was prepared to share.

I skipped the brandy. While drinking my second cup of coffee, I caught Michael Morris checking his watch three different times. Obviously, he had an important previous engagement. Our visit with Moise Rosenthal and Avram Steinman was making him late.

I passed on the waiter's offer of a third cup. I made one abortive attempt to pick up the tab, but Moise waved that aside, telling me it was handled on a direct-billing basis. Thank you, Simon Wiesenthal. Sue, Michael, and I made our joint exit a few minutes later. Because it was cold outside, we stood just inside the entrance while a pair of attendants brought around the cars.

"Do you think those two guys are really on the level?" Sue asked.

"Up to a point," I answered, "but I wouldn't trust them any farther than I can throw them."

"What about old man Gebhardt? Is he alive or dead?"

"Good question," I replied. "It's a crap-shoot either way. If I were you, I wouldn't bet any money one way or the other."

My 928 is always popular when it comes to the young men who work valet-parking concessions. Naturally, the Guard-red Porsche appeared in the hotel driveway long before Sue Danielson's battle-weary Ford Escort. It's possible the parking personnel at the Sorrento might have frowned on handling such lowbrow transportation, but Sue's considerable display of well-turned calf and thigh kept the car jockeys from making snide comments about her car. They did, however, feel free to comment on her looks.

Sue was fully capable of handling herself. She simply ignored their admiring but verging-on-rude leers. Rather than challenge them on it, she merely got in the car and drove away, stiffing the car jockeys out of their expected tip. When Michael Morris and I drove away, one attendant was busy griping to the other about how come she did that. I could have told him, but there are some things in life guys need to be smart enough to figure out for themselves.

Once Michael and I started down Madison, I caught him stealing yet another surreptitious glance at his watch.

"What have you got," I asked, "a hot date?"

He shook his head. "I'm worried about Kari," he said.

"What about her?"

"My mother didn't invite Kari to dinner tonight. She said that under the circumstances, with Mr. Gebhardt dead, she was sure Kari wouldn't want to accept a dinner invitation. The truth is, Mom doesn't like Kari at all. That was just an excuse not to have her over. But I told Kari I'd come over to her place right after dinner. Now I'm worried about showing up so late."

"Ten-thirty isn't all that late," I reassured him.

"As soon as I get you back to your car, you can be at Kari's house in a matter of minutes. There's hardly any traffic this time of night."

Michael's car, a bright blue Geo Storm, was parked on Cherry just east of Third. He was in such a hurry to get where he was going that he leaped out of the Porsche while it was still rolling. He took off without so much as a wave or a thank-you. It's a wonder he didn't break his leg.

Such is love, I thought, watching him scramble into the car, start it, and peel out of the parking place. Love, youth, and raging hormones.

As the pair of bright red taillights sped up Third Avenue, I hoped he'd pay attention to his driving.

It would be too bad if some hard-nosed traffic cop pulled the poor kid over and gave him a ticket, I thought, not because Michael was screwed up on booze or drugs, but because he was an inattentive, lovesick swain.

23

The first few sprinkles of rain dotted the windshield as I headed for Belltown Terrace. Unlike Michael Morris, I could afford to drive at a far more leisurely pace. As I made my way through the broad, flat streets of the Denny Regrade, I was thinking about the few housekeeping chores—washing sheets, remaking the guest-room bed, putting out clean towels—that I needed to handle in advance of Ralph Ames' scheduled arrival the next afternoon.

In fact, I was just putting the load of soiled sheets in my apartment-sized stacked washer/dryer when the phone rang. It was 10:45.

"Detective Beaumont?"

I thought I recognized the voice, although it wasn't entirely steady. "Michael?" I asked. "Is that you? Is something wrong?"

"I'm not sure, but maybe," he answered. "Nobody's here."

"At Kari's house? Maybe they went out," I suggested with reasoned calm calculated to neutralize the rising panic in his voice. "To a friend's house for the evening, or maybe to ' visit a relative."

"Kari said she'd be home all night long," Michael countered. "She said for me to come over whenever I finished up with dinner. But there aren't any lights on anywhere in the house. I tried all the doors, both front and back. Nobody answered." That didn't sound good, even to me. My stomach gave a sharp lurch. "Where are you calling me from?"

"From the house across the street," Michael answered. "Talking to the lady here is what got me so upset."

There was only one house directly across the street from Else Gebhardt's. I happened to know that one belonged to June and John Miller. "What did the lady say?" I asked.

"That her dog was barking like crazy earlier this afternoon. She said there was a big truck parked in the driveway at Kari's house, and that it was backed up all the way to the garage door. She said there were people with dollies carrying stuff out of the house and loading it into the truck."

"Put June Miller on the phone," I said.

"Who's that?" Michael asked.

"June. The lady who lives there."

Michael turned away from the phone. I heard him asking a question, then he came back on the line. "You aren't even here. How did you know her name?" he asked.

"Never mind. Just put her on the phone."

June Miller came on the line a moment later. "This is Detective Beaumont," I said. "What's going on?"

"I'm not sure. I was downstairs with Brett when

Barney started barking his head off. I heard him outside. I tried to get him to shut up or come inside, but he wouldn't stop, and he wouldn't come in either. Barney's terribly nearsighted. I think he saw this big thing sitting there and couldn't figure out what it was. He was so agitated, I was afraid he'd go out of the yard even with his collar working. Finally, I went out to get him. That's when I saw them loading the truck. That's what all the fuss was about—loading a truck.''

''What kind of truck?''

''One of those big rental ones. It starts with an *R*.''

''Ryder? Rollins?''

''Rollins. That's it.''

''You said someone was loading a truck. Who? And could you tell what they were loading?''

''Not really. I only saw two men, although there might have been more.''

''What did they look like?''

''One was older. And then there was a younger one—a middle-aged man, balding, but with reddish hair. And whatever it was they were loading, it must have been heavy. They were using a dolly. You know, the kind of thing appliance-delivery guys use when they're unloading washers and dryers and refrigerators.''

Balding, with reddish hair. That sounded all too familiar.

''Shit!'' I started to say, but then I cut it off and turned it into a discreet cough.

''Excuse me?'' June Miller said. ''Did you say something?''

If I had spoken them aloud, the string of epithets roaring around in my head would have burned June Miller's ears. Whatever was happening, my friend Alan Torvoldsen—good old Champagne Al—was in on it up to his eyeballs. God *damn* it! And I never saw it coming, not at all.

I knew good and well it was too damn early for Else Gebhardt's moving sale, so there could be only one thing that was being spirited out of Else Gebhardt's house. It had to be the gold—all those missing gold teeth from Sobibor.

"I didn't say a thing," I said, coughing again for good measure. "Could you tell exactly what they were loading?"

"Not really, and I didn't want to stare," June Miller said.

"What time did all this happen?"

When I came home and started doing the laundry and household chores, I had slipped out of my clothes and into a heavy-duty terry-cloth robe. Now, though, holding the phone to my ear with one shoulder, I started trying to dress again—clumsily pulling on a pair of Dockers and slipping into my shoes.

"It wasn't dark yet, but it was getting close when Barney started kicking up the fuss," June answered. "That must have been around four or so. And I think I heard the truck engine start up again right around the time I was putting dinner on the table. That would have been a little before seven."

Damn. That meant they had almost a four-hour head start on us. They could be almost anywhere in that length of time. They could be almost through Portland if they had headed South down I-5 or two thirds of the way to Spokane on I-90, or across the international border into Canada, or well on their way to Neah Bay.

"Okay, June," I said, trying to keep a handle on the anger and frustration in my voice. "Thanks a lot. Put Michael back on the phone for a minute, would you?"

A shaky Michael Morris came back on the line. "What do you think?"

He didn't want to hear what I was thinking. "Listen," I said urgently, "and do exactly as I say. As soon as I get off the line with you, I'm going to dial nine-one-one and send a squad car over there. You stay right where you are until one of the officers comes to get you. Under no circumstances are you to go anywhere near Kari's house until I give you the go-ahead. Is that clear?"

"Yes," Michael answered.

"You didn't touch anything while you were over there, did you?"

"Only the doorknobs. To see if they were locked." He paused. "What do you think they'll find?" he asked softly.

By now I feared the worst, but there was no point in telling Michael Morris that. He was scared enough already. On the other hand, I felt morally obliged to give him some advance warning.

"I don't know," I said.

But by now Michael had some idea what we were up against. "It could be real bad, couldn't it?" he said hollowly.

"Yes," I said. "It could. I've got to go, Michael. Remember, you stay put."

"Okay," he said. "I understand. How soon will you be here?"

"As soon as I can," I said. "But I have to make one stop along the way."

One stop. One goddamned stop!

I have no memory of racing into the rest of my clothes, of putting on my shoulder holster, or of fastening my backup ankle holster under my pant leg. I waited until I was out of Belltown Terrace's underground parking garage before I used my cellular phone.

"This is nine-one-one," the lady at the Com Center said. "What are you reporting?"

"This is Detective Beaumont with the Seattle P.D.," I said. "And I wish to God I knew what I was reporting."

I gave her the information I had as quickly and concisely as I could. The operator could have taken the same view I did with Michael initially— that Else and Kari Gebhardt were merely spending the evening with relatives or friends—but something about the urgency in my tone of voice must have convinced her that an innocent, happy ending was most unlikely.

It felt like it took damn near forever for me to drive from Belltown Terrace out to the end of Fishermen's Terminal. I left the Porsche idling in the fire lane and raced on down the slick, timbered dock, hoping against hope that I was wrong about Alan Torvoldsen; praying that *One Day at a Time* would be snugged up against its moorings the way it belonged.

But it wasn't there. The spot where Alan Torvoldsen's old scow had been berthed was empty.

There was nothing there but cold black water reflecting back the sickly yellowish glow of the overhead lights.

"Damn!" I raged.

Sick at heart, I turned and fled back down the dock through what was fast becoming a cold, steady downpour. I barely felt the rain that instantly soaked into my clothing.

"Damn!" was all I could say. "Damn! Damn! Damn!"

I was the one who had gone looking for Alan Torvoldsen earlier that afternoon. I alone had asked him—no, almost begged him—to go over to Blue Ridge and look after Else Gebhardt. Asked *him* to look after her! Jesus Christ. I had invited the damn fox right into the henhouse, handed him a napkin to tie around his neck, passed him a knife and fork, and told him to help himself. Which he had.

Back in the Porsche, I rammed it into gear and skidded my way out of the fire lane and back toward the parking lot. Heading back out of the terminal, I spotted the Rollins truck parked discreetly between net sheds three and four.

I stopped the car, got out, and examined the truck without touching it. The vehicle was parked and locked with the keys still in the ignition. Whoever had rented that truck had no intention of returning for it. If he had, he would have taken the single set of keys with him.

Quickly jotting down the license number, I phoned it in. "Run a check on this one," I told the Records clerk who answered the phone. "Wake up whoever you have to wake up to do it, but I want to know the name of the person who rented that vehicle. In the meantime, I want it impounded ASAP!''

There was always a chance I was wrong and had just impounded some innocent bystander's vehicle. Under the circumstances, however, it was a risk I was willing to take.

I have no idea why the Ballard Bridge was open at that hour of the night. They were most likely testing the drawspan, because there wasn't a boat of any kind in sight. Naturally, I got stuck in the traffic backup while the bridge went up and slowly, ever so slowly, came back down.

The unavoidable stop gave me enough time to call Sue Danielson, break into yet another one of Jared's endless phone calls, and bring her up-to-speed. She said she would get dressed again and meet me at Else's house as soon as she could. I was just ending the call to her when the drawbridge finally returned to its original position, and traffic began to move once more.

Much as I complain about advanced technology, computers do have something to offer, especially in the world of law enforcement. The call on the truck from Records came back long before I ever made it to Culpeper Court.

Records had tracked down and spoken to the manager from the truck-leasing company, who said he didn't have to go into his office to check the name on the rental agreement. He remembered the woman all too well because she had given him and his people a hell of a hard time in the course of making the transaction. She was a foreigner who had rented the truck with an International as well as a German driver's license.

And her name was Erika Weber Schmidt.

Damn! And double damn.

24

As I drove down Greenbrier to Culpeper Court, the entire neighborhood was lit up by the pulsing blue lights of three different blue-and-white squad cars.

Dreading what might be waiting to be discovered inside the house, I parked the Porsche across the street at June and John Miller's house. As I hurried up Else Gebhardt's driveway, a young uniformed patrol officer hustled out of the house to meet me.

"I'm Detective Beaumont," I told her, flashing my badge. "What did you find?"

"Absolutely nothing," she answered. "Nobody's home, but there's no sign of trouble, either. What did you think we'd find?"

Prepared for the worst possible carnage, I now felt weak with relief. "No sign of a struggle?" I repeated lamely.

"None. Captain Riley's on the radio and mad as hell. He wants to know what you think is going on."

I'll just bet he did. And if my fears proved groundless, he was going to be a whole lot madder than he was right then.

"Just let me take a look for myself," I told her. "As soon as I figure out what's gone down, I'll let you know, so you can pass the word. In the meantime, ask him to put a car on an abandoned Rollins truck parked between net sheds three and four down at Fishermen's Terminal. I don't want anyone near that vehicle until the crime lab has a chance to give it a good going-over." I handed over the scribbled license-plate number.

While the officer hurried off to report to her captain, I walked into Else Gebhardt's house. From the moment I had realized *One Day at a Time* was gone, I had been overwhelmed with the weight of my own culpability. But Else's clean and orderly house added something more to the mix.

I don't happen to be one of those gullible people who believes in self-bending forks or miraculously mended watches, and I'm certainly not well versed in the intricacies of ESP. But a sense of hopeless dread filled me as I wandered from room to room. It grew infinitely worse when I stepped into the bedroom that evidently belonged to Else Gebhardt's mother. Inge Didricksen's walker was there, parked beside the bed. But the old lady was nowhere in sight.

As soon as I saw the walker and knew that Inge was gone, too, I realized that all three of them—the old woman, her daughter, and her granddaughter—were missing, even though, in the world of law enforcement, no one enters the ranks of officially missing persons until after a full twenty-four hours have elapsed.

The last part of the house to search was the

basement. Not only was the outside door unlocked, it was open. When I started down the dimly lit stairs, I almost broke my neck. The two railroad ties that had once been out of the way on either side of the staircase now had been moved into the center part of the risers. I slipped and would have fallen if I hadn't managed to catch myself on the banister.

Looking back up the stairway, I saw a twelve-volt battery tucked into the space behind the door. It was connected to an electric winch. It resembled the kind of setup they sometimes mount on the front bumpers of off-road vehicles.

As soon as I saw the winch, I finally understood the railroad ties as well. They were all part of a simple hoist system Gunter Gebhardt must have used to raise and lower equipment into and out of the basement.

The lights were already on. I descended the stairs and stood still for a moment, getting my bearings. I realized almost at once that something about that long, narrow room was different than it had been when I visited it the first time. At first I couldn't tell exactly what it was, but the room seemed larger somehow, more spacious, emptier. But then it's always easier to see what's there in front of your eyes than it is to remember something that was there once but isn't any longer.

One thing that made the room seem bigger was the missing soldiers. That was no surprise. Else had told me about selling them. The lights glared off the bare shelves in the bank of curio cases. The bright fluorescent glow on stark white walls gave the place an abandoned, sterile look. But it was more than just the soldiers. Something else was missing as well.

And that's when I realized what it was. The tools were gone from the shelves at the opposite end of the room. All of them. Every last one. Had Else sold them, too?

And then I understood. Of course. How could I have been so stupid? The tools. Lorenzo had said something about tools, about how they'd brought tools and supplies home with them on board the fishing boat. Tools they'd picked up from Gunter's joint-venture partner.

A wave of gooseflesh swept up my legs when I finally realized the awful truth about all those neatly organized tools that had once been stacked, row upon row, in Gunter Gebhardt's impossibly clean basement.

How many gold teeth did it take to make a vise? I wondered, feeling almost sick to my stomach. Or a sledge hammer? Or a solid-gold wrench? And at a rate of five thousand people a day, how many murderous Sobibor days had it taken to accumulate all the gold hidden in Gunter's hoard of tools.

I said I'm not psychic, and I'm not claustrophobic, either, but suddenly it seemed as though the walls of the basement were closing in on me. Fighting back nausea, I spun around and headed back toward the stairs. And that's when I realized what else was missing.

The engine. The one at the bottom of the stairs—the one I had stumbled over when Else had brought Sue and me down to show us the soldiers. At the time, I had thought it to be some kind of auxiliary power generator. No doubt it was made of gold as well.

Appalled, I rumbled up the stairs and out the back door into the cool comfort of the cold, wet air. I was standing there with my chest heaving when Michael Morris and June Miller found me. Michael hadn't been wearing a jacket when I last saw him, but he was now. It must have belonged to John Miller, because it came almost to the young man's knees.

"What's happened in there?" Michael asked me, his face stark with alarm and worry. "Nobody will tell me anything."

"Nothing," I said.

"What do you mean, nothing?"

There was no sense in making things worse for him. "There's no sign of struggle in there, Michael. It's as though all three of them simply decided to go away for a while. They seem to have left in a very orderly manner. It's like they just stepped outside and locked the door."

"But they didn't do that," Michael objected. "I know Kari wouldn't leave voluntarily, not without calling me or leaving a message."

I turned to June. "When the truck was being loaded, did you see any sign of coercion?" I asked. "Anything to indicate that the people you saw were being forced to do something against their will?"

June Miller shook her head. "No," she said. "Not at all."

Of course not, I thought bitterly. Because Alan Damn Torvoldsen was in it up to his Norwegian eyebrows the whole time he was feeding me his line of pathetic bullshit about how Else Didriksen broke his heart by marrying someone else.

Sue Danielson's Escort showed up on the street, then pulled into the Millers' driveway directly behind the 928. She popped out wearing jeans and a bright yellow slicker. "You look like hell, Beau," she said as soon as she was close enough to catch a glimpse of my face. "What's going on?"

"The tools," I told her, leading her a little away from the others so we could speak privately. "Gunter Gebhardt's tools are gone from the basement."

"So?"

"The soldiers weren't made out of the missing Sobibor gold," I answered. "The tools were."

"Oh," Sue said.

"It looks like Erika Weber Schmidt found herself an accomplice," I added. "Unfortunately his name is Alan Torvoldsen. They're out on his boat right this minute. I'm afraid Else and Kari Gebhardt and Inge Didriksen are out there with them."

Sue frowned. "What makes you think that?"

"Because earlier this afternoon I asked Alan to come over here and look after Else for me. After that fiasco with Moise and Avram walking away with the soldiers, I was worried someone else might try to pull a fast one. I asked Alan not to let any strangers into the house. I don't know how he kept from laughing in my face."

"How do you know for sure he's in on whatever's going on?" Sue asked.

"Because June Miller saw him loading the truck."

Sue Danielson glanced briefly in June Miller's direction and then back at me. "You know, none of this is your fault," she said.

It irked me that I was that transparent, that she could so easily grasp exactly what was going on with me. "The hell it isn't," I responded. "If I had just let things alone . . ." I gave up. There was no point in saying anything more.

By then two of the three squad cars had already left the Gebhardt place. Only two officers were left, one of whom was the young woman I'd spoken to earlier. I was less than eager to chat with either her or with her partner. I knew they were both destined to spend most of the rest of their shift filling out a mountain of paper.

Not that it would do any good. They had broken into Else's Gebhardt's house without a warrant, based on my suspicion that something was amiss, but they had discovered no solid evidence to back up my claim. Consequently, no amount of explaining to Captain Riley would ever square what they had done. He would blame them. They would pass the buck and blame me.

I would live or die depending on whether or not Else Gebhardt took exception to their relatively harmless act of breaking and entering. If she filed a complaint, then there'd be the devil to pay down at Seattle P.D. And the responsibility would fall squarely where it belonged—on me.

A man came walking up to us. He was tall, stoop-shouldered, wearing glasses and a trench coat. "I'm John Miller," he said, offering his hand. "June's taken that poor young man and gone inside to make cocoa. She wanted me to ask you inside. It's cold and wet out here.''

My mother reserved her highest criticism for those she considered too stupid to live. They were always the ones who were ''too dumb to come in out of the rain.'' Which is exactly how stupid her middle-aged son was being right then.

The words John Miller used—''cold and wet''—amounted to gross understatement. A gusting wind drove splinters of icy raindrops into our faces and clothing. And there I stood in the Gebhardts' driveway on Culpeper Court with nothing at all on over my soaking sports jacket. I had failed to notice that I was wet to the skin and shivering.

With John Miller leading the way, we migrated across the street to a house with evidence of recent construction and relandscaping. We entered by walking past what architects are fond of calling a ''water feature.'' The babble of running water burbling noisily over river rocks may sound wonderful on a hot summer's afternoon, but on a cold, wet winter's evening, it only made me that much colder.

Inside the house, John introduced Sue and me to a grizzled, lop-eared black-and-white terrier named Barney. The dog eased over against Sue to demand some attention and petting while John offered me a stack of towels and led me to a bathroom that was fully stocked with a six-year-old's complement of rubber toys.

After toweling myself as dry as possible, I returned to the living room to find John sitting beside the gas-burning fireplace and quizzing Sue about what it was like to be a single parent as well as a police officer. I found it intriguing that he was more interested in that than he was in the details of whatever untoward events had occurred across the street. Meantime, June had taken Michael Morris into the kitchen, where she was busily making a pot of cocoa and administering a dose of TLC to a young man very much in need of both.

I heard her telling him in a calm, soothing voice that he shouldn't worry, that everything was going to be fine. Even though I didn't agree with her—everything wasn't going to be fine—I still gave the woman credit for trying. Michael Morris was almost frantic with worry.

Like somebody else I knew, he was dealing with his own damning set of "if onlys." If only he had insisted that his mother invite Kari over to dinner; if only he had come to Blue Ridge earlier in the evening; if only; if only; if only. *Ad infinitum.*

I felt like telling him he didn't have a corner on the guilt market. Deeply mired in my own storm of self-recrimination, I almost missed Sue Danielson's shrewd suggestion when she broke off her polite conversation with John Miller and abruptly changed the subject back to the case at hand.

"How long ago did they clear the locks?" she asked.

"Why the hell didn't I think of that?" I demanded.

Lake Washington is big, but not big enough to hide a commercial fishing boat loaded with gold bullion disguised as a handyman's garageful of tools. Shilshole Bay, backed first by Puget Sound and by the open ocean far beyond that, is less than two miles from Fishermen's Terminal. Two miles northwest and, at low tide, twenty-seven feet lower.

To get to one from the other, boats have to pass through Salmon Bay and the Hiram M. Chittenden Locks. As Heather Peters told me once in an elegantly simple but apt description, locks are nothing but elevators for boats. And that's true. When heading out to sea, boats come into the lock area from Salmon Bay and then tie up at a pier. When the lock attendants let the water out, the effect is similar to pulling the plug in a bathtub. The water level goes down, and so do any boats inside the lock. When the operation is over, the boats are lower than they were when they started.

In the summer or during peak fishing and boating seasons when hundreds of boats come and go through the locks each day, it would be virtually impossible to learn whether or not a particular boat had cleared the locks. But this was late fall, and traffic was down. Most boaters, recreational and commercial alike, were content to spend the winter months landlocked and couch-bound in front of their glowing television sets.

Not only was it winter, it was night as well. Nighttime traffic on the locks would be even lighter than during the day. In addition, Alan Torvoldsen's *One Day at a Time* was one disreputable-looking tub. Old T-class army lighters, born again and refitted as longliners, aren't all that common in the halibut fishery. If a vessel like that had passed through the locks sometime between 9:00

P.M. and midnight, someone—most likely one of the dockside attendants—was bound to remember.

I borrowed the Millers' nearest phone and placed a call to the Lockmaster. It rang for a long time with no answer. Finally, when I was almost ready to give up, someone came on the line. "Locks," he said.

"This is Detective J. P. Beaumont," I said. "Seattle P.D. We've got an emergency here. I want you to hold all traffic until we get there. It should only take ten minutes or so."

"No problem," the man returned. "We've got almost a half-hour wait right now. What's your name again?"

"Beaumont. Detective J. P. Beaumont."

"You come ahead on down. I'll have someone go over and unlock the gate."

As Sue and I stood up and headed for the door, June Miller walked into the living room carrying a tray loaded with cups full of steaming cocoa. She looked disappointed. "Don't you want to drink some of this before you go?" she asked.

I was grateful when Sue answered for us both. "I'm sorry, we just realized there's something we need to check right away."

But June Miller wasn't about to take no for an answer. "I'll pour it into paper cups for you," she said. "That way you can take it with you. And wouldn't you like to borrow one of John's jackets?" she said to me. "Your clothes are still wet."

At Sue's insistence, I accepted the traveling cup of cocoa with good grace, but I turned down the use of a borrowed coat. After all, wimps wear coats. Cool macho dudes don't.

"No thanks," I said, "I'll be fine."

Famous last words, of course, but I was too intent on noodling out where Alan Torvoldsen might be going to bother with the mundane issue of whether or not to wear a coat. At the time, it didn't seem all that important.

Out in the driveway, Sue and I settled on using one vehicle—mine. We had to back her Escort out of the way in order to get to the 928, but minutes later, properly belted into the Porsche, we were racing back down Fifteenth from Blue Ridge toward the locks. I drove, while Sue sipped quietly on her cocoa for the better part of a mile.

"When you come out of the locks into Shilshole Bay, you only have two choices," she said thoughtfully. "You either have to go north or south, right or left. Which do you think he'd take?"

"It depends on what he wants to accomplish," I answered. "If he wants to head for the open sea, then he has to head north along the shipping lanes and out through the Strait of Juan de Fuca. Every ship out there has an American pilot who comes on board at Port Angeles, and all those ships are in constant radio contact with Marine Traffic Control. Someone would be bound to see them."

"What about south of here?" Sue Danielson asked.

"There's lots less shipping traffic," I answered. "If they wanted to hide out until the heat let up a little or to dock somewhere long enough to refit the *One Day* so she wasn't quite so readily recognizable, they might head south. There must be hundreds of places tucked away in among the islands between here and Olympia at the south end of Puget Sound where a boat could duck in and disappear. Most of those sheltered bays and coves have summer cabins built near them, but in the winter they're pretty much deserted."

By then we were at the locks. We parked in an almost deserted lot. As promised, the gate was closed but unlocked. We made our way into the office, where we found the two on-duty attendants sipping coffee, complaining about the weather, and huddling next to a wall heater to stay warm.

"What can we do for you?" one asked.

The speaker's disembodied voice came through the kind of synthesizer they use on people who've lost a larynx to throat cancer. That must not have made much of an impression on him, however, since he and his colleague were both still smoking. Not only did that defy the rules of good sense, but it was most likely against the law as well. Smoking in the workplace is very much against the rules in Seattle, a place that prides itself on being the secondhand-smoke conscience of the world.

We showed the two men our badges, but they seemed singularly unimpressed. "You could help us by letting us know whether or not a fishing vessel named *One Day at a Time* came through the locks earlier tonight," I said.

The man with the tinny voice shrugged his shoulders. "Don't bother asking me," he said. "How about it, Hank? You were taking lines tonight. Do you remember a boat by that name or not?"

"Not many boats through here tonight," Hank answered, sucking on his smoke. "What's it look like?"

"It's an old T-class freighter."

Hank nodded sagely. "Oh, yeah," he said. "That one. Ugly as sin. Came through long about ten or so."

"Who was on it?" I asked. "Did you see anybody?"

"One guy. Red hair. Going a little bald. He was handling all the lines himself. Really had to scramble."

"Did you see anyone else on board?"

Hank shook his head. "Nope," he said. "Not a soul. Should I have?"

"No," I answered. "I was hoping is all."

"So you're cops," Voice Box said, now mulling the significance of our badges, which had long since been put away. "What's this guy done? Killed somebody or something? How come you're looking for him?"

"Stolen goods," Sue answered quickly, speaking up before I made a botch of it.

Hank laughed outright at that, ending with a rattly, cigarette-induced cough. "Dumb bastard," he said. "Pro'ly stole that godawful boat itself, come to think of it. While he was tying up, I tried to tell him there's a front blowing in from across Vancouver Island. Small-craft advisories. Gale-force winds. But you know those stubborn damn fishermen. 'Been out in lots worse than this,' he tells me."

The hell he has, I thought angrily. Alan Torvoldsen might have been out in some pretty rough seas in his time, but I doubted he'd been in this much hot water.

25

By three o'clock Sunday morning, I was seeing the Seattle Police Department's bureaucratic inaction in action, which is to say, nothing was happening. For one thing, the shit had already hit the officialdom fan over what was now being called the "Culpeper Court break-in." The brass was worried about long-term repercussions from the warrantless search. What is sometimes overlooked down in the south end's Rainier Valley can provoke a firestorm of reaction and protest when it happens elsewhere in the city. It's been my experience that nothing moves slower than a publicity-shy bureaucracy.

What seemed obvious to me—that Else and Kari Gebhardt along with Inge Didriksen were not only missing but also in grave danger—totally eluded the comprehension of Seattle P.D.'s night-time supervisors. One at a time, Sue and I argued our case across desks and up the chain of command. Eventually, so tired we could barely hold our heads up, we landed in the office of the department's night-watch commander, Major John Gray.

Major Gray, whom I had sometimes heard referred to as Major Grim, is a night owl who has

spent years toiling on Seattle P.D.'s graveyard
shift. Although he may be a nice enough guy, I
had heard persistent, ongoing rumors that he was
sometimes a little slow on the uptake. After five
minutes of Sue's and my early-morning session
with the man, I was inclined to agree with that
last assessment.

Although the jigs and jags of the story seemed
simple and straightforward enough to me, Major
Gray was totally incapable of making the necessary and critical connections between other aspects
of the case and the three missing women.

He failed to see any significance in the set of
miniature soldiers that had once been thought to
be made of gold but that had, on examination,
turned out to be made of something else. And he
saw no possible correlation between the soldiers
and Gunter Gebhardt's assortment of tools, which,
although they looked ordinary enough, might very
well turn out to be made of gold. The fact that the
tools were now also unaccountably missing didn't
exactly make Major Gray's day. And he howled
at my theory that this entire debacle might possibly have its origins in a failed romance from Ballard High School some thirty years earlier.

"Wait a minute here," he said. "Are you trying
to tell me that this Norwegian fisherman, Alan
what's-his-name Torvoldsen, got mixed up in all
this because a Ballard girl name Else threw him
over for somebody else way back in the sixties?
Come on, Beau. Get real. You sound more like a
hopeless romantic than a homicide cop."

Maybe it did sound a little improbable. "You
can laugh all you want to, Major Gray," I said,

"but I'm telling you what I believe to be true. Those three missing women are in danger. They're out on a boat with a man who, one way or the other, is involved in the plot surrounding Gunter Gebhardt's murder. Not only that, I have reason to believe this same man is also connected to a fatal house fire up on Camano Island."

"Just for argument's sake," Major Gray said, "let's suppose that's all true. What do you want me to do about it?"

"I want to launch a search. The boat is capable of traveling at a rate of eight to ten knots. The longer we delay, the harder it's going to be to find them."

Major Gray rubbed his chin. Any trained salesman in the world will tell you that's a bad sign.

He said, "Okay, Detective Beaumont, let me play this whole scenario back to you just the way you gave it to me, and you tell me how it sounds. Three women who may or may not be missing and who may or may not have been kidnapped, are possibly—not definitely, but possibly—out on a boat in Puget Sound, traveling in some unspecified direction with an exboyfriend of one of the three women, a guy she jilted a mere thirty years ago. Does this sound a little fishy to you?"

I was beginning to wonder how come anybody ever called the night-watch commander Major Grim instead of Major Laugh-a-Minute. He sounded more like an off-the-wall stand-up comedian from one of those comedy joints down in Pioneer Square.

Major Gray paused as if waiting for me to make some comment, but I was smart enough not to fall

into the trap. Especially not, considering that a
rarely seen expression—an actual grin—was beginning to play around the turned-down corners of
Major Grim's dour mouth.

"And now it gets better," he continued, clearly
enjoying himself. "Although no one else besides
the captain—not a single passenger—was ever
seen on the aforementioned vessel when it cleared
the locks, I'm still supposed to believe that, along
with the three missing women, there are possibly
two other people on board as well, people who
are either this Torvoldsen character's fellow con-
spirators or the Gebhardt woman's fellow victims.
Take your pick.

"One of the invisible extra people is supposedly
a presumed Nazi war criminal who's been missing
for fifty-some years. The other is an unemployed
secret agent from East Germany, a country that no
longer exists."

"It was raining," I argued feebly. "If the passengers were all inside the boat, nobody would
have seen them." Despite that puny attempt at
sidetracking him, I already knew it was hopeless.
By then Major Gray was having far too good a
time.

"Based on all the above—most of which is
solely on your say-so and conjecture—I'm expected to alert the media, call in the Coast
Guard—maybe even the National Guard—and in-
stitute an air-and-ground search."

"An air-and-sea search," I corrected.

"Whatever," Major Gray shook his head. "You
can call it any kind of a search you damn well
please, Detective Beaumont, but I'm telling you,

it ain't a-gonna happen. Not on my watch. Because you've got nothing here to justify it except a few wild figments of your overly active imagination.

"The kind of search-and-rescue operation you want would necessarily cover a large geographical area. Do you have any idea what that would cost? Puget Sound isn't exactly a damn bathtub. We're talking an arm and a leg here—thousands of dollars an hour. That's a lot of cash. We don't happen to have that kind of money sitting around loose in some petty-cash drawer, you know. The only person who could authorize that kind of outlay is the chief himself. I'm sure as hell not calling him in on this. And neither are you. Do I make myself clear?"

"Yes, sir. Loud and clear."

Major Gray shook his head. "Now get out of here, you two. Go home and get some rest. Sleep it off."

Without another word, Sue and I stood up and started toward the door. "Detective Danielson," Major Gray called after us, "if you have any influence on your partner here, you might encourage him to turn off the boob tube. I think he must be watching too many of those World-War-Two era movies on the movie channel."

"What's the movie channel?" I grumbled to Sue when we were out in the hall with the door closed.

"It's on cable," she informed me. "Don't you get cable TV down in that high-flying condo of yours?"

"Who the hell has time to watch television?" I answered irritably.

Sue and I barely spoke as we rode down in the elevator. Once we hit the street level, we hurried to our cars and prepared to go our separate ways. We had picked up Sue's Escort after we left the locks, and both vehicles were parked on Third Avenue, one behind the other.

She stopped beside the Escort and stuck her key in the lock. "You did the best you could," she said, speaking to me over the roof of the car.

I knew she was trying to bolster my flagging spirits and make me feel better, but it didn't help. "It wasn't nearly good enough," I returned glumly. "I feel like the whole system chewed us up and spit us out."

"Maybe Major Gray is right and we're wrong," Sue suggested. "Maybe nothing did happen. Maybe Inge, Else, and Kari will show back up sometime later this morning with a perfectly reasonable explanation for where they've been and what they've been doing."

"You don't believe that," I said, "and neither do I. Erika Weber Schmidt plays for keeps. If anybody ever sees those three women again, they'll probably be as dead as Gunter Gebhardt."

Sue shook her head. "I hope not." She opened the door, started to get in, and then thought better of it. "Give it up for the night," she advised kindly, almost as an afterthought. "We're both too tired to do anything more right now, but call me in the morning. As soon as you wake up. We'll take another crack at it then."

As soon as she said it, I recognized she was

right. I was bone-tired, and she had to be every
bit as worn out as I was. Still, she had stuck with
me all night long; backed me up every futile, bureaucratic inch of the way.

"You've been a brick tonight, Detective Danielson," I said gratefully. "Most guys would have
given up and gone home long before this."

She gave me a wan but game grin. "We're partners, remember? Now go home and get some sleep,
and I will, too."

I did, and so did she. I hauled my weary ass
home, crawled out of my still partially damp
clothes, and heaved myself into a nice warm bed.
The clock radio came on at six-fifteen Sunday
morning, just as it does every morning.

It wasn't that I especially wanted to be up again
at that unreasonable hour. The truth is, my radio
comes on that way every morning. I can tinker
with it for a nap now and again, but I always reset
it. I live in fear of not remembering Sunday night
to reset it for Monday morning.

When the radio came on that Sunday morning,
I'd had so little sleep that I could barely open my
eyes and couldn't get my head screwed on straight.
Blind with fatigue, I got up and staggered for the
bathroom, thinking it was actually Monday.

For one thing, Paul Brendle, The KIRO radio traffic reporter, was in the air giving the helicopter-eye
view of a massive but totally unusual Sunday
morning traffic tie-up on Interstate 5 just north of
downtown Seattle.

Early that morning, a speeding southbound semi
had jackknifed on the rain-slicked pavement of the
Ship Canal Bridge. The truck had plowed through

the Jersey barrier at the south end of the bridge and had taken out two northbound vehicles. One of the wrecked cars, a sedan with one fatality and two seriously injured passengers inside it, had fallen from the northbound lanes into the middle of the express lanes some distance below, while the cab of the truck itself still dangled off the far edge of the raised roadway.

As a result, I-5 was closed to traffic. All lanes were shut down, including the two regular roadways as well as the express lanes. The Department of Transportation's Incident Response team was on the scene. Traffic had been diverted onto surface streets, creating a separate tangle all its own. According to the helicopter-based reporter, even with light weekend traffic volumes, things were a mess in downtown Seattle, and they were likely to remain so for some time—well into daylight hours.

My first thought was that none of this had anything to do with me. I headed back to bed, expecting to close my eyes and go back to sleep. Then the guy back in the studio said something to Paul Brendle to the effect that it sounded like a good day to be up in a helicopter rather than down on the ground. At the sound of those words, something clicked in the back of my head, and I sat bolt upright in bed.

For years, my connection to Paul Brendle—who broadcasts traffic information for the local CBS affiliate—had been exactly the same as that of most other Seattle-area radio listeners. His was a disembodied voice that came to us over the airwaves for several hours each morning and evening, waking us up in the morning—telling us which bridges were screwed up and what alternate routes might work when the one we were accustomed to using turned into an undeclared parking lot.

But my voice-only relationship with him had changed that previous spring when Alexis Downey had invited me to participate in the Seattle Repertory Theatre's first annual charity auction. Along with me, Paul and his wife, JoAnne, had been in attendance at the gala's inaugural event. Both feeling very much like fish out of water, Paul Brendle and I had somehow gravitated to one another and struck up a conversation.

We soon discovered a common bond—we were both moderately disturbed at the idea of being charity-auction cannon fodder. We hid out in a quiet corner of the crowded ballroom. Uncomfortable in my rented monkey suit, I looked to Paul for sympathy. He sighed and nodded, allowing as how he was far more comfortable in a flight jacket, but he advised me to do as he did—to go ahead and buy a tux that actually fit. I told him I'd think about it.

In the course of our few minutes' worth of conversation, the man had proudly told me a little about his company—Puget Sound Helicopters—and about how they had, only the week before, sent three of their twenty-five two-man helicopters up in the air to comb Vashon Island for a missing Alzheimer's patient who had wandered away from home. As I remembered, they had found the man, too, before the elements and hypothermia had a chance to get him.

Search and rescue! As my feet hit the floor,

my fingers were scrabbling in the nightstand table looking for the phone book. Maybe Seattle P.D. couldn't—or wouldn't—afford to spend money on mounting a search-and-rescue operation, but J. P. Beaumont, private citizen, sure as hell could.

I tend to be a slow learner, but gradually I've come to have an understanding about the value of having money. What's taken me more time than anything else is coming to the realization that it's mine now, and I'm free to spend it any damn way I please.

I found the number in the phone book and dialed. At Puget Sound Helicopters, a very polite young man answered the phone.

"I'd like to speak to Paul Brendle," I said.

"I'm sorry, sir. He's out of the office right now. Can I give him a message for you?"

"Yes, you can," I said. "My name's Beaumont, Detective J. P. Beaumont, with the Seattle Police Department."

"Does Mr. Brendle know you?"

"I believe so," I answered. "We met last spring at a charity auction. I need to speak to him as soon as possible regarding a search-and-rescue operation."

"You said detective," the young man responded. "Who are you with?"

"Seattle P.D. If my name doesn't ring a bell, tell him I'm the one who gave away the Bentley at the Seattle Rep auction."

"Do you already have the authorization form?" the young man asked.

"What authorization form?"

"A search-and-rescue requisition," the young

man explained patiently. "Our insurance requires that we have a signed requisition from the requesting agency in our hands before we can put a helicopter and pilot in the air."

"Seattle P.D. isn't authorizing this search," I told him.

"They aren't?" The man sounded confused. "But I thought you said . . . Who is, then?" he asked.

"I am. Me, personally."

"Mr. Beaumont," he said patronizingly, as though I were some kind of nut case, "these kinds of operations are very expensive. . . ."

"How expensive?" I cut in.

"How big an area do you want to search?"

"Puget Sound," I answered.

"That's a big place," he returned. "If we put ten aircraft up, we could pretty well cover the area in three or four hours. At a hundred sixty dollars an hour times four hours times ten aircraft, you're looking at sixty-four hundred dollars plus tax. We'd need a check for seven thousand dollars to launch that kind of operation."

"Do you take American Express?"

"Yes."

"Good. Have Mr. Brendle call me ASAP," I ordered, and followed that by rattling off my phone number. "By the way," I added, "tell him I'm prepared to pay for more than one four-hour shift if that proves necessary. And if I have to cough up overtime pay because it's Sunday? So be it. I'll spring for that, too."

"All right," he said, still sounding a little

guarded. "I'll try to patch Mr. Brendle through to you as soon as possible."

"You do that," I said.

I put down the phone and wondered how long it would take for him to call me back. There was a time in my life when spending seven thousand bucks at a whack would have been inconceivable. Fortunately, those times were past.

Money talks; bullshit walks. Isn't that how the saying goes?

If hiring a team of helicopters and pilots could save those three women's lives—if it wasn't already too late, that is—then a seven-thousand-dollar investment was money well spent. In fact, saving them would have been cheap at twice the price.

Because, after all, what had happened to them was my fault and my responsibility. I was the stupid damn fool who had sent Alan Torvoldsen up to Culpeper Court to look after Else and the others in the first place. And since the problem was all my doing, then it seemed reasonable that the solution should be mine as well.

After all, I thought. Fair is fair.

26.

Professional courtesy to say nothing of good manners dictated that I call Sue Danielson and invite her to come along on my proposed search-and-rescue operation with Puget Sound Helicopters. When she learned that Seattle P.D. wouldn't be paying the freight, she suggested the possibility of calling on the deep-pocket expense account of our friends from Wiesenthal.

My response to that suggestion was instant and negative. "Are you kidding? Absolutely not."

"So who's paying for it, then?"

"I am."

"The whole thing?"

There was a big difference between Sue Danielson's economic reality and my own. I didn't want to rub her nose in it. "It's not that big a deal," I said.

"Seven thousand dollars would be a big deal for me," she returned. "The bottom line is typical territorial homicide dick, isn't it? You'd rather foot the whole bill yourself instead of sharing the glory with somebody else."

Responsibility for Else and the others was what was driving me, not territorial imperative. I couldn't see trying to explain that to Sue Danielson, not right then.

"I'm sharing with you, aren't I?" I volleyed back. "Now cut the lecture, Sue. Are you coming or not?"

"Coming," she answered. "I'll meet you down at the department in twenty minutes."

"That's what you think," I said. "Have you been listening to the news?"

"You woke me up, remember?"

"There's been a bad wreck on I-Five near the Ship Canal Bridge. Whatever you do, don't try coming down the freeway."

"I never drive the freeway," she responded. "And if your car was in the same condition as mine is, you wouldn't either."

After further discussion, we agreed to meet at the Puget Sound Helicopter operations center at Boeing Field. That way, in case Sue did get tied up in traffic, I could go ahead and start the ball rolling without her.

It was dark but edging toward watery, overcast daylight as I wandered around the King County Airport at Boeing Field. It took two passes before I finally located the office, tucked in behind a massive, vine-covered wall. The person behind the reception desk was a young man wearing a white shirt and striped tie.

"Oh, Detective Beaumont," he said. "I'm Roger Hammersmith, Paul's assistant. Paul's still in the air. Would you care for a cup of coffee while you wait?"

At ten past seven, Hammersmith ushered me into a comfortable conference room. Settling in to wait, I noticed that the most striking piece of art was a framed print of a grinning groom carrying his wedding-gown-clad bride toward a waiting helicopter. The picture gave me cause to count my blessings. At least my daughter, Kelly, and my son-in law, Jeremy, hadn't required *that* kind of three-ring circus.

Hammersmith brought in two cups of coffee, one for himself and one for me. Armed with a stack of charts, he set about gathering the necessary information. "How long ago did this missing vessel clear the locks?" he asked.

"Between ten and eleven."

"How fast can they travel?"

"I'd guess eight to ten knots."

It was refreshing to deal with someone who took what I had to say at face value without segueing into a debate about whether or not J. P. Beaumont was off his rocker. Roger Hammersmith simply wanted to get the job done in the most expeditious fashion possible. When I told him that bit of news—about how long *One Day at a Time* had been under way—he sighed and pursed his lips.

"By the time we get our guys in the air—eight-thirty or so at the soonest—that boat could be all the way out to Neah Bay and Cape Flattery. Is it likely the skipper will head for the open seas?"

I nodded. "That's what I think."

"Why?"

I couldn't very well say, "Because he has a load of gold bullion on board and he's making a run for it." What I actually said was, "Alan Torvoldsen is a commercial fisherman. He's been at sea all his life. He's more at home there than he is on land.''

"What kind of boat is it?"

"A T-class lighter."

"Fully fueled?"

"Most likely," I answered.

Commercial fishermen usually top off their tanks when they settle up with their crews at the end of a fishing trip. The boat expenses are paid before the crew can figure their take. Aside from the settlement question, filling the tank helps prevent condensation over the cold winter months.

"How far do you think they can go without refueling?" Hammersmith asked.

I remember hanging around Fishermen's Terminal in the spring when the fleet was getting ready to go out. "I don't know for sure, but most commercial boats have tanks that hold a lot of fuel. Worst-case scenario, I suppose they could go a long way—maybe even as far as the Panama Canal—without refueling."

Hammersmith raised one eyebrow. "When they hit open water, you think they might head south, then?"

Once again, I couldn't very well tell him all my reasons for thinking so, not without giving away too much. "Maybe," I answered.

"Are they loaded with food and water?"

"Again, I couldn't say for sure," I answered, "but I doubt Alan Torvoldsen would be dumb enough to set out without adequate stores of food and water."

Shaking his head, Hammersmith excused himself and disappeared into another part of the building. His absence gave me time to think some bad thoughts about how easy it would be for someone to dispose of hostages once *One Day at a Time* hit that great expanse of blue water known as the Pacific Ocean. Bodies tossed overboard would disappear without a trace. Even if they washed up on land, months might pass before they were discovered on the deserted stretches of Washington's wintertime shore.

I was lost in thought when a recently showered and still wet-haired Sue Danielson blew into the conference room. "So what's the word?" she asked. "What's happening?"

"Not much," I answered. "But at least we're starting to work on the problem."

Roger Hammersmith returned moments later. After a brief introduction to Sue, he sat down to plot strategy.

"I've talked it over with the operations chief up in Everett. He and I agree with you that it's doubtful they'd head for the south end of Puget Sound. Sure, there are plenty of places to hide temporarily, but not forever. If they are trying for the open ocean, as you seem to believe, then they have a couple of choices, especially if they don't want to be seen.

"For one thing, they might head north, dodge between Camano Island and Whidbey, or maybe duck through the Swinomish Channel. The other alternative, especially considering how much lead they've had, is to not worry about being seen in the shipping channels and just make a run for Cape Flattery."

"So what do we do?" I asked.

"We've come up with two separate tactics. Fortunately, we have enough aircraft and pilots at our disposal to execute both plans at once. The first one is based on the assumption that they're putting the pedal to the metal and making a run for it. We counter that maneuver by plotting the most direct route from here through the Strait of Juan de Fuca. We send helicopters out beyond the far end of where they could possibly be by now, going full steam. We have the pilots work their way back to base by doing a track line search."

"And the second one?"

"That scenario assumes that they're going to try to duck into someplace reasonably unobtrusive and wait for the heat to die down some before they head for open water. At this time of year, when most of the tourists are back home for the winter, they might reasonably expect to disappear for days at a time, either up around the San Juans or across the border in Canadian waters.

"But dodging around like that uses up a lot more time than straight-line navigation, where they'd be more likely to stick to the easiest, most tried-and-true courses. That means we'd end up doing a much broader-based grid-pattern search closer to home."

I nodded, another thought occurring to me. "What about calling the Coast Guard Vessel Traffic Center to help with the search?"

Hammersmith shook his head. "I thought about that, too, but I think it's a bad idea," he answered. "If they're operating in the shipping lanes, it would be simple for someone to spot them, call in, and report the sighting. But if whoever's piloting that boat is maintaining any kind of radio contact—which he should be—then, as soon as we call VTC into it, the bad guy knows it, too. What happens to the hostages then? This way, we spot them first, but then we have time enough to marshal our forces before they realize we know where they are.''

''Wouldn't they hear the radio contacts to and from the helicopters?''

''We operate on different frequencies,'' he answered, then looked at me. ''What do you think?'' he asked.

''When do we start?'' I returned.

Hammersmith glanced at his watch. ''Our students fly out of Paine Field up in Everett. We have a bunch of Japanese students who are here learning how to fly helicopters. They're due to report in at eight o'clock sharp. We should be able to have the whole bunch airborne by eight-thirty. This will give them some good practice.'' He looked at me and grinned. ''And help the company make payroll besides.''

He stood up. ''If you'll excuse me, I'll go plot out the flight plans we'll distribute at the preflight briefing.''

As soon as Roger Hammersmith left the room, Sue Danielson turned to me. ''What's going to happen?'' she asked.

''You heard him. Grid-pattern searches until we find them.''

Sue shook her head impatiently. ''Finding them is a foregone conclusion,'' she said. ''What I want to know is what's going to happen once we do.''

I hadn't wanted to think that far ahead. The worst

part about hostage situations is that they're so dangerous. Sure, SWAT teams take out the hostage-takers, but all too often, hostages die as well.

Longtime cops take the position that black humor is better than no humor, so I tried to shrug off Sue's very important question. "I thought I'd have one of the choppers land me on the deck of the boat, maybe swing me in on a rope. I could come out of a crouch with both guns blazing like they used to do on *Sea Hunt,* that old Lloyd Bridges series on TV."

Sue was not amused. "Who's Lloyd Bridges?" she asked. "Any relation to Jeff Bridges?"

"Forget it," I growled. "I can't even talk to you. You're too damn young."

"I get the picture," she answered. "It sounds like the shoot-out at the O.K. Corral, only on a boat. What about a hostage-negotiation team?"

"Right," I said. "And while we're at it, let's have an emergency-response team as well. That's the problem with law enforcement these days. Everybody's a specialist. Whatever happened to general-practitioner cops?"

"I think we should call for reinforcements," she said. "General-practitioner cops went the way of the dodo bird."

The way she said it made it sound as though she considered me right up there on the endangered-species list myself. After that we both lapsed into a sullen silence.

Of course, I knew Sue was right. That's why her saying it irked me so. Young men become police officers because they're idealistic as hell—because they want to ride white horses, save the universe from the forces of evil, and rescue damsels in distress. I suppose these days, young women join up for much the same reasons. They want to make a difference, and they want to do it themselves.

I'm not a remote-control kind of guy. I want to have my own hands on the knobs—my own finger on the trigger, if it comes down to that. Tracking down bad guys and then having to tell somebody else to go get 'em doesn't quite square with my view of myself—of who I am and what I'm all about.

Hammersmith strolled back into the room. "They're about ready for the meeting. I'm going to conference-call it because we've got some guys down here and some up in Everett. I'll be back as soon as the last aircraft is off the ground."

He turned and started away again. "Wait a minute," I called after him. "What about us?"

"What do you mean?"

"Don't we go up in one, too?"

I guess some of those old *Sea Hunt* images were still flickering in the back of my imagination.

"Detective Beaumont," Roger Hammersmith explained patiently, "I thought I made it clear. You guys are command and control." He said it slowly, as though speaking to a wayward child; as though he never expected to have to clarify such a basic concept.

"You and Ms. Danielson stay here until we have a sighting from one of the Robinson helicopters. They're tiny. Cute. They can fly two men, but they can cover a lot more ground if they only have one person on board. Once the pilots find something, that's when Paul will take you two up in one of the big turbines. Then it will be up to you to figure out what to do next.''

"I see," I said. "When will Paul be here?''

"The Department of Transportation has finally hauled the semi off the bridge. Traffic is beginning to move. He should be here within the next half hour or so.''

Once again Hammersmith left the room. When I looked over at Sue Danielson, she drummed her fingers on the table and said nothing. She didn't have to. It was my operation, and she was forcing me to call the shots and do the right thing.

For a time, we sat in silence, waiting and drinking coffee. And after the coffee—incredibly awful swill that must have been made weeks earlier—I paced the floor with my guts at a full boil, wrestled with my indecision, and longed for the physical comfort of an antacid chalk-pill.

Every minute that passed brought us closer to the showdown, the moment when we would find them. It would have been easier to know what to do if we could have predicted in advance exactly where and when we'd find them. Where and when the inevitable confrontation would take place.

Despite my general-practitioner lamentation, I knew damn good and well that not all jurisdictions had trained hostage negotiators available. And even if they had, all such trained individuals are not necessarily created equal. Regardless of whose team was designated to do the job, it might take time—precious time—to assemble team members on a rainy November Sunday morning.

Finally, at ten o'clock, I decided to take my best

shot and called Captain Lawrence Powell at home.
I was glad he answered the phone himself. I
wouldn't have wanted to try explaining the whole
tangled web to Mrs. Powell, only to have to explain it again to her husband a few minutes later.

"Not you, Detective Beaumont," Captain Powell said into the phone, as soon as I identified
myself. "Whenever you call me at home, it usually means trouble. What's going on?"

Unlike my relationship with Major Gray, with
Captain Larry Powell I have a long history of
working together. It's been stormy on occasion,
but we do have a reasonable understanding of how
the other guy thinks and where he stands. Captain
Powell listened to every word I said without
once interrupting.

"Let me get this straight," he said when I finished. "You're there at Boeing Field right now,
waiting for one of the chopper pilots to spot the
boat. When they do, you want me to have a Seattle
P.D. hostage negotiation team assembled at the
airport ready to go, but you don't know where
they'll be going?"

"That's right."

"Jurisdictional lines be damned?" he demanded.

"That's true, too," I conceded, "but we have
letters of mutual aid with most of the other jurisdictions in Washington State, don't we?"

"One would hope," Powell answered thoughtfully, "although whether or not those Memoran-
dums of Agreement are all in order—properly
signed, witnessed, and on file in the right office—
is another question entirely."

"It's always easier to step on toes first and say

you're sorry later," I advised him, speaking with the benefit of my lifelong history of bending, if not actually breaking, the rules. "If we try going for permission in advance, we may end up stuck in some petty jurisdictional squabble when what we need is the ability to take immediate action."

Powell thought about that for a few moments and evidently came to the same conclusion. "All right," he said. "I'll go to work on this and see what I can do. You realize, of course, that I'm going to have to run this by the brass?"

Talking to brass has never been high on my list of skills. If it were, I wouldn't still be a detective after all these years. Just his saying it made the possibility of a successful outcome sound like a hopeless pipe dream.

"All right," I said.

"What about an Emergency Response Team?" he added. "Do you think we'd better haul those guys along as well?"

"With our necks already out that far, why not?" I returned. "If those guys can shoot from a moving helicopter and knock someone off a moving boat, I say let's bring 'em along."

"Helicopter," Powell repeated. "That reminds me. You told me you're planning to pay for the initial search part of this operation, didn't you?"

"Yes."

"From what you've told me, that may or may not be necessary. We've worked with Paul Brendle before. Is he around there somewhere?"

Paul had arrived only moments earlier. He had waved to me through the glass-paned walls of the conference room while I was on the phone with Captain Powell.

"I believe he's out in the hangar area. If you'll wait a minute, I'll go get him."

Paul came in from outside to take the call. Here it comes, I thought, as he took the phone. This is when I'm going to get my ass chewed. But Paul Brendle was smiling broadly at me when he finished the conversation with Larry Powell.

"That captain of yours sounds like an all-right guy. He says he's trying to get permission to send out two specialty teams. If it works, one of them will bring along the city's signed requisition to use the helicopters. Two separate requisitions, if necessary. He did say, though, that if you and your partner—" he nodded toward Sue Danielson— "intend to go up in a helicopter prior to the arrival of that official requisition form, then the two of you will have to buy your own tickets."

Suddenly, my heart felt fully five pounds lighter. "No problem," I said cheerfully. "That's no problem at all."

27

After the phone call to Captain Powell, Sue Danielson's spirits improved immeasurably as well. Ten minutes later, Roger Hammersmith rushed into the window-lined conference room where Sue and I were waiting along with Paul Brendle.

"Got 'em!" he announced. "Sato just radioed into the tower. They're in President's Channel on a southwest heading between Waldron Island and Orcas."

I felt an initial surge of triumph, followed immediately by a rush of concern. On those occasions when I personally have traveled to Orcas, it's been on board Washington State ferries. Because I have an unerring knack for missing ferries by minutes, that kind of travel tends to leave me with a distorted view about how far it is and how long it takes to get there.

"How long will it take?" I asked.

"Not long," Paul said. "Let's go."

Instantly, he was on his feet, pulling on his flight jacket, and heading for the door. Sue and I followed. Walking with a distinct limp, Paul hurried out to the flight line, where a bright red American Eurocopter A-Star helicopter sat at the ready.

Heading there, I glanced at my watch and wondered if I shouldn't rush back into the office long enough to call Captain Powell and let him know what was happening. But it was already too late. While Paul was doing his last-minute visual, preflight check, Roger was already handing Sue into the backseat of the chopper, helping her to don the headset, adjusting the microphone, and showing her the control button on the floor that made it work.

Erroneously assuming helicopters to be similar to automobiles, I headed for the right side of the helicopter. Roger Hammersmith was quick to point out my mistake. In helicopters, the *left-hand* side is always the passenger side. Properly chastised, I headed for the opposite side of the aircraft.

Embarrassed at being shown up for such a helicopter neophyte, I climbed in. The carpeted interior, the plush leather seats, and the myriad of gauges set in a wood-grain panel reminded me of the dashboard of my 928. Except for one thing— the helicopter had a lot more legroom.

Before Hammersmith could give me any further instructions, he was summoned away by yet another telephone call. Following the directions he had given Sue, I put on my own headset. As I waited for us to take off, I tried to keep preflight jitters entirely to myself.

Shameful as it is to admit, as a kid, I never liked carnival rides—not even those as tame as the Ferris wheel. They made me queasy and turned my skin a sickly shade of green. Bearing that in mind, it goes without saying that I don't take to flying. In middle age, I'm a reluctant and generally grouchy airline passenger as opposed to the blasé frequent fliers of the world.

It's easy to understand that prior to that windy, rainy morning I hadn't spent any of my adult life searching for ways to take helicopter rides. Helicopters are noisy. Sitting in a moving plastic bubble high above the ground isn't my idea of a good time.

Paul took several minutes to complete the outside checklist of the helicopter, then he, too, climbed aboard. In his office on the ground, he had been relaxed and easygoing—jovial almost. Once inside the aircraft, he was all business.

"Where exactly did he say they are?" I asked.

Without answering, Paul put on his headset and pressed the Start button of the jet-turbine engine. As the helicopter blades roared into action, they seemed to swallow my question whole. Paul's eyes were busy checking gauges and instruments, and he didn't look in my direction.

"If you want to talk to me," he said, his voice coming through the headset, "you have to push down the black button on the floor. What did you ask?"

"Where are they?"

"Far north end of the San Juans."

"How close to the Canadian border?"

"That depends on how fast the guy is going. From Point Disney on Waldron Island, it's probably only ten miles or so to international waters—ten nautical miles, that is."

Only ten miles? I thought in dismay. By now Captain Powell would be deep in the process of trying to convince Seattle P.D.'s brass that they should take action. Assuming they did that, Powell would have his hands full just coordinating the operation as a joint effort with the law-enforcement folks up in San Juan County on *our* side of the border. Crossing into Canada and working with Canadian authorities as well as with the Royal Canadian Mounted Police would add another whole dimension of complication and difficulty.

Larry Powell has been my squad commander for years. I have considerable faith in his abilities. But since I hadn't been able to make Major John Gray go along with the program—since I couldn't convince him of the validity of my suspicions about what was happening on board *One Day at a Time*—how could Captain Powell possibly expect to pull the RCMP into line?

"Can we beat Alan Torvoldsen to the border?" I asked.

Paul Brendle shrugged and eased the helicopter into the air far enough to take us out to a small landing-pad triangle that had been painted onto the tarmac. "Like I said before, it depends on how fast he's going and on winds aloft."

I tried to say something more, but now, intent on receiving radio transmissions coming in from Air Traffic Control, Paul held up his index finger, motioning for me to be quiet and wait.

Never before having seen a helicopter pilot at work, I confess to being impressed. I've ridden in Metroliners on occasion—the kind of cigar-shaped, one-seat-per-side, sardine-can-type airplane where, if you're lucky, they keep a curtain closed between you and the pilots and their daunting array of instruments and gauges.

The reason I like a closed curtain is that, if something goes wrong and I can't do a damn thing about it, I don't want to know beforehand. I find it reassuring, however, that Metroliners always have two real, reasonably trained, bona-fide pilots.

Paul Brendle's helicopter had only one pilot on board—him. And it was no wonder he didn't want to talk. He didn't have time. Both hands, both feet, both eyes, and his mouth were all working at once in a display of coordination I found nothing short of dazzling. He was talking back and forth to Air Traffic Control when the chopper lifted off, tilted sharply forward, and sped down the runway, quickly gaining altitude.

While the helicopter had been parked without the engine and blades running, a slanting, wind-driven rain had covered the clear plastic bubble, making it almost impossible to see out. As soon as the blades whirled overhead, most of the moisture had been blown away, but now the windshield wipers came on as well.

As the airport tarmac fell away behind us, I was dismayed to realize there was nothing between me and the ground but carpeted metal flooring and a thin—very thin—layer of wraparound, see-through plastic. To my surprise, however, despite what I knew to be serious gusty winds and thick rain, the ride inside the machine was far smoother than I had expected.

I glanced at my watch again. Time was passing too quickly. I felt more and more urgency about getting back to Captain Powell and letting him know what was up.

I pressed down the button on my microphone.

"What about calling . . ." I began, but Paul cut me off once more with his silencing finger while an air-traffic controller advised us to watch out for a medical helicopter inbound across Puget Sound, heading for the landing pad at Harborview Hospital.

Once more I shut up and warily scanned the horizon. I didn't want to die in a midair crash, and I was relieved when I finally managed to spot the incoming chopper through the pouring rain.

We followed the path of the freeway north across the city. Since it was Sunday morning, most of the downtown city streets appeared pretty well deserted, although there was still a residual backup in both directions on the freeway at the Ship Canal Bridge. Somewhere near Northgate we veered northwest and headed toward Puget Sound.

"What was it you wanted back there?" Paul asked.

I was so fascinated by what I was seeing that it took me a minute to remember. "I need to get word back to Captain Powell, about what's going on."

"No problem," Paul Brendle replied. "I'll have Roger handle it. What's his number, and what do you want to tell him?"

Good question. Should I go ahead and trust to Captain Powell's ability to call in the cavalry, or should I try marshaling reinforcements independently? If Powell was actually making progress cutting through regular channels, a call from me to the San Juan Sheriff's Department would only muddy the issue.

Conscious that every moment of delay counted

against us, I gave Paul the number. "Give him the location," I said. "Tell him to try to get us whatever help he can."

Having called for help through official channels, I sat back to worry in silence. What were the chances of our actually catching up with Alan Torvoldsen's boat before it reached Canadian waters? And if we couldn't make it in time, did San Juan County or the Coast Guard have a boat capable of getting there first?

Once we were out over Puget Sound, the clouds began to break up. Whitecaps on the gray-green water showed that the wind had kicked up considerably, but the helicopter bounced very little. Despite my initial misgivings, clearly we were far better off up in the air than we would have been down on the water bobbing around in a boat.

That was discouraging. Rough seas made things tougher, lessening the odds of pulling off a successful rescue mission without someone getting hurt.

What would Alan Torvoldsen do once he realized we were onto him? I wondered. Would he try to run and hide, or would he stand and fight? Was the skipper of *One Day at a Time* armed and dangerous? If so, how much firepower did he have at his disposal? Enough to bring down a helicopter? The plastic bubble of Paul Brendle's cockpit sure as hell wasn't made of bulletproof material.

A garbled-sounding radio transmission came in. I couldn't understand a word of it.

"What did he say?"

"Mr. Sato, one of our R-22 pilots, just took another peek," Paul answered. "He says they just passed Danger Rock. Looks like they're heading on down the Spieden Channel between Spieden Island and San Juan. The international border is in the middle of Haro Strait on the other side of San Juan Island. My guess is that's where they're headed.''

That was my guess, too, even though I didn't possess Paul Brendle's photographic memory for San Juan Island geography.

''We're gaining on them, though,'' he added. ''We've got a thirty-knot tailwind, and they must be running a little slower than we figured.''

''So we might still catch them?''

''Of course.''

''Where?''

''There's a marine atlas in the back pocket behind my seat. Take a look at that, and we'll see.''

Sue, sitting in back, dragged out the oversized book. After spending several minutes studying it, she tapped me on the shoulder and passed it up to me through the space between the two front seats. When I looked back at her, I discovered the skin on her face was a surprising shade of gray-green—almost the same color as the water below us. The same color mine used to be when I stepped off a Tilt-a-Whirl.

''I can't read in moving vehicles,'' she managed. ''It makes me sick.''

''There's a barf bag in that same pocket, if you need it,'' Paul suggested helpfully.

While Sue went rummaging for the air-sickness bag, I busied myself with the atlas. It took some time to sort out the way the atlas worked and to find the proper chart for the area where we were headed. As my eyes ran up the side of San Juan Island, the name Deadman Bay caught my eye. Seeing it seemed like an omen, somehow.

Another radio transmission came through. The basic gist of this one was that San Juan County had a boat heading out from Friday Harbor to offer assistance, but the sheriff was having difficulty assembling his Emergency Response Team. San Juan County's single trained hostage negotiator was leading a religious retreat at Leavenworth up in the Cascades. And the sharpshooter on the San Juan Emergency Response Team was in the hospital in Bellingham giving birth to her second baby.

That meant that our only hope of help was from the two specialty teams dispatched by Captain Powell, and they weren't expected to leave Boeing Field for another ten minutes.

I glanced questioningly back at Sue. Clutching the bag in her hand, she was leaning back in the leather seat with her eyes closed and her face still a pukey shade of green. From the looks of her, it was possible she was out of the game for good.

"What are they up to?" Paul demanded.

Preoccupied with concerns about Sue, I hadn't bothered to listen to the latest radio transmission. "What's going on?"

"They just came around Flattop Island," Paul answered. "Then they sort of eased into a ninety-degree turn and headed northwest."

Once again I picked up the atlas and studied the chart. On it, land masses were colored the same green as Sue's complexion. Water was white with black depth markings that indicated the depth of the water around the various islands and rocky shoals. Suggested courses were lined and numbered in red. Shipping lanes and precautionary areas were marked with purple.

It didn't take long for me to locate the landmarks Paul had mentioned. "What's northwest of Flattop?" he asked.

"Cactus Islands with Spieden before that. Farther north there's John's Island, Stuart Island, and Satellite Island."

"I can't figure out what this guy is up to," Paul said. "Why the sudden course change?"

"Beats the hell out of me," I said, but I had forgotten to push down the microphone button with my foot, so I don't think anyone heard me.

After that, time seemed to slow to a crawl. I tried to follow our course on the charts, struggling to see some correlation between the land masses and water we were seeing below us and the abstract shapes outlined on the charts.

"How do you want to play this one, Detective Beaumont?" Paul asked me finally.

The temptation was there, but I'm a little too old to go around pretending to play the Lone Ranger. It looked as though Sue was out of commission for the duration, but Captain Powell's specialty teams were well on their way by now. It was no time to go in for phony heroics.

"Once we find them," I said, "all I want to do is maintain visual contact until our reinforcements show up."

"Sounds good to me," Paul Brendle answered.

And it would have been a great plan—if things had just worked out that way.

We finally sighted *One Day at a Time* just as

she passed between John's Island and started past the lower outcropping of Reid Island. By then I was familiar enough with the charts that I could actually see the relationship between what was on the maps and what was visible through the plastic bubble.

For a time, we stayed far above them—far enough to stay out of range of a bullet. Some time passed with no visible reaction. The boat continued to stick to her course without the slightest deviation. Then, slowly at first, she began to veer off toward the left.

Prevost Harbor takes a big chunk out of the northeast side of Reid Island. Inside the harbor is a piece of land called Satellite Island. As Paul and I watched, whoever was skippering *One Day at a Time* turned her sharply in that direction, heading toward the easternmost tip of the island where a sandy beach came to a narrow point.

Just as it takes time and distance to slow down a moving train enough to stop it, it takes time to stop a boat as well. As *One Day at a Time* neared the spit of sand, instead of slowing down, she seemed to leap forward. Straight forward.

"Holy shit!" Paul Brendle announced over the intercom a moment later. "She's going aground."

As we hovered far overhead, watching helplessly, the boat seemed to suddenly rise up out of the shallow water. For a moment, it seemed as though it would ride on up the sand onto the narrow strip of beach. Instead, *One Day at a Time* shuddered to a stop, then slowly the aft swung around until it was lying crosswise in the water. Seconds later, it began to list to one side on the curving hull until it seemed as though it would tip over altogether.

"Look at that!" Paul shouted into my ear.

While we watched from above, two figures slipped under the rail, dropped off the lowered side of the listing boat, and fell a couple of feet into the water. After a moment or two, they struggled upright in the waist-deep water and made for shore.

"Go after them," I yelled back to Paul. "Don't let them get away."

The helicopter was low enough that our view of the scene below was surprisingly intimate. As the helicopter bucked forward, I caught sight of a lone figure on deck. A man. I recognized the fringe of red hair, the balding head. It was Alan Torvoldsen, hunkering against the side of the pilothouse, using one hand to keep himself upright on the steeply slanted deck.

Sunlight glinted off something in his other hand—something metal. Instinct more than visual evidence told me the metal object had to be a gun.

I saw Alan Torvoldsen, but only for an instant before he disappeared from my line of vision. Then, instead of seeing the boat, I was staring down at the two escaping figures splashing through the water, churning now in the powerful draft of the helicopter blades.

The two people paused as we passed overhead. They stopped and stared up at us, shading their eyes from the glaring noonday sun, then they both started signaling frantically, beckoning us to come down.

Somehow Sue managed to forget she was seasick. "My God!" she exclaimed from the back-seat. "It's Else. Else Gebhardt and Kari!"

"Quick!" I ordered. "Put this thing down as soon as you can."

Paul brought the helicopter down on a narrow patch of beach just as Else Gebhardt came staggering out of the water. As I opened the door, she came running through the swirling cloud of sand kicked up by the rotating blades and fell into my arms.

"BoBo," Else sobbed. Distraught, soaking wet, and shivering uncontrollably, she sagged against me, shouting to be heard above the roar of the helicopter. "My mother! They've got my mother. They'll kill her!"

Sue Danielson had scrambled out of the helicopter behind me. Glancing over Else's quaking shoulder, I saw Sue assisting Kari out of the water and up onto the beach. Kari was limping on what looked like a severely sprained ankle.

I took off my jacket and wrapped it around Else's shoulders, then I led her a few feet away from the roar of the helicopter in hopes of hearing better. "Where is Inge on the boat?" I asked. "And is she hurt?"

"N-n-not . . . yet," Else answered through chattering teeth. "Sh-she's on one of the b-bunks. B-but they both have g-guns. I'm afraid they'll k-kill her."

After easing Kari down on the ground, Sue joined Else and me. Now that she was back on solid ground, Sue's color was improving. Instead of green, her skin was simply pale. "Who has guns?'' she demanded. ''Alan Torvoldsen and who else? Who all is in on this with him?''

''Not Alan,'' Else returned, glaring at Sue with some of her old ferocity showing in her vivid blue eyes. ''He's done everything he could to help us,'' she said. ''Even wrecked his boat so we'd have a chance to get away.''

I knew what I had seen from above the foundering boat. ''If not Alan, then who?''

''Hans Gebhardt,'' Else answered. ''Gunter's father. And the old man's girlfriend.''

''His girlfriend,'' Sue repeated. ''Erika Weber? Erika Schmidt?''

''Her name's not Erika,'' Else answered, shaking her head. ''The girl's name is Denise. Denise Whitney.''

28

When Paul switched off the helicopter engine, a sudden eerie quiet surrounded us. Gradually, the airfoil blades slowed and stopped rotating. As they did so, the pilot-side door swung open, and Paul Brendle jumped out. Carrying a first-aid kit and a pair of space-age, tinfoil-looking survival blankets, he hurried toward us.

He stopped first beside Kari and covered her with one of the blankets. Then, leaving the first-aid kit on the ground beside her, he came to where the rest of us stood. He wrapped the blanket around Else's shoulders and eased her down onto the sand as well.

"I just heard from Roger," Paul said. "The SWAT team's on its way, but they're still at least twenty minutes out. The San Juan Sheriff's Department police boat should be here about that time as well."

From out on the water, I heard the sharp report of gunfire—a single shot that sounded like a cannon. Ducking reflexively, I quickly scanned the narrow strip of sandy beach for some cover. There wasn't any. Not a scrap. Without cover, and without our knowing what caliber of weapons were on board *One Day at a Time*, twenty minutes could be damned eternity.

"We've got to get out of here," I said.

Else scrambled to her feet. "My mother!" she breathed frantically. "My mother's out there. What if they've shot her?"

Paul Brendle's eyes caught mine. He must have been reading my mind.

"You're right," he said. "Let's get these ladies on the helicopter right away," he said. "At least I can move them out of range."

While Paul led Else to the waiting helicopter, Sue and I supported the injured Kari between us.

"How did this happen?"

Kari shook her head. Each limping step caused a little gasp of pain. "I don't know," she said between steps. "They were there in the house waiting when I brought Granny home from the beauty shop. They were there with Mother and Mr. Torvoldsen. They had guns."

"What kind of guns?" Sue asked.

Kari shook her head. "The woman, Denise. She has one hidden in her purse. The man, the one who says he's my grandfather, has a big one."

"What kind of big one?" Sue persisted. "A rifle? An automatic? A shotgun?"

"I can't help you. I don't know anything at all about guns," Kari Gebhardt answered. "I'm sorry."

There was another report of gunfire out on the water, followed immediately by a woman's piercing shriek. Fortunately, Paul had already helped Else into the backseat of the helicopter. The leather interior may have muffled the sound enough so she didn't hear it. Kari, however, was still outside the helicopter. When she heard the scream, she stiffened but said nothing.

Paul came around behind us just as Sue and I finished boosting Kari into the seat. He closed the door. "Once I drop them off, do you want me to come back?" he asked.

I nodded. "Keep out of range, but stay close enough to guide the cavalry in to the rescue if we need it."

"Sure thing. What about you?" he asked.

I turned to Sue. "Feel like going for a little wade?"

"Not exactly," she replied, "but with two against one, he'll never hold out for another fifteen minutes. Vests on or off?"

Unlike airline seat cushions, Kevlar vests aren't recommended as flotation devices. The water didn't seem that deep, but who could tell whether or not it was shallow all the way out to the boat? If it turned out to be deep, that left us with a hell of a choice. Wear the vest and risk drowning, or don't wear the vest and risk being shot. Heads, you win; tails, I lose.

"That all depends on how good a swimmer you are," I said. "The water doesn't look all that deep. Suit yourself, but I'm leaving mine on."

We stripped off our shoes at the water's edge. As Sue and I stepped into the frigid water, the helicopter's turbine engine roared to life behind us. When it rose overhead, I had the small satisfaction of knowing that Kari and Else were safe, but from the scream we had heard, I was afraid we were already far too late to save Inge.

Wintertime water temperatures in Puget Sound are about forty-five degrees. Stepping into the water was like plunging our feet into a bucket of ice. The water was so cold, it took our breath away. As we splashed along, we had to keep our eyes lowered enough to watch our footing. We also needed to keep an eye on the boat for fear of being shot to death.

The distance between the sand and the stranded boat couldn't have been more than fifty yards. Out in the open like that, fully exposed to anyone who wanted to take a potshot, it felt like fifty miles.

Suddenly, Sue stopped in her tracks. "Look at that!" she exclaimed. "Something's on fire."

I squinted and looked where she was pointing. A thin wisp of smoke rose up over the afterdeck of *One Day at a Time*. It seemed to be coming from a stovepipe on top of the galley. "That's from the stove," I said.

"How do you know that?" Sue wanted to know.

"I've been on fishing boats before. I'm from Ballard, remember?"

"Why would somebody start a fire in the stove at a time like this?"

I wanted to say maybe they're as dumb as we are, standing here arguing about it. I said, "Most likely it's been lit the whole time, and this just happens to be the first time we've noticed the smoke. Come on."

As we started forward again, I noticed that my teeth were chattering. I wondered how long it would take for hypothermia to set in. My feet were already so numb, I could barely walk. Not very long, I thought grimly. Not long at all.

Sue and I covered the remaining distance out to *One Day at a Time* without incident—without seeing anyone move on deck, and without anyone taking a shot at us, either. Once we were standing beside the barnacle-encrusted hull, I realized, with dismay, that the deck of the beached boat was a whole lot higher out of the water than it had appeared to be from shore.

Fortunately, it was low tide. The water we were standing in was little more than waist-deep. I was about to suggest boosting Sue onto my shoulders in hopes of lifting her high enough to clamber aboard when, suddenly, a rope with a life ring attached sailed over the rail. It came whistling through the air so close to my ears that the life ring almost beaned me.

"Get up here, BoBo," an invisible Alan Torvoldsen ordered from above. "What the hell took you so long? I've been bluffing for hours. I didn't think anybody was ever going to come looking for us."

It probably was only a matter of seconds, but it seemed to take forever for Sue and me to scramble aboard. Using the rope, we struggled hand-over-hand, up and over the side. Shivering with cold and gasping for breath, we landed on the slippery, tilting deck.

Alan Torvoldsen knelt in a wary crouch in the narrow walkway between the pilothouse and the rail, using the wall of the pilothouse as cover. A huge .44 revolver—a cocked, single-action antique—lay on the deck beside him. As soon as Sue and I were safely aboard, Alan picked up the Colt and held it aimed aft, in the general direction of the galley.

"Help me," a woman's voice mumbled plaintively from somewhere nearby. "Please help me. I can't move."

"Who's that?" I demanded.

"The old man's girlfriend," Alan responded. "I think her name's Denise Something. She wanted to get away. She tried to make a run for the rail, but he shot her in the back. Nice guy."

"And Inge Didricksen?" I asked. "What about her?"

"Last time I saw Inge, he was using her as a human shield," Alan answered. "He's holed up with her inside the galley. If I could have gotten off a clear shot a little earlier, I'd have plugged the sorry son of a bitch."

"Did he say what he wants?" Sue asked. "We've got hostage negotiators coming. An Emergency Response Team is en route."

I looked down at my waterproof watch. I thought at first maybe it had stopped, but when I held it up to my ear, it was still ticking. I couldn't believe that barely ten minutes had passed.

"Reinforcements should be here within minutes," I said.

"Oh, my God," Denise moaned. "I'm so cold. I can't move at all, and I'm bleeding. There's blood everywhere. Someone please help me."

Alan Torvoldsen looked at me and shook his head. "The girl may not have minutes," he said. "We should do something now."

I racked my brain. "Are there portholes on the sides of the galley?" I asked finally.

Alan nodded. "Two on either side."

Without waiting for me to suggest it, Sue sidled backward along the side of the pilothouse. "I'm on the way," she said. "Cover me when I need it."

"I know something about first aid," Alan offered. "If you can keep him occupied, maybe I can drag the girl around here and out of the line of fire."

It was both a brave and foolhardy suggestion. As plans went, it wasn't much, but it was marginally better than no plan at all. Peeking around the corner of the pilothouse, I could see that the door to the galley stood slightly ajar.

"Hans!" I shouted. "Hans Gebhardt. Can you hear me? This is Detective Beaumont with the Seattle Police Department. Give it up. Let the woman go, then come out with your hands up."

"She will die, and I will die," Hans Gebhardt asserted calmly. "I have chosen not to die alone."

That's when I realized that no matter what he had done, Hans Gebhardt—noted Nazi war criminal—was nothing but a coward. He might have idly stood by and watched, unmoved, while thousands of innocent victims were marched to their deaths. He might have coldly plundered their naked corpses afterward. But Hans Gebhardt himself wasn't nearly as brave as his victims. He was afraid to face death without the comfort of taking someone else along with him. Because he wanted company.

"There's no reason for either one of you to

die," I called back. "Let Inge go. We'll give you whatever you want."

"What I want is my innocence back," Hans returned. "And that's not in your power to give. It's fifty years too late."

"Don't make it any worse than it already is," I argued. "Don't take the life of another innocent victim."

Hans Gebhardt laughed aloud. "You hear that, Inge? This *dumkopf* thinks you're a poor innocent, that you don't deserve to die right along with me. He doesn't know that you and your precious Henrik were in on it from the beginning, does he? He doesn't know you two were willing to barter your own daughter for a chance at a share of my gold."

"Gunter was as good a husband as Else deserved," Inge said.

"What?" Alan said. It was half question/half exclamation. As though he couldn't trust his ears with the words he was hearing.

". . . just wasn't supposed to take thirty years for me to get it out, now, was it?" Hans Gebhardt continued, unaware of Alan's involuntary reaction to what was being said.

Inge Didricksen was equally unaware. "Shut up!" she rasped. "Just shut up!"

"Why should I shut up? You don't want me to tell this man the truth about you, do you? You don't want him to know how, with both the Jews and the Nazis looking for me, with both sets of hunters after my gold, I needed all the help I could get right after the war. You don't want him to know about Henrik Didricksen's greedy cousin back in Norway who took in my wife and my son.

For a share of the gold, of course. Not out of the kindness of his heart. For enough gold, that stupid jerk was even willing to overlook bigamy.

"You don't want me to tell him how you and your husband agreed to help me as well—for another share. Except I think you thought you'd get the use of two shares—yours and Gunter's both."

"Don't listen to this stupid man," Inge shrilled. "He doesn't know what he's talking about."

"Don't I, now. Now, I'm stupid. But you were glad enough to talk to me when you were afraid Erika Weber Schmidt would come looking for you next. And she would have, too, if I hadn't been smart enough to take care of her myself."

"If you were so smart," Inge said fiercely, "we wouldn't be here now."

"Better here than in Israel, don't you think?"

"The Jews don't want me," Inge retorted angrily. "I never killed anybody."

Stunned beyond words by what I was hearing, for a moment I said nothing, then the silence was broken by the first faint thumps of arriving helicopters. Somewhere in the distance I thought I also heard the crash of waves against a fast-moving hull.

The helicopters were coming. So was the San Juan County police boat. It didn't matter now if, in the process of keeping them talking, Inge Didricksen and Hans Gebhardt had revealed fifty years' worth of terrible secrets I never wanted to hear. In terms of doing my job, I had kept the two of them talking long enough for reinforcements to arrive. Within minutes I'd be able to pass the negotiations over into the capable hands of a trained hostage negotiator, although by then, I have to admit, I didn't much care how those negotiations turned out.

"Do you hear those helicopters?" I asked. "You could just as well give up. Stop this now—before it's too late, before anyone else gets hurt."

I didn't know it, but even as I spoke the cautioning words, it was already too late. With a groan of outrage that grew out of thirty years of shattered dreams, with an anger fueled and made fierce by Else Didricksen's lifetime of betrayal at the hands of both her husband and her parents, Alan Torvoldsen surged to his feet.

Before I could stop him, he charged across the few feet of open deck between the pilothouse and the galley. Gun in hand and finger on the trigger, he crashed through the half-open door of the galley. Belching smoke, the ancient Colt revolver roared to life.

As I recalled the incident later, I believe there were three distinctly separate shots in all. Two of them were almost simultaneous. The third came a second or so later.

The smell of burned cordite was still thick in the air when Alan Torvoldsen reappeared in the doorway. Emerging through a haze of swirling smoke, he leaned against the door casing for a moment, then staggered forward, the gun trailing loosely in his hand. When he doubled over in front of me, I thought sure he'd been shot.

Instead, he straightened up and stood gazing at me. When I looked down, I realized he'd placed the still-smoking Colt on the deck at my feet.

"I tried to hit him, but I guess my aim was

bad,'' Alan said. ''I think I must have hit them both.''

Sue Danielson, with her semiautomatic in hand, came screeching around the far side of the galley.

''What the hell happened?'' she demanded. ''There are curtains on all those portholes. I couldn't see a damn thing!''

Alan's steady gaze held mine, his clear blue eyes never straying from my face. His look was resigned, his whole manner surprisingly calm.

''Go ahead and arrest me if you have to, BoBo,'' he said quietly. ''I understand, but I'm warning you right now. If this case ever goes to court, I'm pleading self-defense. Either that, or temporary insanity.''

For a moment, the three of us stood there in stricken silence, without any of us knowing what to say or do. Then a voice broke in on our paralyzed stupor.

''Help me,'' Denise Whitney whimpered.

I stepped out onto the deck far enough to see her. Gravely wounded, she lay directly between the pilothouse and the galley. Because of the steep slope of the slanted deck, her feet were higher than her head. A pool of bright red blood had dammed up briefly under her flattened cheek. Now a thin stream of it trickled away across the metal deck.

''Please help me,'' she said again, her voice diminished to a mere whisper. ''I'm so cold. I think I'm dying.''

And it turned out she was.

29

There wasn't all that much to be done for Denise Whitney. While helicopters circled overhead, Alan brought some blankets. Sue and I used those to cover her as best we could, but we couldn't staunch the bleeding.

"... tell my parents I'm sorry ..." were the last words she murmured. At least those were the last ones we were able to understand. Sue promised she would.

One of the problems with training is that you get caught up in an incident and you go on automatic pilot. Sometimes you keep on going much longer than you ought to.

It wasn't until Alan showed up with a second armload of blankets and ordered Sue and me to use them on ourselves that we realized just how cold we were. Not frostbitten, but cold enough that it took a hell of a long time to warm back up.

By the time we made it back to Seattle, finished up the worst of the paper, and headed home it was close to midnight—Sunday night and Monday morning. The lights were all off in my apartment, but I knew Ralph Ames had arrived safely. I found a note from him posted on my bedroom door. He said Alexis Downey had called, wondering why I had stood her up for dinner. Ralph's note also mentioned that he, Ralph, had taken my grandmother out to dinner—to the King's Table in Ballard—obviously not his usual choice. That man is nothing if not a gentleman.

I slept around the clock. What finally woke me up, around midnight Tuesday, was a severe case of chills, followed immediately by the cold sweats.

"You're coming down with pneumonia," Ralph said the next morning, when I tried to take a sip of coffee. My chattering teeth kept clicking on the side of the cup.

Ralph was right, of course, as he usually is. His instant diagnosis was confirmed later that afternoon by a chest X ray. Before I had a chance to object, someone had slapped me into a bed in Swedish Hospital for a three-day stay. I don't remember much about it. I think I must have slept most of the time.

When Thanksgiving weekend rolled around a week and a half later, I had recuperated enough to sit up and take nourishment, as they say. As soon as Jeremy and Kelly had heard I was sick, they had tried to waffle out of their proposed Turkey Day visit. I wouldn't let them off the hook. The doctor had assured me that I couldn't possibly still be contagious by then. Besides, as I told them during that last begging phone call—the one that finally turned the tide—I wanted to see my granddaughter, Kayla, at least once more before she was ready to graduate from junior high.

Kelly finally agreed to come, but only on the condition that they stay in a hotel so they wouldn't "be any trouble." I rented a two-room suite for them down at the Mayflower Park Hotel. It was nearby, small enough not to be intimidating and nice enough for them to feel like staying there was a real treat.

As I said, for the first several days after I got sick, I was totally out of it. Then, after I came home from the hospital, I was so weak, I could barely hold my head up. Consequently, Ralph Ames put himself in charge of holiday planning. He and his girlfriend, Mary Greengo, combined forces with my grandmother, Beverly Piedmont.

Before I knew it, plans for Thanksgiving were entirely out of hand. Within minutes the proposed guest list had far outstripped the seating capacity of my penthouse apartment. Undaunted, Ralph reserved Belltown Terrace's party room for the day, and plans moved forward.

When the day arrived, Alexis Downey was among those invited, but she didn't show. I guess she was still mad about being stood up for dinner two Sundays earlier. But there were plenty of other guests to take her place.

In addition to Kelly and Jeremy, the list of attendees included Ron and Amy Peters, their two kids—Heather and Tracy—as well as Amy's widowed mother. My grandmother brought along three of her friends from church, saying they didn't have anywhere else to go. I suspect that of being a blatant lie. Belltown Terrace is a very nice place, and I think she wanted to show off a little, but I figured she was entitled. Mary Greengo and Ralph did the lion's share of the cooking, and she brought along both her parents.

In addition to those from outside the building, Heather had gathered up some Belltown Terrace holiday ''orphans'' to round out the roster. These included a middle-aged gay couple named Ted and David whose plans to go back East for a family Thanksgiving had been stymied—along with those of thousands of other holiday travelers—by a huge blizzard that had virtually shut down the entire eastern seaboard. The same held true for Gail Richardson, owner of Charley, Belltown Terrace's legendary Elevator Dog.

After dinner was over and while people were busy cleaning up, I sat down on a couch to hold Kayla for a few minutes. Gail Richardson joined Kayla and me on the couch.

Gail is a tall, square-jawed woman, in her mid-forties. Her hair is absolutely white. She has a serious way about her that is offset by sudden bursts of deep-throated laughter. During dinner I had learned that she was the producer of a hit television sitcom—one I had never seen or even heard of—which was being filmed in Seattle and had just been renewed for a second season. From what I had been able to ascertain so far, Charley comprised Gail's entire family.

When she sat down on the couch, I had just discovered that five-month-old, one-toothed Kayla would giggle aloud in delight if I made a series of goofy faces. Naturally, I made a fool of myself. I was concentrating so much on Kayla's delighted crowing, that when Heather Peters came over to stand beside us, I didn't notice her at first.

''Babies are a lot of trouble, aren't they?''

Heather said sourly. Saying that, she stalked off, without another word.

"Whoa," I said. "I believe I detect the smallest trace of jealousy here."

"It's not surprising, considering," Gail said. "After all, not only is Heather being booted out of her position at home, it looks like she's losing your undivided attention as well."

"What do you mean she's losing her position?"

"Didn't you know?" Gail asked. "Amy's pregnant. It's going to be a boy."

I was thunderstruck. "I'll be damned!" I exclaimed. "How did that happen?"

There was a momentary pause (Dare I say a pregnant pause?) followed by the hoot of Gail Richardson's infectious laughter. "I believe it happened in the usual way," Gail managed, wiping the tears of laughter from her face.

Embarrassed, I found myself flushing and then laughing as well. "I guess I've been out of the loop for a while," I said.

"I guess you have," she agreed.

Much later that night, after all the other guests had gone home, Ralph and I found ourselves alone in my apartment. "Great dinner, Ralph," I said. "My compliments to the chefs. You guys do good work."

"Mary and I couldn't have done it without Beverly's supervision," Ralph returned. "Considering her age, that grandmother of yours is truly remarkable. Did you know she invited Mary and me to drop by sometime so she can show us the clipping file she has on you? Do you know about that?"

I nodded. "She's been keeping it for years."

"Even when you were . . . estranged?"

"That's right."

Worn out, I went to bed a few minutes later. As I lay there, I thought about Kari and Else Gebhardt for the first time in days. I kicked myself for not thinking about them earlier, for not calling them to wish them well. No doubt this had been a tough and anything but joyous holiday for them.

I couldn't help comparing Kari Gebhardt's grandmother, Inge Didricksen, to mine, Beverly Piedmont. Kari had been thoroughly convinced that her grandmother was a nice, upstanding woman. Kari had loved Inge and had expected that love to be returned. I, on the other hand, had spent years despising my grandmother—hating her for what I regarded as her unfeeling betrayal of both my mother and me.

It turned out that both Kari Gebhardt and I were dead wrong.

Poor Kari, I thought, as I drifted off to sleep. Poor, poor Kari. She could decline to inherit her grandfather's ill-gotten gain. She could throw the awful Sobibor gold into the court system and let the various claimants fight for it, but walking away from it wouldn't free her of the gold, of her grandfather, or of the nightmare of Sobibor.

Alan Torvoldsen called me early the next afternoon from Friday Harbor. "Hey, BoBo," he said. "The San Juan County prosecutor just announced that they're not going to press charges against me. She called it justifiable homicide. I thought ya'd want to know."

"That's great, Al. Glad to hear it."

"Say, how're ya doing? I heard ya were sick."

"Pneumonia," I answered. "But I'm on the mend."

We talked for a few more minutes. Then, just as we were getting ready to hang up, I remembered a question I had meant to ask him earlier.

"Al," I said, "tell me how you happened to know about that sandbar? Was it just a happy accident, or did you know you could run aground on that beach instead of being smashed to pieces on rocks?"

"Oh, that," Champagne Al replied with a laugh. He sounded happy. "That was easy. I did it years ago, ya see, with Lars. Ran the *Norwegian Princess* right up on the beach. I was drunker'an nine hundred dollars at the time. My brother almost killed me over it, but I didn't hurt a thing. Alls we had to do was wait for high tide. The boat floated right off, same as *One Day at a Time* did this last time."

"You mean you were planning on beaching the boat there all along?" I asked.

"I was planning on beaching somewhere," he answered. "Alls I was waiting for was some assurance of help. By the time you guys finally showed up, I was almost out of options. I figured it was just dumb luck that I ended up there, in a spot I knew. It was like that damn sand spit had been lying in wait for me all along. Like it had my name on it. Know what I mean?"

"I think I do, Al," I said. "I really think I do. By the way," I added, "how's Else?"

Alan Torvoldsen paused for a moment. When he answered—slathering on a thick but phony

Norwegian brogue—I could almost hear the smile in his voice. "*Ja,* sure, ya betcha," he said. "I tink Else's gonna be yust fine."

And suddenly so did I.

Author's Note

The death camp at Sobibor, Poland, did exist, and a mass escape did occur there in October of 1943. During the Nazi war crime trials at Nuremburg, some of the German officers in charge of the camp did, indeed, receive minimal sentences. The rest of the story, including the pursuit of an escaped Nazi guard, is entirely fictional.

The author wishes to thank the many wonderful people who supported the effort that went into writing this book—readers and consultants alike. In addition, I want to acknowledge the wonderful folks who made generous donations to local charities in order to be part of this story. As my mother would say, "Whoever you are, you know who you are." Thanks.

JAJ
Seattle, Washington

Now, for the first time ever—
Beau Meets Brady!

When a twisted case brings them together,
J.P. Beaumont and Joanna Brady
learn what it really means to be a
PARTNER IN CRIME.

Available in hardcover
wherever books are sold.